Jack Reacher –
a hero for our time

'Clint East... ...is
all rolled into on... ...*Times*

'Thinking girl's beefcake'
The Times

'TOUGH-BUT-FAIR'
Mirror

'ONE OF THE GREAT ANTIHEROES'
Independent

'**Admired** by his male
readers and **lusted** after
by his female ones'
Daily Express

'Arms the size of **Popeye's**'
Independent

'The lonest of **lone wolves**...
too cool for school'
San Francisco Chronicle

'Part-**Robin Hood**,
part-**gorilla**'
Sunday Times

'One of the truly memorable
tough-guy heroes' **Jeffery Deaver**

'This is Jack **Reacher** for pity's sake,
he'll **eat you** for breakfast!' *Los Angeles Times*

Have you read them all?

The Jack Reacher thrillers by Lee Child – in the order in which they first appeared.

KILLING FLOOR

Jack Reacher gets off a bus in a small town in Georgia. And is thrown into the county jail, for a murder he didn't commit.

DIE TRYING

Reacher is locked in a van with a woman claiming to be FBI. And ferried right across America into a brand new country.

TRIPWIRE

Reacher is digging swimming pools in Key West when a detective comes round asking questions. Then the detective turns up dead.

THE VISITOR

Two naked women found dead in a bath filled with paint. Both victims of a man just like Reacher.

ECHO BURNING

In the heat of Texas, Reacher meets a young woman whose husband is in jail. When he is released, he will kill her.

WITHOUT FAIL

A Washington woman asks Reacher for help. Her job? Protecting the Vice-President.

PERSUADER

A kidnapping in Boston. A cop dies. Has Reacher lost his sense of right and wrong?

Jack Reacher: CV

Name: Jack Reacher
(no middle name)

Born: 29 October

Height:
6 foot 5 inches/
1.95 metres

Weight:
220-250 lbs/
100-113 kg

Size:
50-inch/127cm chest,
3XLT coat, 37-inch/
95cm inside leg

Eyes: Blue

Distinguishing marks:
scar on corner of left
eye, scar on upper lip

Education:
US Army base schools in
Europe and the Far East;
West Point Military Academy

Service:
US Military Police,
thirteen years; first CO
of the 110th Division;
demoted from Major to
Captain after six years,
mustered out with rank
of Major after seven

Service awards:
Top row: Silver Star, Defense
Superior Service Medal,
Legion of Merit
Middle row: Soldier's Medal,
Bronze Star, Purple Heart
Bottom row: 'Junk awards'

Last known address:
Unknown

Family:
Mother, Josephine Moutier
Reacher, French national;
Father, Career US
Marine, served in
Korea and Vietnam;
Brother, Joe, five years in
US Military Intelligence,
Treasury Dept.

Special skills:
Small arms expert, outstanding
on all man-portable
weaponry and
hand-to-hand combat

Languages:
Fluent English and French,
passable Spanish

What he doesn't have:
Driver's licence; credit cards;
Federal benefits; tax returns;
dependents

THE AFFAIR

Lee Child

BANTAM BOOKS

LONDON · TORONTO · SYDNEY · AUCKLAND · JOHANNESBURG

TRANSWORLD PUBLISHERS
61–63 Uxbridge Road, London W5 5SA
A Random House Group Company
www.transworldbooks.co.uk

THE AFFAIR
A BANTAM BOOK: 9780553825503
9780553825510

First published in Great Britain
in 2011 by Bantam Press
an imprint of Transworld Publishers
Bantam edition published 2012

Copyright © Lee Child 2011

Lee Child has asserted his right under the Copyright, Designs
and Patents Act 1988 to be identified as the author of this work.

This book is a work of fiction and, except in the case of historical fact, any
resemblance to actual persons, living or dead, is purely coincidental.

A CIP catalogue record for this book
is available from the British Library.

This book is sold subject to the condition that it shall not,
by way of trade or otherwise, be lent, resold, hired out,
or otherwise circulated without the publisher's prior
consent in any form of binding or cover other than that
in which it is published and without a similar condition,
including this condition, being imposed on the
subsequent purchaser.

Addresses for Random House Group Ltd companies outside the UK
can be found at: www.randomhouse.co.uk
The Random House Group Ltd Reg. No. 954009

The Random House Group Limited supports The Forest Stewardship
Council (FSC®), the leading international forest-certification
organization. Our books carrying the FSC label are printed on
FSC®-certified paper. FSC is the only forest-certification scheme endorsed
by the leading environmental organizations, including Greenpeace.
Our paper procurement policy can be found
at www.randomhouse.co.uk/environment.

Typeset in 11/14pt Times by
Kestrel Data, Exeter, Devon.
Printed in Great Britain by
Clays Ltd, St Ives plc

2 4 6 8 10 9 7 5 3 1

Dedicated to the memory of
David Thompson, 1971–2010.
A fine bookseller and a good friend.

THE AFFAIR

ONE

The Pentagon is the world's largest office building, six and a half million square feet, thirty thousand people, more than seventeen miles of corridors, but it was built with just three street doors, each one of them opening into a guarded pedestrian lobby. I chose the southeast option, the main concourse entrance, the one nearest the Metro and the bus station, because it was the busiest and the most popular with civilian workers, and I wanted plenty of civilian workers around, preferably a whole long unending stream of them, for insurance purposes, mostly against getting shot on sight. Arrests go bad all the time, sometimes accidentally, sometimes on purpose, so I wanted witnesses. I wanted independent eyeballs on me, at least at the beginning. I remember the date, of course. It was Tuesday, the eleventh of March, 1997, and it was the last day I walked into that place as a legal employee of the people who built it.

A long time ago.

The eleventh of March 1997 was also by chance exactly four and a half years before the world changed, on that other future Tuesday, and so like a lot of things in the old days the security at the main concourse entrance was serious without being hysterical. Not that I invited hysteria. Not from a distance. I was wearing my Class A uniform, all of it clean, pressed, polished and spit-shined, all of it covered with thirteen years' worth of medal ribbons, badges, insignia and citations. I was thirty-six years old, standing tall and walking ramrod straight, a totally squared away U.S. Army Military Police major in every respect, except that my hair was too long and I hadn't shaved for five days.

Back then Pentagon security was run by the Defense Protective Service, and from forty yards I saw ten of their guys in the lobby, which I thought was far too many, which made me wonder whether they were all theirs or whether some of them were actually ours, working undercover, waiting for me. Most of our skilled work is done by Warrant Officers, and they do a lot of it by pretending to be someone else. They impersonate colonels and generals and enlisted men, and anyone else they need to, and they're good at it. All in a day's work for them to throw on DPS uniforms and wait for their target. From thirty yards I didn't recognize any of them, but then, the army is a very big institution, and they would have chosen men I had never met before.

I walked on, part of a broad wash of people heading across the concourse to the doors, some men and women in uniform, either Class As like my own or the old woodland-pattern BDUs we had back then, and some men and women obviously military but out of uniform, in suits or work clothes, and some obvious civilians, some of each category carrying bags or briefcases or

12

packages, all of each category slowing and sidestepping and shuffling as the broad wash of people narrowed to a tight arrowhead and then narrowed further still to lonely single file or collegial two-by-two, as folks got ready to stream inside. I lined up with them, on my own, single file, behind a woman with pale unworn hands and ahead of a guy in a suit that had gone shiny at the elbows. Civilians, both of them, desk workers, probably analysts of some kind, which was exactly what I wanted. Independent eyeballs. It was close to noon. There was sun in the sky and the March air had a little warmth in it. Spring, in Virginia. Across the river the cherry trees were about to wake up. The famous blossom was about to break out. All over the innocent nation airline tickets and SLR cameras lay on hall tables, ready for sightseeing trips to the capital.

I waited in line. Way ahead of me the DPS guys were doing what security guys do. Four of them were occupied with specific tasks, two manning an inquiry counter and two checking official badge holders and then waving them through an open turnstile. Two were standing directly behind the glass inside the doors, looking out, heads high, eyes front, scanning the approaching crowd. Four were hanging back in the shadows behind the turnstiles, just clumped together, shooting the shit. All ten were armed.

It was the four behind the turnstiles that worried me. No question that back in 1997 the Department of Defense was seriously puffed up and overmanned in relation to the threats we faced then, but even so it was unusual to see four on-duty guys with absolutely nothing to do. Most commands at least made their surplus personnel look busy. But these four had no obvious role. I stretched up tall and peered ahead and tried to get a look at their shoes. You can learn a lot from shoes. Undercover disguises often don't get that far, especially in a uniformed environment. The DPS was basically a beat cop role, so to the extent that a choice was available, DPS guys would go for cop shoes, big comfortable things appropriate for walking and standing all day. Undercover MP Warrant Officers might use their own shoes, which would be subtly different.

But I couldn't see their shoes. It was too dark inside, and too far away.

The line shuffled along, at a decent pre-9/11 clip. No sullen impatience, no frustration, no fear. Just old-style routine. The woman in front of me was wearing perfume. I could smell it coming off the nape of her neck. I liked it. The two guys behind the glass noticed me about ten yards out. Their gaze moved off the woman and on to me. It rested on me a beat longer than it needed to, and then it moved on to the guy behind.

Then it came back. Both men looked me over quite openly, up and down, side to side, four or five seconds, and then I shuffled forward and their attention moved behind me again. They didn't say anything to each other. Didn't say anything to anyone else, either. No warnings, no alerts. Two possible interpretations. One, best case, I was just a guy they hadn't seen before. Or maybe I stood out because I was bigger and taller than anyone within a hundred yards. Or because I was wearing a major's gold oak leaves and ribbons for some heavy-duty medals including a Silver Star, like a real poster boy, but because of the hair and the beard I also looked like a real caveman, which visual dissonance might have been enough reason for the long second glance, just purely out of interest. Sentry duty can be boring, and unusual sights are always welcome.

Or two, worst case, they were merely confirming to themselves that some expected event had indeed happened, and that all was going according to plan. Like they had prepared and studied photographs and were saying to themselves: *OK, he's here, right on time, so now we just wait two more minutes until he steps inside, and then we take him down.*

Because I was expected, and I was right on time. I had a twelve o'clock appointment and matters to discuss with a particular colonel in a third-floor office in the C ring, and I was certain I would never get there. To walk head-on into a hard arrest was a pretty blunt tactic, but sometimes if you want to know for sure whether the stove is hot, the only way to find out is to touch it.

The guy ahead of the woman ahead of me stepped inside the doors and held up a badge that was attached to his neck by a lanyard. He was waved onward. The woman in front of me moved and then stopped short, because right at that moment the two DPS watchers chose to come out from behind the glass. The woman paused in place and let them squeeze out in front of her, against the pressing flow. Then she resumed her progress and stepped inside, and the two guys stopped and stood exactly where she had been, three feet in front of me, but facing in the opposite direction, towards me, not away from me.

They were blocking the door. They were looking right at me. I was pretty sure they were genuine DPS personnel. They were wearing cop shoes, and their uniforms had eased and stretched and moulded themselves to their individual physiques over a long period of time. These were not disguises, snatched from a locker and put on for the first time that morning. I looked beyond the two guys, inside, at their four partners who were doing nothing, and I tried to judge the fit of their clothes, by way of comparison. It was hard to tell.

In front of me the guy on my right said, 'Sir, may we help you?'

I asked, 'With what?'

'Where are you headed today?'

'Do I need to tell you that?'

'No, sir, absolutely not,' the guy said. 'But we could speed you along a little, if you like.'

Probably via an inconspicuous door into a small locked room, I thought. I figured they had civilian witnesses on their mind too, the same way I did. I said, 'I'm happy to wait my turn. I'm almost there, anyway.'

The two guys said nothing in reply to that. Stalemate. Amateur hour. To try to start the arrest outside was dumb. I could push and shove and turn and run and be lost in the crowd in the blink of an eye. And they wouldn't shoot. Not outside. There were too many people on the concourse. Too much collateral damage. This was 1997, remember. March eleventh. Four and a half years before the new rules. Much better to wait

16

until I was inside the lobby. The two stooges could close the doors behind me and form up shoulder to shoulder in front of them while I was getting the bad news at the desk. At that point theoretically I could turn back and fight my way past them again, but it would take me a second or two, and in that second or two the four guys with nothing to do could shoot me in the back about a thousand times.

And if I charged forward they could shoot me in the front. And where would I go anyway? To escape *into* the Pentagon was no kind of a good idea. The world's largest office building. Thirty thousand people. Five floors. Two basements. Seventeen miles of corridors. There are ten radial hallways between the rings, and they say a person can make it between any two random points inside a maximum seven minutes, which was presumably calculated with reference to the army's official quick-march pace of four miles an hour, which meant if I was running hard I could be anywhere within about three minutes. But where? I could find a broom closet and steal bag lunches and hold out a day or two, but that would be all. Or I could take hostages and try to argue my case, but I had never seen that kind of thing succeed.

So I waited.

The DPS guy in front of me on my right said, 'Sir, you be sure and have a nice day now,' and then he moved past me, and his partner moved past me on my other side, both of them just strolling slow, two guys happy to be out in the air, patrolling, varying their viewpoint. Maybe not so dumb after all. They were doing their jobs and following their plan. They had tried to decoy me into a small locked room, but they had failed, no harm, no foul, so now they were turning the page straight to plan B. They would wait until I was inside and the doors were closed, and then they would jump into crowd control mode, dispersing the incoming people, keeping them safe in case shots had to be fired inside. I assumed the lobby glass was supposed to be bulletproof, but the smart money never bets on the DoD having gotten exactly what it paid for.

The door was right in front of me. It was open. I took a breath and stepped into the lobby. *Sometimes if you want to know for sure whether the stove is hot, the only way to find out is to touch it.*

TWO

The woman with the perfume and the pale hands was already deep into the corridor beyond the open turnstile. She had been waved through. Straight ahead of me was the two-man inquiry desk. To my left were the two guys checking badges. The open turnstile was between their hips. The four spare guys were still doing nothing beyond it. They were still clustered together, quiet and watchful, like an independent team. I still couldn't see their shoes.

I took another breath and stepped up to the counter.

Like a lamb to the slaughter.

The desk guy on the left looked at me and said, 'Yes, sir.' Fatigue and resignation in his voice. A response, not a question, as if I had already spoken. He looked young and reasonably smart. Genuine DPS, presumably. MP Warrant Officers are quick studies, but they wouldn't be running a Pentagon inquiry desk, however deeply under they were supposed to be.

The desk guy looked at me again, expectantly, and I said, 'I have a twelve o'clock appointment.'

'Who with?'

'Colonel Frazer,' I said.

The guy made out like he didn't recognize the name. The world's largest office building. Thirty thousand people. He leafed through a book the size of a telephone directory and asked, 'Would that be Colonel John James Frazer? Senate Liaison?'

I said, 'Yes.'

Or: *Guilty as charged.*

Way to my left the four spare guys were watching me. But not moving. Yet.

The guy at the desk didn't ask my name. Partly because he had been briefed, presumably, and shown photographs, and partly because my Class A uniform included my name on a nameplate, worn as per regulations on my right breast pocket flap, exactly centred, its upper edge exactly a quarter of an inch below the top seam.

Seven letters: *REACHER.*

Or, eleven letters: *Arrest me now.*

The guy at the inquiry desk said, 'Colonel John James Frazer is in 3C315. You know how to get there?'

I said, 'Yes.' Third floor, C ring, nearest to radial corridor number three, bay number fifteen. The Pentagon's version of map coordinates, which it needed, given that it covered twenty-nine whole acres of floor space.

The guy said, 'Sir, you have a great day,' and his guileless gaze moved past my shoulder to the next in line. I stood still for a moment. They were tying it up with a bow. They were making it perfect. The general common law test for criminal culpability is expressed by the Latin *actus non facit reum nisi mens sit rea*, which means, roughly, doing things won't necessarily get you in trouble unless you actually mean to do them. Action plus intention is the standard. They were waiting for me to prove my intention. They were waiting for me to step through the turnstile and into the labyrinth. Which explained why the four spare guys were on their side of the gate, not mine. Crossing the line would make it real. Maybe there were jurisdiction issues. Maybe lawyers had been consulted. Frazer wanted my ass gone for sure, but he wanted his own ass covered just as much.

I took another breath and crossed the line and made it real. I walked between the two badge checkers and squeezed between the cold alloy flanks of the turnstile. The bar was retracted. There was nothing to hit with my thighs. I stepped out on the far side and paused. The four spare guys were on my right. I looked at their shoes. Army regulations are surprisingly vague about shoes. Plain black lace-up Oxfords or close equivalents, conservative, no designs on them, minimum of three pairs of eyelets, closed toe, maximum two-inch heel. That's all the fine print says. The four guys on my right were all in compliance, but they weren't wearing cop shoes. Not like the two guys outside. They were sporting four variations on the same classic theme. High shines, tight laces, a little creasing and wear here and there. Maybe they were genuine DPS. Maybe they weren't. No way of telling. Not right then.

I was looking at them, and they were looking at me, but no one spoke. I looped around them and headed deeper into the building. I used the E ring counterclockwise and turned left at the first radial hallway.

The four guys followed.

They stayed about sixty feet behind me, close enough to keep me in sight, far enough back not to crowd me. A maximum seven minutes between any two points. I was the meat in a sandwich. I figured there would be another crew waiting outside 3C315, or as close to it as they decided to let me get. I was heading straight for them. Nowhere to run, nowhere to hide.

I used some stairs on the D ring and went up two flights to the third floor. I changed to a clockwise direction, just for the fun of it, and passed radial corridor number five, and then four. The D ring was busy. People were bustling from place to place with armfuls of khaki files. Blank-eyed men and women in uniform were stepping smartly. The place was congested. I dodged and sidestepped and kept on going. People looked at me every step of the way. The hair, and the beard. I stopped at a water fountain and bent down and took a drink. People passed me by. Sixty feet behind me the four spare DPS guys were nowhere to be seen. But then, they didn't really need to tail me. They knew where I was going, and they knew what time I was supposed to get there.

I straightened up and got going again and turned right into radial number three. I made it to the C ring. The air smelled of uniform wool and linoleum polish and very faintly of cigars. The paint on the walls was thick and institutional. I looked left and right. There were people in the corridor, but no big cluster outside bay fifteen. Maybe they were waiting for me inside. I was already five minutes late.

22

I didn't turn. I stuck with radial three and walked all the way across the B ring to the A ring. The heart of the building, where the radial corridors finish. Or start, depending on your rank and perspective. Beyond the A ring is nothing but a five-acre pentagonal open courtyard, like the hole in an angular doughnut. Back in the day people called it Ground Zero, because they figured the Soviets had their biggest and best missile permanently targeted on it, like a big fat bull's-eye. I think they were wrong. I think the Soviets had their five biggest and best missiles targeted on it, just in case strikes one through four didn't work. The smart money says the Soviets didn't always get what they paid for, either.

I waited in the A ring until I was ten minutes late. Better to keep them guessing. Maybe they were already searching. Maybe the four spare guys were already getting their butts kicked for losing me. I took another big breath and pushed off a wall and tracked back along radial three, across the B ring, to the C. I turned without breaking stride and headed for bay fifteen.

THREE

There was no one waiting outside bay fifteen. No special crew. No one at all. The corridor was entirely empty, too, both ways, as far as the eye could see. And quiet. I guessed everyone else was already where they wanted to be. Twelve o'clock meetings were in full swing.

Bay fifteen's door was open. I knocked on it once, as a courtesy, as an announcement, as a warning, and then I stepped inside. Originally most of the Pentagon's office space was open plan, boxed off by file cabinets and furniture into bays, hence the name, but over the years walls had gone up and private spaces had been created. Frazer's billet in 3C315 was pretty typical. It was a small square space with a window without a view, and a rug on the floor, and photographs on the walls, and a metal DoD desk, and a chair with arms and two without, and a credenza and a double-wide storage unit.

And it was a small square space entirely empty of people, apart from Frazer himself in the chair behind the desk. He looked up at me and smiled.

He said, 'Hello, Reacher.'

I looked left and right. No one there. No one at all.

There was no private bathroom. No large closet. No other door of any kind. The corridor behind me was empty. The giant building was quiet.

Frazer said, 'Close the door.'

I closed the door.

Frazer said, 'Sit down, if you like.'

I sat down.

Frazer said, 'You're late.'

'I apologize,' I said. 'I got hung up.'

Frazer nodded. 'This place is a nightmare at twelve o'clock. Lunch breaks, shift changes, you name it. It's a zoo. I never plan to go anywhere at twelve o'clock. I just hunker down in here.' He was about five-ten, maybe two hundred pounds, wide in the shoulders, solid through the chest, red-faced, black-haired, in his middle forties. Plenty of old Scottish blood in his veins, filtered through the rich earth of Tennessee, which was where he was from. He had been in Vietnam as a teenager and the Gulf as an older man. He had combat pips all over him like a rash. He was an old-fashioned warrior, but unfortunately for him he could talk and smile as well as he could fight, so he had been posted to Senate Liaison, because the guys with the purse strings were now the real enemy.

He said, 'So what have you got for me?'

I said nothing. I had nothing to say. I hadn't expected to get that far.

He said, 'Good news, I hope.'

'No news,' I said.

'Nothing?'

I nodded. 'Nothing.'

'You told me you had the name. That's what your message said.'

'I don't have the name.'

'Then why say so? Why ask to see me?'

I paused a beat.

'It was a shortcut,' I said.

'In what way?'

'I put it around that I had the name. I wondered who might crawl out from under a rock, to shut me up.'

'And no one has?'

'Not so far. But ten minutes ago I thought it was a different story. There were four spare men in the lobby. In DPS uniforms. They followed me. I thought they were an arrest team.'

'Followed you where?'

'Around the E ring to the D. Then I lost them on the stairs.'

Frazer smiled again.

'You're paranoid,' he said. 'You didn't lose them. I told you, there are shift changes at twelve o'clock. They come in on the Metro like everyone else, they shoot the shit for a minute or two, and then they head for their squad room. It's on the B ring. They weren't following you.'

I said nothing.

He said, 'There are always groups of them hanging around. There are always groups of everyone hanging around. We're seriously overmanned. Something is going to have to be done. It's inevitable. That's all I hear about on the Hill, all day, every day. There's nothing we can do to stop it. We should all bear that in mind. People like you, especially.'

26

'Like me?' I said.

'There are lots of majors in this man's army. Too many, probably.'

'Lots of colonels too,' I said.

'Fewer colonels than majors.'

I said nothing.

He asked, 'Was I on your list of things that might crawl out from under a rock?'

You were the list, I thought.

He said, 'Was I?'

'No,' I lied.

He smiled again. 'Good answer. If I had a beef with you, I'd have you killed down there in Mississippi. Maybe I'd come on down and take care of it myself.'

I said nothing. He looked at me for a moment, and then a smile started on his face, and the smile turned into a laugh, which he tried very hard to suppress, but he couldn't. It came out like a bark, like a sneeze, and he had to lean back and look up at the ceiling.

I said, 'What?'

His gaze came back level. He was still smiling. He said, 'I'm sorry. I was thinking about that phrase people use. You know, they say, that guy? He couldn't even get arrested.'

I said nothing.

He said, 'You look terrible. There are barbershops here, you know. You should go use one.'

'I can't,' I said. 'I'm supposed to look like this.'

Five days earlier my hair had been five days shorter, but apparently still long enough to attract attention.

Leon Garber, who at that point was once again my commanding officer, summoned me to his office, and because his message read in part *without repeat without attending to any matters of personal grooming* I figured he wanted to strike while the iron was hot and dress me down right then, while the evidence was still in existence, right there on my head. And that was exactly how the meeting started out. He asked me, 'Which army regulation covers a soldier's personal appearance?'

Which I thought was a pretty rich question, coming from him. Garber was without a doubt the scruffiest officer I had ever seen. He could take a brand-new Class A coat from the quartermaster's stores and an hour later it would look like he had fought two wars in it, then slept in it, then survived three bar fights in it.

I said, 'I can't remember which regulation covers a soldier's personal appearance.'

He said, 'Neither can I. But I seem to recall that whichever, the hair and the fingernail standards and the grooming policies are in chapter one, section eight. I can picture it all quite clearly, right there on the page. Can you remember what it says?'

I said, 'No.'

'It tells us that hair grooming standards are necessary to maintain uniformity within a military population.'

'Understood.'

'It mandates those standards. Do you know what they are?'

'I've been very busy,' I said. 'I just got back from Korea.'

'I heard Japan.'

28

'That was a stopover on the way.'

'How long?'

'Twelve hours.'

'Do they have barbers in Japan?'

'I'm sure they do.'

'Do Japanese barbers take more than twelve hours to cut a man's hair?'

'I'm sure they don't.'

'Chapter one, section eight, paragraph two, says the hair on the top of the head must be neatly groomed, and that the length and the bulk of the hair may not be excessive or present a ragged, unkempt, or extreme appearance. It says that, instead, the hair must present a tapered appearance.'

I said, 'I'm not sure what that means.'

'It says a tapered appearance is one where the outline of the soldier's hair conforms to the shape of his head, curving inward to a natural termination point at the base of his neck.'

I said, 'I'll get it taken care of.'

'These are mandates, you understand. Not suggestions.'

'OK,' I said.

'Paragraph two says that when the hair is combed, it *will not* fall over the ears or the eyebrows, and it *will not* touch the collar.'

'OK,' I said again.

'Would you not describe your current hairstyle as ragged, unkempt, or extreme?'

'Compared to what?'

'And how are you doing in relation to the thing with

29

the comb and the ears and the eyebrows and the collar?'

'I'll get it taken care of,' I said again.

Then Garber smiled, and the tone of the meeting changed completely.

He asked, 'How fast does your hair grow, anyway?'

'I don't know,' I said. 'A normal kind of speed, I suppose. Same as anyone else, probably. Why?'

'We have a problem,' he said. 'Down in Mississippi.'

FOUR

Garber said the problem down in Mississippi concerned a twenty-seven-year-old woman named Janice May Chapman. She was a problem because she was dead. She had been unlawfully killed a block behind the main street of a town called Carter Crossing.

'Was she one of ours?' I asked.

'No,' Garber said. 'She was a civilian.'

'So how is she a problem?'

'I'll get to that,' Garber said. 'But first you need the story. It's the back of beyond down there. Northeastern corner of the state, over near the Alabama line, and Tennessee. There's a north–south railroad track, and a little backwoods dirt road that crosses it east–west near a place that has a spring. The locomotives would stop there to take on water, and the passengers would get out to eat, so the town grew up. But since the end of World War Two there's only been about two trains a day, both freight, no passengers, so the town was on its way back down again.'

'Until?'

'Federal spending. You know how it was. Washington

couldn't let large parts of the South turn into the Third World, so we threw some money down there. A lot of money, actually. You ever notice how the folks who talk loudest about small government always seem to live in the states with the biggest subsidies? Small government would kill them dead.'

I asked, 'What did Carter Crossing get?'

Garber said, 'Carter Crossing got an army base called Fort Kelham.'

'OK,' I said. 'I've heard of Kelham. Never knew where it was, exactly.'

'It used to be huge,' Garber said. 'Ground was broken in about 1950, I think. It could have ended up as big as Fort Hood, but ultimately it was too far east of I-55 and too far west of I-65 to be useful. You have to drive a long way on small roads just to get there. Or maybe Texas politicians have louder voices than Mississippi politicians. Either way, Hood got the attention and Kelham withered on the vine. It struggled on until the end of Vietnam, and then they turned it into a Ranger school. Which it still is.'

'I thought Ranger training was at Benning.'

'The 75th sends their best guys to Kelham for a time. It's not far. Something to do with the terrain.'

'The 75th is a special ops regiment.'

'So they tell me.'

'Are there enough special ops Rangers in training to keep a whole town going?'

'Almost,' Garber said. 'It's not a very big town.'

'So what are we saying? An Army Ranger killed Janice May Chapman?'

32

'I doubt it,' Garber said. 'It was probably some local hillbilly thing.'

'Do they have hillbillies in Mississippi? Do they even have hills?'

'Backwoodsmen, then. They have a lot of trees.'

'Whichever, why are we even talking about it?'

At that point Garber got up and came out from behind his desk and crossed the room and closed the door. He was older than me, naturally, and much shorter, but about as wide. And he was worried. It was rare for him to close his door, and rarer still for him to go more than five minutes without a tortured little homily or aphorism or slogan, designed to sum up a point he was trying to make in an easily remembered form. He stepped back and sat down again with a hiss of air from his cushion, and he asked, 'Have you ever heard of a place called Kosovo?'

'Balkans,' I said. 'Like Serbia and Croatia.'

'There's going to be a war there. Apparently we're going to try to stop it. Apparently we'll probably fail, and we'll end up just bombing the shit out of one side or the other instead.'

'OK,' I said. 'Always good to have a plan B.'

'The Serbo-Croat thing was a disaster. Like Rwanda. A total embarrassment. This is the twentieth century, for God's sake.'

'Seemed to me to fit right in with the twentieth century.'

'It's supposed to be different now.'

'Wait for the twenty-first. That's my advice.'

'We're not going to wait for anything. We're going to try to do Kosovo right.'

'Well, good luck with that. Don't come to me for help. I'm just a policeman.'

'We've already got people over there. You know, intermittently, in and out.'

I asked, 'Who?'

Garber said, 'Peacekeepers.'

'What, the United Nations?'

'Not exactly. Our guys only.'

'I didn't know that.'

'You didn't know because nobody is supposed to know.'

'How long has this been happening?'

'Twelve months.'

I said, 'We've been deploying ground troops to the Balkans in secret for a whole year?'

'It's not such a big deal,' Garber said. 'It's about reconnaissance, partly. In case something has to happen later. But mostly it's about calming things down. There are a lot of factions over there. If anyone asks, we always say it was the other guy who invited us. That way everyone thinks everyone else has got our backing. It's a deterrent.'

I asked, 'Who did we send?'

Garber said, 'Army Rangers.'

Garber told me that Fort Kelham was still operating as a legitimate Ranger training school, but in addition was being used to house two full companies of grown-up Rangers, both handpicked from the 75th Ranger Regiment, designated Alpha Company and Bravo Company, who deployed covertly to Kosovo on a rotating basis, a month at a time. Kelham's relative isolation made it a perfect clandestine location. Not, Garber said, that we should really feel the need to hide anything. Very few personnel were involved, and it was a humanitarian mission driven by the purest of motives. But Washington was Washington, and some things were better left unsaid.

I asked, 'Does Carter Crossing have a police department?'

Garber said, 'Yes, it does.'

'So let me guess. They're getting nowhere with their homicide investigation, so they want to go fishing. They want to list some Kelham personnel in their suspect pool.'

Garber said, 'Yes, they do.'

'Including members of Alpha Company and Bravo Company.'

Garber said, 'Yes.'

'They want to ask them all kinds of questions.'

'Yes.'

'But we can't afford to let them ask anyone any questions, because we have to hide all the covert comings and goings.'

'Correct.'

'Do they have probable cause?'

I hoped Garber was going to say no, but instead he said, 'Slightly circumstantial.'

I said, 'Slightly?'

He said, 'The timing is unfortunate. Janice May Chapman was killed three days after Bravo Company got back from Kosovo, after their latest trip. They fly in

35

direct from overseas. Kelham has an airstrip. I told you, it's a big place. They land under cover of darkness, for secrecy's sake. Then a returning company spends the first two days locked down and debriefing.'

'And then?'

'And then on the third day a returning company gets a week's leave.'

'And they all go out on the town.'

'Generally.'

'Including Main Street and the blocks behind.'

'That's where the bars are.'

'And the bars are where they meet the local women.'

'As always.'

'And Janice May Chapman was a local woman.'

'And known to be friendly.'

I said, 'Terrific.'

Garber said, 'She was raped and mutilated.'

'Mutilated how?'

'I didn't ask. I didn't want to know. She was twenty-seven years old. Jodie is twenty-seven years old, too.'

His only daughter. His only child. Much loved.

I asked, 'How is she?'

'She's fine.'

'Where is she now?'

'She's a lawyer,' he said, like it was a location, not an occupation. Then in turn he asked, 'How's your brother?'

I said, 'He's OK, as far as I know.'

'Still at Treasury?'

'As far as I know.'

'He was a good man,' Garber said, like leaving the army was the same thing as dying.

I said nothing.

Garber asked, 'So what would you do, down there in Mississippi?'

This was 1997, remember. I said, 'We can't shut out the local PD. Not under those circumstances. But we can't assume any level of expertise or resources on their part, either. So we should offer some help. We should send someone down there. We can do all the work on the base. If some Kelham guy did it, we'll serve him up on a platter. That way justice is done, but we can hide what we need to hide.'

'Not that simple,' Garber said. 'It gets worse.'

'How?'

'Bravo Company's commander is a guy called Reed Riley. You know him?'

'The name rings a bell.'

'And so it should. His father is Carlton Riley.'

I said, 'Shit.'

Garber nodded. 'The senator. The chairman of the Armed Services Committee. About to be either our best friend or our worst enemy, depending on which way the wind is going to blow. And you know how it is with guys like that. Having an infantry captain for a son is worth a million votes to him. Having a hero for a son is worth twice that. I don't want to think about what happens if one of young Reed's guys turns out to be a killer.'

I said, 'We need someone at Kelham right now.'

Garber said, 'That's why you and I are having this meeting.'

'When do you want me there?'

'I don't want you there,' Garber said.

FIVE

Garber told me his top pick for the Kelham job wasn't me. It was a newly minted MP major named Duncan Munro. Military family, Silver Star, Purple Heart, and so on and so forth. He had recently completed some good work in Korea, and was currently doing some great work in Germany. He was five years younger than me, and from what I was hearing he was exactly what I had been five years in the past. I had never met him.

Garber said, 'He's flying down there tonight. ETA late morning.'

'Your call,' I said. 'I guess.'

'It's a delicate situation,' he said.

'Evidently,' I said. 'Too delicate for me, anyway.'

'Don't get your panties in a wad. I need you for something else. Something I hope you'll see as just as important.'

'Like what?'

'Undercover work,' he said. 'That's why I'm happy about your hair. Ragged and unkempt. There are two things we do very badly when we're undercover. Hair, and shoes. Shoes, you can buy at Goodwill. You can't buy messy hair at a moment's notice.'

'Undercover where?'

'Carter Crossing, of course. Down in Mississippi. Off post. You're going to blow into town like some kind of aimless ex-military bum. You know the type. You're going to be the kind of guy who feels right at home there, because it's the kind of environment he's familiar with. So you're going to stay put a spell. You're going to develop a relationship with local law enforcement, and you're going to use that relationship in a clandestine fashion to make sure that both they and Munro are doing this thing absolutely right.'

'You want me to impersonate a civilian?'

'It's not that hard. We're all members of the same species, more or less. You'll figure it out.'

'Will I be actively investigating?'

'No. You'll be there to observe and report only. Like a training assessment. You've done it before. My eyes and ears. This thing has got to be done absolutely right.'

'OK,' I said.

'Any other questions?'

'When do I leave?'

'Tomorrow morning, first light.'

'And what's your definition of doing this thing absolutely right?'

Garber paused and shuffled in his chair and didn't answer that question.

I went back to my quarters and took a shower, but I didn't shave. Going undercover is like method acting, and Garber was right. I knew the type. Any soldier does. Towns near bases are full of guys who washed out for some reason or other and never got further than a mile. Some stay, and some are forced to move on, and the ones who move on end up in some other town near some other base. The same, but different. It's what they know. It's what they're comfortable with. They retain some kind of ingrained, deep-down military discipline, like old habits, like stray strands of DNA, but they abandon regular grooming. Chapter one, section eight, paragraph two no longer rules their lives. So I didn't shave, and I didn't comb my hair either. I just let it dry.

Then I laid stuff out on my bed. I didn't need to go to the Goodwill for shoes. I had a pair that would do. About twelve years previously I had been in the U.K. and I had bought a pair of brown brogues at an old-fashioned gentleman's store in a village miles from anywhere. They were big, heavy, substantial things. They were well cared for, but a little worn and creased. Down at heel, literally.

I put them on my bed, and they sat there alone. I had no other personal clothing. None at all. Not even socks. I found an old army T-shirt in a drawer, olive drab, cotton, originally of a hefty grade, now washed pale and as thin as silk. I figured it was the kind of thing a guy might keep around. I put it next to the shoes. Then I hiked over to the PX and poked around the aisles I usually don't frequent. I found a pair of mud-coloured canvas pants and a long-sleeved shirt that was basically maroon, but it had been pre-washed so that the seams had faded to a kind of pink. I wasn't thrilled with it, but it was the only choice in my size. It was reduced in price, which made sense to me, and it looked basically civilian. I had seen people wearing worse things. And it was versatile. I wasn't sure what the temperatures were going to be, in March in the northeastern corner of Mississippi. If it was warm, I could roll the sleeves up. If it was cold, I could roll them down.

I chose white underwear and khaki socks and then stopped in the toiletries section and found a kind of half-size travel toothbrush. I liked it. The business end was nested in a clear plastic case, and it pulled out and reversed and clipped back in, to make it full-length and ready to use. It was obviously designed for a pocket. It would be easy to carry and the bristle part would stay clean. A very neat idea.

I sent the clothing straight to the laundry, to age it a little. Nothing ages stuff like on-base laundries. Then I walked off-post to a hamburger place for a late lunch. I found an old friend in there, an MP colleague, a guy called Stan Lowrey. We had worked together many times. He was sitting at a table in front of a tray holding the wreckage of a half-pounder and fries. I got my meal and slid in opposite him. He said, 'I hear you're on your way to Mississippi.'

I asked, 'Where did you hear that?'

'My sergeant got it from a sergeant in Garber's office.'

'When?'

'About two hours ago.'

'Terrific,' I said. 'I didn't even know two hours ago. So much for secrecy.'

'My sergeant says you're going as second fiddle.'

41

'Your sergeant is right.'

'My sergeant says the lead investigator is some kid.'

I nodded. 'I'm babysitting.'

'That sucks, Reacher. That blows big time.'

'Only if the kid does it right.'

'Which he might.'

I took a bite of my burger, and a sip of my coffee. I said, 'Actually I don't know if anyone could do it right. There are sensitivities involved. There may be no right way of doing it at all. It could be that Garber is protecting me and sacrificing the kid.'

Lowrey said, 'Dream on, my friend. You're an old horse and Garber is pinch-hitting for you in the bottom of the ninth with the bases loaded. A new star is about to be born. You're history.'

'You too, then,' I said. 'If I'm an old horse, you're already waiting at the glue factory gate.'

'Exactly,' Lowrey said. 'That's what I'm worried about. I'm going to start looking at the want ads tonight.'

Nothing much happened during the rest of the afternoon. My laundry came back, a little bleached and battered by the giant machines. It was steam-pressed, but a day's travelling would correct that. I left it on the floor, piled neatly on my shoes. Then my phone rang, and a switchboard operator patched me into a call from the Pentagon, and I found myself talking to a colonel named John James Frazer. He said he was currently with Senate Liaison, but he preceded that embarrassing announcement with his whole prior combat bio, so I wouldn't write him off as a jerk. Then he said, 'I need to know immediately if there's the slightest shred or scintilla of a hint or a rumour about anyone in Bravo Company. Immediately, OK? Night or day.'

I said, 'And I need to know how the local PD even knows Bravo Company is based at Kelham. I thought it's supposed to be a secret.'

'They fly in and out on C5 transports. Noisy airplanes.'

'In the dead of night. So they could be supply runs, for all anyone knows. Beans and bullets.'

'There was a weather problem a month ago. Storms over the Atlantic. They were late. They landed after dawn. They were observed. And it's a base town anyway. You know how it is. The locals pick up on the patterns. Faces they know, there one month, gone the next. People aren't dumb.'

'There already are hints and rumours,' I said. 'The timing is suggestive. Like you said, people aren't dumb.'

'The timing could be entirely coincidental.'

'Could be,' I said. 'Let's hope it is.'

Frazer said, 'I need to know immediately if there's anything Captain Riley could have, or should have, or might have, or ought to have known. Anything at all, OK? No delay.'

'Is that an order?'

'It's a request from a senior officer. Is there a difference?'

'Are you in my chain of command?'

'Consider that I am.'

'OK,' I said.

'Anything at all,' he said again. 'To me, immediately and personally. My ears only. Night or day.'

'OK,' I said again.

'There's a lot riding on this. Do you understand? The stakes are very high.'

'OK,' I said, for the third time.

Then Frazer said, 'But I don't want you to do anything that makes you feel uncomfortable.'

I went to bed early, my hair matted, my unshaven face scratchy on the pillow, and the clock in my head woke me at five, two hours before dawn, on Friday, the seventh of March, 1997. The first day of the rest of my life.

SIX

I showered and dressed in the dark, socks, boxers, pants, my old T, my new shirt. I laced my shoes and put my toothbrush in my pocket with a pack of gum and a roll of bills. I left everything else behind. No ID, no wallet, no watch, no nothing. Method acting. I figured that was how I would do it, if I was doing it for real.

Then I headed out. I walked up the post's main drag and got to the guardhouse and Garber came out to meet me in the open. He had been waiting for me. Six o'clock in the morning. Not yet light. Garber was in BDUs, presumably fresh on less than an hour ago, but he looked like he had spent that hour rolling around in the dirt on a farm. We stood under the glow of a yellow vapour light. The air was very cold.

Garber said, 'You don't have a bag?'

I said, 'Why would I have a bag?'

'People carry bags.'

'What for?'

'For their spare clothing.'

'I don't own spare clothing. I had to buy these things especially.'

45

'You *chose* that shirt?'

'What's wrong with it?'

'It's pink.'

'Only in places.'

'You're going to Mississippi. They'll think you're queer. They'll beat you to death.'

'I doubt it,' I said.

'What are you going to do when those clothes get dirty?'

'I don't know. Buy some more, I suppose.'

'How are you planning to get to Kelham?'

'I figured I'd walk into town and get a Greyhound bus to Memphis. Then hitchhike the rest of the way. I imagine that's how people do these things.'

'Have you eaten breakfast?'

'I'm sure I'll find a diner.'

Garber paused a beat and asked, 'Did John James Frazer get you on the phone yesterday? From Senate Liaison?'

I said, 'Yes, he did.'

'How did he sound?'

'Like we're in big trouble unless Janice May Chapman was killed by another civilian.'

'Then let's hope she was.'

'Is Frazer in my chain of command?'

'Probably safest to assume he is.'

'What kind of a guy is he?'

'He's a guy under a whole lot of stress right now. Five years' work could go down the pan, just when it gets important.'

'He told me not to do anything that makes me feel uncomfortable.'

'Bullshit,' Garber said. 'You're not in the army to feel comfortable.'

I said, 'What some guy on leave does after he gets drunk in a bar is not a company commander's fault.'

'Only in the real world,' Garber said. 'But this is politics we're talking about.' Then he went quiet again, just for a moment, as if he had many more points to make and was trying to decide which one of them to start with. But in the end all he said was, 'Well, have a safe trip, Reacher. Stay in touch, OK?'

The walk to the Greyhound depot was long but not difficult. Just a case of putting one foot in front of the other. I was passed by a few vehicles. None of them stopped to offer me a ride. They might have if I had been in uniform. Off-post citizens are usually well disposed towards their military neighbours, in the heartland of America. I took their neglect as proof that my civilian disguise was convincing. I was glad to pass the test. I had never posed as a civilian before. It was unknown territory. Something new for me. I had never even been a civilian. I suppose technically I was, for eighteen years between birth and West Point, but those years had been spent inside a blur of Marine Corps bases, one after another, because of my father's career, and living on-post as part of a military family had nothing to do with civilian life. Absolutely nothing at all. So that morning's walk felt fresh and experimental to me. The sun came up behind me and the air went warm and dewy and a ground mist rose off the road to my knees. I walked on through it and thought of my old pal Stan Lowrey, back on the base. I wondered if he had looked at the want ads. I wondered if he needed to. I wondered if I needed to.

There was a coach diner a half mile short of downtown and I stopped there for breakfast. I had coffee, of course, and scrambled eggs. I felt I integrated pretty well, visually and behaviourally. There were six other customers in there. All of them were civilians, all of them were men, and all of them were ragged and unkempt by the standards required to maintain uniformity within a military population. All six of them were wearing hats on their heads. Six mesh caps, printed with the names of what I took to be agricultural equipment manufacturers, or seed merchants. I wondered if I should have gotten such a hat. I hadn't thought about it, and I hadn't seen any in the PX.

I finished my meal and paid the waitress and walked on bareheaded to where the Greyhounds came and went. I bought a ticket and sat on a bench and thirty minutes later I was in the back of a bus, heading south and west.

SEVEN

The bus ride was magnificent, in its way. Not a radical distance, no more than a small portion of the giant continent, no more than an inch on a one-page map, but it took six hours. The view out the window changed so slowly it seemed never to change at all, but even so the landscape at the end of the journey was very different than at the beginning. Memphis was a slick city, laced with wet streets, boxed in by low buildings painted muted pastel colours, heaving and bustling with furtive unexplained activity. I got out at the depot and stood a moment in the bright afternoon and listened to the hum and throb of people at work and at play. Then I kept the sun on my right shoulder and walked south and east. First priority was the mouth of a wide road leading out of town, and second priority was something to eat.

I found myself in a built-up and insalubrious quarter full of pawn shops and porn shops and bail bond offices, and I figured getting a ride there would be next to impossible. The same driver who might stop on the open road would never stop in that part of town. So I put my second priority first and fuelled up at a greasy spoon café, and resigned myself to a lengthy hike thereafter. I wanted a corner with a road sign, a big green rectangle marked with an arrow and *Oxford* or *Tupelo* or *Columbus*. In my experience a guy standing under such a sign with his thumb out left no doubt about what he wanted and where he was going. No explanation was required. No need for a driver to stop and ask, which helped a lot. People are bad at saying no face to face. Often they just drive on by, purely to avoid the possibility. Always better to reduce confusion.

I found such a corner and such a sign at the end of a thirty-minute walk, on the front edge of what I took to be a leafy suburb, which would mean 90 per cent of passing drivers would be respectable matrons returning home, which would mean they would ignore me completely. No suburban matron would stop for a stranger, and no driver with just a mile more to go would offer a ride. But to walk on would have been illusory progress. A false economy. Better to waste time standing still than to waste it walking and burning energy. Even with nine cars out of ten wafting on by, I figured I would be mobile within an hour.

And I was. Less than twenty minutes later an old pick-up truck eased to a stop next to me and the driver told me he was heading for a lumber yard out past Germantown. It must have been clear that I didn't grasp the local geography, so the guy told me if I rode with him I would end up outside of the urban tangle with nothing but a straight shot into northeastern Mississippi ahead of me. So I climbed aboard and another twenty minutes later

I was alone again, on the shoulder of a dusty two-lane that headed unambiguously in the direction I wanted to go. A guy in a sagging Buick sedan picked me up and we crossed the state line together and drove forty miles east. Then a guy in a stately old Chevy truck took me twenty miles south on a minor road and let me out at what he said was the turn I wanted. By that point it was late in the afternoon and the sun was heading for the far horizon, pretty fast. The road ahead was die-straight with low forest on both sides and nothing but darkness in the distance. I figured Carter Crossing straddled that road, perhaps thirty or forty miles away to the east, which put me close to completing the first part of my mission, which was simply to get there. The second part was to make contact with the local cops, which might be harder. There was no cogent reason for a transient bum to pal up with people in police uniforms. No obvious mechanism either, short of getting arrested, which would start the whole relationship on the wrong foot.

But in the event both objectives were achieved in one fell swoop, because the first eastbound car I saw was a police cruiser heading home. I had my thumb out, and the guy stopped for me. He was a talker and I was a listener, and within minutes I found out that some of what Garber had told me was wrong.

EIGHT

The cop's name was Pellegrino, like the sparkling water, although he didn't say that. I got the impression that people drank from the tap in that part of Mississippi. On reflection it was no surprise he stopped for me. Small-town cops are always interested in unexplained strangers heading into their territory. The easiest way to find out who they are is simply to ask, which he did, immediately. I told him my name and spent a minute on my cover story. I said I was recent ex-military, heading to Carter Crossing to look for a friend who might be living there. I said the friend had last served at Kelham and might have stuck around. Pellegrino had nothing to say in response to that. He just took his eyes off the empty road for a second and looked me up and down, calibrating, and then he nodded and faced front again. He was moderately short and very overweight, maybe French or Italian way back, with black hair buzzed short and olive skin and broken veins both sides of his nose. He was somewhere between thirty and forty, and I guessed if he didn't stop eating and drinking he wasn't going to make it much beyond fifty or sixty.

I finished saying my piece and he started talking, and the first thing I found out was that he wasn't a small-town cop. Garber had been wrong, technically. Carter Crossing had no police department. Carter Crossing was in Carter County, and Carter County had a County Sheriff's Department, which had jurisdiction over everything inside an area close to five hundred square miles. But there wasn't much inside those five hundred square miles except Fort Kelham and the town, which was where the Sheriff's Department was based, which made Garber right again, in a sense. But Pellegrino was indisputably a deputy sheriff, not a police officer, and he seemed very proud of the distinction.

I asked him, 'How big is your department?'

Pellegrino said, 'Not very. We got the sheriff, who we call the chief, we got a sheriff's detective, we got me and another deputy in uniform, we got a civilian on the desk, we got a woman on the phones, but the detective is out sick long term with his kidneys, so it's just the three of us, really.'

I asked him, 'How many people live in Carter County?'

'About twelve hundred,' he said. Which I thought was a lot, for three functioning cops. Apples to apples, it would be like policing New York City with a half-sized NYPD. I asked, 'Does that include Fort Kelham?'

'No, they're separate,' he said. 'And they have their own cops.'

I said, 'But still, you guys must be busy. I mean, twelve hundred citizens, five hundred square miles.'

'Right now we're real busy,' he said, but he didn't mention anything about Janice May Chapman. Instead he talked about a more recent event. Late in the evening the day before, under cover of darkness, someone had parked a car on the train track. Garber was wrong again. He had said there were two trains a day, but Pellegrino told me in reality there was only one. It rumbled through at midnight exactly, a mile-long giant hauling freight north from Biloxi on the Gulf Coast. That midnight train had smashed into the parked vehicle, wrecking it completely, hurling it way far up the line, bouncing it into the woods. The train had not stopped. As far as anyone could tell it hadn't even slowed down. Which meant the engineer had not even noticed. He was obliged to stop if he struck something on the line. Railroad policy. Pellegrino thought it was certainly possible the guy hadn't noticed. So did I. Thousands of tons against one, moving fast, no contest. Pellegrino seemed captivated by the senselessness of it all. He said, 'I mean, who would do that? Who would park an automobile on the train track? And why?'

'Kids?' I said. 'For fun?'

'Never happened before. And we've always had kids.'

'No one in the car?'

'No, thank God. Like I said, as far as we know it was just parked there.'

'Stolen?'

'Don't know yet. There's not much of it left. We think it might have been blue. It set on fire. Burned some trees with it.'

'No one called in a missing car?'

'Not yet.'

I asked, 'What else are you busy with?'

And at that point Pellegrino went quiet and didn't answer, and I wondered if I had pushed it too far. But I reviewed the back-and-forth in my head and figured it was a reasonable question. Just making conversation. A guy says he's real busy but mentions only a wrecked car, another guy is entitled to ask for more, right? Especially while riding through the dusk in a companionable fashion.

But it turned out Pellegrino's hesitation was based purely on courtesy and old-fashioned Southern hospitality. That was all. He said, 'Well, I don't want to give you a bad impression, seeing as you're here for the first time. But we had a woman murdered.'

'Really?' I said.

'Two days ago,' he said.

'Murdered how?'

And it turned out that Garber's information was inaccurate again. Janice May Chapman had not been mutilated. Her throat had been cut, that was all. And delivery of a fatal wound was not the same thing as mutilation. Not the same thing at all. Not even close.

Pellegrino said, 'Ear to ear. Real deep. One big slice. Not pretty.'

I said, 'You saw it, I guess.'

'Up close and personal. I could see the bones inside her neck. She was all bled out. Like a lake. It was real bad. A good-looking woman, real pretty, all dressed up for a night out, neat as a pin, just lying there on her back in a pool of blood. Not right at all.'

I said nothing, out of respect for something Pellegrino's tone seemed to demand.

He said, 'She was raped, too. The doctor found that out when he got her clothes off and got her on the slab. Unless you could say she'd been into it enough at some point to throw herself down and scratch up her ass on the gravel. Which I don't think she would be.'

'You knew her?'

'We saw her around.'

I asked, 'Who did it?'

He said, 'We don't know. A guy off the base, probably. That's what we think.'

'Why?'

'Because those are who she spent her time with.'

I asked, 'If your detective is out sick, who is working the case?'

Pellegrino said, 'The chief.'

'Does he have much experience with homicides?'

'She,' Pellegrino said. 'The chief is a woman.'

'Really?'

'It's an elected position. She got the votes.' There was a little resignation in his voice. The kind of tone a guy uses when his team loses a big game. *It is what it is.*

'Did you run for the job?' I asked.

'We all did,' he said. 'Except the detective. He was already bad with his kidneys.'

I said nothing. The car rocked and swayed. Pellegrino's tyres sounded worn and soft. They set up a dull baritone roar on the blacktop. Up ahead the evening gloom had gone completely. Pellegrino's headlights lit the way fifty yards in front. Beyond that was nothing but darkness. The road was straight, like a tunnel through the trees. The trees were twisted and opportunistic, like weeds competing for light and air and minerals, like they had seeded themselves a hundred years ago on abandoned arable land. They flashed past in the light spill, as if frozen in motion. I saw a tin sign on the shoulder, lopsided and faded and pocked with rusty coin-sized spots where the enamel had flaked loose. It advertised a hotel called Toussaint's. It promised the convenience of a Main Street location, and rooms of the highest quality.

Pellegrino said, 'She got elected because of her name.'

'The sheriff?'

'That's who we were talking about.'

'Why? What's her name?'

'Elizabeth Deveraux,' he said.

'Nice name,' I said. 'But no better than Pellegrino, for instance.'

'Her daddy was sheriff before her. He was a well-liked man, in certain quarters. We think some folks voted out of loyalty. Or maybe they thought they were voting for the old guy himself. Maybe they didn't know he was dead. Things take time to catch on, in certain quarters.'

I asked, 'Is Carter Crossing big enough to have quarters?'

Pellegrino said, 'Halves, I guess. Two of them. West of the railroad track, or east.'

'Right side, wrong side?'

'Like everywhere.'

'Which side is Kelham?'

'East. You have to drive three miles. Through the wrong side.'

'Which side is the Toussaint's hotel?'

'Won't you be staying with your friend?'

'When I find him. If I find him. Until then I need a place.'

'Toussaint's is OK,' Pellegrino said. 'I'll let you out there.'

And he did. We drove out of the tunnel through the trees and the road broadened and the forest itself died back to stunted saplings left and right, all choked with weeds and trash. The road became an asphalt ribbon laid through a wide flat area of earth the size of a football field. It led through a right turn to a straight street between low buildings. Main Street, presumably. There was no architecture. Just construction, a lot of it old, most of it wood, with some stone at the foundation level. We passed a building marked Carter County Sheriff's Department, and then a vacant lot, and then a diner, and then we arrived at Toussaint's hotel. It had been a fancy place once. It had green paint and trim and mouldings and iron railings on the second-floor balconies. It looked like it had been copied from a New Orleans design. It had a faded signboard with its name on it, and a row of dim lights washing the exterior facade, three of which were out.

Pellegrino eased the cruiser to a stop and I thanked him for the ride and got out. He pulled a wide U-turn behind me and headed back the way we had come, presumably to park in the Sheriff's Department lot. I used a set of wormy wooden steps and crossed a bouncy wooden veranda and pushed in through the hotel door.

NINE

Inside the hotel I found a small square lobby and an unattended reception desk. The floor was worn boards partially covered by a threadbare rug of Middle Eastern design. The desk was a counter made of hardwood polished to a high shine by years of wear and labour. There was a matrix of pigeonholes on the wall behind it. Four high, seven wide. Twenty-eight rooms. Twenty-seven of them had their keys hanging in place. None of the pigeonholes contained letters or notes or any other kind of communication.

There was a bell on the desk, a small brass thing going green around the edges. I hit it twice, and a polite *ding ding* echoed around for a spell, but it produced no results. No one came. There was a closed door next to the pigeonholes, and it stayed closed. A back office, I guessed. Empty, presumably. I saw no reason why a hotel owner would deliberately avoid doubling his occupancy rate.

I stood still for a moment and then checked a door on the left of the lobby. It opened to an unlit lounge that smelled of damp and dust and mildew. There were humped shapes in the dark that I took to be armchairs. No activity. No people. I stepped back to the desk and hit the bell again.

No response.

I called out, 'Hello?'

No response.

So I gave up for the time being and went back out, across the shaky veranda, down the worn steps, and I stood in a shadow on the sidewalk under one of the busted lamps. There was nothing much to see. Across Main Street was a long row of low buildings. Stores, presumably. All of them were dark. Beyond them was blackness. The night air was clear and dry and faintly warm. March, in Mississippi. Meteorologically I could have been anywhere. I could hear the thrill of breeze in distant leaves, and tiny granular sounds, like moving dust, or termites eating wood. I could hear an extractor fan in the wall of the diner up the street. Beyond that, nothing. No human sounds. No voices. No revelry, no traffic, no music.

Tuesday night, near an army base.

Not typical.

I had eaten nothing since lunch in Memphis, so I headed for the diner. It was a narrow building, but deep, set end-on to Main Street. The kitchen entrance was probably on the block behind. Inside the front door was a pay phone on the wall and a register and a hostess station. Beyond that was a long straight aisle with tables for four on the left and tables for two on the right. Tables, not booths, with freestanding chairs. Like a café. The only customers in the place were a couple about twice my age. They were face to face at a table for four. The guy had a newspaper and the woman had a book. They were settled in, like they were happy to linger over their meal. The only staff on view was a waitress. She was close to the swing door in back that led to the kitchen. She saw me step in and she hustled the whole length of the aisle to greet me. She put me at a table for two, about halfway into the room. I sat facing the front, with my back to the kitchen. Not possible to watch both entrances at once, which would have been my preference.

'Something to drink?' the waitress asked me.

'Black coffee,' I said. 'Please.'

She went away and came back again, with coffee in a mug, and a menu.

I said, 'Quiet night.'

She nodded, unhappy, probably worried about her tips.

She said, 'They closed the base.'

'Kelham?' I said. 'They closed it?'

She nodded again. 'They locked it down this afternoon. They're all in there, eating army chow tonight.'

'Does that happen a lot?'

'Never happened before.'

'I'm sorry,' I said. 'What do you recommend?'

'For what?'

'To eat.'

'Here? It's all good.'

'Cheeseburger,' I said.

'Five minutes,' she said. She went away and I took my coffee with me and headed back past the hostess station

61

to the pay phone. I dug in my pocket and found three quarters from my lunchtime change, which were enough for a short conversation, which was the kind I liked. I dialled Garber's office and a duty lieutenant put him on the line and he asked, 'Are you there yet?'

I said, 'Yes.'

'Trip OK?'

'It was fine.'

'Got a place to stay?'

'Don't worry about me. I've got seventy-five cents and four minutes before I eat. I need to ask you something.'

'Fire away.'

'Who briefed you on this?'

Garber paused.

'I can't tell you that,' he said.

'Well, whoever it was, he's kind of hazy about the details.'

'That can happen.'

'And Kelham is locked down.'

'Munro did that, as soon as he got there.'

'Why?'

'You know how it is. There's a risk of bad feeling between the town and the base. It was a commonsense move.'

'It was an admission of guilt.'

'Well, maybe Munro knows something you don't. Don't worry about him. Your only job is to eavesdrop on the local cops.'

'I'm on it. I rode in with one.'

'Did he buy the civilian act?'

'He seemed to.'

'Good. They'll clam up if they know you're connected.'

'I need you to find out if anyone from Bravo Company owns a blue car.'

'Why?'

'The cop said someone parked a blue car on the railroad track. The midnight train wrecked it. Could have been an attempt to hide evidence.'

'He'd have burned it out, surely.'

'Maybe it was the kind of evidence that burning wouldn't conceal. Maybe a big dent in the fender or something.'

'How would that relate to a woman getting carved up in an alley?'

'She wasn't carved up. Her throat was cut. That was all. Deep and wide. One pass, probably. The cop I talked to said he saw bone.'

Garber paused a beat.

He said, 'That's how Rangers are taught to do it.'

I said nothing.

He asked, 'But how would that relate to a car?'

'I don't know. Maybe it doesn't relate. But let's find out, OK?'

'There are two hundred guys in Bravo Company. Law of averages says there's going to be about fifty blue cars.'

'And all fifty of them should be parked on the base. Let's find out if one isn't.'

'It was probably a civilian vehicle.'

'Let's hope it was. I'll work that end. But either way, I need to know.'

'This is Munro's investigation,' Garber said. 'Not yours.'

I said, 'And we need to know if someone got a gravel rash. Hands, knees, and elbows, maybe. From the rape. The cop said Chapman had matching injuries.'

'This is Munro's investigation,' Garber said again.

I didn't answer that. I saw the waitress push in through the kitchen door. She was carrying a plate piled high with an enormous burger in a bun and a tangle of shoe-lace fries as big and untidy as a squirrel's nest. I said, 'I have to go, boss. I'll call you tomorrow,' and I hung up and carried my coffee back to my table. The waitress put my plate down with a degree of ceremony. The meal looked good and smelled good.

'Thanks,' I said.

'Can I get you anything else?'

'You can tell me about the hotel,' I said. 'I need a room, but there was nobody home.'

The waitress half-turned and I followed her gaze to the old couple settled in at their table for four. They were still reading. The waitress said, 'They usually sit a spell in here, and then they go back. That would be the best time to catch them.'

Then she went away and left me to it. I ate slowly and enjoyed every bite. The old couple sat still and read. The woman turned a page every couple of minutes. Much less often the guy made a big loud production out of snapping the spine of his paper and refolding it ready for the next section. He was studying it intently. He was practically reading the print off it.

Later the waitress came back and picked up my plate and offered me dessert. She said she had great pies. I said, 'I'm going to take a walk. I'll look in again on my way back and if those two are still here, then I'll stop in for pie. I guess there's no hurrying them.'

'Not usually,' the waitress said.

I paid for the burger and the coffee and added a tip that didn't compare to a roomful of hungry Rangers, but it was enough to make her smile a little. Then I headed back to the street. The night was turning cold and there was a little mist in the air. I turned right and strolled past the vacant lot and the Sheriff's Department building. Pellegrino's car was parked outside and there was a glow in one window suggesting an interior room was occupied. I kept on going and came to the T where we had turned. To the left was the way Pellegrino had brought me in, through the forest. To the right that road continued east into the darkness. Presumably it crossed the railroad line and then led onward through the wrong side of town to Kelham. Garber had described it as a dirt track, which it might have been once. Now it was a standard rural road, with a stony surface bound with tar. It was dead straight and unlit. There were deep ditches either side of it. There was a thin moon in the sky, and a little light to see by. I turned right and walked on into the gloom.

TEN

Two minutes and two hundred yards later I found the railroad track. First came the warning sign on the shoulder of the road, two diagonal arms bolted together at ninety degrees, one marked RAILROAD and the other marked CROSSING. There were red lights attached to the pole and somewhere beyond it there would be an electric bell in a box. Twenty yards farther on the ditches either side of the road ended abruptly, and the track itself was up on a hump, gleaming faintly in the moonlight, two parallel rails running not very level and not completely straight north and south, looking old and worn and short on maintenance. The gravel bed was lumpy and compacted and matted with weeds. I stood on a tie between the rails and looked first one way and then the other. Twenty yards to the north, on the left, was the shadowy bulk of an old ruined water tower, still with a wide soft hose like an elephant's trunk, which once must have been connected to Carter Crossing's freshwater spring, and once must have stood ready to replenish the greedy steam locomotives that halted there.

I turned a full 360 in the dark. There was absolute stillness and silence everywhere. I could smell charcoal on the night air, maybe from where the blue car had burned the trees to the north. I could smell barbecue faintly in the east, where I guessed the rest of the township was, on the wrong side of the tracks. But I could see only darkness in that direction. Just the suggestion of a hole through the woods, where the road ran, and then nothing more.

I turned back the way I had come, the hard road under my feet, thinking about pie, and I saw headlights in the distance. A large car or a small truck, coming straight at me, moving slow. At one point it looked ready to make the turn into Main Street, and then it seemed to change its mind. Maybe it had picked me up in its beams. It straightened again and kept on coming. I kept on walking. It was a blunt-nosed pick-up truck. It dipped and wallowed over the humps in the road. Its lights rose and fell in the mist. I could hear a low wet burble from a worn V-8 motor.

It came over into the wrong lane and stopped twenty feet from me and idled. I couldn't see who was in it. Too much glare. I walked on. I wasn't about to step into the weeds, and the shoulder was narrow anyway, because of the ditch on my right, so I held my course, which was going to take me close to the driver's door. The driver saw me coming, and when I was ten feet out he dropped his window and put his left wrist on the door and his left elbow in my path. By that point there was enough light spill to make him out. He was a civilian, white, heavy, wearing a T-shirt with the sleeve rolled above a thick arm covered in fur and ink. He had long hair that hadn't been washed for a week or more.

Three choices.

First, stop and chat.

Second, step into the weeds between the pavement and the ditch, and pass him by.

Third, break his arm.

I chose the first option. I stopped. But I didn't chat. Not immediately. I just stood there.

There was a second man in the passenger seat. Same type of a guy. Fur, ink, hair, dirt, grease. But not identical. A cousin, maybe, not a brother. Both men looked right at me, with the kind of smug, low-wattage insolence some kinds of strangers get in some kinds of bars. I looked right back at them. I'm not that kind of stranger.

The driver said, 'Who are you and where are you going?'

I said nothing. I'm good at saying nothing. I don't like talking. I could go the rest of my life without saying another word, if I had to.

The driver said, 'I asked you a question.'

I thought: *two questions, actually.* But I said nothing. I didn't want to have to hit the guy. Not with my hands. I'm no hygiene freak, but even so, with a guy like that, I would feel the need to wash up afterwards, extensively, with good soap, especially if there was pie in my future. So I planned on kicking him instead. I saw the moves in my head: he opens his door, he steps out, he comes around the door towards me, and then he goes down, puking and retching and clutching his groin.

No major difficulty.

He said, 'Do you speak English?'

I said nothing.

The guy in the passenger seat said, 'Maybe he's a Mexican.'

The driver asked me, 'Are you a Mexican?'

I didn't answer.

The driver said, 'He doesn't look like a Mexican. He's too big.'

Which was true in a general sense, although I had heard of a guy from Mexico called Jose Calderon Torres, who had stood seven feet six and a quarter inches, which was more than a foot taller than me. And I remembered a Mexican guy called Jose Garces from the LA Olympics, who had cleaned-and-jerked more than four hundred and twenty pounds, which was probably what the two guys in the truck weighed both together.

The driver asked, 'Are you coming in from Kelham?'

There's a risk of bad feeling between the town and the base, Garber had said. People are always tribal, when it comes right down to it. Maybe these guys had known Janice May Chapman. Maybe they couldn't understand why she had dated soldiers, and not them. Maybe they had never looked in a mirror.

I said nothing. But I didn't walk on. I didn't want the truck loose behind me. Not in a lonely spot, not on a dark country road. I just stood there, looking directly at the two guys, at their faces, first one, then the other, with nothing much in my own face except frankness and scepticism and a little amusement. It's a look that usually works. It usually provokes something, out of a certain type of person.

It provoked the passenger first.

He wound his window down and reared up through it, almost all the way out to his waist, twisting and leaning so he could face me directly across the hood of the truck. He held on to the pillar with one hand and moved the other through a fast violent arc, like he was cracking a whip or throwing something at me. He said, 'We're *talking* to you, asshole.'

I said nothing.

He said, 'Is there a reason I don't get out of this truck and kick your butt?'

I said, 'Two hundred and six reasons.'

He said, 'What?'

'That's how many bones you got in your body. I could break them all before you put a glove on me.'

Which got his buddy going. His instinct was to stick up for his friend and face down a challenge. He leaned further out his own window and said, 'You think?'

I said, 'Often all day long. It's a good habit to have.' Which shut the guy up, while he tried to piece together what I meant. He went back over our conversation in his head. His lips were moving.

I said, 'Let's all go about our legitimate business and leave each other alone. Where are you guys staying?'

Now I was asking the questions, and they weren't answering.

I said, 'It looked to me like you were about to turn into Main Street. Is that your way home?'

No answer.

I said, 'What, you're homeless?'

The driver said, 'We got a place.'

'Where?'

'A mile past Main Street.'

'So go there. Watch TV, drink beer. Don't worry about me.'

'Are you from Kelham?'

'No,' I said. 'I'm not from Kelham.'

The two guys went quiet and kind of deflated themselves, like parade balloons, back through their windows, back into the cab, back into their seats. I heard the truck's transmission engage, and then it took off backwards, fast, and then it slewed and lurched through a 180 turn, with dust coming up and tyre squeal, and then it drove away and braked hard and turned into Main Street. Then it was lost to sight behind the dark bulk of the Sheriff's Department. I breathed out and started walking again. No damage done. *The best fights are the ones you don't have*, a wise man once said to me. It was not advice I always followed, but on that occasion I was pleased to walk away with clean hands, both literally and figuratively.

Then I saw another car coming towards me. It did the same thing the truck had done. It went to turn, and then it paused and straightened and headed in my direction. It was a cop car. I could tell by the shape and the size, and I could make out the silhouette of a light bar on the roof. At first I thought it was Pellegrino out on patrol, but when the car got closer it killed its lights and I saw a woman behind the wheel, and Mississippi suddenly got a lot more interesting.

71

ELEVEN

The car came over into the wrong lane and stopped alongside me. It was an old Chevy Caprice police cruiser painted up in the Carter County Sheriff's Department colours. The woman behind the wheel had an unruly mass of dark hair, somewhere between wavy and curly, tied back in an approximate ponytail. Her face was pale and flawless. She was low in the seat, which meant either she was short or the seat was caved in by long years of use. I decided the seat must be caved in, because her arms looked long and the set of her shoulders didn't suggest a short person. I pegged her at somewhere in her middle thirties, old enough to show some mileage, young enough to still find some amusement in the world. She was smiling slightly, and the smile was reaching her eyes, which were big and dark and liquid and seemed to have some kind of a glow in them. Although that might have been a reflection from the Chevy's instrument panel.

She wound down her window and looked straight at me, first my face, then a careful up-and-down, side-to-side appraisal all the way from my shoes to my hair, with nothing but frankness in her gaze. I stepped in closer to give her a better look, and to take a better look. She was more than flawless. She was spectacular. She had a revolver in a holster on her right hip, and next to it was a shotgun stuffed muzzle-down in a scabbard mounted between the seats. There was a big radio slung under the dash on the passenger side, and a microphone on a curly wire in a clip near the steering wheel. The car was old and worn, almost certainly bought secondhand from a richer municipality.

She said, 'You're the guy Pellegrino brought in.'

Her voice was quiet but clear, warm but not soft, and her accent sounded local.

I said, 'Yes, ma'am, I am.'

She said, 'You're Reacher, right?'

I said, 'Yes, ma'am, I am.'

She said, 'I'm Elizabeth Deveraux. I'm the sheriff here.'

I said, 'I'm very pleased to meet you.'

She paused a beat and said, 'Did you eat dinner yet?'

I nodded. 'But not dessert,' I said. 'As a matter of fact I'm heading back to the diner for pie right now.'

'Do you usually take a walk between courses?'

'I was waiting out the hotel people. They didn't seem in much of a hurry.'

'Is that where you're staying tonight? The hotel?'

'I'm hoping to.'

'You're not staying with the friend you came to find?'

'I haven't found him yet.'

She nodded in turn. 'I need to talk to you,' she said. 'Find me in the diner. Five minutes, OK?'

73

There was authority but no menace in her voice. No agenda. Just the kind of easy command I guessed came from being first a sheriff's daughter and then a sheriff herself.

'OK,' I said. 'Five minutes.'

She wound up her window again and reversed away and turned around, in a slower version of the same manoeuvre the two guys in the truck had used. She switched her headlights back on and drove away. I saw her brake lights flare red and she turned into Main Street. I followed on foot, in the weeds, between the pavement and the ditch.

I got to the diner well inside the five minutes I had been given and found Elizabeth Deveraux's cruiser parked at the kerb outside. She herself was at the same table I had used. The old couple from the hotel had finally decamped. The place was empty apart from Deveraux and the waitress.

I went in and Deveraux said nothing specific but used one foot under the table to shove the facing chair out a little. An invitation. Almost a command. The waitress got the message. She didn't try to seat me elsewhere. Clearly Deveraux had already ordered. I asked the waitress for a slice of her best pie and another cup of coffee. She went through to the kitchen and silence claimed the room.

Up close and personal I was prepared to concede that Elizabeth Deveraux was a seriously good looking woman. Truly beautiful. Out of the car she was relatively tall, and her hair was amazing. There must have been five pounds of it in her ponytail alone. She had all the right parts in all the right proportions. She looked great in her uniform. But then, I liked women in uniform, possibly because I had known very few of the other kind. But best of all was her mouth. And her eyes. Together they put a kind of wry, amused animation into her face, as if whatever happened to her she would stay cool and calm and collected through it all, and then she would find some quality in it to make her smile. There was still light in her eyes. Not just a reflection from the Caprice's speedometer.

She said, 'Pellegrino told me you've been in the army.'

I paused a beat. Undercover work is all about lying, and I hadn't minded lying to Pellegrino. But for some unknown reason I found myself not wanting to lie to Deveraux. So I said, 'Six weeks ago I was in the army,' which was technically true.

'What branch?'

'I was with an outfit called the 110th, mostly,' I said. Also true.

'Infantry?'

'It was a special unit. Combined operations, basically.' Which was true, technically.

'Who's your local friend?'

'A guy called Hayder,' I said. An outright invention.

Deveraux said, 'He must have been infantry. Kelham is all infantry.'

I nodded. '75th Ranger Regiment,' I said.

'Was he an instructor?' she asked.

'Yes,' I said.

She nodded. 'They're the only ones who are here long enough to want to stick around afterwards.'

I said nothing.

She said, 'I've never heard of him.'

'Then maybe he moved on again.'

'When might he have done that?'

'I'm not sure. How long have you been sheriff?'

'Two years,' she said. 'Long enough to get to know the locals, anyway.'

'Pellegrino said you'd been here all your life. I mean, as far as getting to know the locals is concerned.'

'Not true,' she said. 'I haven't been here all my life. I was here as a kid, and I'm here now. But there were years in between.'

There was something wistful about her tone. *There were years in between.* I asked her, 'How did you spend those years?'

'I had a rich uncle,' she said. 'I toured the world at his expense.'

And at that point I suspected I was in trouble. At that point I suspected my mission was about to fail. Because I had heard that answer before.

TWELVE

The waitress brought out Elizabeth Deveraux's main course and my dessert both together. Deveraux had ordered the same thing I had eaten, the fat cheeseburger and the squirrel's nest of fries. My pie was peach and the slice I got was about half the size of a Major League home plate. It was bigger than the dish it was in. My coffee was in a tall stoneware mug. Deveraux had plain water in a chipped glass.

It's easier to let a pie go cold than a cheeseburger, so I figured I had a chance to talk while Deveraux had no choice but to eat and listen and comment briefly. So I said, 'Pellegrino told me you guys are real busy.'

Deveraux chewed and nodded.

I said, 'A wrecked car and a dead woman.'

She nodded again and chased an errant pearl of mayonnaise back into her mouth with the tip of her little finger. An elegant gesture, for an inelegant act. She had short nails, nicely trimmed and polished. She had slender hands, a little tanned and sinewy. Good skin. No rings. None at all. Especially not on her left ring finger.

I asked, 'Any progress on any of that?'

She swallowed and smiled and held her hand up like a traffic cop. *Stop. Wait.* She said, 'Give me a minute, OK? No more talking.'

So I ate my pie, which was good. The crust was sweet and the peaches were soft. Probably local. Or maybe over from Georgia. I didn't know much about the cultivation of fruit. She ate, with the burger in her right hand, her left taking fries one by one from her plate, her eyes on mine most of the time. The grease from the meat made her lips glisten. She was a slim woman. She must have had a metabolism like a nuclear reactor. She took occasional long sips of water. I drained my mug. The coffee was OK, but not as good as the pie.

She asked, 'Doesn't coffee keep you awake?'

I nodded. 'Until I want to go to sleep. That's what it's for.'

She took a last sip of water and left a rind of bun and six or seven fries on her plate. She wiped her mouth and then her hands on her napkin. She folded her napkin and laid it down next to her plate. Dinner was over.

I asked, 'So are you making progress?'

She smiled at some inner amusement and then leaned sideways away from the table, hands braced to increase her angle, and she looked me over again, slowly, a crooked path, all the way from my feet in the shadows to my head. She said, 'You're pretty good. Nothing to be ashamed about, really. It's not your fault.'

I asked, 'What isn't?'

She leaned back in her chair. She kept her eyes on mine. She said, 'My daddy was sheriff here before me. Since before I was born, actually. He won about twenty consecutive elections. He was firm, but fair. And honest. No fear or favour. He was a good public servant.'

I said, 'I'm sure he was.'

'But I didn't like it here very much. Not as a kid. I mean, can you imagine? It's the back of beyond. We got books in the mail. I knew there was a big wide world out there. So I had to get away.'

I said, 'I don't blame you.'

She said, 'But some ideas get ingrained. Like public service. Like law enforcement. It starts to feel like a family business, the same as any other.'

I nodded. She was right. Kids follow their parents into law enforcement far more than most other professions. Except baseball. The son of a pro ballplayer is eight hundred times more likely to make the Majors than some other random kid.

She said, 'So look at it from my point of view. What do you think I did when I turned eighteen?'

I said, 'I don't know,' although by that point I was pretty sure I did know, more or less, and I wasn't happy about it.

She said, 'I went to South Carolina and joined the Marine Corps.'

I nodded. Worse than I had expected. For some reason I had been betting on the air force.

I asked her, 'How long were you in?'

'Sixteen years.'

Which made her thirty-six years old. Eighteen years at home, plus sixteen as a jarhead, plus two as Carter County Sheriff. Same age as me.

I asked her, 'What branch of the Corps?'

'Provost Marshal's office.'

I looked away. 'You were a military cop,' I said.

She said, 'Public service and law enforcement. I killed two birds with one stone.'

I looked back, beaten. 'Terminal rank?'

'CWO5,' she said.

Chief Warrant Officer 5. An expert in a specific specialized field. The sweet spot, where the real work was done.

I asked her, 'Why did you leave?'

'Rumblings,' she said. 'The Soviets are gone, reductions in force are coming. I figured it would feel better to step up than be thrown out. Plus my daddy died, and I couldn't let some idiot like Pellegrino take over.'

I asked her, 'Where did you serve?'

'All over,' she said. 'Uncle Sam was my rich uncle. He showed me the world. Some parts of it were worth seeing, and some parts of it weren't.'

I said nothing. The waitress came back and took away our empty plates.

'Anyway,' Deveraux said, 'I was expecting you. It's exactly what we would have done, frankly, under the same circumstances. A homicide behind a bar near a base? Some kind of big secrecy or sensitivity *on* the base? We would have put an investigator on the post, and we would have sent another into town, undercover.'

I said nothing.

She said, 'The idea being, of course, that the undercover guy in town would keep his ear to the ground and then step in and stop the locals embarrassing the Corps. If strictly necessary, that is. It was a policy I supported

80

back then, naturally. But now I *am* the locals, so I can't really support it any more.'

I said nothing.

'Don't feel bad,' she said. 'You were doing it better than some of our guys did. I love the shoes, for instance. And the hair. You're fairly convincing. You ran into a bit of bad luck, that's all, with me being who I am. Although the timing wasn't subtle, was it? But then, it never is. I don't see how it ever could be. And to be honest, you're not a very fluent liar. You shouldn't have said the 110th. I know about the 110th, of course. You were nearly as good as we were. But really, Hayder? Far too uncommon a name. And the khaki socks were a mistake. Obvious PX. You probably bought them yesterday. I wore socks just like them.'

'I didn't want to lie,' I said. 'Didn't seem right. My father was a Marine. Maybe I sensed it in you.'

'He was a Marine but you joined the army? What was that, mutiny?'

'I don't know what it was,' I said. 'But it felt right at the time.'

'How does it feel now?'

'Right this minute? Not so great.'

'Don't feel bad,' she said again. 'You gave it a good try.'

I said nothing.

She asked, 'What rank are you?'

I said, 'Major.'

'Should I salute?'

'Only if you want to.'

'Still with the 110th?'

'Temporarily. Home base right now is the 396th MP. The Criminal Investigation Division.'

'How many years in?'

'Thirteen. Plus West Point.'

'I'm honoured. Maybe I *should* salute. Who did they send to Kelham?'

'A guy called Munro. Same rank as me.'

'That's confusing,' she said.

I said, 'Are you making progress?'

She said, 'You don't give up, do you?'

'Giving up was not in the mission statement. You know how it is.'

'OK, I'll trade,' she said. 'One answer for one answer. And then you ship back out. You hit the road at first light. In fact I'll get Pellegrino to drive you back to where he picked you up. Do we have a deal?'

What choice did I have? I said, 'We have a deal.'

'No,' she said. 'We're not making progress. Absolutely none at all.'

'OK,' I said. 'Thanks. Your turn.'

'Obviously it would give me an insight to know if you're the ace, or if the guy they sent to Kelham is the ace. I mean, in terms of the army's current thinking. About the balance of probabilities here. As in, do they think the problem is inside the gates or outside? So, are you the big dog? Or is the other guy?'

'Honest answer?'

'That's what I would expect from the son of a fellow Marine.'

'The honest answer is I don't know,' I said.

THIRTEEN

Elizabeth Deveraux paid for her burger and my pie and coffee, which I thought was generous, so I left the tip, which made the waitress smile again. We stepped out to the sidewalk together and stood for a moment next to the old Caprice. The moon had gotten brighter. A thin layer of high cloud had moved away. There were stars out.

I said, 'Can I ask you another question?'

Deveraux was immediately guarded. She said, 'About what?'

'Hair,' I said. 'Ours is supposed to conform to the shape of our heads. Tapered, they call it. Curving inward to a natural termination point at the base of the neck. What about yours?'

'I wore a buzz cut for fifteen years,' she said. 'I started growing it out when I knew I was going to quit.'

I looked at her in the moonlight and the spill from the diner window. I pictured her with a buzz cut. She must have looked sensational. I said, 'Good to know. Thanks.'

She said, 'I had no chance, right from the beginning. The regulation for women in the Corps required what

83

they called a non-eccentric style. Your hair could touch your collar, but it couldn't fall below the bottom edge. You were allowed to pin it up, but then I couldn't get my hat on.'

'Sacrifices,' I said.

'It was worth it,' she said. 'I loved being a Marine.'

'You still are,' I said. 'Once a Marine, always a Marine.'

'Is that what your daddy said?'

'He never got the chance. He died in harness.'

She asked, 'Is your mom still alive?'

'She died a few years later.'

'Mine died when I was in boot camp. Cancer.'

'Really? Mine too. Cancer, I mean. Not boot camp.'

'I'm sorry.'

'Not your fault,' I said, automatically. 'She was in Paris.'

'So was I. Parris Island, anyway. Did she emigrate?'

'She was French.'

'Do you speak French?'

I said, '*Un peu, mais lentement.*'

'What does that mean?'

'A little, but slowly.'

She nodded and put her hand on the Caprice's door. I took the hint and said, 'OK, goodnight, Chief Deveraux. It was a pleasure meeting you.'

She just smiled.

I turned left and walked down towards the hotel. I heard the big Chevy motor start up, and I heard the tyres start to roll, and then the car passed me, going slow, and then it pulled a wide U-turn across the width of the street and stopped again, just ahead of me, facing me, at the kerb right next to the Toussaint's hotel. I walked on and got there just as Deveraux opened her door and got out again. Naturally I assumed she had something more to say to me, so I stopped walking and waited politely.

'I live here,' she said. 'Goodnight.'

She had already gone upstairs before I got into the lobby. The old guy I had seen in the diner was behind the reception counter. He was open for business. I could tell he was disconcerted by my lack of luggage, but cash money is cash money, and he took eighteen dollars of mine and in return he gave me the key to room twenty-one. He told me it was on the second floor, at the front of the building, overlooking the street, which he said was quieter than the back, which made no sense at all until I remembered the railroad track.

On the second floor the staircase came up in the centre of a long north–south corridor, which was uncarpeted and dimly lit by four mean and ungenerous bulbs. It had eight doors off the back side and nine off the street side. There was a slim bar of brighter yellow light showing through the crack under room seventeen's door, which was on the street side. Deveraux, presumably, getting ready for bed. My room was four doors further north. I unlocked it and went in and turned on the light and found the kind of still air and dusty chill that indicates long disuse. It was a rectangular space with a high ceiling and what would have been pleasant proportions, except that at some point in the last decade an attached bathroom had been shoehorned into one corner. The window was a pair of glazed doors that gave out on to the iron balcony I had seen from the street. There was a bed and a chair and a dressing table, and on the floor there was a threadbare Persian rug worn thin by use and beating.

I pulled the drapes closed and unpacked, which consisted solely of assembling my new toothbrush and propping it upright in a milky glass on the bathroom shelf. I had no toothpaste, but then I had never been convinced that toothpaste was anything more than a pleasant-tasting lubricant. An army dentist I had known swore that the mechanical action of the brush's bristles was all that was needed for perfect oral health. And I had chewing gum for freshness. And I still had all my teeth, apart from a top row molar knocked out many years before by a lucky knuckle in a street fight in Cleveland, Ohio.

The clock in my head said it was about twenty after eleven. I sat on the bed for a spell. I had been up early and was moderately tired, but not exhausted. And I had things to do, and limited time to do them in, so I waited long enough to let an average person get off to sleep, and then I went out to the corridor again. Deveraux's light was off. There was nothing showing under her door. I crept down the stairs to the lobby. The reception desk was once again unattended. I went out to the street and turned left, towards territory as yet unexplored.

FOURTEEN

I looked at the whole length of Main Street as carefully as was possible in the grey moonlight. It ran on south for about two hundred yards, as straight as a die, and then it narrowed a little and started to meander and became residential, with modest homes randomly spaced in yards of varying sizes. The west side of the straight downtown stretch had stores and commercial operations of various kinds, punctuated with narrow alleys, some of which led onward into the scrub and had more small houses on the left and the right. Those stores and commercial operations were matched by similar establishments on the east side of Main Street, neatly in line with the diner and the hotel, and the alleys to the west were matched by broader paved passageways opposite, which linked all the way through to a one-sided street built parallel to and behind Main Street. I guessed that one-sided street had been the whole point of the town in the early days, and was certainly the point in my being there that night.

It ran north and south and had a long line of establishments that faced the railroad track across nothing but a blank width of beaten earth. I imagined old passenger trains wheezing to a stop, with their panting locomotives next to the water tower a little ways up the line, the trains' long windowed sides stretching south. I imagined restaurant staff and café owners running across the beaten earth and placing wooden steps below the train doors. I imagined passengers stepping down, spilling out, dry and hungry from their long haul, hundreds of them eagerly crossing the width of earth, and then eating and drinking their fill. I imagined coins clattering, cash registers ringing, the train whistles blowing, the passengers returning, the trains moving onward, the wooden steps being retrieved, then stillness returning for an hour, then the next train easing in, and the whole process repeating itself endlessly.

That single-sided street had powered the local economy, and it still did.

The passenger trains were long gone, of course, and so were the cafés and the restaurants. But the cafés and the restaurants had been replaced by bars, and auto parts stores, and bars, and loan offices, and bars, and gun shops, and bars, and secondhand stereo stores, and bars, and the trains had been replaced by streams of cars coming in from Kelham. I imagined the cars parking on the beaten earth, and small groups of Rangers-in-training spilling out and spending Uncle Sam's money up and down the row. A captive market, miles from anywhere like Garber had said, just like the railroad passengers back in the day. I had seen the proposition repeated at a hundred bases all around the world. The cars would be old Mustangs or Gran

Torinos or GTOs, or secondhand BMWs or Mercedes in Germany, or strange Toyota Crowns or Datsuns in the Far East, and the beer would be different brands and different strengths, and the loans would be in different currencies, and the guns would be chambered for different loads in different calibres, and the used stereo equipment would operate on different voltages, but other than that the give and take was exactly the same everywhere.

I found the spot where Janice May Chapman had been killed easily enough. Pellegrino had said she had bled out like a lake, which meant sand would have been used to soak up the spill, and I found a fresh spreading pile of it in a paved alley near the rear left-hand corner of a bar called Brannan's. Brannan's was about in the centre of the one-sided street, and the alley in question ran along its left flank before dog-legging twice and exiting on Main Street between an old-style pharmacy and a hardware store. Maybe the hardware store was where the sand had come from. Three or four sixty-pound bags would have done the job. It was spread in a neat teardrop shape over the smooth flagstones, about three or four inches deep.

The spot was not directly overlooked. Brannan's rear door was about fifteen feet away, and the bar had no side windows. The back of the pharmacy was a blank wall. Brannan's neighbour was a loan office with a Western Union franchise, and its right flank had a window towards the rear, but the place would have been closed at night. No witnesses. Not that there would have been much to witness. Cutting a throat doesn't take much time. Given a decent blade and enough weight and force, it takes as long as it takes to move your hand eight inches. That's all.

I stepped out of the alley and walked halfway to the railroad track and stood on the beaten earth and judged the light. No point in looking for things I wouldn't be able to see. But the moon was still high and the sky was still clear, so I kept on going and stepped over the first rail and turned left and hiked north, walking on the ties like guys used to way back, when they were leaving the land and heading to Chicago or New York. I passed over the road crossing, and I passed the old water tower.

Then the ground began to shake.

Just faintly at first, a mild constant tremor, like the edge of a distant earthquake. I stopped walking. The tie under my feet trembled. The rails either side of me started to sing. I turned around and saw a tiny pinpoint of light far in the distance. A single headlight. The midnight train, a couple of miles south of me, coming on fast.

I stood there. The rails hummed and keened. The ties hammered up and down through tiny microscopic distances. The gravel under them clicked and hopped. The ground tremors deepened to big bass shudders. The distant headlight twinkled like a star, jumping minutely left and right through hard constrained limits.

I stepped off the track and looped back to the old water tower and leaned against a tarred wooden upright. It shook against my shoulder. The ground shook under my feet. The rails howled. The train whistle blew, long and loud and forlorn in the distance. The warning bells at the roadside twenty yards away started ringing. The red lights started flashing.

The train kept on coming towards me, for a long time resolutely distant, then all of a sudden right next to me, right on top of me, huge, just insanely massive, and impossibly loud. The ground shook so hard that the old water tower next to me danced mutely in place and I was bounced up and down whole inches. Moving air whipped and battered at me. The locomotive flashed past, and then began an endless sequence of cars, hammering, juddering, strobing in the moonlight, hurtling north without pause, ten of them, twenty, fifty, a hundred. I clung to the tarred pole for a whole long minute, sixty long seconds, deafened by squealing metal, beaten numb by the throbbing ground, scoured by the slipstream.

Then the train was gone.

The butt end of a bulk silo car rolled away from me at sixty miles an hour, and the howl of the wind dropped a half tone, and the earthquake subsided to mild tremors again, and then to nothing, and the screaming rails quieted to a low hiss. The manic bells stopped dead.

Silence came back.

The first thing I did was change my mind about how far I was going to have to walk to find the wreckage of the blue car. I had assumed it would be close by. But after that awesome display of power I figured it might be somewhere in New Jersey. Or Canada.

FIFTEEN

In the end I found most of the car about two hundred yards north. It was preceded by a debris field that stretched most of the intervening distance. There were pebbles of broken windshield glass, glistening and glinting in the dew and the moonlight. The glass had been flung along random curved trajectories, as if by a giant hand. There was a chrome bumper, torn off and folded capriciously in half, a tight V, like a drinking straw. It had embedded itself in the ground, like a lawn dart. There was a wheel with no hub cap. The impact had been colossal. The car had been smashed forward like a baseball off a tee. Zero to sixty, instantaneously.

I guessed it had been parked on the track about twenty yards north of the water tower. That was where the first of the glass was located. The locomotive had hit the car, and it had flown fifty or more yards through the air, and then it had landed and cartwheeled. Maybe wheels to roof to wheels to roof, or end over end. I guessed the initial impact had more or less disassembled it. Like an explosion. Then the rolling action had flung its constituent parts all over the place. Including its fuel, which had ignited. There were narrow black tongues of burned scrub all over the last fifty yards, and what was left of the vehicle itself was nested against the trees in the epicentre of a starburst of blackened trunks and branches. Arson investigators I had met could have worked out its rate of rotation from the fuel splatter alone.

Pellegrino had seen the car in daylight and called it blue. In the moonlight it looked ash grey to me. I couldn't find an intact painted surface. I couldn't find an intact anything larger than a square inch. It was a burned-out mess, crushed and crumpled to the point of being virtually unrecognizable. I was prepared to accept it was a car, but only because I couldn't imagine what else it could be.

If someone's intention had been to conceal evidence, then that someone had succeeded, big time, and comprehensively.

I got back to the hotel at one o'clock exactly, and went straight to bed. I set the alarm in my head for seven in the morning, which was when I figured Deveraux would be getting up for work. I figured her day would start at eight. Clearly she was not neglectful of her appearance, but she was a Marine and a pragmatic person, so she wouldn't budget more than an hour to get ready. I figured I could match her shower time with my own, and then I could find her in the diner for breakfast. Which was as far ahead as my planning extended. I wasn't sure what I was going to say to her.

*　　　*　　　*

93

But I didn't sleep until seven in the morning. I was woken up at six. By someone knocking loudly on my door. I wasn't thrilled. I rolled out of bed and pulled on my pants and opened up. It was the old guy. The hotel keeper.

He said, 'Mr Reacher?'

I said, 'Yes?'

He said, 'Good. I'm glad I got the right person. At this hour, I mean. It's always better to be sure.'

'What do you want?'

'Well, initially, as I said, I'm confirming who you are.'

'I sincerely hope there's more to it than that. At this hour. You only have two guests. And the other one isn't *mister* anything.'

'You have a phone call.'

'Who from?'

'Your uncle.'

'My *uncle*?'

'Your uncle Leon Garber. He said it was urgent. And judging by his tone, it's important, too.'

I put my T-shirt on and followed the guy downstairs, barefoot. He led me through a side door into the office behind the counter. There was a worn mahogany desk with a phone on it. The handset was off the hook, resting on the desk top.

The old guy said, 'Please make yourself at home,' and left, and closed the door on me. I sat down in his chair and picked up the phone.

I said, 'What?'

Garber said, 'You OK?'

'I'm fine. How did you find me?'

94

'Phone book. There's only one hotel in Carter Crossing. Everything going well?'

'Terrific.'

'You sure?'

'Positive.'

'Because you're supposed to check in every morning at six.'

'Am I?'

'That's what we agreed.'

'When?'

'We spoke yesterday at six. As you were leaving.'

'I know,' I said. 'I remember. But we didn't agree we'd talk at six every day.'

'You called me yesterday. At dinnertime. You said you would call again today.'

'I didn't specify the time.'

'I think you did.'

'Well, you're wrong, you old coot. What do you want?'

'You're cranky this morning.'

'I was up late last night.'

'Doing what?'

'Looking around.'

'And?'

'There are a couple of things,' I said.

'Like what?'

'Just two specific items. Matters of interest.'

'Do they represent progress?'

'At this point they're just questions. The answers might represent progress, eventually. If I ever get them.'

Garber said, 'Munro is getting nowhere at Kelham.

95

Not so far. This whole thing might be more complicated than we thought.'

I didn't answer that. Garber was quiet for a beat.

'Wait,' he said. 'What do you mean, *if* you ever get the answers?'

I didn't answer.

Garber said, 'And why were you looking around in the dark? Wouldn't it have been better to wait for first light?'

I said, 'I met the chief here.'

'And?'

'Different from what you might expect.'

'How?' Garber asked. 'Is he honest?'

'He's a she,' I said. 'Her father was sheriff before her.'

Garber paused again.

'Don't tell me,' he said. 'She figured you out.'

I didn't answer.

'Christ on a bike,' he said. 'This has got to be a new world record. How long did it take her? Ten minutes? Five?'

'She was a Marine MP,' I said. 'One of us, practically. She knew all along. She was expecting me. To her it was a predictable move.'

'What are you going to do?'

'I don't know.'

'Is she going to shut you out?'

'Worse. She wants to throw me out.'

'Well, you can't let her do that. No way. You have to stay there. That's for damn sure. In fact, I'm ordering you not to come back. You hear me? Your orders are to stay. She can't throw you out anyway. It's a question of civil rights. The First Amendment, or something. Free association. Mississippi is part of the Union, same as anywhere else. It's a free country. So stay there, OK?'

I hung up with Garber and sat in the little office for a moment. I found a dollar bill in my pocket and left it on the desk, to cover the cost of an outgoing call, and I dialled the Pentagon. The Pentagon has a lot of numbers and a lot of operators, and I chose one that always answered. I asked the guy to try John James Frazer's billet, just on the off chance. The Senate Liaison guy. I wasn't expecting him to be there not long after six in the morning, but he was. Which told me something. I introduced myself and told him I had no news.

'You must have something,' he said. 'Or you wouldn't have called.'

'I have a warning,' I said.

'What kind?'

'I've seen a couple of things, and they're enough to tell me this situation is going to turn out bad. It's going to turn out sick and weird and it's going to be all over every newspaper for a month. Even if it's nothing to do with Kelham, we could end up tainted. Just because of the proximity.'

Frazer paused. 'How sick?'

'Potentially very sick.'

'Gut feeling? *Is* it anything to do with Kelham?'

'Too early to say.'

'Help me out here, Reacher. Best guess?'

'At this stage, I'd say no. No military involvement.'

'That's good to hear.'

97

'It's only a guess,' I said. 'Don't break out the cigars just yet.'

I didn't go back to bed. No point. Too late. I just brushed my teeth and showered and chewed some gum and got fully dressed. Then I stood by my window and watched the dawn. The creeping daylight enlarged the world. I saw Main Street in all its detailed glory. I saw scrub and fields and forest extending in every direction.

Then I sat in my chair to wait. I figured I would hear Deveraux go out to her car. I was more or less right above where it was parked at the kerb.

SIXTEEN

I heard Deveraux leave the hotel at twenty past seven exactly. First the street door creaked open and slammed shut, and then her car door creaked open and slammed shut. I got up and looked out the window. She was behind the wheel, low in the seat, in what looked like a clean version of the same uniform she had worn the day before. Her riot of hair was still wet from the shower. She was talking on the radio. Probably telling Pellegrino that job one for the day was to haul my ass halfway back to Memphis.

I went down the stairs and stepped out to the sidewalk. The morning air was fresh and cold. I looked up the street and saw that Deveraux's car was parked again, right outside the diner. So far, so good. I walked in that direction and pushed in through the door, past the pay phone, past the hostess station. There were six customers inside, including Deveraux. The other five were men, four of them in work clothes and the fifth in a pale-coloured suit. A professional gentleman. Maybe a country lawyer or a country doctor, or the guy that ran the loan office next to Brannan's bar. The waitress was the same woman as the night before. She was busy toting plates of food, so I didn't wait for her. I just walked up to Deveraux's table and said, 'Would you mind if I joined you?'

She was sipping coffee. She didn't have her food yet. She smiled and said, 'Good morning.'

Her tone was warm. She seemed happy to see me.

I said, 'Yes, good morning.'

She said, 'Have you come to say goodbye? That's very polite and very formal.'

I said nothing in reply to that. She did her thing with her foot again, under the table, and kicked the facing chair out. I sat down. She asked, 'Did you sleep well?'

I said, 'Fine.'

'The train didn't wake you at midnight? It takes some getting used to.'

'I was still up,' I said.

'Doing what?'

'This and that,' I said.

'Inside or out?'

'Out,' I said.

'You found the crime scene?'

I nodded.

She nodded in turn.

'And you found two things of note,' she said. 'So you thought you'd stop by and make sure I appreciated their significance before you got on your way. That's very public-spirited of you.'

The waitress came by and put a heaping plate of French toast on the table. Then she turned to me and I ordered the same thing, with coffee. Deveraux waited until she was gone, and asked, 'Or was it entirely private-spirited? Is this your one last attempt to protect the army before you go?'

'I'm not going,' I said.

She smiled again. 'Are you going to give me your civil rights speech now? Free country, and all that bullshit?'

'Something like that.'

She paused a beat.

'I'm all for civil rights,' she said. 'And certainly there's room at the inn, as they say. So, sure, by all means, please stay. Enjoy yourself. There are trails to hike, and there are things to hunt, and there are sights to see. Knock yourself out. Do whatever you want to. Just don't get between me and my investigation.'

I asked her, 'How do you explain the two things?'

'Do I need to? To you?'

'Two heads are better than one.'

'I can't trust you,' she said. 'You're here to steer me wrong, if you have to.'

'No, I'm here to warn the army if things start to look bad. Which I will, if I have to. But we're a long way from any kind of a conclusion here. We've barely even started. It's too early to steer anybody anywhere, even if I was going to. Which I'm not.'

'We?' she said. '*We're* a long way from a conclusion? What is this, a democracy?'

'OK, you,' I said.

'Yes,' she said. 'Me.'

At that point the waitress came back with my meal. And my coffee. I sniffed the steam and took a long first sip. A little ritual. Nothing better than just-made

101

coffee, early in the morning. Across the table from me Deveraux continued eating. She was cleaning her plate. A metabolism like a nuclear plant.

She said, 'OK, time out. Convince me. Put your cards on the table. Tell me about the first thing, and spin it so it looks bad for the army. Which it does, by the way, spin or no spin.'

I looked straight at her. 'Have you been on the base?'

'All over it.'

'I haven't. Therefore apparently you know what I'm only guessing.'

She nodded. 'So bear that in mind. Tread carefully. Don't blow smoke.'

I said, 'Janice May Chapman was not raped in that alley.'

'Because?'

'Because Pellegrino reported gravel abrasions on the corpse. And there's no gravel in that alley. Nor any-where else that I could see. It's all dirt or blacktop or smooth paving stones for miles around.'

'The railroad track has gravel,' she said.

A test. She wanted me to jump all over it.

'Not really gravel,' I said. 'The railroad track has larger stones. Ballast, they call it, in a rail bed. Pieces of granite, bigger than a pebble, smaller than a fist. The injuries would look completely different. They wouldn't look like gravel rash.'

'The roads are gravel.'

Another test.

'Bound with tar and rolled,' I said. 'Not the same at all.'

'So?'

The final test.

Spin it so it looks bad for the army.

'Kelham is for the elite,' I said. 'It's a finishing school for the 75th, which is special ops support. It's a big place. They must have all kinds of simulated terrain. Sand, to simulate the desert. Concrete, like the frozen steppes. Fake villages, all that kind of shit. I'm sure they have plenty of gravel there, for one reason or another.'

Deveraux nodded again. 'They have a running track made of gravel. For endurance training. Ten laps is like ten hours on a road surface. Plus low-scoring individuals get to rake it smooth every morning. As a punishment. Two birds with one stone.'

I said nothing.

Deveraux said, 'She was raped on the base.'

I said, 'Not impossible.'

Deveraux said, 'You're an honest man, Reacher. The son of a Marine.'

'Marines have got nothing to do with it. I'm a commissioned officer in the United States Army. We have standards too.'

I started to eat my breakfast just as she finished hers. She said, 'The second thing is more problematical, though. I can't make it fit.'

'Really?' I said. 'Isn't it basically the same as the first thing?'

She looked at me, blankly.

She said, 'I don't see how.'

I stopped eating and looked back at her.

I said, 'Talk me through it.'

'It's a simple question,' she said. 'How did she get there? She left her car at home, and she didn't walk. For one thing, she was wearing four-inch heels, and for another thing, no one walks anywhere any more. But she wasn't picked up from home either. Her neighbours are the worst busybodies in the world, and both of them swear no one came calling on her. And I believe them. And no one saw her arrive in town with a soldier. Or with a civilian, for that matter. Or even on her own. And trust me, those barkeeps watch the traffic. All of them. It's a habit. They want to know if they can afford to eat tomorrow. So she just materialized in that alley, unexplained.'

I was quiet for a second.

Then I said, 'That wasn't my second thing.'

'Wasn't it?'

'Your two things and my two things are not the same two things. Which means there are three things in total.'

'So what's your second thing?'

I said, 'She wasn't killed in that alley, either.'

SEVENTEEN

I finished my breakfast before I spoke again. French toast, maple syrup, coffee. Protein, fibre, carbohydrates. And caffeine. All the essential food groups, except nicotine, but I had already quit by then. I put my silverware down and said, 'There's really only one obvious way to cut a woman's throat. You stand behind her and use one hand in her hair to pull her head back. Or you hook your fingers in her eye sockets, or if you're sure your hands are steady you could use your palm under her chin. But whichever, you expose her throat and you put some tension in the ligaments and the blood vessels. Then you get busy with the blade. You're taught to expect major resistance to the cut, because there's some pretty tough stuff in there. And you're taught to start an inch earlier and finish an inch later than you think is really necessary. Just to be absolutely sure.'

Deveraux said, 'I'm assuming that's exactly what happened in the alley. But suddenly, I hope. So it was all over before she realized it was happening at all.'

I said, 'It didn't happen in the alley. It can't have.'

'Why not?'

'One of the side benefits of doing it from behind is you don't get covered in blood. And there's a lot of blood. You're talking about carotids and jugulars, and a young healthy person suddenly agitated and struggling, maybe even fighting. Her blood pressure must have been spiking sky high.'

'I know there's a lot of blood. I saw it. There was a huge pool of it. She was all bled out. As white as a sheet. I assume you saw the sand. That's how big the pool was. It looked like a gallon or more.'

'You ever cut a throat?'

'No.'

'You ever seen it done?'

She shook her head. 'No,' she said.

'The blood doesn't just seep out like you slit your wrists in the bathtub. It comes out like a fire hose. It sprays everywhere, ten feet or more, great gouts of it, splattering all over the place. I've seen it on ceilings, even. Crazy patterns, like someone took a paint can and threw it around. Like that guy Jackson Pollock. The painter.'

Deveraux said nothing.

I said, 'There would have been blood all over the alley. On the loan office's wall, for sure. And on the bar's wall, and maybe on the pharmacy's wall. On the floor, too, yards away. Crazy thin patterns. Not a neat pool right underneath her. That's just not possible. She wasn't killed there.'

Deveraux linked her hands on the table and bowed her head over them. She was doing something I had never seen a person do before. Not literally. She was

106

hanging her head. She breathed in, breathed out, and five seconds later she looked up again and said, 'I'm an idiot. I suppose I must have known all that, but I didn't remember it. I just didn't see it.'

'Don't feel bad,' I said. 'You never saw it happen, so you don't have anything to remember.'

'No, it's basic,' she said. 'I'm an idiot. I've wasted days.'

'It gets worse,' I said. 'There's more.'

She didn't want to hear about how it got worse. She didn't want more. Not immediately. Not right then. She was still beating herself up for missing the thing with the blood. I had seen that kind of reaction many times. I had *had* that kind of reaction many times. Smart, conscientious people hate making mistakes. Not just because of ego. Because mistakes of a certain type have the kinds of consequences that people with consciences don't like to live with.

She frowned and ground her teeth and growled at herself for a minute, and then she shook her head and stopped and came up with a brave smile, tighter and grimmer than her normal sunny radiance. She said, 'OK, tell me more. Tell me how it gets worse. But not in here. I have to eat here three times a day. I don't want the associations.'

So we paid for our breakfasts and stepped out to the sidewalk. We stood there for a long moment, near her car, saying nothing. I could tell by her body language she wasn't going to invite me to her office. She didn't want me near the Sheriff's Department. This wasn't a democracy. In the end she said, 'Let's go back to the

107

hotel. We can use the lounge. We're guaranteed privacy there, after all. Since we're the only two guests.'

We walked back down the street, and up the shaky steps, and across the old veranda. We went in and used the door on the left of the lobby. I smelled the same damp and dust and mildew as the night before. In the daylight the humped shapes I had seen in the dark turned out to be armchairs, as I had thought. There were twelve of them, grouped in various combinations, twos and fours. We took a matched pair, either side of a cold fireplace.

I asked her, 'Why do you live here?'

'Good question,' she said. 'I thought it would be a month or two. But it extended.'

'What about your old man's house?'

'Rented,' she said. 'The lease died with him.'

'You could rent another one. Or buy one. Isn't that what people do?'

She nodded. 'I looked at some. Couldn't pull the trigger. Have you seen the houses around here?'

I said, 'Some of them look OK.'

'Not to me,' she said. 'I wasn't ready, anyway. I hadn't decided how long I was going to stay. Still haven't, really. No doubt it will turn out to be the rest of my life, but I guess I don't want to admit that to myself. I'd rather let it creep up on me day by day, I suppose.'

I thought about my pal Stan Lowrey, and his want ads. There was a lot more to leaving the service than getting a job. There were houses, and cars, and clothes. There were a hundred strange, unknown details, like the customs of a remote foreign tribe, glimpsed only in passing, and never fully understood.

Deveraux said, 'So let's hear it.'

I said, 'Her throat *was* cut, right? We're clear on that?'

'Definitely. Unmistakably.'

'And that was the only wound?'

'The doctor says so.'

'So somewhere there's blood all over the place. Wherever it was actually done. In a room, maybe, or out in the woods. It's impossible to clean up properly. Literally impossible. So there's evidence out there, just waiting for you.'

'I can't search the base. They won't let me. It's a jurisdiction thing.'

'You don't know for sure it happened on the base.'

'She was raped on the base.'

'It's not impossible she was raped on the base. That's not quite the same thing.'

'I can't search five hundred square miles of Mississippi, either.'

'So zoom in on the perpetrator. Narrow it down.'

'How?'

'No woman can bleed out twice,' I said. 'Her throat was cut in some unknown location, blood sprayed everywhere, she died, and that's all she wrote. Then she was dumped in the alley. But whose blood was she lying in? Not her own, because she'd left it all back in the unknown location.'

'Oh, God,' Deveraux said. 'Don't tell me the guy collected it and brought it with him.'

'Possible,' I said. 'But a little unlikely. It would be tricky to cut someone's throat while simultaneously dancing around with a bucket, trying to catch the spray.'

'There could have been two guys.'

'Possible,' I said again. 'But still unlikely. It's like a fire hose, flipping all around. Here, there, and everywhere. The second guy would be lucky to gather a pint.'

'So what are you saying? Whose blood was it?'

'An animal's, possibly. Maybe a deer. Freshly slaughtered, but not quite fresh enough. There was some time lag. That blood was already congealing. A gallon of liquid blood would have spread much farther than that pile of sand. A little goes a long way, where blood is concerned.'

'A hunter?'

'That's my guess.'

'Based on not very much. You didn't see the blood. You didn't test it. It could have been fake blood from a joke store. Or it *could* have been hers. Someone might have figured out a way to collect it. Just because you can't see a way doesn't mean a way doesn't exist. Or they could have bled her out first and then cut her throat afterwards.'

'Still a hunter,' I said.

'Why?'

'There's more,' I said. 'It continues to get worse.'

EIGHTEEN

At that point the old lady I had seen in the diner stuck her head in the door. The hotel's co-owner. She asked if she could bring us anything. Elizabeth Deveraux shook her head. I asked for coffee. The old lady said sorry, she didn't have any. She said I could get it to go from the diner, if I really needed it. I wondered what exactly she was offering, therefore, if anything. But I didn't ask. The old lady left again, and Deveraux said, 'Why are you fixated on hunters?'

'Pellegrino told me she was all dressed up for a night out, as neat as a pin, just lying there on her back in a pool of blood. Those were his words. Is that a fair summary?'

Deveraux nodded. 'That's exactly what I saw. Pellegrino is an idiot, but a reliable one.'

'That's more proof she wasn't killed there. She would have fallen forward on her face, not on her back.'

'Yes, I missed that too. Don't rub it in.'

'What was she wearing?'

'A dark-blue sheath dress with a low white collar. Underwear and pantyhose. Dark-blue shoes with spike heels.'

111

'Clothes in disarray?'

'No. They looked neat as a pin. Like Pellegrino told you.'

'So she wasn't put into those clothes postmortem. You can always tell. Clothes never go on a corpse just right. Especially not pantyhose. So she was still dressed when she was killed.'

'I accept that.'

'Was there blood on the white collar? At the front?'

Deveraux closed her eyes, presumably to recall the scene. She said, 'No, it was immaculate.'

'Was there blood anywhere on her front?'

'No.'

'OK,' I said. 'So her throat was cut in an unknown location, while she was dressed in those clothes. But she had gotten no blood on her, until she was dumped on her back in a pool that was separately transported. Tell me how that isn't a hunter.'

'Tell me how it is. If you can. You can help the army all you want, but you don't have to believe your own bullshit.'

'I'm not helping the army. Soldiers can be hunters too. Many of them are.'

'Why is it a hunter at all?'

'Tell me how you cut a woman's throat without getting a drop of blood on her front.'

'I don't know how.'

'You string her up on a deer trestle. That's how. By her ankles. Upside down. You tie her hands behind her. You haul her arms up until her back is arched and her throat is presented as the lowest point.'

*   *   *

112

We sat in the shadowed silence for a minute, not saying a word. I guessed Deveraux was picturing the scene. I sure was. A clearing in the woods somewhere, remote and lonely, or a room far from anywhere, with improvised equipment, or a hut or a shack with roof beams, Janice May Chapman hanging upside down, her hands hauled up behind her back, towards her feet, her shoulders straining, her back curving painfully. She was probably gagged, too, the gag tied in to a third rope looped over the trestle's top rail. That third rope must have been pulled tight, arching her head up and back, keeping it well out of the way, leaving her throat completely accessible.

I asked, 'How did she wear her hair?'

'Short,' Deveraux said. 'It wouldn't have gotten in the way.'

I said nothing.

Deveraux asked, 'Do you really think that's how it was done?'

I nodded. 'Any other method, she wouldn't have bled out all the way. Not white as a sheet. She would have died, and her heart would have stopped pumping, and there would have been something left inside her. Two, three pints, maybe. It was being upside down that finished the job. Gravity, plain and simple.'

'The ropes would have left marks, wouldn't they?'

'What did the medical examiner say? Have you had his report?'

'We don't have a medical examiner. Just the local doctor. One step up from when all we had was the local undertaker, but not a very big step.'

113

Not a democracy. I said, 'You should go take a look for yourself.'

She said, 'Will you come with me?'

We walked back to the diner and took Deveraux's car from the kerb and U-turned and headed back down Main Street, past the hotel again, past the pharmacy and the hardware store, and onward to where Main Street turned into a wandering rural route. The doctor's place was half a mile south of the town. It was a regular clapboard house, painted white, set in a large untidy yard, with a shingle next to the mailbox at the end of the driveway. The name on the shingle was Merriam, and it was lettered crisply in black over a rectangle of white paint that was brighter and newer than the surrounding surface. A new arrival, not long in town, new to the community.

The house had its ground floor given over to the medical practice. The front parlour was a waiting room, and the back room was where patients were examined and treated. We found Merriam in there, at a desk, doing paperwork. He was a florid man close to sixty. New in town, perhaps, but not new to doctoring. His greeting was languid and his pace was slow. I got the impression he regarded the Carter Crossing position as semi-retirement, maybe after a pressurized career in a big-city practice. I didn't like him much. A snap judgement, maybe, but generally those are as good as any other kind.

Deveraux told the guy what we wanted to see and he got up slowly and led us through the house to what

114

might once have been a kitchen. It was now tiled in cold white, and it had no-nonsense medical-style sinks and cupboards all over it. In the centre of the floor it had a stainless-steel mortuary table, and on the table was a corpse. The light over it was bright.

The corpse was Janice May Chapman. She had a tag on her toe with her name written on it in a spidery hand. She was naked. Deveraux had called her as white as a sheet, but by that point she was pale blue and light purple, blotched and mottled with the characteristic marbling of the truly bloodless. She had been perhaps five feet seven inches tall, and she might once have weighed about a hundred and twenty pounds, neither fat nor excessively thin. She had dark hair bobbed short. It was thick and heavy, well cut, and still in good condition. Pellegrino had called her pretty, and it didn't require much imagination to agree. The flesh on her face was collapsed and empty, but her bone structure was good. Her teeth were white and even.

Her throat was a mess. It was laid open from side to side and the wound had dried to a rubbery gape. Flesh and muscle had shrunk back, and tendons and ligaments had curled, and empty veins and arteries had retracted. White bone was visible, and I could see a single horizontal score mark on it.

The knife had been substantial, the blade had been sharp, and the killing stroke had been forceful, confident, and fast.

Deveraux said, 'We need to examine her wrists and ankles.'

The doctor made a *have at it* gesture.

115

Deveraux took Chapman's left arm and I took her right. Her wrist bones were light and delicate. The skin lying over them had no abrasions. No rope burns. But there was faint residual marking. There was a two-inch-wide band that was slightly bluer than the rest. Very slightly bluer. Almost not there at all. But perceptible. And very slightly swollen, compared to the rest of her forearm. Definitely raised. The exact opposite of a compression.

I looked at Merriam and asked, 'What do you make of this?'

'The cause of death was exsanguination through severed carotid arteries,' he said. 'That was what I was paid to determine.'

'How much were you paid?'

'The fee structure was agreed between my predecessor and the county.'

'Was it more than fifty cents?'

'Why?'

'Because fifty cents is all that conclusion is worth. Cause of death is totally obvious. So now you can earn your corn by helping us out a little.'

Deveraux looked at me and I shrugged. Better that I had said it than her. She had to live with the guy afterwards. I didn't.

Merriam said, 'I don't like your attitude.'

I said, 'And I don't like twenty-seven-year-old women lying dead on a slab. You want to help or not?'

He said, 'I'm not a pathologist.'

I said, 'Neither am I.'

The guy stood still for a moment, and then he sighed

116

and stepped forward. He took Janice May Chapman's limp and lifeless arm from me. He looked at the wrist very closely, and then ran his fingers up and down, gently, from the back of her hand to the middle of her forearm, feeling the swelling. He asked, 'Do you have a hypothesis?'

I said, 'I think she was tied up tight. Wrists and ankles. The bindings started to bruise her, but she didn't live long enough for the bruises to develop very much. But they definitely started. A little blood leaked into her tissues, and it stayed there when the rest of it drained out. Which is why we're seeing compression injuries as raised welts.'

'Tied up with what?'

'Not ropes,' I said. 'Maybe belts or straps. Something wide and flat. Maybe silk scarves. Something padded, perhaps. To disguise what had been done.'

Merriam said nothing. He moved past me to the end of the table and looked at Chapman's ankles. He said, 'She was wearing pantyhose when she was brought in. The nylon was undamaged. Not torn or laddered at all.'

'Because of the padding. Maybe it was foam rubber. Something like that. But she was tied up.'

Merriam was quiet for another moment.

Then he said, 'Not impossible.'

I asked, 'How plausible?'

'Postmortem examination has its limits, you know. You'd need an eyewitness to be certain.'

'How do you explain the complete exsanguination?'

'She could have been a haemophiliac.'

'Suppose she wasn't?'

'Then gravity would be the only explanation. She was hung upside down.'

'By belts or straps, or ropes over some kind of padding?'

'Not impossible,' Merriam said again.

'Turn her over,' I said.

'Why?'

'I want to see the gravel rash.'

'You'll have to help me,' he said, so I did.

NINETEEN

The human body is a self-healing machine, and it doesn't waste time. Skin is crushed or split or cut, and blood immediately rushes to the site, the red cells scabbing and knitting a fibrous matrix to bind the parted edges together, the white cells seeking out and destroying germs and pathogens below. The process is under way within minutes, and it lasts as many hours or days as are necessary to return the skin to its previous unbroken integrity. The process causes a bell curve of inflammation, peaking as the suffusion of blood peaks, and as the scab grows thickest, and as the fight against infection reaches its most intense state.

The small of Janice May Chapman's back was peppered with tiny cuts, as was the whole of her butt, as were her upper arms just above her elbows. The cuts were small, thinly scabbed incisions, all surrounded by small areas of crushing, which were colourless due to her bloodlessness. The cuts were all inflicted in random directions, as if by loose and rolling items of similar size and nature, small and hard and neither razor-sharp nor completely blunt.

Classic gravel rash.

I looked at Merriam and asked, 'How old do you think these injuries are?'

He said, 'I have no idea.'

'Come on, doctor,' I said. 'You've treated cuts and grazes before. Or have you? What were you before? A psychiatrist?'

'I was a paediatrician,' he said. 'I have no idea what I'm doing here. None at all. Not in this area of medicine.'

'Kids get cuts and grazes all the time. You must have seen hundreds.'

'This is a serious business. I can't risk unsupported guesses.'

'Try educated guesses.'

'Four hours,' he said.

I nodded. I figured four hours was about right, judging by the scabs, which were more than nascent, but not yet fully mature. They had been developing steadily, and then their development had stopped abruptly when the throat was cut and the heart had stopped and the brain had died and all metabolism had ceased.

I asked, 'Did you determine the time of death?'

Merriam said, 'That's very hard to know. Impossible, really. The exsanguination interferes with normal biological processes.'

'Best guess?'

'Some hours before she was brought to me.'

'How many hours?'

'More than four.'

'That's obvious from the gravel rash. How many more than four?'

120

'I don't know. Fewer than twenty-four. That's the best I can do.'

I said, 'No other injuries. No bruising. No sign of a defensive struggle.'

Merriam said, 'I agree.'

Deveraux said, 'Maybe she didn't fight. Maybe she had a gun to her head. Or a knife to her throat.'

'Maybe,' I said. I looked at Merriam again and asked, 'Did you do a vaginal examination?'

'Of course.'

'And?'

'I judged she had had recent sexual intercourse.'

'Any bruising or tearing in that area?'

'None visible.'

'Then why did you conclude she was raped?'

'You think it was consensual? Would you lie down on gravel to make love?'

'I might,' I said. 'Depending on who I was with.'

'She had a home,' Merriam said. 'With a bed in it. And a car, with a back seat. Any putative boyfriend would have a home and a car, too. And there's a hotel here in town. And there are other towns, with other hotels. No one needs to conduct a tryst outdoors.'

'Especially not in March,' Deveraux said.

The small room went quiet, and it stayed quiet until Merriam asked, 'Are we done here?'

'We're done,' Deveraux said.

'Well, good luck, chief,' Merriam said. 'I hope this one turns out better than the last two.'

* * *

121

Deveraux and I walked down the doctor's driveway, past the mailbox, past the shingle, to the sidewalk, where we stood next to Deveraux's car. I knew she was not going to give me a ride. This was not a democracy. Not yet. I said, 'Did you ever see a rape victim with intact pantyhose?'

'You think that's significant?'

'Of course it is. She was attacked on gravel. Her pantyhose should have been shredded.'

'Maybe she was forced to undress first. Slowly and carefully.'

'The gravel rash had edges. She was wearing something. Pulled up, pulled down, whatever, but she was partially clothed. And then she changed afterwards. Which is possible. She had four hours.'

'Don't go there,' Deveraux said.

'Go where?'

'You're trying to plead the army down to rape only. You're going to say she was killed by someone else, separately, later.'

I said nothing.

'And that dog won't hunt,' Deveraux said. 'You stumble into someone and get raped, and then within the next four hours you stumble into someone else completely different and get your throat cut? That's a really bad day, isn't it? That's the worst day ever. It's too coincidental. No, it was the same guy. But he had himself an all-day session. He took hours. He had plans and equipment. He had access to her clothes. He made her change. This was all highly premeditated.'

122

'Possible,' I said.

'They teach effective tactical planning in the army. So they claim, anyway.'

'True,' I said. 'But they don't give you all day off very often. Not in a training environment. Not usually.'

Deveraux said, 'But Kelham is not just about training, is it? Not from what I've been able to piece together. There are a couple of rifle companies there. In and out on rotation. And they get leave when they come back. Days off. Plenty of them. All in a row. One after the other.'

I said nothing.

Deveraux said, 'You should call your CO. Tell him it's looking bad.'

I said, 'He already knows. That's why I'm here.'

She paused a long moment and said, 'I want you to do me a favour.'

'Like what?'

'Go look at the car wreck again. See if you can find a licence plate or identify the vehicle. Pellegrino got nowhere with it.'

'Why would you trust me?'

'Because you're the son of a Marine. And because you know if you conceal or destroy evidence I'll put you in jail.'

I asked, 'What did Merriam mean when he wished you better luck with this one than the other two?'

She didn't answer.

I said, 'The other two what?'

She paused a beat and her beautiful face fell a little

and she said, 'Two girls were killed last year. Same MO. Throats cut. I got nowhere with them. They're cold cases now. Janice May Chapman is the third in nine months.'

TWENTY

Elizabeth Deveraux said nothing more. She just climbed into her Caprice and drove away. She pulled a wide U-turn in front of me and headed north, back to town. I lost sight of her after the first curve. I stood still for a long moment and then set off walking. Ten minutes later I was through the last of the rural meanders and the road widened and straightened in front of me. Main Street, in fact as well as name. Some daytime activity was starting up. The stores were opening. I saw two cars and two pedestrians. But that was all. Carter Crossing was no kind of a bustling metropolis. That was for damn sure.

I walked on the right-hand sidewalk and passed the hardware store, and the pharmacy, and the hotel, and the diner, and the empty space next to it. Deveraux's car was not parked in the Sheriff's Department lot. No police vehicles were. There were two civilian pick-up trucks there, both of them old and battered and modest. The desk clerk and the dispatcher, presumably. Locally recruited, no union, no benefits. I thought again about my friend Stan Lowrey and his want ads. He would aim higher, I guessed. He would have to. He had girlfriends. Plural. He had mouths to feed.

I made it to the T-junction and turned right. In the daylight the road speared dead straight ahead of me. Narrow shoulders, deep ditches. The traffic lanes banked up and over the rail crossing and then the shoulders and the ditches resumed and the road ran onward through the trees.

There was a truck parked my side of the crossing. Facing me. A big, blunt-nosed thing. Brush-painted in a dark colour. Two guys in it. Staring at me. Fur, ink, hair, dirt, grease.

My two pals, from the night before.

I walked on, not fast, not slow, just strolling. I got within about twenty yards. Close enough for me to see detail in their faces. Close enough for them to see detail in mine.

This time they got out of their truck. The doors opened as one and they climbed out and down. They skirted the hood and stood together in front of the grille. Same height, same build. Like cousins. They were each about six-two and around two hundred or two hundred and ten pounds. They had long knotted arms and big hands. Work boots on their feet.

I walked on. I stopped ten feet away. I could smell them from there. Beer, cigarettes, rancid sweat, dirty clothes.

The guy on my right said, 'Hello again, soldier boy.'

He was the alpha dog. Both times he had been driving, and both times he was the first to speak. Unless the

126

other guy was some kind of a silent mastermind, which seemed unlikely.

I said nothing, of course.

The guy asked, 'Where are you going?'

I didn't answer.

The guy said, 'You're going to Kelham. I mean, where the hell else does this road go?'

He turned and swept his arm through an extravagant gesture, indicating the road, and its relentless straightness, and its lack of alternative destinations. He turned back and said, 'Last night you told us you weren't from Kelham. You lied to us.'

I said, 'Maybe I live on that side of town.'

'No,' the guy said. 'If you'd tried living on that side of town, we'd have visited you before.'

'For what purpose?'

'To explain the facts of life. Different places are for different folks.' He came a little closer. His buddy came with him. The smell grew stronger.

I said, 'You guys need to take a bath. Not necessarily together.'

The guy on my right asked, 'What have you been doing this morning?'

I said, 'You don't want to know.'

'Yes, we do.'

'No, you really don't.'

'You're not welcome here. Not any more. None of you.'

'It's a free country,' I said.

'Not for people like you.' Then he paused, and his gaze suddenly shifted and focused into the far distance

127

over my shoulder. The oldest trick in the book. Except this time he wasn't faking. I didn't turn, but I heard a car on the road behind me. Far away. A big car, quiet, with wide highway tyres. Not a cop car, because no recognition dawned in the guy's eyes. No familiarity. It was a car he hadn't seen before. A car he couldn't explain.

I waited and it swept past us. It was going fast. It was a black town car. Urban. Dark windows. It thumped up the rise, pattered across the tracks, and thumped back down again. Then it kept on going straight. A minute later it was tiny in the haze. Effectively lost to sight.

An official visitor, heading to Kelham. Rank and prestige.

Or panic.

The guy on my right said, 'You need to get back on the base. And then stay there.'

I said nothing.

'But first you need to tell us what you've been doing. And who you've been seeing. Maybe we should go check she's still alive.'

I said, 'I'm not from Kelham.'

The guy took a step forward. He said, 'Liar.'

I took a breath and made like I was going to speak. Then I head-butted the guy full in the face. No warning. I just braced my feet and snapped forward from the waist and crashed my forehead into his nose. *Bang*. It was perfectly done. Timing, force, impact. It was all there in full measure. Plus surprise. No one expects a head butt. Humans don't hit things with their heads. Some inbuilt atavistic instinct says so. A head butt changes the game. It adds a kind of unhinged savagery to the mix.

An unprovoked head butt is like bringing a sawed-off shotgun to a knife fight.

The guy went down like an empty suit. His brain told his knees it was out of business and he folded up and fell over backwards. He was unconscious before he hit the floor. I could tell by the way the back of his head hit the road. No attempt to soften the blow. It just smacked down with a thud. Maybe he added some fractures in back, to match the ones I had given him in front. His nose was bleeding badly. It was already starting to swell. The human body is a self-healing machine, and it doesn't waste time.

The other guy just stood there. The silent mastermind. Or the beta dog. He was staring at me. I took a long step to my left and head-butted him too. *Bang.* Like a double bluff. He was completely unprepared. He was expecting a fist. He went down in the same kind of heap. I left him there, on his back, six feet from his buddy. I would have taken their truck, to save myself some time and effort, but I couldn't stand the stink in the cab. So I walked on, to the railroad track, where I turned left on the ties and headed north.

I came off the track a little earlier than I had the night before and traced the wreck's debris field from its very beginning. The smaller and lighter pieces had travelled shorter distances. Less momentum, I supposed. Less kinetic energy. Or more air resistance. Or something. But the smaller beads of glass and the smaller flakes of metal were the first to be found. They had stalled and fluttered and fallen to earth and come to rest well before the heavier items, which had barrelled onward.

It had been a fairly old car. The collision had exploded it, like a diagram, but some parts hadn't put up much of a fight. There were squares and flakes of rust, from the underbody. They were layered and scaly and caked with dirt.

An old car, with significant time spent in cold climates where they salt the roads in winter. Not a Mississippi native. A car that had been hauled from pillar to post, six months here, six months there, regularly, unpredictably.

A soldier's car, probably.

I walked on and turned and tried to gauge the general vector. Debris had sprayed through a fan shape, narrow at first, widening later. I pictured a licence plate, a small rectangle of thin featherweight alloy, bursting free of its bolts, sailing through the night-time air, stalling, falling, maybe end over end. I tried to figure out where it might have landed. I couldn't see it anywhere, not inside the fan shape, not on its edges, not beyond its edges. Then I remembered the howling gale that had accompanied the train, and I widened my area of search. I pictured the plate caught in a miniature tornado, whipping and spiralling through the roiled air, going high, maybe even going backward.

In the end I found it still attached to the chrome bumper I had seen the night before. The bumper had folded up just left of the plate, and made a point, which had half buried itself in the scrub. Like a spear. I rocked it loose and pulled it out and turned it over and saw the plate hanging from a single black bolt.

It was an Oregon plate. It featured a drawing of a salmon behind the number. Some kind of a wildlife initiative. Protect the natural environment. The tags were current and up to date. I memorized the number and reburied the bent bumper in its hole. Then I walked on, to where the bulk of the wreck had burned against the trees.

By bright daylight I agreed with Pellegrino. The car had been blue, a light powdery shade like a winter sky. Maybe it had started life that way, or maybe it had faded a little with age. But either way I found enough unblemished paint to be sure. There was an intact patch inside what had been the glove box. There was an overspray stripe under melted plastic trim inside one of the doors. Not much else had survived. No personal items. No paperwork of any kind. No discarded material. No hairs, no fibres. No ropes, no belts, no straps, no knives.

I wiped my hands on my pants and walked back the way I had come. The two guys and their truck had gone. I guessed the silent mastermind had woken up first. The beta dog. I had hit him less hard. I guessed he had hauled his buddy into the truck and taken off, slow and shaky. No harm done. No major harm, anyway. Nothing permanent. For him, at least. The other one would have a headache, for six months or so.

I stood on the spot where they had gone down and saw another black car coming towards me from the west. Another town car, fast and purposeful, wallowing and wandering a little on the uneven road. It had a good wax shine and black window glass. It blew past me at speed, thumped up, pattered over the rail line, thumped down again, and rushed onward towards Kelham. I turned and watched it, and then I turned back and started walking again. No particular place to go, except I was hungry by that point, so I headed for Main Street and the diner. The place was empty. I was the only customer. The same waitress was on duty. She met me at the hostess station and asked, 'Is your name Jack Reacher?'

I said, 'Yes, ma'am, it is.'

She said, 'There was a woman in here an hour ago, looking for you.'

TWENTY-ONE

The waitress was a typical eyewitness. She was completely unable to describe the woman who had been looking for me. Tall, short, heavy, slender, old, young, she had no reliable recollection. She hadn't gotten a name. She had formed no impression of the woman's status or profession or her relationship to me. She hadn't seen a car or any other mode of transportation. All she could remember was a smile and the question. Was there a new guy in town, very big, very tall, answering to the name Jack Reacher?

I thanked her for the information and she sat me at my usual table. I ordered a piece of sweet pie and a cup of coffee and I asked her for coins for the phone. She opened the register and gave me a wrapped roll of quarters in exchange for a five-dollar bill. She brought my coffee and told me my pie would be right along in a moment. I walked across the silent room to the phone by the door and split the roll with my thumbnail and dialled Garber's office. He answered the phone himself, instantly.

I asked, 'Have you sent another agent down here?'

'No,' he said. 'Why?'

'There's a woman asking for me by name.'

'Who?'

'I don't know who. She hasn't found me yet.'

'Not one of mine,' Garber said.

'And I saw two cars heading for Kelham. Limousines. DoD or politicians, probably.'

'Is there a difference?'

I asked, 'Have you heard anything from Kelham?'

'Nothing about the Department of Defense or politicians,' he said. 'I heard that Munro is pursuing something medical.'

'Medical? Like what?'

'I don't know. Is there a medical dimension here?'

'With a potential perpetrator? Not that I've seen. Apart from the gravel rash question I asked before. The victim is covered in it. The perp should have some too.'

'They've all got gravel rash. Apparently there's some crazy running track there. They run till they drop.'

'Even Bravo Company right after they get back?'

'Especially Bravo Company right after they get back. There's some serious self-image at work there. These are seriously hard men. Or so they like to think.'

'I got the licence plate off the wreck. Light-blue car, from Oregon.' I recited the number from memory, and I heard him write it down.

He said, 'Call me back in ten minutes. Don't speak to a soul before that. No one, OK? Not a word.'

I ignored the letter of the law by speaking to the waitress. I thanked her for my pie and coffee. She hung around a

134

beat longer than she needed to. She had something on her mind. Turned out she was worried she might have gotten me in trouble by telling a stranger she had seen me. She was prepared to feel guilty about it. I got the impression Carter Crossing was the kind of place where private business stayed private. Where a small slice of the population didn't want to be found.

I told her not to worry. By that point I was pretty sure who the mystery woman was. A process of elimination. Who else had the information and the imagination to find me?

The pie was good. Blueberries, pastry, sugar and cream. Nothing healthy. No vegetable matter. It hit the spot. I took the full ten minutes to eat it, a little at a time. I finished my coffee. Then I walked over to the phone again and called Garber back.

He said, 'We traced the car.'

I said, 'And?'

'And what?'

'Whose is it?'

He said, 'I can't tell you that.'

'Really?'

'Classified information, as of five minutes ago.'

'Bravo Company, right?'

'I can't tell you that. I can't confirm or deny. Did you write the number down?'

'No.'

'Where's the plate?'

'Where I found it.'

'Who have you told?'

'Nobody.'

'You sure?'

'Completely.'

'OK,' Garber said. 'Here are your orders. Firstly, do not, repeat, do *not* give that number to local law enforcement. Not under any circumstances. Secondly, return to the wreck and destroy that plate immediately.'

TWENTY-TWO

I obeyed the first part of Garber's order, by not immediately rushing around to the Sheriff's Department and passing on the news. I disobeyed the second part, by not immediately rushing back to the debris field. I just sat in the diner and drank coffee and thought. I wasn't even sure how to destroy a licence plate. Burning it would conceal the state of origin, but not the number itself, which was embossed. In the end I figured I could fold it twice and stamp it flat and bury it.

But I didn't go do that. I just sat there. I figured if I sat in a diner long enough, drinking coffee, my mystery woman would surely find me.

Which she did, five minutes later.

I saw her before she saw me. I was looking out at a bright street, and she was looking in at a dim room. She was on foot. She was wearing black pants and black leather shoes, a black T-shirt, and a leather jacket the colour and texture of an old baseball glove. She was carrying a briefcase made of the same kind of material. She was lean and lithe and limber, and she seemed to be moving slower than the rest of the world, like fit strong people always do. Her hair was still dark, still cut short, and her face was still full of fast intelligence and rapid glances. Frances Neagley, First Sergeant, United States Army. We had worked together many times, tough cases and easy, long hauls and short. She was as close to a friend as I had, back in 1997, and I hadn't seen her in more than a year.

She came in scanning for the waitress, ready to ask for an update. She saw me at my table and changed course immediately. No surprise in her face. Just fast assimilation of new information, and satisfaction that her method had worked. She knew the state and she knew the town, and she knew I drank a lot of coffee, and therefore a diner was where she would find me.

I used my toe and poked the facing chair out, like Deveraux had twice done for me. Neagley sat down, smooth and easy. She put her briefcase on the floor by her feet. No greeting, no salute, no handshake, no peck on the cheek. There were two things people needed to understand about Neagley. Despite her personal warmth she couldn't bear to be physically touched, and despite her considerable talents she refused to become an officer. She had never given reasons for either thing. Some folks thought she was smart, and some folks thought she was crazy, but all agreed that with Neagley no one would ever know for sure.

'Ghost town,' she said.

'The base is closed,' I said.

'I know. I'm up to speed. Closing the base was their first mistake. It's as good as a confession.'

138

'Story is they were worried about tension with the town.'

Neagley nodded. 'Wouldn't take much to start some, either way around. I saw the street behind this one. All those stores, lined up like a row of teeth, facing the base? Very predatory. Our people must be sick of getting laughed at and ripped off.'

'Seen anything else?'

'Everything. I've been here two hours.'

'How are you, anyway?'

'We have no time for social chit-chat.'

'What do you need?'

'Nothing,' she said. 'It's you that needs.'

'What do I need?'

'You need to get a damn clue,' she said. 'This is a suicide mission, Reacher. Stan Lowrey called me. He's worried. So I asked around. And Lowrey was right. You should have turned this whole thing down.'

'I'm in the army,' I said. 'I go where I'm told.'

'I'm in the army too. But I avoid sticking my head in a noose.'

'Kelham is the noose. Munro is the one risking his neck. I'm on the sidelines here.'

'I don't know Munro,' she said. 'Never met him. Never even heard of him before. But dollars to doughnuts he'll do what he's told. He'll cover it up and swear black is white. But you won't.'

'A woman was killed. We can't ignore that.'

'Three women were killed.'

'You know about that already?'

'I told you, I've been here two hours. I'm up to speed.'

'How did you find out?'

'I met the sheriff. Chief Deveraux herself.'

'When?'

'She dropped by her office. I happened to be there. I was asking for you.'

'And she told you stuff?'

'I gave her the look.'

'What look?'

Neagley blinked and composed herself and then tilted her face down a little and looked up at me, her eyes on mine, hers open wide and serious and frank and sympathetic and understanding and encouraging, her lips parted a fraction as if imminently ready to exhale a murmur of absolute empathy, her whole demeanour astonished and marvelling at how bravely I was bearing the many heavy burdens my lot in life had brought me. She said, 'This is the look. Works great with women. Kind of conspiratorial, right? Like we're in the same boat?'

I nodded. It was a hell of a look. But I found myself disappointed that Deveraux had fallen for it. Some damn jarhead she was. I asked, 'What else did she tell you?'

'Something about a car. She's assuming it's critical to the case and that it belonged to a Kelham guy.'

'She's right. I just found the plate. Garber ran it and told me to sit on it.'

'And are you going to?'

'I don't know. Might not be a lawful order.'

'See what I mean? You're going to commit suicide. I knew it. I'm going to stick around and keep you out of trouble. That's why I came.'

140

'Aren't you deployed?'

'I'm in D.C. At a desk. They won't miss me for a day or two.'

I shook my head. 'No,' I said. 'I don't need help. I know what I'm doing. I know how the game is played. I won't sell myself cheap. But I don't want to bring you down with me. If that's the way it has to turn out.'

'Nothing *has* to turn out any which way, Reacher. It's a choice.'

'You don't really believe that.'

She made a face. 'At least pick your battles.'

'I always do. And this one is as good as any.'

At that point the waitress came out of the kitchen. She saw me, saw Neagley, recognized her from before, saw that we weren't rolling around on the floor tearing each other's eyes out, and her earlier guilt evaporated. She refilled my coffee mug. Neagley ordered tea, Lipton's breakfast blend, water properly boiling. We sat in silence until the order was filled. Then the waitress went away again and Neagley said, 'Chief Deveraux is a very beautiful woman.'

I said, 'I agree.'

'Have you slept with her yet?'

'Certainly not.'

'Are you going to?'

'I guess I can dream. Hope dies last, right?'

'Don't. There's something wrong with her.'

'Like what?'

'She doesn't care. She's got three unsolved homicides and her pulse is as slow as a bear in winter.'

'She was a Marine MP. She's been digging the same ditch we have, all her life. How excited do you get about three dead people?'

'I get professionally excited.'

'She thinks a Kelham guy did it. Therefore she has no jurisdiction. Therefore she has no role. Therefore she can't get professionally excited.'

'Whatever, there's a bad vibe there. That's all I'm saying. Trust me.'

'Don't worry.'

'I mentioned your name and she looked at me like you owe her money.'

'I don't.'

'Then she's crazy about you. I could tell.'

'You say that about every woman I meet.'

'But this time it's true. I mean it. Her cold little heart was going pitter patter. Be warned, OK?'

'Thanks anyway,' I said. 'But I don't need a big sister on this occasion.'

'Which reminds me,' she said. 'Garber is asking about your brother.'

'My brother?'

'Scuttlebutt on the sergeants' network. Garber has put a watch on your office, for notes or calls from your brother. He wants to know if you're in regular contact.'

'Why would he?'

'Money,' Neagley said. 'That's all I can think of. Your brother is still at Treasury, right? Maybe there's a financial issue with Kosovo. Got to be warlords and gangsters over there. Maybe Bravo Company is bringing money home for them. You know, laundering it. Or stealing it.'

'How would that tie in with a woman named Janice May Chapman, from the armpit of Mississippi?'

'Maybe she found out. Maybe she wanted some for herself. Maybe she was a Bravo Company girlfriend.'

I didn't reply.

'Last chance,' Neagley said. 'Do I stay or do I go?'

'Go,' I said. 'This is my problem, not yours. Live long and prosper.'

'Parting gift,' she said. She leaned down and opened her briefcase and came out with a slim green file folder. It was printed on the outside with the words *Carter County Sheriff's Department*. She laid it on the table and put her hand flat on it, ready to slide it across. She said, 'You'll find this interesting.'

I asked, 'What is it?'

'Photographs of the three dead women. They've all got something in common.'

'Deveraux gave this to you?'

'Not exactly. She left it unattended.'

'You stole it?'

'Borrowed it. You can return it when you're done. I'm sure you'll find a way.' She slid the file across to me, she stood up, and she walked away. No handshake, no kiss, no touch. I watched her push out through the door, watched her turn right on Main Street, and watched her disappear.

The waitress heard the door as Neagley left. Maybe there was a repeater bell in the kitchen. She came out to check if there was a new arrival and saw that there wasn't. She contented herself with refilling my mug for

143

the second time, and then she went back to the kitchen. I squared the green file in front of me and opened it up.

Three women. Three victims. Three photographs, all taken in the last weeks or months of their lives. Nothing sadder. Cops ask for a recent likeness, and distraught relatives scurry to choose from what they have. Usually they come up with joy and smiles, prom pictures or studio portraits or vacation snapshots, because joy and smiles are what they want to remember. They want the long grim record to start with life and energy.

Janice May Chapman had showed plenty of both. Her photograph was a waist-up colour shot taken at what looked like a party. She was half-turned towards the camera, looking directly into the lens, smiling in the first seconds of spontaneity. A well-timed click. The photographer had not caught her unawares, but neither had he made her pose too long.

Pellegrino had been wrong. He had called her real pretty, but that was like calling America fairly big. Real pretty was a serious underestimate. In life Chapman had been absolutely spectacular. It was hard to imagine a more beautiful woman. Hair, eyes, face, smile, shoulders, figure, everything. Janice May Chapman had had it all going on, that was for sure.

I shuffled her to the bottom of the pack and looked at the second woman. She had died in November 1996. Four months ago. A note pasted to the bottom corner of the photograph told me so. The photograph was one of those rushed, semi-formal colour portraits like you see from a college service at the start of the academic year, or from a hard-worked hack on a cruise ship. A murky canvas background, a stool, a couple of umbrella flashes, three, two, one, *pop*, thank you. The woman in the picture was black, probably in her middle twenties, and every bit as spectacular as Janice May Chapman. Maybe even more so. She had flawless skin and the kind of smile that starts the AC running. She had the kind of eyes that start wars. Dark, liquid, radiant. She wasn't looking at the camera. She was looking right through it. Right at me. Like she was sitting across the table.

The third woman had died in June 1996. Nine months ago. She was also black. Also young. Also spectacular. *Truly* spectacular. She had been photographed outside, in a yard, in the shade, with late-afternoon light coming off a white clapboard wall and bathing her in its glow. She had a short natural hairstyle and a white blouse with three buttons undone. She had liquid eyes and a shy smile. She had magnificent cheekbones. I just stared. If some white-coated lab guy had fed an IBM supercomputer with all we had ever known about beauty, from Cleopatra to the present day, the circuits would have hummed for an hour and then printed this exact image.

I moved my mug and laid all three pictures side by side on the table. *They've all got something in common*, Neagley had said. They were all roughly the same age. Two or three years might have covered them all. But Chapman was white, and the other two were black. Chapman was at least economically comfortable, judging by her dress and her jewellery, and the first black woman looked less so, and the second looked close to marginal, in a rural way, judging by her clothes and her unadorned neck and ears, and by the yard she was sitting in.

Three lives, lived in close geographic proximity, but separated by vast gulfs. They may never have met or spoken. They may never have even laid eyes on each other. They had absolutely nothing in common.

Except that all three were amazingly beautiful.

TWENTY-THREE

I repacked the file and tucked it in the back of my pants under my shirt. I paid my bill and left a tip and walked out to the street. I figured I would walk up to the Sheriff's Department. I figured it was time for some reconnaissance. Time for an initial foray. Time for an exploratory penetration. A toe in the water. Not a democracy, but it was a public building. And I had a legitimate reason to be there. I had lost property to return. I figured if Deveraux was out, I could leave the file with the desk clerk. And if Deveraux was in, I could play it by ear.

She was in.

Her old Caprice was in the lot, slotted neatly in the parking bay closest to the door. A privilege of rank, presumably. Office cultures all work the same way. I walked past it and hauled open a heavy glass door and found myself in a dowdy, beat-up lobby. Plastic tile on the floor, scarred paint on the walls, and an inquiry desk facing me, with an old guy behind it. He had no hair and a toothless, caved-in face, and he was wearing a suit vest with no coat, like an old-time newspaperman. As soon as he saw me he picked up a phone and hit a button and said, 'He's here.' He listened to a reply and then he pointed with the phone, using it like a baton, stretching its cord, and he said, 'End of the corridor on the right. She's expecting you.'

I walked the corridor and got a glimpse through a half-closed door of a stout woman at a telephone switch-board, and then I arrived at Deveraux's billet. Her door was open. I knocked on it once as a courtesy and went in.

It was a plain square space in no better condition than the lobby. Same tile, same battered paint, same grime. It was full of stuff bought cheap at the end of the last geological era. Desk, chairs, file cabinets, all plain and municipal and well out of date. There were grip-and-grin pictures on the wall, of an old guy in uniform that I took to be Deveraux's father, the previous incumbent. There was a stand-up hat rack with an old cardigan sweater on one of the pegs. It had hung there so long it looked crusted and rigid with age.

At first glance, not a wonderful room.

But it had Deveraux in it. I had pictures of three stunning women digging into my back, but she held her own with any of them. She was right up there. Maybe she even beat them all. *A very beautiful woman*, Neagley had said, and I was glad my subjectivity had been confirmed by someone else's objectivity. She looked small in the desk chair, slender in the shoulders, lithe and relaxed. As usual, she was smiling.

She asked, 'Did you ID the car for me?'

148

I didn't answer that question, and her phone rang. She picked it up and listened for a moment, and then she said, 'OK, but it's still a felony assault. Keep it on the front burner, OK?' Then she put the phone down and said, 'Pellegrino,' by way of explanation.

I said, 'Busy day?'

'Two guys were beaten up this morning by someone they swear was a soldier from Kelham. But the army says the base is still closed. I don't know what's going on. The doctor is working overtime. Concussions, he says. But it's my budget that's going to be concussed.'

I said nothing.

Deveraux smiled again and said, 'Anyway, first of all, tell me about your friend.'

'My friend?'

'I met her. Frances Neagley. I'm guessing she's your sergeant. She was very army.'

'She was my sergeant once. Many years, on and off.'

'I'm wondering why she came.'

'Maybe I asked her to come.'

'No, in that case she'd have known where and when to meet you. It would have been prearranged. She wouldn't have had to ask all over town.'

I nodded. 'She came to warn me. Apparently I'm in a lose-lose situation. She called it a suicide mission.'

'She's right,' Deveraux said. 'She's a smart woman. I liked her. She was good. She does this thing with her face. Like a special look, all collegial and confiding. I bet she's a great interrogator. Did she give you the photographs?'

'You meant her to take them?'

'I hoped she would. I left them accessible, and ducked out for a minute.'

'Why?'

'It's complicated,' Deveraux said. 'I wanted you to see them, alone and on your own time. Like a controlled experiment. No pressure from me, and especially no influence from me. No context. I wanted a completely unguarded first impression.'

'From me?'

'Yes.'

'Is this a democracy now?'

'Not yet. But any port in a storm, as they say.'

'OK,' I said.

'So what was it? Your first impression?'

'All three of them were amazingly beautiful.'

'Is that all they had in common?'

'I imagine so. Apart from all being women.'

Deveraux nodded.

'Good,' she said. 'I agree. They were all amazingly beautiful. I'm very glad to have confirmation from an independent point of view. It was a hard thing for me to articulate, even to myself. And I'd certainly avoid saying it out loud. It would sound very weird, like some gay thing.'

'Is that an issue for you?'

'I live in Mississippi,' she said. 'I was in the Marine Corps and I'm not married.'

'OK,' I said.

'And I'm not currently dating.'

'OK,' I said.

'I'm not gay,' she said.

'Understood.'

'But even so, for a woman cop to be seen obsessing over a female victim's looks never goes down well.'

'Understood,' I said again. I leaned forward to let my back clear the chair, and I pulled the file out of my waistband. I laid it on the desk.

'Mission accomplished,' I said. 'Nice moves, by the way. Not many people beat Neagley in a mind game.'

'Takes one to know one,' she said. She slid the file closer and ran her palm over it, left and right, and her hand came to rest at one end, and she kept it there. Maybe where it was warm from the small of my back.

She asked, 'Did you ID the car?'

TWENTY-FOUR

She kept her palm pressed on the file folder, and looked straight at me. Her question hung in the air between us. *Did you ID the car?* In my head I heard Garber's emphatic squawk in my ear, on the phone in the diner: *do not, repeat, do not give that number to local law enforcement.*

My commanding officer.

Orders are orders.

Deveraux said, 'Did you?'

I said, 'Yes.'

'And?'

'I can't tell you.'

'Can't or won't?'

'Both. Classified information, as of five minutes after I called it in.'

She didn't respond.

I said, 'Well, what would you do in this situation?'

'Now?'

'Not now. Then. When you were in the Corps.'

'As a Marine I would have done exactly what you're doing.'

'I'm glad you understand.'

She nodded. She kept her hand on the file. She said, 'I didn't tell you the truth before. Not the whole truth, anyway. About my father's house. It wasn't always rented. He owned it, from when he was married. But when my mother got sick, they found out they didn't have insurance. They were supposed to. It was supposed to come with the job. But the county guy who was responsible had run into trouble and had been stealing the premiums. Just a two-year hiatus, but that happened to be when my mother got sick. After that, it was a pre-existing condition. My father refinanced, things got worse, and he defaulted. The bank took the title, but they let him live there as a renter. I admired both parties. The bank did the right thing, as far as it could, and my daddy kept on serving his community, even though it had kicked him in the teeth. Honour and obligation are things I appreciate.'

'*Semper Fi*,' I said.

'You bet your ass. And you answered my question anyway, as I'm sure you intended. If the ID is classified, then it's a Kelham car. That's all I really need to know.'

'Only if there's a connection,' I said. 'Between the car and the homicide.'

'Unlikely to be a coincidence.'

I said, 'I'm sorry about your father.'

'Me too. He was a nice man, and he deserved better.'

I said, 'It was me who beat on those civilians.'

Deveraux said, 'Really? How on earth did you get there?'

'I walked.'

153

'You can't have. You didn't have time, surely. It's more than twelve miles. Almost past Kelham's northern limit. Practically in Tennessee.'

'What happened there?'

'Two guys were out doing something. Maybe just taking a walk. They could see the woods around Kelham's fence, but they weren't particularly close to it. A guy came out of the woods, the two hikers got rousted, it turned bad, they got hit. They claim the guy that hit them was a soldier.'

'Was he in uniform?'

'No. But he had the look, and he had an M16 rifle.'

'That's bizarre.'

'I know. It's like they're establishing a quarantine zone.'

'Why would they? They've already got about a million acres all to themselves.'

'I don't know why. But what else are they doing? They're chasing anyone that gets anywhere near the fence.'

I said nothing.

Deveraux said, 'Wait. Who did *you* beat on?'

'Two guys in a pick-up truck. They harassed me last night, they harassed me again this morning. Once too often.'

'Description?'

'Dirt, grease, hair and tattoos.'

'In an old black truck painted with a housepainter's brush?'

'Yes.'

'Those are the McKinney cousins. In an ideal world

154

they should be beat on at least once a week, regular as clockwork. So I thank you for your full and frank confession, but I propose to take no action at this time.'

'But?'

'Don't do it again. And watch your back. I'm sure that right now they're planning to get the whole family together and come looking for you.'

'There are more of them?'

'There are dozens of them. But don't worry. Not yet, at least. It will take time for them to assemble. None of them has a phone. None of them knows how to use a phone.'

And at that point phones started ringing all throughout the building. And I heard urgent radio chatter from the dispatcher's hutch, where the stout woman sat. Ten seconds later she appeared in the doorway, out of breath, holding both jambs to steady herself, and she said, 'Pellegrino is calling in from near the Clancy place. Near the split oak. He says we got ourselves another homicide.'

TWENTY-FIVE

Both Deveraux and I glanced instinctively at the file folder on her desk. Three photographs. Soon to be four. Another sad visit to grieving relatives. Another request for a good recent likeness. The worst part of the job.

Then Deveraux glanced at me, and hesitated. *Not a democracy.* I said, 'You owe it to me. I need to see this. I need to know what I'm committing suicide over.'

She hesitated another second, and then she said, 'OK,' and we ran for her car.

The Clancy place turned out to be more than ten miles north and east of the town. We crossed the silent railroad and headed towards Kelham for a mile, deep into the hidden half of Carter Crossing. The wrong side of the tracks. Out there the road had no shoulders and no ditches. I guessed the ditches had silted up and the shoulders had been ploughed. Flat fields full of dirt came right up to the edge of the blacktop. I saw old frame houses standing in yards, and low barns, and swaybacked sheds, and tumbledown shacks. I saw old women on porches and raggedy kids on bikes. I saw old trucks moving slow and a solitary shopper with a straw hat and a straw basket. Every face I saw was black. *Different places are for different folks*, the McKinney cousins had told me. Rural Mississippi, in 1997.

Then Deveraux turned due north on a washboard two-lane and left the dwellings behind us. She hit the gas. The car responded. The Chevy Caprice was every working cop's favourite car for a reason. It was a perfect *what if* proposition. What if we took a roomy sedan and put a Corvette motor in it? What if we beefed up the suspension a little? What if we used four disc brakes? What if we gave it a top speed of 130 miles an hour? Deveraux's example was well used and worn, but it still motored along. The rough surface pattered under the tyres, and the body wallowed and shuddered, but we got where we were going pretty fast.

Where we were going turned out to be a large hard-scrabble acreage with a battered house in its centre. We turned in and used a two-rut driveway that became a plain farm track as it passed the house. Deveraux blipped her siren once as a courtesy. I saw an answering wave from a window. An old man. A black face. We headed onward across flat barren land. Way far in the distance I could see a lone tree, chopped vertically by lightning down two-thirds of its height. Each half was leaning away from the other in a dramatic Y shape. Both halves were dusted with pale green springtime leaves. The split oak, I assumed. Still alive and in business. Still enduring. Near it was parked a police cruiser, right out on the dirt. Pellegrino's, I assumed.

Deveraux put her car next to it and we got out.

157

Pellegrino himself was fifty yards away, just standing there, at ease, facing us, with his hands clasped behind his back.

Like a sentry.

Ten yards farther on was a shape on the ground.

We hiked across the fifty yards of dirt. There were turkey vultures in the air, three of them, looping lazily high above us, just waiting for us to be gone. Far to my right I could see a line of trees, thick in parts, and thin in others. Through the thin parts I could see a wire fence. Kelham's northwestern boundary, I guessed. The left shoulder of whatever vast acreage the DoD had requisitioned fifty years before. And a small portion of what some well-connected fencing contractor had been overpaid to install.

Halfway to Pellegrino I could see some details in the shape behind him. A back, facing towards me. A short brown jacket. A suggestion of dark hair and white skin. The empty slump of a corpse. The absolute stillness of the recently dead. The impossible relaxation. Unmistakable.

Deveraux did not pause for a verbal report. She walked straight past Pellegrino and kept on going. She looped around wide and approached the collapsed shape from the far side. I stopped five yards short and hung back. Her case. Not a democracy.

She shuffled closer to the shape, slowly and carefully, watching where she was putting her feet. She got close enough to touch and squatted down with her elbows on her knees and her hands clasped together. She looked right to left, at the head, the torso, the arms, the legs. Then she looked left to right, the same sequence all over again, but in reverse.

Then she looked up and said, 'What the hell *is* this?'

TWENTY-SIX

I followed the same long loop Deveraux had used and tiptoed in from the north side. I squatted down next to her. I put my elbows on my knees. I clasped my hands together.

I looked, right to left, and then left to right.

The corpse was male.

And white.

Forty-five years old, maybe a little less, maybe a little more.

Maybe five-ten, maybe a hundred and eighty pounds. Dark hair, going mousy. Two or three days' stubble, going white. A green work shirt, a brown canvas windbreaker jacket. Blue jeans. Brown engineer boots, creased and cracked and starved of polish and caked with dirt.

I asked Deveraux, 'Do you know him?'

She said, 'I never saw him before.'

He had bled to death. He had taken what I guessed was a high-velocity rifle round through the meat of his right thigh. His pants were soaked with blood. Almost certainly the round had torn his femoral artery. The femoral artery is a high-capacity vessel. Absolutely crucial. Any significant breach will be fatal within minutes, absent prompt and effective emergency treatment.

But what was extraordinary about the scene in front of us was that prompt and effective emergency treatment had been attempted. The guy's pants leg had been slit with a knife. The wound was partially covered with an absorbent bandage pad.

The absorbent bandage pad was a general-issue military field dressing.

Deveraux stood up and backed away, short mincing tiptoe steps, her eyes on the corpse, until she got ten or twelve feet away. I did the same thing and joined her. She talked low, as if noise was disrespectful. As if the corpse could hear us. She asked, 'What do you make of that?'

'There was a dispute,' I said. 'A shot was fired. Probably a warning shot that went astray. Or a giddy-up shot that came too close.'

'Why not a killing shot that missed?'

'Because the shooter would have tried again right away. He would have stepped in closer and put one through the guy's head. But he didn't do that. He tried to help the guy instead.'

'And?'

'And he saw that he was failing in his attempt. So he panicked and ran away. He left the guy to die. Won't have taken long.'

'The shooter was a soldier.'

'Not necessarily.'

'Who else carries GI field dressings?'

'Anyone who shops at surplus stores.'

Deveraux turned around. Turned her back on the corpse. She raised her arm and pointed at the horizon on our right. A short sweep of her arm.

She asked, 'What do you see?'

I said, 'Kelham's perimeter.'

'I told you,' she said. 'They're enforcing a quarantine zone.'

Deveraux headed back to her car for something and I stood still and looked at the ground around my feet. The earth was soft and there were plenty of footprints. The dead guy's looped and staggered, some of them backward like an old-fashioned dance chart. Their curving sequence ended where he lay. All around the lower half of his body were toe marks and round depressions from knees, where his assailant had first squatted and then knelt to work on him. Those marks were at the head of a long straight line of partial prints, mostly toe, not much heel, all widely spaced. The shooter had run in fast. A reasonably tall person. Not a giant. Not especially heavy. There were identical prints facing the other way, where the shooter had run away again. I didn't recognize the tread patterns. They were unlike any army boot I had ever seen.

Deveraux came back from her car with a camera. It was a silver SLR. She got ready to take her crime scene pictures and I followed the line of panicked running prints away from the area. I kept them three feet to my right and tracked them a hundred yards, and then they petered out on a broad vein of bone-hard dirt. Some kind of a geological issue, or an irrigation thing, or I had reached the limit of what old man Clancy liked to plough. I saw no reason why a fleeing man would change direction at that point, so I kept on going straight, hoping to pick up the prints again, but I didn't. Within fifty yards the ground became matted with low wiry weeds of some description. Ahead of me they grew a little taller, and then they shaded into the brush that had grown up at the base of Kelham's fence. I saw no bruised stalks, but it was tough vegetation and I wouldn't have expected it to show much damage.

I turned back and took a step and saw a glint of light twelve feet to my right. Metallic. Brassy. I detoured and bent down and saw a cartridge case lying on the dirt. Bright and fresh. New. Long, from a rifle. Best case, it was a .223 Remington, made for a sporting gun. Worst case, it was a 5.56 millimetre NATO round, made for the military. Hard to tell the difference with the naked eye. The Remington case has thinner brass. The NATO case is heavier.

I picked it up and weighed it in my palm.

Dollars to doughnuts, it was a military round.

I looked ahead at Deveraux and Pellegrino and the dead guy in the distance. They were about a hundred and forty yards away. Practically touching distance, for a rifleman. The 5.56 NATO round was designed to penetrate one side of a steel helmet at six hundred metres, which works out to about six hundred and fifty yards. The dead guy was more than four times closer than that. An easy shot. Hard to miss, which was my only real consolation. The kind of guy that gets sent from Benning to Kelham for finishing school isn't the kind of guy that misplaces a round at point-blank range. Yet this was clearly an unintentional hit. The bandage proved it. It was a warning shot gone wrong. Or a giddy-up shot. But the kind of guy that gets sent from Benning to Kelham has worked out his testosterone issues long ago. He puts his warning shots high and wide. And his giddy-up shots. All the subject needs is to see the muzzle flash and hear the noise of the gun. That's all the situation requires. And no soldier does more than he has to. No soldier ever has, since Alexander the Great first put his army together. Initiative in the ranks usually ends in tears. Especially where live ammunition is involved. And civilians.

I put the brass in my pocket and hiked back. I saw nothing else of significance. Deveraux had snapped a whole roll of film, and she rewound it and took it out of her camera and sent Pellegrino back to the pharmacy to get it printed. She told him to ask for rush service, and then she told him to bring the doctor back with him, with the mortuary wagon. He departed on cue and Deveraux and I were left standing together in a thousand acres of emptiness, with nothing for company except a corpse and a blasted tree.

I asked, 'Did anyone hear a shot?'

She said, 'Mr Clancy is the only one who could. Pellegrino talked to him already. He claims not to have heard anything.'

'Any yelling? A warning shot presupposes some yelling first.'

'If he didn't hear a shot, he wouldn't have heard yelling.'

'A single NATO round far away and outdoors isn't necessarily loud. The yelling could have been louder. Especially if it was two-way yelling, which it might have been, back and forth. You know, if there was a dispute or an argument.'

'You accept it was a NATO round now?'

I put my hand in my pocket and came out with the shell case. I held it in my open palm. I said, 'I found it a hundred and forty yards out, twelve feet off the straight vector. Exactly where an M16 ejection port would have put it.'

Deveraux said, 'It could be a Remington .223,' which was kind of her. Then she took it from me. Her nails felt sharp on the skin of my palm. It was the first time we had touched. The first physical contact. We hadn't shaken hands when we met.

She did what I had done. She weighed the brass in her palm. Unscientific, but long familiarity can be as accurate as a laboratory instrument. She said, 'NATO for sure. I've fired a lot of these, and picked them up afterwards.'

'Me too,' I said.

'I'm going to raise hell,' she said. 'Soldiers against civilians, on American soil? I'll go all the way to the Pentagon. The White House, if I have to.'

'Don't,' I said.

'Why the hell not?'

'You're a county sheriff. They'll crush you like a bug.'

She said nothing.

'Believe me,' I said. 'If they've gotten as far as deploying soldiers against civilians, they've gotten as far as working out ways to beat local law enforcement.'

TWENTY-SEVEN

The guy was finally pronounced dead thirty minutes later, at one o'clock in the afternoon, when the doctor showed up with Pellegrino. Pellegrino was in his cruiser and the doctor was in a fifth-hand meat wagon that looked like something out of a history book. I guessed it was a riff on a 1960s hearse, but built on a Chevrolet platform, not Cadillac, and devoid of viewing windows or other funereal hoo-hah of any kind. It was like a half-height panel van, painted dirty white.

Merriam checked pulse and heartbeat and poked around the wound for a minute. He said, 'This man bled out through his femoral artery. Death by gunshot.' Which was obvious, but then he added something interesting. He teased up the slit edge of the guy's pants leg and said, 'Wet denim is not easy to cut. Someone used a very sharp knife.'

I helped Merriam put the guy on a canvas gurney, and then we loaded him in the back of the truck. Merriam drove him away, and Deveraux spent five minutes on the radio in her car. I stood around with Pellegrino. He didn't say anything, and neither did I. Then Deveraux got out of her car again and sent him about his business. He drove away, and Deveraux and I were alone once more, except for the blasted tree and a patch of dark tone on the ground, where the dead guy's blood had soaked into the soil.

Deveraux said, 'Butler claims no one came out of Kelham's main gate at any time this morning.'

I said, 'Who's Butler?'

'My other deputy. Pellegrino's opposite number. I've had him stationed outside the base. I wanted a quick warning, in case they cancel the lockdown. There's going to be all kinds of tension. People are very upset about Chapman.'

'But not about the first two?'

'Depends who you ask, and where. But the soldiers never stop short of the tracks. The bars are all on the other side.'

I said nothing.

She said, 'There must be more gates. Or holes in the fence. It's got to be, what? Thirty miles long? And it's fifty years old. Got to be weak spots. Someone came out somewhere, that's for sure.'

'And went back in again,' I said. 'If you're right, that is. Someone went back in bloody to the elbows, with a dirty knife, and at least one round short in his magazine.'

'I am right,' she said.

'I never heard of a quarantine zone before,' I said. 'Not inside the United States, anyway. I just don't buy it.'

'I buy it,' she said.

Something in her tone. Something in her face.

I said, 'What? Did the Marines do this once?'

'It was no big thing.'

'Tell me all about it.'

'Classified information,' she said.

'Where was it?'

'I can't tell you that.'

'When was it?'

'I can't tell you that either.'

I paused a beat and asked, 'Have you spoken to Munro yet? The guy they sent to the base?'

She nodded. 'He called and left a message when he arrived. First thing. As a courtesy. He gave me a number to reach him.'

'Good,' I said. 'Because now I need to speak to him.'

We drove back together, across Clancy's land, out his gate, south on the washboard two-lane, then west through the black half of town, away from Kelham, towards the railroad. I saw the same old women on the same front porches, and the same kids on the same bikes, and men of various ages moving slow between unknown starting points and unknown destinations. The houses leaned and sagged. There were abandoned work sites. Slabs laid, with no structures built on them. Tangles of rusted rebar. Weedy piles of bricks and sand. All around was flat tilled dirt and trees. There was a kind of hopeless crushed torpor in the air, like there probably had been every day for the last hundred years.

'My people,' Deveraux said. 'My base. They all voted for me. I mean it, practically a hundred per cent.

Because of my father. He was fair to them. They were voting for him, really.'

I asked, 'How did you do with the white folks?'

'Close to a hundred per cent with them too. But that's all going to change, on both ends of the deal. Unless I get some answers for all concerned.'

'Tell me about the first two women.'

Her response to that was to brake sharply and twist in her seat and back up twenty yards. Then she nosed into the turning she had just passed. It was a dirt track, well smoothed and well scoured. It had a humped camber and shallow bar ditches left and right. It ran straight south, and was lined on both sides with what might once have been slave shacks. Deveraux passed by the first ten or so, passed by a gap where one had burned out, and then she turned into a yard I recognized from the third photograph I had seen. The poor girl's house. The unadorned neck and ears. The amazing beauty. I recognized the shade tree she had been sitting under, and the white wall that had reflected the setting sun softly and obliquely into her face.

We parked on a patch of grass and got out. A dog barked somewhere, and its chain rattled. We walked under the limbs of the shade tree and knocked on the back door. The house was small, not much bigger than a cabin, but it was well tended. The white siding was not new, but it had been frequently painted. It was stained auburn at the bottom, the colour of hair, where heavy rains had bounced up out of the mud.

The back door was opened by a woman not much older than Deveraux and me. She was tall and thin and she moved slow, with a kind of sun-beat languor, and with the kind of iron stoicism I imagined all her neighbours shared. She smiled a resigned smile at Deveraux, and shook her hand, and asked her, 'Any news about my baby?'

Deveraux said, 'We're still working on it. We'll get there in the end.'

The bereaved mother was too polite to respond to that. She just smiled her wan smile again and turned to me. She said, 'I don't believe we've met.'

I said, 'Jack Reacher, ma'am,' and shook her hand.

She said, 'I'm Emmeline McClatchy. I'm delighted to meet you, sir. Are you working with the Sheriff's Department?'

'The army sent me to help.'

'Now they did,' she said. 'Not nine months ago.'

I didn't answer that.

The woman said, 'I have some deer meat in the pot. And some tea in the pitcher. Would you two care to join me for lunch?'

Deveraux said, 'Emmeline, I'm sure that's your dinner, not your lunch. We'll be OK. We'll eat in town. But thanks anyway.'

It was the answer the woman seemed to have been expecting. She smiled again and backed away into the gloom behind her. We walked back to the car. Deveraux backed out to the street, and we drove away. Further down the row was a shack much like the others, but it had electric beer signs in the windows. A bar of some kind. Maybe music. We threaded through a matrix of dirt streets. I saw another abandoned construction project.

171

Knee-high foundation walls had been built out of cinder blocks, and four vertical wooden posts had been raised at the corners. But that was all. Building materials were scattered around the rest of the lot in untidy piles. There were surplus cinder blocks, there were bricks, there was a pile of sand, there was a stack of bagged cement, gone all smooth and rigid with dew and rain.

There was also a pile of gravel.

I turned and looked at it as we drove past. Maybe two yards of it, the small sharp grey kind they mix with sand and cement to make into concrete. The pile had spread and wandered into a low hump about the size of a double bed, all weedy at the edges. It had pockmarks and divots in its top surface, as if kids had walked on it.

I didn't say anything. Deveraux's mind was already made up. She drove on and turned left into a broader street. Bigger houses, bigger yards. Picket fences, not hurricane wire. Cement paths to the doors, not beaten earth. She slowed and then eased to a stop outside a place twice the size of the shack we had just left. A decent one-storey house. Expensive, if it had been in California. But shabby. The paint was peeling and the gutters were broken-backed. The roof was asphalt and some of the tiles had slipped. There was a boy in the yard, maybe sixteen years old. He was standing still and doing nothing. Just watching us.

Deveraux said, 'This is the other one. Shawna Lindsay was her name. That's her baby brother right there, staring at us.'

The baby brother was no oil painting. He had lucked out with the genetic lottery. That was for damn sure. He

172

was nothing like his sister. Nothing at all. He had fallen out of the ugly tree, and hit every branch. He had a head like a bowling ball, and eyes like the finger holes, and about as close together.

I asked, 'Are we going in?'

Deveraux shook her head. 'Shawna's mom told me not to come back until I could tell her who slit her first-born's throat. Those were her words. And I can't blame her for them. Losing a child is a terrible thing. Especially for people like this. Not that they thought their girls would grow up to be models and buy them a house in Beverly Hills. But to have something truly special meant a lot to them. You know, after having nothing else, ever.'

The boy was still staring. Quiet, baleful, and patient.

'So let's go,' I said. 'I need to use the phone.'

TWENTY-EIGHT

Deveraux let me use the phone in her office. Not a democracy, not yet, but we were getting there. She found the number Munro had left for her, and she dialled it for me, and she told whoever answered that Sheriff Elizabeth Deveraux was on the line for Major Duncan Munro. Then she handed the receiver to me and vacated her chair and the room.

I sat down behind her desk with nothing but dead air in my ear and the remnant of her body heat on my back. I waited. The silence hissed at me. The army did not play hold music. Not back in 1997. Then a minute later there was a plastic click and clatter as a handset was scooped up off a desk, and a voice said, 'Sheriff Deveraux? This is Major Munro. How are you?'

The voice was hard, and brisk, and hyper-competent, but it had an undertone of good cheer in it. But then, I figured anyone would be happy to get a call from Elizabeth Deveraux.

I said, 'Munro?'

He said, 'I'm sorry, I was expecting Elizabeth Deveraux.'

'Well, sadly you didn't get her,' I said. 'My name is Reacher. I'm using the sheriff's phone right now. I'm with the 396th, currently TDY with the 110th. We're of equal rank.'

Munro said, 'Jack Reacher? I've heard of you, of course. How can I help you?'

'Did Garber tell you he was sending an undercover guy to town?'

'No, but I guessed he would. That would be you, right? Tasked to snoop on the locals? Which must be going pretty well, seeing as you're calling from the sheriff's phone. Which must be fun, in a way. People here say she's a real looker. Although they also say she's a lesbian. You got an opinion on any of that?'

'That stuff is none of your business, Munro.'

'Call me Duncan, OK?'

'No, thanks. I'll call you Munro.'

'Sure. How can I help you?'

'We've got shit happening out here. There was a guy shot to death this morning, close to your fence, north-western quadrant. Unknown assailant, but probably a military round, and definitely a half-assed attempt to patch the fatal wound with a GI field dressing.'

'What, someone shot a guy and then gave him first aid? Sounds like a civilian accident to me.'

'I hoped you weren't going to be that predictable. How do you explain the round and the dressing?'

'Remington .223 and a surplus store.'

'And two guys were beat up before that, by someone they swear was a soldier.'

'Not a soldier based at Kelham.'

'Really? How many Kelham personnel can you vouch for? In terms of their exact whereabouts this morning?'

'All of them,' Munro said.

'Literally?'

'Yes, literally,' he said. 'We've got Alpha Company overseas as of five days ago, and I've got everyone else confined to quarters, or else sitting in the mess hall or the officers' club. There's a good MP staff here, and they're watching everyone, while also watching each other. I can guarantee no one left the base this morning. Or since I got here, for that matter.'

'Is that your standard operating procedure?'

'It's my secret weapon. Sitting down all day, no reading, no television, no nothing. Sooner or later someone talks, out of sheer boredom. Never fails. My arm-breaking days are over. I learned that time is my friend.'

'Tell me again,' I said. 'This is very important. You're absolutely sure no one left the base this morning? Or last night? Not even under secret orders, maybe local, or from Benning, or maybe even from the Pentagon? I'm serious here. And don't bullshit a bullshitter.'

'I'm sure,' Munro said. 'I guarantee it. On my mother's grave. I know how to do this stuff, you know. Give me that, at least.'

'OK,' I said.

Munro asked, 'Who was the dead guy?'

'No ID at this time. Civilian, almost certainly.'

'Near the fence?'

'Same as the guys that got beat up. Like a quarantine zone.'

'That's ridiculous. That's not happening. I know that for sure.'

We both went quiet for a second, and then I asked, 'What else do you know for sure?'

'I can't tell you. Orders are to keep this thing tighter than a fish's butt.'

'Let's play Twenty Questions.'

'Let's not.'

'The short version. Three questions. Yes or no answers.'

'Don't put me on the spot, OK?'

'We're both on the spot already. Don't you see that? We've got a real mess here. And either it's in there with you or it's out here with me. So sooner or later one of us is going to have to help the other. We might as well start now.'

Silence. Then: 'OK, Jesus, three questions.'

'Did they tell you about the car?'

'Yes.'

'Did anyone mention money from Kosovo as a possible motive?'

'Yes.'

'Did they tell you about two other dead women?'

'No. What other dead women?'

'Last year. Local. Same MO. Cut throats.'

'Connected?'

'Probably.'

'Jesus. No, nobody said a word.'

'Do you have written records of Bravo Company's movements? June and November last year?'

'That's your fourth question.'

'We're just chatting now. Two officers, equal rank, just shooting the shit. The game is over.'

'There are no records of Bravo Company's movements here. They're operating under special ops protocols. Therefore everything is filed at Fort Bragg. It would take the biggest subpoena you ever saw just to get a look at the outside of the file cabinet.'

I asked, 'You making any general progress there?'

No answer.

I asked, 'How long does it normally take for your secret weapon to work?'

He said, 'It's usually much faster than this.'

I didn't answer, and there was more dead air, and some quiet breathing, and then Munro said, 'Listen, Reacher, I guess this is hardly worth talking about, because you're just going to think well, what else would I say, because we both know I was sent here to cover someone's ass. But I'm not like that. Never have been.'

'And?'

'From what I know so far, none of our guys killed any women. Not this month, or November, or June. That's how it looks right now.'

TWENTY-NINE

I put the phone down on Munro, and Deveraux came back into the office immediately. Maybe she had been watching a light on the switchboard. She said, 'Well?'

'No quarantine patrols. No one has left Kelham since Munro arrived.'

'He would say that, though, wouldn't he?'

'And he's not smelling anything. He thinks the perp is not on the base.'

'Ditto.'

I nodded. Smoke and mirrors. Politics and the real world. Utter confusion. I said, 'You want to get lunch?'

She said, 'After.'

'After what?'

'You have a problem to deal with. The McKinney cousins are out on the street. They're waiting for you. And they've brought reinforcements.'

Deveraux led me across the corridor to a dim corner room with windows in two walls. The view across Main Street was empty. Nothing happening. But the view north towards the T-junction showed four figures. My two old friends, plus two more similar guys. Dirt, hair, fur and ink. They were standing around in the wide area where the two roads met, hands in pockets, kicking the dirt, doing nothing at all.

My first reaction was a kind of dumbfounded admiration. A head butt is a serious blow, especially one of mine. To be walking and talking just a few hours later was impressive. My second reaction was annoyance. With myself. I had been too gentle. Too new in town, too reluctant, too proper, too ready to see mitigating circumstances in sheer animal stupidity. I looked at Deveraux and asked, 'What do you want me to do?'

She said, 'You could apologize and make them go away.'

'What's my second choice?'

'You could let them hit you first. Then I could arrest them for unprovoked assault. I'd love to get the chance to do that.'

'They won't hit me at all if you're there.'

'I'll stay out of sight.'

'I'm not sure I want to do either thing.'

'One or the other, Reacher. Your choice.'

I stepped out to Main Street like some guy in an old movie. There should have been music playing. I turned right and faced north. I stood still. The four guys saw me. They showed a moment of surprise, and then a moment of warm anticipation. They formed up in a side-to-side line, all four of them strung out west to east, about four feet apart. They all took a step towards me, and then they all stopped and waited. There were two trucks

180

parked on the Kelham road, behind them and to the right. There was the brush-painted pick-up I had seen before, and in front of it was another one just as bad.

I walked on, like a fish towards a net. The sun was about as high as it was going to get in March. The air was warm. I could feel heat on my skin. I could feel the road surface under the soles of my shoes. I put my hands in my pockets. Nothing in there, except most of the roll of quarters I had gotten in the diner. I closed my fist around the paper tube. A five-dollar punch, less what I had spent on the phone.

I walked on and stopped ten feet from the skirmish line. The two guys I had met before were on the left. The silent mastermind was on the outside, and the alpha dog was in second position. Both of them had noses like spoiled eggplants. Both of them had two black eyes. Both of them had crusted blood on their lips. Neither one of them exhibited much in the way of balance or focus. Right of the alpha dog was a guy slightly smaller than the others, and next to him was a big guy in a biker vest.

I looked at the alpha dog and said, 'This is your plan?'

He didn't answer.

I said, 'Four guys? Is that all?'

He didn't answer.

I said, 'I was told there were dozens of you.'

No answer.

'But I guess logistics and communications were difficult. So you settled on a lighter force, quickly assembled and rapidly deployed. Which is very up to date, actually. You should go to the Pentagon and sit in on some seminars. You'd feel right at home with their thinking.'

The new guy second from the right was drunk. He had a low-level buzz going on. It was oozing from his pores. I could practically smell it. Beer for breakfast. Maybe with chasers. A decade-long diet, judging by the look of him. So he would be slow to react, and then wild and unaimed afterwards. No big problem. The new guy with the biker vest was carrying some kind of back pain. Low down, base of his spine. I could tell because he was standing with his pelvis rolled forward, taking the pressure off. Some kind of rupture or strain. A dozen possible causes. He was a country boy. He could have lifted a bale, or fallen off a horse. No major threat. He would defeat himself. One enthusiastic swing, and all kinds of things would tear loose inside. He would hobble away like a cripple. By which time his drunken friend would already be down. And the other two were already in no kind of good shape. The two I knew. The two that knew me. The alpha dog was slightly on my left, and I'm a right-handed fighter. He was practically volunteering.

Overall, an encouraging situation.

I said, 'It's a shame one of you isn't bigger. Or two or three of you. Or all of you, actually.'

No answer.

I said, 'But hey, a plan's a plan. Did it take long to work out?'

No answer.

I said, 'You know what we used to say about plans, up at West Point?'

'What?'

'Everyone has a plan until they get punched in the mouth.'

No answer. No movement. I unwrapped my hand from around the roll of quarters. I wasn't going to need them. I took my hands out of my pockets. I said, 'The problem with light forces is if things go bad, they go real bad real quick. Look at what happened in Somalia. So you should think very carefully about this choice. You're at a fork in the road here. You have to decide which way to go. You could wade in, just the four of you, right now. But the next stop after that will be the hospital. That's a promise. That's a cast-iron guarantee. You'll get hit harder than you've ever been hit before. I'm talking broken bones. I can't promise brain damage. Looks like someone already beat me to that.'

No response.

I said, 'Or you could attempt a tactical withdrawal now, and then you could take your time putting that big force together. You could come back in a couple of days. Dozens of you. You could find your granddaddy's varmint gun. You could start the painkillers early.'

No response. Nothing verbal, anyway. But shoulders slumped a fraction, and feet started shuffling.

'Good decision,' I said. 'Overwhelming force is always better. You really should go to the Pentagon. You could walk them through your reasoning. They'd listen to you. They're listening to everyone except us.'

The alpha dog said, 'We'll be back.'

'I'll be here,' I said. 'Whenever you're ready.'

They walked away, trying to be casual about it, trying

to be haughty, trying to salvage some dignity. They climbed into their trucks and made a big show of revving their engines and squealing their tyres through tight 180 turns. They drove off west into the forest, towards Memphis, towards the rest of the world. I watched them go, and then I walked back to the Sheriff's Department.

Deveraux had seen the whole thing from the window in the dim corner room. Like a silent movie. No dialogue. She said, 'You made them go away. You apologized. I can't believe it.'

'Not exactly,' I said. 'I took a rain check. They're coming back later, dozens of them.'

'Why did you do that?'

'More arrests for you. They'll look good for your re-election campaign.'

'You're crazy.'

'You want to get lunch now?'

'I already have a lunch date,' she said.

'Since when?'

'Five minutes ago. Major Duncan Munro called back and asked me to dine with him in the Kelham Officers' Club.'

THIRTY

Deveraux left for Kelham in her car and I was left alone on the sidewalk. I walked past the vacant lot to the diner. Lunch, for one. I ordered the cheeseburger again, and then stepped over to the phone by the door and called the Pentagon. Colonel John James Frazer. Senate Liaison. He answered on the first ring. I asked him, 'What genius decided to classify that plate number?'

He said, 'I can't tell you that.'

'Whoever, it was a bad mistake. All it did was confirm the car belongs to a Kelham guy. It was practically a public announcement.'

'We had no alternative. We couldn't put it in the public domain. Journalists would have gotten it five minutes after local law enforcement. We couldn't allow that.'

'Now it sounds like you're telling me it belonged to a Bravo Company guy.'

'I'm not telling you anything. But believe me, we had no choice. The consequences would have been catastrophic.'

Something in his voice.

'Please tell me you're kidding,' I said. 'Because

right now you're making it sound like it was Reed Riley's own personal vehicle.'

No response.

I asked, 'Was it?'

No answer.

'Was it?'

'I can't confirm or deny,' Frazer said. 'And don't ask again. And don't use that name again, either. Not on an unsecured line.'

'Does the officer in question have an explanation?'

'I can't comment on that.'

I said, 'This is getting out of control, Frazer. You need to rethink. The cover-up is always worse than the crime. You need to stop it now.'

'Negative on that, Reacher. There's a plan in place, and it will stay in place.'

'Does the plan include an exclusion zone around Kelham? Maybe for journalists especially?'

'What the hell are you talking about?'

'I've got circumstantial evidence here of boots on the ground outside of Kelham's fence. Part of the circumstantial evidence is a corpse. I'm telling you, this thing is out of control now.'

'Who's the corpse?'

'A scrappy middle-aged guy.'

'A journalist?'

'I don't know how to recognize a journalist by sight alone. Maybe that's a skill they teach to the infantry, but they don't teach it to MPs.'

'No ID on him?'

'We haven't looked yet. The doctor hasn't finished with him.'

Frazer said, 'There is no exclusion zone around Fort Kelham. That would be a major policy shift.'

'And illegal.'

'Agreed. And stupid. And counterproductive. It isn't happening. It never has.'

'I think the Marine Corps did it once.'

'When?'

'Within the last twenty years.'

'Well, Marines. They do all kinds of things.'

'You should check it out.'

'How? You think they put it in their official history?'

'Do it obliquely. Look for an officer who got canned overnight with no other explanation. Maybe a colonel.'

I hung up with Frazer and ate my burger and drank some coffee and then I set out to do what Garber had ordered me to do mid-morning, which was to return to the wreck and destroy the offending licence plate. I turned east on the Kelham road and then north on the railroad ties. I passed by the old water tower. Its elephant's trunk was made from some kind of black rubberized canvas, gone all perished and patchy with age. The whole thing was swaying a little in a soft southerly breeze. I walked on fifty yards and then stepped off the line and headed for where I had seen the half-buried bumper.

The half-buried bumper was gone.

It was nowhere to be seen. It had been dug up and taken away. The hole its lance-like point had made had been filled with earth, which had been stamped down by boot soles and then tamped flat by the backs of shovels.

The boot prints were like nothing I had ever seen in the military. But the shovel marks could have been made by GI entrenching tools. It was difficult to be sure. Couldn't rule it out, couldn't rule it in.

I walked on, deeper into the debris field. It had all been tampered with. It had been sifted, and examined, and turned over, and checked, and evaluated. Almost two hundred linear yards. Maybe a thousand individual fragments had been displaced. No doubt ten times as many smaller items had been eyeballed. A wide area. A big task. A lot of work. Slow and painstaking. Six men, I figured. Maybe eight. I pictured them advancing in a line, under effective command, working with great precision.

With military precision.

I walked back the way I had come. I got to the middle of the railroad crossing and saw a car in the east, coming from the direction of Kelham. It was still far away on the straight road. Small to the eye, but not a small car. At first I thought it might be Deveraux coming back after lunch, but it wasn't. It was a black car, and big, and fast, and smooth. A town car. A limousine. It was right out on the crown of the road, straddling the line, staying well away from the ragged shoulders. It was swaying and wafting and wandering.

I came off the track on the Kelham side and stood in the middle of the road, feet apart, arms out, big and obvious. I let the car get within a hundred yards and then I crossed my arms above my head and waved the universal distress semaphore. I knew the driver would stop. This was 1997, remember. Four and a half years before the new rules. A long time ago. A much less suspicious world.

The car slowed and stopped in front of me. I went to my right, around the hood, down the flank, towards the driver's window, holding back a little, trying to perfect my angle. I wanted to get a look at the passenger. I figured he would be in the back, on the far side, with the front passenger seat scooted forward for leg room. I knew how these things were done. I had been in town cars before. Once or twice.

The driver's window came down. I bent forward from the waist. Took a look. The driver was a big fat guy with the kind of belly that forced his knees wide apart. He was wearing a black chauffeur's cap and a black jacket and a black tie. He had watery eyes. He said, 'Can we help you?'

I said, 'I'm sorry. My mistake. I thought you were someone else. But thanks anyway for stopping.'

'Sure,' the guy said. 'No problem.' His window went back up and I stepped aside and the car drove on.

The passenger had been male, older than me, grey-haired, prosperous, in a fine suit made of wool. There had been a leather briefcase on the seat beside him.

He was a lawyer, I thought.

THIRTY-ONE

I was facing east, towards the black part of town, and there were things over there that I wanted to see again, so I set off walking in that direction. The road felt good under my feet. I guessed once upon a time during the glory days of the railroad it had been a simple dirt track, but it had been updated since then, almost certainly in the 1950s, almost certainly on the DoD's dime. The foundation had been dug down, for armour on flat-bed transporters, and the line had been straightened, because if an army engineer sees a ruled line on a map, then a straight road is what appears on the ground. I had walked on many DoD roads. There are a lot of them, all around the world, all built a lifetime ago, during the long and spectacular blaze of American military power and self-confidence, when there was nothing we couldn't or wouldn't do. I was a product of that era, but not a part of it. I was nostalgic for something I had never experienced.

Then I thought about my old pal Stan Lowrey, talking about want ads in the hamburger place near where we were based. Changes were coming, for sure, but I wasn't

190

unhappy. That straight road through the low Mississippi forest was helping me. The sun was out, and the air was warm. There were miles behind me, and miles ahead, and plenty of time on the clock. I had no ambitions and very few needs. I would be OK, whatever came next. No choice. I would have to be.

I made the same turn Deveraux had made in her car, south on the dirt road between the bar ditches and the slave shacks. Towards Emmeline McClatchy's place. At walking speed I was seeing different things than from the car. Poverty, mostly, and up close. There were patched clothes on lines, washed so thin they were almost transparent. There were no new cars. There were chickens in some of the yards, and goats, and the occasional pig. There were mangy dogs on chains. There were duct tape and baling wire fixes everywhere, to electric lines, to rain gutters, to plumbing outlets. And I was seeing suspicion too, to a degree. There were barefoot children briefly visible, staring at me, their fingers in their mouths, until they were snatched back out of sight by anxious mothers who wouldn't meet my eye.

I kept on going and passed by Emmeline McClatchy's place. I didn't see her. I didn't see anybody on that stretch of the road. No kids, no adults. Nobody. I passed by the house with the beer signs in the windows. I followed the same turns Deveraux had steered me through before, left and right and left, until I found the abandoned work site and its pile of gravel.

The house planned for the lot was small, and its

foundation was set at an angle according to ancient practice and wisdom, to take advantage of prevailing breezes and to avoid the full impact of the southwestern sun in the summer. The foundation itself was built of recycled blocks and sand-heavy cement. A sewer pipe and a water line had been roughed in. The corner posts were already weathering. Nothing else had been completed. Money had run out, I supposed.

The gravel in the pile was waiting to be made into concrete, I assumed. Maybe the ground floor of the new place was intended to be a solid slab, not boards. Maybe there were advantages to doing it that way, perhaps related to termites. I had no idea. I had never built a house. I had never had to consider housing-related issues.

The gravel pile itself had spread and settled during the idle months. Weeds were showing through the edges where it was thin. It was knee-high over most of its area, and up close it was about the size of a queen bed. The divots and the pockmarks in its top surface were like a Rorschach test. It was entirely possible to see them as the result of innocent children running and jumping and stomping. It was equally possible to see them as the result of a grown woman being thrown down and raped, in a violent flurry of knees and elbows and backs.

I squatted down and ran a fingertip through the tiny stones. They were surprisingly hard to move. They were packed down tight, and some kind of a dusty residue on them seemed to have mixed with rain or dew to form a weak adhesive. I made a furrow about an inch wide and an inch deep, and then I turned my hand over.

I pressed the back of my hand into the pile and held it there for a minute. Then I looked at the result. Small white marks, but no indentations, because there was no real flesh on the back of my hand. So I pulled up my sleeve and pressed the inside of my forearm against the pile. I put the flat of my other hand on it and leaned on it hard. I bounced it up and down a couple of times, and scrabbled it around. Then I looked at it.

The result was some small red marks, some small white marks, and a whole lot of dust, dirt, and mud. I spat on my arm and wiped it on my pants and the resulting clean stripe looked both very like and very unlike the small of Janice May Chapman's back. Another Rorschach test. Inconclusive.

But I did come to one minor conclusion. I cleaned up my arm as well as I could, which was not perfectly, and I decided that whatever gravel patch Chapman had been raped on, she had not only dressed afterwards, but showered too.

I walked on and found the wider street where Shawna Lindsay had lived. The second victim. The middle-class girl, comparatively. Her baby brother was still in his yard. Sixteen years old. The ugly boy. He was just standing there. Doing nothing. Watching the street. Watching me approach. His eyes tracked me all the way. I stepped up on the shoulder and came to a stop face to face with him, with only his low picket fence between us.

I said, 'How's life, kid?'

He said, 'My mom's out.'

'Good to know,' I said. 'But that wasn't what I asked.'

'Life's a bitch,' he said.

'And then you die,' I said. Which I regretted, instantly. Insensitive, given his family's recent history. But he took no notice. Which I was glad about. I said, 'I need to talk to you.'

'Why? You earning a whitey merit badge? You need to find a black person to talk with today?'

'I'm in the army,' I said. 'Which means half my friends are black, and more important it means half my bosses are black. I talk to black people all the time, and they talk to me. So don't give me that ghetto shit.'

The boy was quiet for a second. Then he asked, 'What part of the army are you in?'

'Military Police.'

'Is that a tough job?'

'Tougher than tough,' I said. 'Think about it logically. Any soldier could kick your ass, and I could kick any soldier's ass.'

'For real?'

'More than real,' I said. 'Real is for other people. Not for us.'

He asked, 'What do you want to talk about?'

'A hunch.'

'What kind?'

I said, 'My guess is no one ever talked to you about your sister's death.'

He looked down.

I said, 'Normally with a homicide victim, they talk to everyone who knew her. They ask for insights and opinions. They want to know what kinds of things she did, where she went, who she hung with. Did they ever talk to you about that kind of stuff?'

'No,' he said. 'Nobody ever talked to me.'

'They should have,' I said. 'I would have. Because brothers know things about sisters. Especially at the ages you two were. I bet you knew things about Shawna that no one else did. I bet she told you things she couldn't tell your mom. And I bet you figured out some stuff on your own.'

The kid shuffled in place a little. Bashful, and a little proud. Like saying: *Yeah, maybe I did figure some things out.* Out loud he said, 'No one ever talks to me about anything.'

'Why not?'

'Because I'm deformed. They think I'm slow, too.'

'Who says you're deformed?'

'Everybody.'

'Even your mom?'

'She doesn't say it, but she thinks it.'

'Even your friends?'

'I don't have any friends. Who would want to be friends with me?'

'They're all wrong,' I said. 'You're not deformed. You're ugly, but you're not deformed. There's a difference.'

He smiled. 'That's what Shawna used to tell me.'

I pictured the two of them together. Beauty and the beast. A tough life, for both of them. Tough for him, with the endless implied comparisons. Tough for her, with the endless need for tact and patience. I said, 'You should join the army. You'd look like a movie star compared to half the people I know. You should see the guy that sent me here.'

'I'm going to join the army,' he said. 'I talked to some-one about it.'

'Who did you talk to?'

'Shawna's last boyfriend,' he said. 'He was a soldier.'

THIRTY-TWO

The kid invited me inside. His mom was out, and there was a pitcher of iced tea in the refrigerator. The house was dim and shuttered. It smelled stale. It was mean and narrow inside, but it had plenty of rooms. An eat-in kitchen, a living room, and what I guessed were three bedrooms in back. Space for two parents and two kids, except I saw no sign of a father, and Shawna was never coming home again.

The kid told me his name was Bruce. We took glasses of tea and sat at the kitchen table. There was an old wall phone next to the refrigerator. Pale yellow plastic. Its cord had been stretched about twelve feet long. There was an old television set on the countertop. Small, but colour, with chrome accents on the cabinet. Practically an antique, probably rescued from a trash pile somewhere and polished up like an old Cadillac.

Up close and personal the kid was no better looking than he had been outside. But if you ignored his head, then the rest of him was in pretty good shape. He was all bone and muscle, broad through the chest and the shoulders, thick in the arms. Deep down he seemed patient and cheerful. I liked him, basically.

He asked me, 'Would they really let me join the army?'

'Who is they?'

'The army, I mean. The army itself. Would they let me in?'

'Do you have felony convictions?'

'No, sir.'

'An arrest record of any kind?'

'No, sir.'

'Then of course they'll let you in. They'd take you today if you were old enough.'

'The others would laugh at me.'

'Probably,' I said. 'But not for the reason you think. Soldiers aren't like that. They'd find something else. Something you never even thought of yet.'

'I could wear my helmet all the time.'

'Only if they find one big enough.'

'And night-vision goggles.'

'Maybe a bomb-disposal hood,' I said. I figured bomb disposal was the coming thing. Small wars and booby traps. But I didn't say so. Not the kind of message a potential recruit wants to hear.

I sipped my tea.

The boy asked me, 'Do you watch television?'

'Not much,' I said. 'Why?'

'They have commercials,' he said. 'Which means they have to fit an hour's story into forty-some minutes. So they get right to it.'

'You think that's what I should do now?'

'That's what I'm saying.'

'So who do you think killed your sister?'

The boy took a sip of tea and a serious breath and then he started in on everything he had been thinking about, and everything he had never been asked about. It all came tumbling out, fast, coherent, responsive, and thoughtful. He said, 'Well, her throat was cut, so we need to think about who is trained to do that kind of thing, or experienced with that kind of thing, or both.'

That kind of thing. His sister's throat.

I asked, 'So who fits the bill?'

'Soldiers,' he said. 'Especially here. And ex-soldiers, especially here. Fort Kelham is field training for special ops guys. They know those skills. And hunters. And most people in town, to be honest. Including me.'

'You? Are you a hunter?'

'No, but I have to eat. People keep pigs.'

'And?'

'You think pigs commit suicide? We cut their throats.'

'You've done that?'

'Dozens of times. Sometimes I get a dollar.'

I asked, 'When and where did you last see Shawna alive?'

'It was the day she was killed. It was a Friday in November. She left here about seven o'clock. After dark, anyway. She was all dressed up.'

'Where was she going?'

'Across the tracks. To Brannan's bar, probably. That's where she usually went.'

'Is Brannan's the most popular bar?'

'They're all popular. But Brannan's is where most folk start out and finish up.'

'Who did Shawna go with that night?'

'She left on her own. Probably she was going to meet her boyfriend at the bar.'

'Did she ever get there?'

'No. She was found two streets from here. Where someone started to build a house.'

'The place with the gravel pile?'

The boy nodded. 'She was dumped right on it. Like a human sacrifice in a history book.'

We got up from the table and poked around the kitchen for a minute. Then we took more tea and sat down again. I said, 'Tell me about Shawna's last boyfriend.'

'First white boyfriend she ever had.'

'Did she like him?'

'Pretty much.'

'Did they get along?'

'Pretty good.'

'No problems?'

'Didn't see any.'

'Did he kill her?'

'He might have.'

'Why do you say that?'

'Can't rule him out.'

'Gut feeling?'

'I want to say no, but someone killed her. It could have been him.'

'What was his name?'

'Reed. That was all Shawna ever said. Reed this, Reed that. Reed, Reed, Reed.'

'Last name?'

'I don't know.'

'We wear name tapes,' I said. 'Battledress uniform, above the right breast pocket.'

'I never saw him in uniform. They all wear jeans and T-shirts to town. Jackets, sometimes.'

'Officer or enlisted man?'

'I don't know.'

'You talked to him. Didn't he say?'

The kid shook his head. 'He said his name was Reed. That's all.'

'Was he an asshole?'

'A bit.'

'Did he look like he worked hard for a living?'

'Not really. He didn't take things very seriously.'

'Probably an officer then,' I said. 'What did he tell you about joining the army?'

'He said serving your country was a noble thing to do.'

'Definitely an officer.'

'He said I could learn a skill. He said I might make specialist.'

'You could do better than that.'

'He said they would explain it all at the recruiting office. He said there's a good one in Memphis.'

'Don't go there,' I said. 'Way too dangerous. Recruiting offices are shared between all four branches of the service. The Marines might grab you first. Fate worse than death.'

'So where should I go?'

'Go straight to Kelham. There are recruiters on every post.'

'Will that work?'

'Sure it will. As soon as you've got something in your hand that proves you're eighteen years old, they'll let you in and never let you out again.'

'But they say the army is getting smaller.'

'Thanks for pointing that out, kid.'

'So why would they want me?'

'They're still going to have hundreds of thousands of people. Tens of thousands will still leave every year. They'll always need to be replaced.'

'What's wrong with the Marines?'

'Nothing really. It's a traditional rivalry. They say stuff, we say stuff.'

'They do amphibious landings.'

'History shows the army has done many more all on its own.'

'Sheriff Deveraux was a Marine.'

'Is a Marine,' I said. 'They never stop being Marines, even after they leave. It's one of their things.'

'You like her,' the kid said. 'I could tell. I saw you riding in her car.'

'She's OK,' I said. 'Did Reed have a car? Shawna's boyfriend?'

The kid nodded. 'They all have cars. I'm going to have a car too, after I join.'

'What kind of car did Reed have?'

'He had a 1957 Chevy Bel-Air two-door hardtop. Not really a classic. It was kind of beat up.'

'What colour was it?'

The kid said, 'It was blue.'

THIRTY-THREE

The kid showed me his sister's room. It was clean and tidy. Not preserved as a shrine, but not yet cleared out, either. It spoke of loss, and bewilderment, and lack of energy. The bed was made and small piles of clothes were neatly folded. No decision had been taken about its future fate.

There was none of Shawna Lindsay's personality on display. She had been a grown woman, not a teenager. There were no posters on the walls, no souvenirs of anything, no breathless diary. No keepsakes. She had owned some clothes, some shoes, and two books. That was all. One book was a thin thing explaining how to become a notary public. The other was an out-of-date tourist guide to Los Angeles.

'Did she want to be in the movies?' I asked.

'No,' the kid said. 'She wanted to travel, that's all.'

'To LA specifically?'

'Anywhere.'

'Did she have a job?'

'She worked part time at the loan office. Next to Brannan's bar. She could do her numbers pretty good.'

203

'What did she tell you that she couldn't tell your mom?'

'That she hated it here. That she wanted to get out.'

'Your mom didn't want to hear that stuff?'

'She wanted to keep Shawna safe. My mom is afraid of the world.'

'Where does your mom work?'

'She's a cleaner. At the bars in town. She gets them ready for happy hour.'

'What else do you know about Shawna?'

The kid started to say something, and then he stopped. In the end he just shrugged and said nothing. He moved towards the centre of the plain square space and stood there, as if he was soaking something up. Something in the still air. I got the feeling he had rarely been in that room. Not often before Shawna's death, and not often since.

He said, 'I know I really miss her.'

We went back to the kitchen and I asked, 'If I left the money, do you think your mom would mind if I used her phone?'

'You need to make a call?' the kid asked back, as if that was an extraordinary thing.

'Two calls,' I said. 'One I need to make, and one I want to make.'

'I don't know how much it costs.'

'Pay phones cost a quarter,' I said. 'Suppose I left a dollar a call?'

'That would be too much.'

'Long distance,' I said.

'Whatever you think is right. I'm going outside again.'

I waited until I saw him emerge in the front yard. He took up a position near the fence, just standing there, watching the street, infinitely patient. Some kind of a perpetual vigil. I tucked a dollar bill between the phone's plastic casing and the wall and took the receiver off the hook. I dialled the call I needed to make. Stan Lowrey, back on our shared home base. I went through his sergeant and a minute later he came on the line.

I said, 'Well, there's a surprise. You're still there. You've still got a job.'

He said, 'I think I'm safer than you are right now. Frances Neagley just reported back.'

'She worries too much.'

'You don't worry enough.'

'Is Karla Dixon still working financial stuff?'

'I could find out.'

'Ask her a question for me. I want to know if I should be concerned about money coming in from a place called Kosovo. Like gangsters laundering bales of cash. That kind of a thing.'

'Doesn't sound very likely. That's the Balkans, right? They're middle class if they own a goat. Rich, if they own two. Not like America.'

I looked out the window and said, 'Not so very different from parts of it.'

Lowrey said, 'I wish I was working financial stuff. I might have picked up some necessary skills. Like how to have savings.'

'Don't worry,' I said. 'You'll get unemployment. For a spell, at least.'

'You sound cheerful.'

'I've got a lot to be cheerful about.'

'Why? What's going on down there?'

'All kinds of wonderful things,' I said, and hung up. Then I trapped a second dollar bill between the phone and the wall and dialled the call I wanted to make. I used the Treasury Department's main switchboard and got a woman who sounded middle-aged and elegant. She asked, 'How may I direct your inquiry?'

I said, 'Joe Reacher, please.'

There was some scratching and clicking and a minute of dead air. No hold music at Treasury, either, back in 1997. Then a woman picked up and said, 'Mr Reacher's office.' She sounded young and bright. Probably a magna cum laude graduate from a prestigious college, full of shining eyes and idealism. Probably good-looking, too. Probably wearing a short plaid skirt and a white turtleneck sweater. My brother knew how to pick them.

I asked, 'Is Mr Reacher there?'

'I'm afraid he's out of the office for a few days. He had to go to Georgia.' She said it like she would have said Saturn or Neptune. An incomprehensible distance, and barren when you got there. She asked, 'May I take a message?'

'Tell him his brother called.'

'How exciting. He never mentioned he had brothers. But actually, you sound just like him, did you know that?'

'So people say. There's no message. Tell him I just wanted to say hello. To touch base, you know. To see how he is.'

206

'Will he know which brother?'

'I hope so,' I said. 'He's only got one.'

I left immediately after that. Shawna's brother did not break his lonely vigil. I waved and he waved back, but he didn't move. He just kept on watching the far horizon. I hiked back to the Kelham road and turned left for town. I got some of the way towards the railroad and heard a car behind me, and a blip of a siren, like a courtesy. I turned and Deveraux pulled up right alongside me, neat and smooth. A short moment later I was in her front passenger seat, with nothing between us except her holstered shotgun.

THIRTY-FOUR

The first thing I said was, 'Long lunch.' Which was supposed to be just a descriptive comment, but she took it as more. She said, 'Jealous?'

'Depends what you ate. I had a cheeseburger.'

'We had rare roast beef and horseradish sauce. With roast potatoes. It was very good. But you must know that. You must eat in the OC all the time.'

'How was the conversation?'

'Challenging.'

'In what way?'

'First tell me what you've been doing.'

'Me? I've been eating humble pie. Metaphorically, at least.'

'How so?'

'I went back to the wrecked car. I was under orders to destroy the licence plate. But it was already gone. The debris field had been picked clean, very methodically. There was a big force out there at some point this morning. So I think you're right. There are boots on the ground outside Kelham's fence. They're operating an exclusion zone. They were diverted to the clean-up because someone at the Pentagon didn't trust me to do it.'

Deveraux didn't answer.

'Then I took a long walk,' I said.

Deveraux asked, 'Did you see the gravel pile?'

'I saw it this morning,' I said. 'I went back for a closer look.'

'Thinking about Janice May Chapman?'

'Obviously.'

'It's a coincidence,' she said. 'Black-on-white rapes are incredibly rare in Mississippi. No matter what folks want to believe.'

'A white guy could have taken her there.'

'Unlikely. He'd have stuck out like a sore thumb. He'd have been risking a hundred witnesses.'

'Shawna Lindsay's body was found there. I talked to her kid brother.'

'Where else would it be found? It's a vacant lot. That's where bodies get dumped.'

'Was she killed there?'

'I don't think so. There was no blood.'

'At the scene or inside her?'

'Neither one.'

'What do you make of that?'

'Same guy.'

'And?'

'Addiction to risk,' she said. 'June, November, March, the bottom of the socio-economic scale, then the middle, then the top. By Carter County standards, that is. He started safe and got progressively riskier. No one cares about poor black girls. Chapman was the first really visible victim.'

'You care about poor black girls.'

'But you know how it is. An investigation can't sustain itself all on its own. It needs an external source of energy. It needs outrage.'

'And there wasn't any?'

'There was pain, obviously. And sorrow, and suffering. But mostly there was resignation. And familiarity. Business as usual. If all the murdered women of Mississippi rose up tonight and marched through town, you'd notice two things. It would be a very long parade, and most of the marchers would be black. Poor black girls have been getting killed here for ever. White women with money, not so often.'

'What was the McClatchy girl's name?'

'Rosemary.'

'Where was her body found?'

'In the ditch near the crossing. West of the tracks.'

'Any blood?'

'None at all.'

'Was she raped?'

'No.'

'Was Shawna Lindsay?'

'No.'

'So Janice May Chapman was another kind of escalation.'

'Apparently.'

'Did Rosemary McClatchy have a connection with Kelham?'

'Of course she did. You saw her photograph. Kelham guys were lining up at her door with their tongues hanging out. She stepped out with a string of them.'

'Black guys or white guys?'

'Both.'

'Officers or enlisted men?'

'Both.'

'Any suspects?'

'I had no probable cause even to ask questions. She wasn't seen with anyone from Kelham for at least two weeks before she was killed. My jurisdiction ends at Kelham's fence. They wouldn't have let me through the gate.'

'They let you through the gate today.'

'Yes,' she said. 'They did.'

'What is Munro like?' I asked.

'Challenging,' she said again.

We thumped up over the tracks and parked just beyond them, with the straight road west in front of us, and the ditch where Rosemary McClatchy had been found on our right, and the turn into Main Street ahead and on our left. A standard cop instinct. If in doubt, pull over and park where people can see you. It feels like doing something, even when it isn't.

Deveraux said, 'Obviously I started out with the baseline assumption that Munro would be lying through his teeth. Job one for him is to cover the army's ass. I understand that, and I don't blame him for it. He's under orders, the same way you are.'

'And?'

211

'I asked him about the exclusion zone. He denied it, of course.'

'He would have to,' I said.

She nodded. 'But then he went ahead and tried to prove it to me. He toured me all over. That's why I was gone so long. He's running a very tight ship. Every last man is confined to quarters. There are MPs everywhere. The MPs are watching each other, as well as everyone else. The armoury is under guard. The logs show no weapons in or out for two solid days.'

'And?'

'Well, naturally I assumed I was getting conned big time. And sure enough, there were two hundred empty beds. So naturally I assumed they've got a shadow force bivouacked in the woods somewhere. But Munro said no, that's a full company currently deployed elsewhere for a month. He swore blind. And I believed him, ultimately, because like everyone else I've heard the planes come in and out, and I've seen the faces come and go.'

I nodded. *Alpha Company*, I thought. *Kosovo*.

She said, 'So in the end it all added up. Munro showed me a lot of evidence and it was all very consistent. And no one can run a con that perfect. So there is no exclusion zone. I was wrong. And you must be wrong about the debris field. It must have been local kids, scavenging.'

'I don't think so,' I said. 'It looked like a very organized search.'

She paused a beat. 'Then maybe the 75th is sending people directly from Benning. Which is entirely possible.

Maybe they're living in the woods around the fence. All Munro proved is that no one is leaving Kelham. He could be one of those guys who tells you a small truth in order to hide a bigger lie.'

'Sounds like you didn't like him much.'

'I liked him well enough. He's smart and he's loyal to the army. But if we'd both been Marine MPs at the same time I'd have been worried. I'd have seen him as a serious rival. There's something about him. He's the type of guy you don't want to see moving into your office. He's too ambitious. And too good.'

'What did he say about Janice May Chapman?'

'He gave me what appeared to be a very expert summary of what appeared to be a very expert investigation which appeared to prove no one from Kelham was ever involved with anything.'

'But you didn't believe it?'

'I almost did,' she said.

'But?'

'He couldn't hide the rivalry. He made it clear. It's him against me. It's the army against the local sheriff. That's the challenge. He wants the world to think the bad guy is on my side of the fence. But I wasn't born yesterday. What the hell else would he want the world to think?'

'So what are you going to do?'

'I'm not sure yet.'

'What do you want to do?'

'He doesn't respect the Marines, either. Him against me means the army against the Corps. Which is a bad fight to pick. So if he wants rivalry, I want to give it right

213

back. I want to take him on. I want to beat him like a rented mule. I want to find the truth somehow and stick it up his ass.'

'Do you think you can do that?'

She said, 'I can if you help me.'

THIRTY-FIVE

We sat in the idling Caprice for a long minute, saying nothing. The car must have had ten thousand hours of stake-out duty on it. From its previous life, in Chicago or New Orleans or wherever. Every pore of every interior surface was thick with sweat and odour and exhaustion. Grime was crusted everywhere. The floor mats had separated into hard tufts of fibre, each one like a flattened pearl.

Deveraux said, 'I apologize.'

I said, 'For what?'

'For asking you to help me. It wasn't fair. Forget I said anything.'

'OK.'

'Can I let you out somewhere?'

I said, 'Let's go talk to Janice May Chapman's nosy neighbours.'

'No,' she said. 'I can't let you do that. I can't let you turn against your own people.'

'Maybe I wouldn't be turning against my own people,' I said. 'Maybe I would be doing exactly what my own people wanted me to do all along. Because maybe I would be helping Munro, not you. Because he might be right, you know. We still have no idea who did what here.'

We. She didn't correct me. Instead she said, 'But what's your best guess?'

I thought about the limousines scurrying in and out of Fort Kelham, carrying expensive lawyers. I thought about the exclusion zone, and the panic in John James Frazer's voice, on the phone from the Pentagon. Senate Liaison. I said, 'My best guess is it was a Kelham guy.'

'You sure you want to take the risk of finding out for sure?'

'Talking to a man with a gun is a risk. Asking questions isn't.'

I believed that then, back in 1997.

Janice May Chapman's house was a hundred yards from the railroad track, one of the last three dwellings on a dead-end lane a mile south and east of Main Street. It was a small place, set back in a wedge-shaped yard off a circular bulge where traffic could turn around at the end of the street. It was facing two other houses, as if it was nine o'clock on a dial and they were two and four. It was maybe fifty years old, but it had been updated with new siding and a new roof and some diligent landscaping. Both of its neighbours were in a similar state of good repair, as had been all the previous houses on the street. Clearly this was Carter Crossing's middle-class enclave. Lawns were green and weed-free. Driveways were paved and uncracked. Mailbox posts were exactly vertical. The only real-estate negative was the train, but there was only one of those a day. One minute out of fourteen hundred and forty. Not a bad deal.

Chapman's house had a full-width front porch, roofed over for shade, railed in with fancy millwork spindles, and equipped with a matched pair of white rocking chairs and a rag mat in various muted colours. Both her neighbours had the exact same thing going on, the only difference being that both their porches were occupied, each by a white-haired old lady wearing a floral-print housedress and sitting bolt upright in a rocker and staring at us.

We sat in the car for a minute and then Deveraux rolled forward and parked right in the middle of the turnaround. We got out and stood for a second in the afternoon light.

'Which one first?' I asked.

'Doesn't matter,' Deveraux said. 'Whichever, the other one will be right over within about thirty seconds.'

Which is exactly what happened. We chose the right-hand house, the one at four o'clock on the dial, and before we were three steps on to its porch the neighbour from the two o'clock house was right behind us. Deveraux made the introductions. She gave the ladies my name and said I was an investigator from the army. Up close the ladies were slightly different from one another. One was older, the other was thinner. But they were broadly similar. Thin necks, pursed lips, haloes of white hair. They welcomed me respectfully. They were from a generation that liked the army, and knew something about it. No question they had had husbands or brothers or sons in uniform, World War Two, Korea, Vietnam.

217

I turned and checked the view from the porch. Chapman's house was neatly triangulated by her two neighbours. Like a focal point. Like a target. The two neighbours' porches were exactly where the infantry would set up machine-gun nests for effective enfilade fire.

I turned back and Deveraux ran through what she had already discussed. She asked for confirmation of every point and got it. All negative. No, neither of the two ladies had seen Chapman leave her house on the day she died. Not in the morning, not in the afternoon, not in the evening. Not on foot, not in her car, not in anybody else's car. No, nothing new had come to either one of them. They had nothing to add.

The next question was tactically difficult, so Deveraux left it to me. I asked, 'Were there intervals when something could have happened that you didn't see?' In other words: *Just exactly how nosy are you? Were there moments when you weren't staring at your neighbour?*

Both ladies saw the implication, of course, and they clucked and pursed and fussed for a minute, but the gravity of the situation meant more to them than their wounded feelings, and they came out and admitted that, no, they had the situation pretty much sewn up around the clock. Both liked to sit on their porches when they weren't otherwise occupied, and they tended to be otherwise occupied at different times. Both had bedrooms at the front of their houses, and neither tried to sleep until the midnight train had passed, and then afterwards both were light sleepers anyway, so not much escaped them at night, either.

I asked, 'Was there usually much coming and going over there?'

The ladies conferred and launched a long, complicated narrative that threatened to go all the way back to the American Revolution. I started to tune it out until I realized they were describing a fairly active social calendar that about half a year ago had settled into a month-on, month-off pattern, first of social frenzy, and then of complete inactivity. Feast or famine. Chapman was either never out, or always out, first four or five weeks in one condition, and then four or five weeks in the other.

Bravo Company, in Kosovo.

Bravo Company, at home.

Not good.

I asked, 'Did she have a boyfriend?'

She had several, they said, with prim delight. Sometimes all at once. Practically a parade. They listed sequential glimpsed sightings, all of polite young men with short hair, all in what they called dungaree pants, all in what they called undershirts, some in what they called motorcycle coats.

Jeans, T-shirts, leather jackets.

Soldiers, obviously, off duty.

Not good.

I asked, 'Was there anyone in particular? Anyone special?'

They conferred again and agreed a period of relative stability had commenced three or perhaps four months earlier. The parade of suitors had slowed, first to a trickle, and then it had stopped altogether and been replaced by the attentions of a lone man, once again described as polite, young, short-haired, but always inappropriately dressed on the many occasions they had seen him. Jeans, T-shirts, leather jackets. In their day, a gentleman called on his belle in a suit and a tie.

I asked, 'What did they do together?'

They went out, the ladies said. Sometimes in the afternoons, but most often in the evenings. Probably to bars. There was very little in the way of alternative entertainment in that corner of the state. The nearest picture house was in a town called Corinth. There had been a vaudeville theatre in Tupelo, but it had closed many years ago. The couple tended to come back late, sometimes after midnight, after the train had passed. Sometimes the suitor would stay an hour or two, but to their certain knowledge he had never spent the night.

I asked, 'When was the last time you saw her?'

The day before she died, they said. She had left her house at seven o'clock in the evening. The same suitor had come calling for her, right at the top of the hour, quite formally.

'What was Janice wearing that night?' I asked.

A yellow dress, they said, knee-length but low-cut.

'Did her friend show up in his own car?' I asked.

Yes, they said, he did.

'What kind of a car was it?'

It was a blue car, they said.

THIRTY-SIX

We left both ladies on one porch and crossed the street to take a closer look at Chapman's house. It was very much the same as the neighbours' places. It was classic tract housing, built fast in uniform batches for returning military and their new baby-boom families right after the end of World War Two. Then each individual example had grown slightly different from all the others over the passing years, the same way identical triplets might evolve differently with age. Chapman's choice had ended up modest and unassuming, but pleasant. Someone had put neat gingerbread trim all over it, and the front door had been replaced.

We stood on the porch and I looked in a window and saw a small square living room, full of furniture that looked pretty new. There was a loveseat and an armchair and a small television set on a low chest of drawers. There was a VHS player and some tapes next to it. The living-room door was open and I could see part of a narrow hallway beyond. I shifted position and craned my neck for a better look.

'Go inside if you want,' Deveraux said, behind me.

'Really?'

'The door is unlocked. It was unlocked when we got here.'

'Is that usual?'

'Not unusual. We never found her key.'

'Not in her pocketbook?'

'She didn't have a pocketbook with her. She seems to have left it in the kitchen.'

'Is *that* usual?'

'She didn't smoke,' Deveraux said. 'She certainly didn't pay for drinks. Why would she need a pocketbook?'

'Make-up?' I said.

'Twenty-seven-year-olds don't powder their noses halfway through the evening. Not like they used to. Not any more.'

I opened the front door and stepped inside the house. It was neat and clean, but the air was still and heavy. The floors and the rugs and the paint and the furniture were all fresh, but not brand new. There was an eat-in kitchen across the hall from the living room, with two bedrooms behind, and presumably a bathroom.

'Nice place,' I said. 'You could buy it. It would be better than the Toussaint's hotel.'

Deveraux said, 'With those old biddies across the street, watching me all the time? I'd go crazy inside a week.'

I smiled. She had a point.

She said, 'I wouldn't buy it even without the biddies. I wouldn't want to live like this. Not at all what I'm used to.'

I nodded. Said nothing.

Then she said, 'Actually I couldn't buy it even if I wanted to. We don't know who the next of kin is. I wouldn't know who to talk to.'

'No will?'

'She was twenty-seven years old.'

'No paperwork anywhere?'

'We haven't found any so far.'

'No mortgage?'

'Nothing on record with the county.'

'No family?'

'No one recalls her mentioning any.'

'So what are you going to do?'

'I don't know.'

I moved on down the hallway.

'Look around,' Deveraux called after me. 'Feel free. Make yourself at home. But tell me if you find something I should see.'

I walked from room to room, feeling the kind of trespass feelings I get every time I walk through a dead person's house. There were minor examples of disarray here and there, the kind of things that would have been cleaned up and tidied away before an expected guest's arrival. They humanized the place a little, but on the whole it was a bland and soulless home. There was too much uniformity. All the furniture matched. It looked like it had been selected from the same range from the same manufacturer, all at the same time. All the rugs went well together. All the paint was the same colour. There were no pictures on the walls, no photographs on the shelves. No books. No souvenirs, no prized possessions.

The bathroom was clean. The tub and the towels were dry. The medicine cabinet above the sink had a mirrored door, and behind it were over-the-counter analgesics, and toothpaste, and tampons, and dental floss, and spare soap and shampoo. The main bedroom had nothing of interest in it except a bed, which was made, but not well. The second bedroom had a narrower bed that looked like it had never been used.

The kitchen was fitted out with a range of useful stuff, but on balance I doubted that Chapman had been a gourmet cook. Her pocketbook was stowed neatly on the counter, resting upright against the side of the refrigerator. It was basically a small leather pouch, with a flap lid designed to close magnetically. It was navy blue in colour, which might or might not have been the reason it had been left behind. I wasn't sure of the current protocol involved in matching a blue bag with a yellow dress. Maybe not permitted. Although plenty of medals had blue and yellow in their ribbons, and the women soldiers I knew would have killed to get one, literally.

I opened the flap and looked in the bag. There was a slim leather wallet, dark red, and a convenience pack of tissues, unopened, and a pen, and some coins, and some crumbs, and a car key. The car key had a long serrated shaft, and a black plastic head moulded to feel good to the thumbs, and embossed with a large letter H.

'Honda,' Deveraux said, beside me. 'A Honda Civic. Bought new three years ago from a dealer in Tupelo. All up to date in terms of maintenance.'

'Where is it?' I asked.

Deveraux pointed to a door. 'In her garage.'

I took the wallet out of the bag. It had nothing in it except cash money and a Mississippi driver's licence, issued three years before. The picture on it dimmed about half of Chapman's allure, but it was still well worth looking at. The money added up to less than thirty dollars.

I put the wallet back and restacked the bag where it had been, next to the refrigerator. I opened the door Deveraux had pointed out, and behind it I found a tiny mud room that had two more doors in it, one letting out to the back yard on my left, and another to the garage straight ahead. The garage was completely empty apart from the car. The Honda. A small import, silver in colour, clean and undamaged, sitting there cold and patient and smelling faintly of oil and unburnt hydrocarbons. All around it was nothing but empty swept concrete. No unopened moving boxes, no chairs with the stuffing coming out, no abandoned projects, no junk, no clutter.

Nothing at all.

Unusual.

I opened the door to the back yard and stepped out. Deveraux came out with me and asked, 'So, was there anything in there I should have seen?'

'Yes,' I said. 'There were things in there anyone should have seen.'

'So what did I miss?'

'Nothing,' I said. 'They weren't there to *be* seen. That's my point. We should have seen certain things, but we didn't. Because certain things were missing.'

'What things?' she asked.

'Later,' I said, because by that point I had seen something else.

THIRTY-SEVEN

Janice May Chapman's back yard was not maintained to the same standard as her front yard. In fact it was barely maintained at all. It was almost completely neglected. It was mostly lawn, and it looked a little sad and sunken. It was mowed, but what had been mowed was basically weed, not grass. At the far end was a low panel fence, made of wood, starved of stain or protection, with the centre panel fallen out and laid aside.

What I had seen from the door was a faint narrow path through the mowed weeds. It was almost imperceptible. Almost not there at all. Only the late-afternoon sun made it visible. The light came in low from one side and showed a ghostly trail, where the weeds were a little brushed and crushed and bruised. A little darker than the rest of the lawn. The path led through a curved trajectory straight to the hole in the fence. It had been made by feet, going back and forth.

I got two steps along it and stopped again. The ground was crunching under my soles. I looked down. Deveraux bumped into my back.

The second time we had ever touched.

'What?' she said.

I looked up again.

'One thing at a time,' I said, and started walking again.

The path led off the weeds, through the gap in the fence, and out into a barren abandoned field about a hundred yards in width. At the far edge of the field was the railroad track. Halfway along the right-hand edge of the field were two tumbled gateposts, and beyond them was a dirt road which ran east and west. West, I guessed, towards more old field entrances and a link to the winding continuation of Main Street, and east towards the railroad track, where it dead-ended.

The old field had tyre tracks all the way across it. They came in between the ruined gateposts and ran through a wide right-angle turn straight towards the gap in Chapman's fence. They ended close to where I was standing, in a wide looping triangle, where cars had backed up and turned, ready for the return trip.

'She got sick of the old biddies,' I said. 'She was playing games with them. Sometimes she came out the front, and sometimes she came out the back. And I bet sometimes the boyfriends said goodnight and drove right around the block for more.'

Deveraux said, 'Shit.'

'Can't blame her. Or the boyfriends. Or the biddies, really. People do what they do.'

'But it makes their evidence meaningless.'

'That's what she wanted. She didn't know it was ever going to be important.'

228

'Now we don't know when she came and went on that last day.'

I stood in the silence and looked all around. Nothing to see. No other houses, no other people. An empty landscape. Total privacy.

Then I turned and looked back at the weed patch that passed for a lawn.

'What?' Deveraux said again.

'She bought this place three years ago, right?'

'Yes.'

'She was twenty-four at the time.'

'Yes.'

'Is that usual? Twenty-four-year-olds owning real estate?'

'Maybe not very usual.'

'With no mortgage?'

'Definitely not very usual. But what has that got to do with her yard?'

'She wasn't much of a gardener.'

'That's not a crime.'

'The previous owner wasn't much of a gardener either. Did you know him? Or her?'

'I was still in the Corps three years ago.'

'Not a long-time resident, that you remember from being a kid? Maybe a third old biddy, like a matched set?'

'Why?'

'No reason. Not important. But whoever, they didn't like mowing their lawn. So they dug it up and replaced it with something else.'

'With what?'

'Go take a look.'

She backtracked through the gap in the fence and walked halfway along the path and squatted down. She parted the weedy stalks and dug her fingertips into the surface underneath. She raked them back and forth and then she looked up at me and said, 'Gravel.'

The previous owner had tired of lawn care and opted for raked stones. Like a Japanese garden, maybe, or like the low-water-use yards conscientious Californians were starting to put in. Maybe there had been earthenware tubs here and there, full of cheerful flowers. Or maybe not. It was impossible to tell. But it was clear the gravel had not been a total success. Not a labour-saving cure-all. It had been laid thin. The subsoil had been full of weed roots. Regular applications of herbicide had been called for.

Janice May Chapman had not continued the herbicide applications. That was clear. No hosepipe in her garage. No watering can. Rural Mississippi. Agricultural land. Rain and sun. Those weeds had come boiling up like madmen. Some boyfriend had brought over a gasoline mower and hacked them back. Some nice guy with plenty of energy. The kind of guy who doesn't like mess and disarray. A soldier, almost certainly. The kind of guy who does things for people, gets things neat, and then keeps them neat.

Deveraux asked, 'So what are you saying? She was raped here?'

'Maybe she wasn't raped at all.'

Deveraux said nothing.

'It's possible she wasn't,' I said. 'Think about it. A sunny afternoon, total privacy. They're sitting out back because they don't want to sit on the front porch with the old biddies watching every move. They're on the stoop, they're feeling good, they get right to it.'

'On the lawn?'

'Wouldn't you?'

She looked right at me and said, 'Like you told the doctor, it would depend on who I was with.'

We spent the next few minutes talking about injuries. I did the thing with my forearm again. I pressed it down and mashed it around. I simulated the throes of passion. I came up with plenty of green chlorophyll stains and a smear of dry stony mud. When I wiped off the dirt we both saw the same kind of small red marks we had seen on Janice May Chapman's corpse. They were superficial and there was no broken skin, but we both agreed Chapman might have been at it longer, and harder, with more weight and force.

'We need to go inside again,' I said.

We found Chapman's laundry basket in the bathroom. It was a rectangular wicker thing, with a lid. Painted white. On top of the pile inside was a short sundress. It had cap sleeves and was printed with red and white pinstripes. It was rucked and creased at the waist. It had grass stains on the upper back. Next item down in the laundry pile was a hand towel. Then a white blouse.

'No underwear,' Deveraux said.

'Evidently,' I said.

'The rapist kept a souvenir.'

'She wasn't wearing any. Her boyfriend was coming over.'

'It's March.'

'What was the weather like that day?'

'It was warm,' Deveraux said. 'And sunny. It was a nice day.'

'Rosemary McClatchy wasn't raped,' I said. 'Nor was Shawna Lindsay. Escalation is one thing. A complete change in MO is another.'

Deveraux didn't answer that. She stepped out of the bathroom into the hallway. The centre point of the little house. She looked all around. She asked, 'What did I miss here? What should be here that isn't?'

'Something more than three years old,' I said. 'She moved here from somewhere else, and she should have brought things with her. At least a few things. Books, maybe. Or photographs. Maybe a favourite chair or something.'

'Twenty-four-year-olds aren't very sentimental.'

'They keep some little thing.'

'What did you keep when you were twenty-four?'

'I'm different. You're different.'

'So what are you saying?'

'I'm saying she showed up here three years ago out of the blue and brought nothing with her. She bought a house and a car and got a local driver's licence. She bought a houseful of new furniture. All for cash. She doesn't have a rich daddy or his picture would be next to the TV in a silver frame. I want to know who she was.'

THIRTY-EIGHT

I followed Deveraux from room to room while she checked for herself. Paint on the walls, still fresh. Loveseat and armchair in the living room, still new. A recent television set. A fancy VHS player. Even the pots and pans and knives and forks in the kitchen showed no nicks or scratches from long-term use.

There were no clothes in the closet older than a couple of seasons. No old prom dress wrapped in plastic. No old cheerleader outfit. No photographs of family. No keepsakes. No old letters. No softball trophies, no jewellery box with a busted ballerina. No battered stuffed animals preserved from childhood years.

'Does it matter?' Deveraux said. 'She was just a random victim, after all.'

'She's a loose end,' I said. 'I don't like loose ends.'

'She was already here when I got back to town. I never thought about it. I mean, people come and go all the time. This is America.'

'Did you ever hear anything about her background?'

'Nothing.'

'No rumours or assumptions?'

233

'None at all.'

'Did she have a job?'

'No.'

'Accent?'

'The Midwest, maybe. Or just south of it. The heartland, anyway. I only spoke to her once.'

'Did you fingerprint the corpse?'

'No. Why would we? We knew who she was.'

'Did you know?'

'Too late now.'

I nodded. By now Chapman's skin would be sloughing off her fingers like a soft old glove. It would be wrinkling and tearing like a wet paper bag. I asked, 'Do you have a fingerprint kit in the car?'

She shook her head. 'Butler does the fingerprinting here. The other deputy. He took a course with the Jackson PD.'

'You should get him here. He can take prints from the house.'

'They won't all be hers.'

'Nine out of ten will be. He should start with the tampon box.'

'She won't be on file anywhere. Why would she be? She was a kid. She didn't serve and she wasn't a cop.'

I said, 'Nothing ventured, nothing gained.'

Deveraux used the radio in her car out in the middle of the turnaround. She had chess pieces to move. Pellegrino had to replace Butler at Kelham's gate. She came back in and said, 'Twenty minutes. I have to get back. I have work to do. You wait here. But don't worry. Butler should do it right. He's a reasonably smart guy.'

'Smarter than Pellegrino?'

'Everyone is smarter than Pellegrino. My car is smarter than Pellegrino.'

I asked, 'Will you have dinner with me?'

She said, 'I have to work pretty late.'

'How late?'

'Nine o'clock, maybe.'

'Nine would be fine.'

'Are you paying?'

'Absolutely.'

She paused a beat.

'Like a date?' she asked.

'We might as well,' I said. 'There's only one restaurant in town. We'd probably end up eating together anyway.'

'OK,' she said. 'Dinner. Nine o'clock. Thank you.'

Then she said, 'Don't shave, OK?'

I said, 'Why not?'

She said, 'You look good like that.'

And then she left.

I waited on Janice May Chapman's front porch, in one of her rocking chairs. Both old ladies watched me from across the street. Deputy Butler showed up just inside his allotted twenty minutes. He was in a car like Pellegrino's. He left it where Deveraux had left hers, and unfolded himself from the interior, and stepped around to the trunk. He was a tall guy, and well put together, somewhere in his middle twenties. He had long hair for a cop, and a square, solid face. First glance, he wouldn't be the easiest guy in the world to manage. But maybe not impossible.

He took a black plastic box out of his trunk and walked up Chapman's driveway towards me. I got out of my chair and held out my hand. Always better to be polite. I said, 'Jack Reacher. I'm pleased to meet you.'

He said, 'Geezer Butler.'

'Really?'

'Yes, really.'

'You play bass guitar?'

'Like I haven't heard that one before.'

'Was your dad a Black Sabbath fan?'

'My mom too.'

'Are you?'

He nodded. 'I've got all their records.'

I led him inside. He stood in the hallway, looking around. I said, 'The challenge here is to get her prints and no one else's.'

'To avoid confusion?' he said.

No, I thought. *To avoid a Bravo Company guy lighting up the system. Better safe than sorry.*

I said, 'Yes, to avoid confusion.'

'The chief said I should start in the bathroom.'

'Good plan,' I said. 'Toothbrush, toothpaste, tampon box, personal things like that. Things that were boxed up or wrapped in cellophane in the store. No one else will have touched them.'

I hung back so as not to crowd him, but I watched him pretty carefully. He was extremely competent. He took twenty minutes and got twenty good prints, all small neat ovals, all obviously a woman's. We agreed that was

236

an adequate sample, and he packed up his gear and gave me a ride back to town.

I got out of Butler's car outside the Sheriff's Department and walked south to the hotel, where I stood on the sidewalk and wrestled with a dilemma. I felt I should go buy a new shirt, but I didn't want Deveraux to feel that dinner was supposed to be more than just dinner. Or in reality I did want her to feel dinner could be more than just dinner, but I didn't want her to see me wanting it. I didn't want her to feel pushed into anything, and I didn't want to appear over-eager.

But in the end I decided a shirt was just a shirt, so I hiked across to the other side of Main Street and looked at the stores. Most of them were about to close. It was after five o'clock. I found a men's outfitters three enterprises south of where I started. It didn't look promising. In the window was a jacket made from some kind of synthetic denim. It glittered and shone in the lights. It looked like it had been knitted out of atomic waste. But the only other shopping choice was the pharmacy, and I didn't want to show up at dinner wearing a dollar T. So I went in and looked around.

There was plenty more stuff pieced together from dubious fabrics, but there was plenty of plainer stuff too. There was an old guy behind the counter who seemed happy to let me poke around. He had a tape measure draped around his neck. Like a badge of office. Like a doctor wears a stethoscope. He didn't say anything, but he seemed to understand I was looking for shirts and he either frowned and tutted or beamed and nodded as

I moved around from pile to pile, as if I was playing a parlour game, getting warmer and colder in my search.

Eventually I found a white button-down made of heavy cotton. The collar was an eighteen and the sleeves were thirty-seven inches long, which was about my size. I hauled my choice to the counter and asked, 'Would this be OK for a job in an office?'

The old guy said, 'Yes, sir, it would.'

'Would it impress a person at dinner?'

'I think you'd want something finer, sir. Maybe a pin-point.'

'So it's not what you'd call formal?'

'No, sir. Not by a long chalk.'

'OK, I'll take it.'

It cost me less than the pink shirt from the PX. The old guy wrapped it in brown paper and taped it up into a little parcel. I carried it back across the street. I planned to dump it in my room. I made it into the hotel lobby just in time to see the owner setting off up the stairs in a big hurry. He turned when he heard the door, and he saw it was me and he stopped. He was out of breath. He said, 'Your uncle is on the phone again.'

THIRTY-NINE

I took the call alone in the back office, as before. Garber was tentative from the get-go, which made me uneasy. His first question was, 'How are you?'

'I'm fine,' I said. 'You?'

'How's it going down there?'

'Bad,' I said.

'With the sheriff?'

'No, she's OK.'

'Elizabeth Deveraux, right? We're having her checked out.'

'How?'

'We're having a quiet word with the Marine Corps.'

'Why?'

'Maybe we can get you something you can use against her. You might need leverage at some point.'

'Save your effort. She's not the problem.'

'So what is?'

'We are,' I said. 'Or you are. Or whoever. The army, I mean. They're patrolling outside of Kelham's fence and shooting people.'

'That's categorically impossible.'

'I've seen the blood. And the car wreck has been sanitized.'

'That can't be happening.'

'It is happening. And you need to stop it happening. Because right now you've got a big problem, but you're going to turn it into World War Three.'

'You must be mistaken.'

'There are two guys beat up and one guy dead down here. I'm not mistaken.'

'Dead?'

'As in no longer alive.'

'How?'

'He bled out through a gunshot wound to the thigh. There was a half-assed attempt to patch it up with a GI field dressing. And I found a NATO shell case at the scene.'

'That's not us. I would know.'

'Would you?' I said. 'Or would I? You're up there guessing and I'm down here looking.'

'It's not legal.'

'Tell me about it. Worst case, it's a policy decision. Best case, someone's gone rogue. You need to find out which and get it stopped.'

'How?' Garber said. 'You want me to walk up to a random selection of senior officers and accuse them of an egregious breach of the law? Maybe the worst ever in American military history? I'd be locked up before lunch and court-martialled the next morning.'

I paused. Breathed. Asked, 'Are there names I shouldn't say on an open line?'

Garber said, 'There are names you shouldn't even know.'

'This whole thing is drifting out of control. It's going from bad to worse. I've seen three lawyers heading in and out of Kelham. Someone needs to make a decision. The officer in question needs to be pulled out and redeployed. Right now.'

'That's not going to happen. Not as long as Kosovo is important. This guy could stop a war single-handed and all by himself.'

'He's one of four hundred men, for Christ's sake.'

'Not according to the political ad campaigns two years from now. Think about it. He's going to be the Lone Ranger.'

'He's going to be locked up in Leavenworth.'

'Munro doesn't think so. He says the officer in question is likely innocent.'

'Then we should act like it. We should stop with the lawyers and we should stop patrolling outside the fence.'

'We're not patrolling outside the fence.'

I gave up. 'Anything else?'

'One thing,' Garber said. 'I have to do this. I hope you understand.'

'Try me.'

'You got a postcard from your brother.'

'Where?'

'At your office.'

'And you read it?'

'An army officer has no reasonable expectation of privacy.'

'Is that in the regulations too? Along with the hair-styles?'

'You need to explain the message to me.'

'Why? What does it say?'

'The picture on the front is downtown Atlanta. The card was mailed from the Atlanta airport eleven days ago. The text reads: Heading to a town called Margrave, south of here, business, but heard a story Blind Blake died there, will let you know. Then it's signed Joe, his name.'

'I know my brother's name.'

'What does the message mean?'

'It's a personal note.'

'I'm ordering you to explain it to me. I apologize, but I have to do this.'

'You went to elementary school. You can read.'

'What does it mean?'

'It means what it says. He's heading south of Atlanta to a town called Margrave.'

'Who was Blind Blake?'

'A guitar player, from way back. Blues music. One of the first legends.'

'Why would Joe make a point of informing you about that?'

'Shared interest.'

'What does Joe mean when he says he will let you know?'

'He means what he says.'

'Let you know about what?'

'About the Blind Blake legend, of course. About whether he died there.'

'Why does it matter where this man died?'

'It doesn't matter. It's just a thing. Like collecting baseball cards.'

'So this is really about baseball cards?'

'What the hell are you talking about?'

'Is this a code for something else?'

'A code? Why the hell would it be a code?'

Garber said, 'You called his office today.'

'You know about that?'

'There's a reporting mechanism in place.'

'That kid? The girl in his office?'

'I'm not at liberty to discuss the details. But I need to know why you called him.'

'He's my brother.'

'But why now? Were you going to ask him something?'

'Yes,' I said. 'I was going to ask him how he's doing. Purely social.'

'Why now? Did something at Kelham provoke the inquiry?'

'This is none of your business.'

'Everything is my business. Help me out here, Reacher.'

I said, 'Two black women were killed here before Janice May Chapman. Did you even know that? Because that's something you should be bearing in mind, if you're thinking about political campaigns. We ignored them and then our heads exploded when a white woman got killed.'

'How does this relate to Joe?'

'I met the second victim's brother. Made me think about family. That's all it was.'

'Did Joe tell you anything about money from Kosovo?'

'I didn't get him. He was out of the office. He was in Georgia.'

'Atlanta again? Or Margrave?'

'I have no idea. Georgia is a big state.'

'OK,' Garber said. 'I apologize for the intrusion.'

I asked, 'Who exactly is worried about money from Kosovo?'

He said, 'I'm not at liberty to discuss that.'

I hung up with Garber and breathed in and out for a spell, and then I carried my new shirt upstairs and left it on my bed. I started to think about dinner with Elizabeth Deveraux. Three hours to go, and only one more thing to do beforehand.

FORTY

I came out of the front of the hotel and looped back through the dog-leg alley between the pharmacy and the hardware store and came out the other end between the loan office and Brannan's bar. Where Janice May Chapman's body had been found. The sand pile was still there, dry and crusted and powdery and a little redistributed by the breeze. I stepped around it and checked activity on the one-sided street. Not much was going on. Some of the bars were closed, because the base was closed. No point in opening without customers. A simple economic calculation.

But Brannan's bar was open. Defiantly optimistic, or maybe just maintaining some longstanding tradition. I went in and found nobody there except two similar guys fussing with stuff in the drinks well. They looked like brothers. Middle thirties, maybe two years apart, like Joe and me. Wise to the ways of the world, which was going to give me the advantage. Their place was like a thousand base-town bars I had seen before, a complex boxed-in machine designed to turn boredom into cash. It was a decent size. I guessed it had been a small restaurant in the past, but small restaurants make big bars. The decor was maybe a little better than most. There were travel posters on the walls, of the world's great cities photographed at night. No local stuff, which was smart. If you're stuck for six months in the back of beyond, you don't want to be reminded of it at every turn.

'Got coffee?' I asked.

They said no, which didn't surprise me very much.

I said, 'My name is Jack Reacher and I'm an MP with a dinner date coming up.'

They didn't follow.

I said, 'Which means that usually I'd have time to hang around all night and weasel stuff out of you in the normal course of conversation, but I don't have time for that on this occasion, so we'll have to rely on a straight-forward question-and-answer session, OK?'

They got the message. Base-town bar owners worry about MPs. Easiest thing in the world to put a particular establishment on a local no-go list, for a week, or a month. Or for ever. They introduced themselves as Jonathan and Hunter Brannan, brothers, inheritors of a business started by their grandmother back in the railroad days. She had sold tea and fancy cakes, and she had made a nice living. Their father had switched to alcohol when the trains stopped and the army arrived. They were a nice enough pair of guys. And realistic. They ran the best bar in town, so they couldn't deny they saw everybody from time to time.

'Janice Chapman came here,' I said. 'The woman who got killed.'

They agreed that, yes, she did. No evasion. Everyone comes to Brannan's.

I asked, 'With the same guy every recent time?'

They agreed that, yes, that was the case.

I asked, 'Who was he?'

Hunter Brannan said, 'His name was Reed. Don't know much about him apart from that. But he was a big dog. You can always tell, by the way the others react.'

'Was he a regular customer?'

'They all are.'

'Was he in here that night?'

'That's a tough question. This place is usually packed.'

'Try to remember.'

'I would say he was. For the early part of the evening, at least. I don't recall seeing him later.'

'What car does he drive?'

'Some old thing. Blue, I think.'

I asked, 'How long has he been coming here?'

'A year or so, I guess. But he's one of the in-and-out guys.'

'What does that mean?'

'They've got a couple of squads over there. They go somewhere, and then they come back. A month on, a month off.'

'Did you see him with previous girlfriends?'

Jonathan Brannan said, 'A guy like that, he always has arm candy.'

'Who in particular?'

'Whoever was the prettiest. Whoever was willing to put out, I guess.'

'Black or white?'

'Both. He's pretty much an equal opportunities type of guy.'

'Remember any names?'

'No,' Hunter Brannan said. 'But I remember feeling pretty jealous a couple of times.'

I went back to the hotel. Two hours until dinner. I spent the first hour taking a nap, because I was tired, and because I was figuring I wouldn't be sleeping again too soon. Hoping I wouldn't be, anyway. Hope springs eternal. I woke myself up at eight o'clock and unpacked my new shirt. I brushed my teeth with water and chewed some gum. Then I took a long hot shower, plenty of soap, plenty of shampoo.

I put on my new shirt and rolled the sleeves level with my elbows. The shirt was tight across the shoulders, so I left the top two buttons undone. I tucked the tails into my pants and put my shoes on and shined them one at a time against the backs of my calves.

I checked the mirror.

I looked exactly like a guy who wants to get laid. Which I was. There was nothing to be done about it.

I dumped my old shirts in the trash can and left my room and went down the stairs and stepped out to the darkness of the street. A voice from the shadows behind me said, 'Hello again, soldier boy.'

FORTY-ONE

Ahead of me across the street were three pick-up trucks parked at the kerb. Two that I recognized, and one that I didn't. All the doors were open. Legs were dangling. Cigarettes were glowing. Smoke was drifting. I stepped left and half-turned and saw the alpha dog. The McKinney cousin. His face was still a mess. He was standing under one of the hotel's busted lamps. His arms were down by his sides, and his hands were away from his hips, and his thumbs were away from his fingers. He was all fired up and ready.

Across the street five guys slipped out of the pick-up trucks. They started towards me. I saw the beta dog, and the beer-for-breakfast guy, and the biker with the bad back, and two guys I hadn't seen before, each of them looking like the other four. Same region, same family, or both.

I stayed on the sidewalk. With six guys, I didn't want any of them behind me. I wanted a wall at my back. The alpha dog stepped off the sidewalk into the gutter and met the others as the right-hand item in a neat six-man arc. They all stayed in the street, eight or ten feet from me. Out of reach, but I could smell them. They were all doing the ape thing with their arms and hands and thumbs. Like gunfighters with no guns.

'Six of you?' I said. 'Is that it?'

No answer.

'That's kind of incremental, isn't it?' I said. 'I was hoping for something a little more radical. Like the difference between an airborne company and an armoured division. I guess we were thinking along different lines. I have to say, I'm kind of disappointed.'

No answer.

I said, 'Anyway, guys, I'm sorry, but I have a dinner date.'

They all took a step forward, bringing them closer to each other and closer to me. Six pale faces, sallow in what little light there was.

I said, 'I'm wearing a brand-new shirt.'

No answer.

Basic rule of thumb with six guys: you have to be quick. You can't spend more than the bare minimum of time on any one individual. Which means you have to hit each of them one time only. Because that's the minimum. You can't hit a guy less than once.

I rehearsed my moves. I figured I would start in the middle. One two three, bang bang bang. The third hit would be the hardest. The third guy would be moving. The first two wouldn't. They would be rooted to the spot. Shock and surprise. They would go down easy. But the third guy would be reacting by the time I got to him. And unpredictably. He might have a coherent plan in mind, but it wouldn't be in motion yet. He would still be jerking around with uncontrolled reflex panic.

So I was prepared to miss out on the third guy. Maybe jump straight to the fourth. The third guy might run. Certainly at least one of them would. I have never seen a pack that stayed together after the first few heads hit the pavement.

I said, 'Guys, please, I just took a shower.'

There was no answer, which was what I had privately predicted. They all stepped forward again, which is what I expected them to do. So I met them halfway, which seemed polite. I took two long strides, the second of them powering off the edge of the kerbstone, 250 pounds of moving mass, and I hit the third guy from the left with a straight right that would have taken his teeth out if he'd had any to start with. As it was it snapped his head back and turned his spine and shoulders to jelly and he was gone, from the fight and from my vision, because by then I was already jerking left and scything my right elbow into the second guy, horizontal across the bridge of his nose, a colossal blow full of torque from my waist and full of force from the fact that I was basically falling into him. I saw blood in the air and stamped down hard and reversed my momentum and used the same elbow backward on a guy I sensed behind me. I could tell by the impact he was flinching away and I had caught him on the ear, so I made a mental note he might need more attention later, and then I jerked forward again and changed the angle of attack by kicking the fourth guy full on in the groin, a satisfying bone-and-flesh *crunch* that simultaneously folded him in half and lifted him off his feet.

Three seconds, three down, one taking an eight count.
Nobody ran.

Another mental note: Mississippi hooligans are made of sterner stuff than most. Or else they're just plain dumber.

The fifth guy got as far as scrabbling at my shoulder. Some kind of an attempt at a punch, or maybe he was going for a choke hold. Maybe he planned to keep me still while the sixth guy landed some blows. I couldn't tell. But whatever, he was sorely disappointed in his ambitions. I exploded backward at him, my whole body moving, my torso twisting, my elbow whipping back, and I caught him in the cheek, and then I used the bounce to jam forward once more, in search of the lone survivor. The sixth guy. He caught his heel on the kerb and his arms came up like a scarecrow, which I took as an invitation to pop him in the chest, right in the solar plexus, which was like plugging him into an electrical outlet. He hopped and danced and went down in a heap.

The guy I had hit on the ear was pawing at it like it was coming off. His eyes were closed, which made it not much of a fair fight, but those are always my favourite kind. I lined up and smacked a left hook into his chin.

He went down like a dropped marionette.

I breathed out.

Six for six.

End of story.

I coughed twice and spat on the ground. Then I hustled north. The clock in my head said it was already one minute past nine.

FORTY-TWO

I pushed in through the diner door and found the place empty apart from the waitress and the old couple from Toussaint's. They looked to be about halfway through their nightly marathon. The woman had a book, the man had a paper. Deveraux wasn't there yet.

I told the waitress I was expecting company. I asked her for a table for four. I figured the tables for two would be cramped for a long social engagement. She set me up in a spot near the front and I headed for the bathroom.

I rinsed my face and washed my hands and forearms and elbows with hot water and soap. I ran wet fingers through my hair. I breathed in and breathed out. Adrenalin is a bitch. It doesn't know when to quit. I flapped my hands and rolled my shoulders. I took a look in the mirror. My hair was OK. My face was clean.

There was blood on my shirt.

On the pocket. And above. And below. Not much, but some. A definite comma-shaped curl of droplets. Like it had been flung at me. Or like I had walked into a mist. Which I had. The second guy. I had hit him on

253

the bridge of his nose. His nose had bled like a flushing toilet.

I said, 'Shit,' quietly, to myself.

My old shirts were in the trash in my room.

The stores were all closed.

I edged closer to the sink and took another look in the mirror. The droplets were already drying. Turning brown. Maybe they would end up looking deliberate. Like a logo. Or a pattern. Like a single element taken from a swirling fabric. I had seen similar things. I wasn't sure what they were called. Paisley?

I breathed in, breathed out.

Nothing to be done.

I headed back to the dining room and got there just as Deveraux stepped in through the door.

She wasn't in uniform. She had changed her clothes. She was wearing a silver silk shirt and a black knee-length skirt. High-heeled shoes. A silver necklace. The shirt was thin and tight and tiny. It was open at the top. The skirt sat at her waist. I could have spanned her waist with my hands. Her legs were bare. And slim. And long. Her hair was wet from the shower. It was loose on her shoulders. It was spilling down her back. No ponytail. No elastic band. She was smiling, all the way up to her amazing eyes.

I showed her to our table and we sat down facing each other. She was small and neat, centred on her bench. She was wearing perfume. Something faint and subtle. I liked it.

She said, 'I'm sorry I'm late.'

I said, 'No problem.'

She said, 'You have blood on your shirt.'

I said, 'Is that what it is?'

'Where did you get it?'

'Across the street from the hotel. There's a store.'

'Not the shirt,' she said. 'The blood. You didn't cut yourself shaving.'

'You told me not to.'

'I know,' she said. 'I like you like that.'

'You look great too.'

'Thank you. I decided to quit early. I went home to change.'

'I see that.'

'I live in the hotel.'

'I know.'

'Room seventeen.'

'I know.'

'Which has a balcony overlooking the street.'

'You saw?'

'Everything,' she said.

'Then I'm surprised you didn't break the date.'

'Is it a date?'

'It's a dinner date.'

She said, 'You didn't let them hit you first.'

'I wouldn't be here if I had.'

'True,' she said, and smiled. 'You were pretty good.'

'Thank you,' I said.

'But you're killing my budget. Pellegrino and Butler are getting overtime to haul them away. I wanted them gone before the hotel folks finish their dinner. Voters don't like mayhem in the streets.'

The waitress came by. She brought no menus. Deveraux had been eating there three times a day for two years. She knew the menu. She asked for the cheeseburger. So did I, with coffee to drink. The waitress made a note and went away.

I said, 'You had the cheeseburger yesterday.'

Deveraux said, 'I have it every day.'

'Really?'

She nodded. 'Every day I do the same things and eat the same things.'

'How do you stay thin?'

'Mental energy,' she said. 'I worry a lot.'

'About what?'

'Right now about a guy from Oxford, Mississippi. That's the guy who got shot in the thigh. The doctor brought his personal effects to my office. There was a wallet and a notebook. The guy was a journalist.'

'Big paper?'

'No, freelance. Struggling, probably. His last press pass was two years old. But Oxford has a couple of alternative papers. He was probably trying to sell something to one of them.'

'There's a school in Oxford, right?'

Deveraux nodded again. 'Ole Miss,' she said. 'About as radical as this state gets.'

'Why did the guy come here?'

'I would have loved the chance to ask him. He might have had something I could use.'

The waitress came back with my coffee and a glass of water for Deveraux. Behind my back I heard the old guy from the hotel grunt and turn a page in his paper.

I said, 'My CO still denies there are boots on the ground outside the fence.'

Deveraux asked, 'How does that make you feel?'

'I don't know. If he's lying to me, it will be the first time ever.'

'Maybe someone's lying to him.'

'Such cynicism in one so young.'

'But don't you think?'

'More than likely.'

'So how does *that* make you feel?'

'What are you, a psychiatrist now?'

She smiled. 'Just interested. Because I've been there. Does it make you angry?'

'I never get angry. I'm a very placid type of a guy.'

'You looked angry twenty minutes ago. With the McKinney family.'

'That was just a technical problem. Space and time. I didn't want to be late for dinner. I wasn't angry, really. Well, not at first. I got a bit frustrated later. You know, mentally. I mean, when there were four of them, I gave them the chance to come back in numbers. And what did they do? They added two more guys. That's all. They showed up with a total of six. What is *that* about? It's deliberate disrespect.'

Deveraux said, 'I think most people would consider six against one to be fairly respectful.'

'But I warned them. I told them they'd need more. I was trying to be fair. But they wouldn't listen. It was like talking to the Pentagon.'

'How's that going, by the way?'

'Not good. They're as bad as the McKinney family.'

'Are you worried?'

'Some people are.'

'They should be. The army is going to change.'

'The Marines too, then.'

She smiled. 'A little, maybe. But not much. The army is the big target. And the easy target. Because the army is boring. The Marines aren't.'

'You think?'

'Come on,' she said. 'We're glamorous. We have a great dress uniform. We do great close-order drill. We do great funerals. You know why we do all that? Because Marines are very good at PR. And we get good advice. Our consultants are better than yours, basically. That's what I'm saying. That's what it comes down to. So you'll lose a lot, and we'll lose a little.'

'You have consultants?' I said.

'And lobbyists,' she said. 'Don't you?'

'I don't think so,' I said. I thought about my old pal Stan Lowrey, and his want ads. The waitress brought our meals. Just like the night before. Two big cheeseburgers, two big tangles of fries. I had had the same thing for lunch. I hadn't remembered that. But I was hungry. So I ate. And I watched Deveraux eat. Which was some kind of a threshold. It has to mean something, if you can stand to watch another person eat.

She chewed and swallowed and said, 'Anyway, what else did your CO tell you?'

'That he's having you checked out.'

She stopped eating. 'Why would he?'

'To give me something to use against you.'

258

She smiled. 'There's not much there, I'm afraid. I was a good little jarhead. But don't you see? They're proving my case for me. The more desperate they get, the more I know for sure it's some Kelham guy's ass on the line.' She started eating again.

I said, 'My CO was also quizzing me on my mail.'

'They're reading your letters?'

'A postcard from my brother.'

'Why?'

'They must think it might help.'

'Did it?'

'Not in the least. It was nothing.'

'They *are* desperate, aren't they?'

'My CO kept apologizing about it.'

'So he should.'

'He asked if there was a code in the postcard. But really I think *he* was talking in code. I think he has been all along. Right back at the beginning he wasted ten minutes giving me a hard time about my hair. That's not like him, which I think was the point. He's telling me this isn't him. He's telling me he's in the dark, under orders, doing something he doesn't want to do.'

'Nice of him to dump his problems on you. He could have sent someone else.'

'Could he though? Maybe this whole thing was a package deal, soup to nuts, planned up above. Like when the owner picks the team. Me and Munro. Maybe they're getting ready to thin the herd, and we're being given a loyalty test.'

'Munro told me he knows you by reputation.'

I nodded. 'We've never met.'

'Reputations are dangerous things to have, in times like these.'

I said nothing.

She said, 'If I asked my old buddies to check *you* out, what would they find?'

'Parts of it aren't pretty,' I said.

'So this is payback time,' she said. 'It's a win-win for somebody. Either they break you or they get rid of you. You've got an enemy somewhere. Any idea who?'

'No,' I said.

We ate in silence for a moment, and finished up. Clean plates. Meat, bread, cheese, potatoes, all gone. I felt full. Deveraux was half my size. Or less. I didn't know how she did it. She said, 'Anyway, tell me about your brother.'

'I'd rather talk about you.'

'Me? There's nothing to say. Carter Crossing, the Marine Corps, Carter Crossing again. That's the story of my life. No sisters, no brothers. How many do you have?'

'Just the one.'

'Older or younger?'

'Two years older. Born way far away in the Pacific. I haven't seen him for a long time.'

'Is he like you?'

'We're like two alternative versions of the same person. We look alike. He's smarter than me. I get things done better. He's more cerebral, I'm more physical. He was good and I was bad, according to our parents. Like that.'

'What does he do for a living?'

I paused.

'I can't tell you that,' I said.

'His job is classified?'

'Not really,' I said. 'But it might give you a clue about one of the things the army is worried about here.'

She smiled. She was a very tolerant woman. She said, 'Should we get pie?'

We ordered two peach pies, the same as I had eaten the night before. And coffee, for both of us, which I took to be a good sign. She wasn't worried about being kept awake. Maybe she was planning on it. The old couple from the hotel got up and left while the waitress was still in the kitchen. They stopped by our table. No real conversation. Just a lot of nodding and smiling. They were determined to be polite. Simple economics. Deveraux was their meal ticket, and I was temporarily the icing on their cake.

The clock in my head hit ten in the evening. The pies arrived, and so did the coffee. I didn't pay much attention to either. I spent most of my time looking at the third button on Deveraux's shirt. I had noticed it before. It was the first one that was done up. Therefore it was the first one that would need to be undone. It was a tiny mother-of-pearl thing, silvery grey. Behind it was skin, neither pale nor dark, and very three-dimensional. Left to right it curved towards me, then away from me, then towards me again. It was rising and falling as she breathed.

The waitress came by and offered more coffee. For possibly the first time in my life I turned it down.

Deveraux said no, too. The waitress put the check on the table, face down, next to me. I flipped it over. Not bad. You could still eat well on a soldier's pay, back in 1997. I dropped some bills on it and looked across at Deveraux and said, 'Can I walk you home?'

She said, 'I thought you'd never ask.'

FORTY-THREE

Pellegrino and Butler had done their work. They had earned their overtime payments. The McKinney boys were gone. Main Street was silent and completely deserted. The moon was out and the air was soft. Deveraux was taller in her heels. We walked side by side, close enough for me to hear the whisper of silk on skin, and to catch the scent of her perfume.

We got to the hotel and went up the worn steps and crossed the porch. I held the door for her. The old guy was working behind the counter. We nodded goodnight to him and headed for the stairs. At the top Deveraux paused and said, 'Well, goodnight, Mr Reacher, and thanks again for your company at dinner.'

Loud and clear.

I just stood there.

She crossed the corridor.

She took out her key.

She put it in room seventeen's lock.

She opened the door.

Then she closed it again loudly and tiptoed back to me and stretched up and put her hand on my shoulder.

She put her lips close to my ear and whispered, 'That was for the old man downstairs. I have to think about my reputation. Mustn't shock the voters.'

I breathed out.

I took her hand and we headed for my room.

We were both thirty-six years old. All grown up. Not teenagers. We didn't rush. We didn't fumble. We took our time, and what a time it was. Maybe the best ever.

We kissed as soon as my door was closed. Her lips were cool and wet. Her teeth were small. Her tongue was agile. It was a great kiss. I had one hand in her hair, and one on the small of her back. She was jammed hard against me, and moving. Her eyes were open. So were mine. We kept that first kiss going for whole minutes. Five of them, or maybe ten. We were patient. We took it slow. We were very good at it. I think we both understood that the first time happens only once. We both wanted to savour it.

Eventually we came up for air. I took my shirt off. I didn't want McKinney blood between us. I have a big shrapnel scar low down on my front. It looks like a pale octopus crawling up out of my waistband. Ugly white stitches. Usually a conversation starter. Deveraux saw it and ignored it. She moved right along. She was a Marine. She had seen worse. Her hand went to her top button.

I said, 'No, let me.'

She smiled and said, 'That's your thing? You like undressing women?'

'More than anything in the world,' I said. 'And I've

264

been staring at that particular button since a quarter past nine.'

'Since ten past nine,' she said. 'I paid attention to the time line. I'm a cop.'

I took her left hand and got her to hold it out, palm up. She kept it there, patiently. I undid her cuff button. I did the same with her right hand. The silk fell back over slim wrists. She put her hands on my chest. She slid them up behind my head. We kissed again, five whole minutes. Another great kiss. Better than the first.

We came up for air again and I moved on to the button on the front of her shirt. Like all the others it was small. And slippery. My fingers are big. But I got the job done. The button popped open, helped on its way by the swell of her breasts. I moved down to the fourth button. Then the fifth. I eased the silk out of the waistband of her skirt, all the way around, little by little, slowly and carefully. She was looking at me and smiling the whole time. Her shirt fell open. She was wearing a bra. A tiny black thing, with lace, and delicate straps. It barely covered her nipples. Her breasts were fantastic.

I eased the shirt back off her shoulders and it sighed and parachuted to the floor behind her. Her scent came up at me. We kissed again, long and hard. I kissed the curve where her neck met her shoulder. She had a cleft down her back. Her bra strap spanned it like a little bridge. She put her head back and her hair spilled everywhere. I kissed her throat.

'Now your shoes,' she said, and her throat buzzed against my lips.

She turned me around and pushed me backward and sat me down on the edge of the bed. She knelt in front of me. She untied my right shoe, and then my left. She eased them off. She hooked her thumbs in my socks and peeled them down.

'PX for sure,' she said.

'Less than a dollar,' I said. 'Couldn't resist.'

We stood up again and kissed again. By that point in my life I had kissed hundreds of girls, but I was ready to admit Deveraux was the finest of them all. She was spectacular. She moved and quivered and trembled. She was strong, but gentle. Passionate, but not aggressive. Hungry, but not demanding. The clock in my head took a break. We had all the time in the world, and we were going to use every last minute of it.

She hooked her fingers behind the front of my waistband. She tugged on it. She undid the button, one finger, one thumb. We kept on kissing. She found my zipper tab and eased it down, slowly, slowly, small hand, neat thumb, precise finger. She put her hands flat on my shoulder blades and slid them side to side, warm, dry, soft, and then she moved them down, slowly, to my waist, and then down again. She slid the tips of her fingers under my loosened waistband and tented the fabric. She went deeper. She pushed back and down and my pants slid over my hips. We were still kissing.

We came up for air and she turned me around and sat me down again. She pulled my pants off and dumped them on top of her shirt. She left me on the bed and stepped back a pace and held her arms out wide and said, 'Tell me what to take off next.'

'I get to pick?'

She nodded. 'Your choice.'

I smiled. A hell of a choice. Bra, skirt, shoes. I figured she could keep her shoes on. For a spell, anyway. Maybe all night long.

I said, 'Skirt.'

She obliged. There was a button and a zipper at the side. She popped the button and slid the zipper down, slowly, an inch, two inches, three, four. I heard its sound quite clearly in the silence. The skirt fell to the ground. She stepped out of it, one foot, then the other. Her legs were long and smooth and toned. She was wearing tiny black panties. Not much to them. Just a wisp of dark fabric.

Bra, panties, shoes. I was still sitting on the bed. She climbed into my lap. I lifted her hair away and kissed her ear. I traced its shape with my tongue. I could feel her cheek against mine. I could feel the smile. I kissed her mouth, she kissed my ear. We spent twenty minutes learning every contour above our necks.

Then we moved lower.

I unsnapped her bra. It fell away, insubstantial. I ducked my head. Her head went back, arching her breasts towards me. They were firm and round and smooth. Her nipples were sensitive. She moaned a little. So did I. She moved and kissed my chest. I lifted her off my lap and rolled her on her back on the bed. Then she rolled me. Twenty fabulous minutes, spent getting to know each other above the waist.

Then we moved lower.

I was on my back. She knelt over me and slid my

267

boxers down. She smiled. So did I. Ten amazing minutes later we changed places. Her panties came down over her hips, and then she lifted her knees to let me finish the job. I buried my face between her thighs. She was wet and sweet. She moved, uninhibited. She rolled her head from side to side and squirmed her shoulders and pressed herself down on the mattress. She ran her fingers through my hair.

Then it was time. We started tenderly. Long and slow, long and slow. Deep and easy. She flushed and gasped. So did I. Long and slow.

Then faster and harder.

Then we were panting.

Faster, harder, faster, harder.

Panting.

'Wait,' she said.

'What?'

'Wait, wait,' she said. 'Not now. Not yet. Slow down.'

Long and slow, long and slow.

Breathing hard.

Panting.

'OK,' she said. 'OK. Now. Now. *Now!*'

Faster and harder.

Faster, harder, faster, harder.

The room began to shake.

Just very faintly at first, like a mild constant tremor, like the edge of a far distant earthquake. The French door trembled in its frame. A glass rattled on the bathroom shelf. The floor quivered. The hall door creaked and stuttered. My shoes hopped and moved. The bedhead hammered against the wall. The floor shook hard. The walls boomed. Coins in my abandoned pocket tinkled. The bed shook and bounced and walked tiny fractions across the moving floor.

Then the midnight train was gone, and so were we.

FORTY-FOUR

Afterward we lay side by side, sweat pooling, naked, breathing hard, holding hands. I stared up at the ceiling. Deveraux said, 'I've wanted to do that for two whole years. That damn train. Might as well make use of it.'

I said, 'If I ever buy a house it's going to be next to a railroad track. That's for damn sure.'

She moved her position and snuggled next to me. I put my arm around her. We lay quiet, and spent, and satisfied. I heard Blind Blake in my head. I had once listened to a cassette tape of all his songs, transferred from beat-up old 78s, the absurd roar and scratch of ancient shellac surface noise almost drowning out the quiet, wistful voice and the agile guitar, as it picked out the rhythms of the railroad. A blind man. Blind from birth. He had never seen a train. But he had heard plenty. That was clear.

Deveraux asked me what I was thinking about, and I told her. I said, 'That's the guy my brother's note was about.'

'Are you still mad about it?'

'I'm sad about it,' I said.

'Why?'

'This mission was a mistake,' I said. 'They shouldn't have put me on the outside. Not for this kind of thing. It's making me think of them as . . . *them*. Not *us* any more.'

Later we had a languid conversation about whether she should go back to her own room. Reputations. Voters. I said the old guy had come upstairs for me when Garber had called. He had gotten a good look inside the room. She said if that happened again I could delay a second and she could hide in the bathroom. She said they rarely knocked on her door. And if by some chance they did the next morning and there was no reply, they would assume she was out on a case. Which would be entirely plausible. She wasn't short of work to do, after all.

Then she said, 'Maybe Janice Chapman was doing what we just did. With the gravel scratches, I mean. With her boyfriend, whoever he was. Out in her back yard, at midnight. Under the stars. The railroad track is pretty close by. Must be amazing out of doors.'

'It must be,' I said. 'I was right next to the track at midnight last night. It's like the end of the world.'

'Would the timing work? With the scabs?'

'If she had sex at midnight she was killed about four in the morning. What time was she found?'

'Ten the next evening. That's eighteen hours. I guess there would have been some decomposition by then.'

'Probably. But bled-out bodies can look pretty weird. It would have been fairly hard to tell. And your department doctor isn't exactly Sherlock Holmes.'

'So it's possible?'

'We'd have to explain why she put on a nice dress and pantyhose some time between midnight and four in the morning.'

We pondered that for a moment. Then we surrendered to inertia. We said nothing more, about dresses or pantyhose, or voters or rooms or reputations, and then we fell asleep, in each other's arms, outside the covers, naked, in the still silence of the Mississippi night.

Four hours later I was awake again and confirming my longest-held belief: there is no better time than the second time. All the first time's semi-formal niceties can be forgotten. All the first time tricks we used to impress each other can be abandoned. There's new familiarity, and no loss of excitement. There's a general sense of what works and what doesn't. Second time around, you're ready to rock and roll.

And we did.

Afterwards Deveraux yawned and stretched and said, 'You're not bad for a soldier boy.'

I said, 'You're excellent for a Marine.'

'We'd better be careful. We might develop feelings for each other.'

'What are those?'

'What are what?'

'Feelings.'

She paused a beat.

She said, 'Men should be more in touch with their feelings.'

I said, 'If I ever have one, you'll be the first to know, I promise.'

She paused again. Then she laughed. Which was good. This was already 1997, remember. It was touch and go in those days.

I woke up for the second time at seven o'clock in the morning, thinking about pregnancy.

FORTY-FIVE

Elizabeth Deveraux was sitting upright in the bed when I woke. She was on my left, in the centre of her space, facing me, back straight, legs crossed, like yoga. She was naked and unselfconscious. She was very beautiful. Just spectacularly good looking. One of the best looking women I had ever seen, and certainly the best looking I had ever seen naked, and definitely the best looking I had ever slept with.

But by that point she was mentally preoccupied. Seven o'clock in the morning. The start of the work day. No third time lucky for me. Not right then. She said, 'They must have had something else in common. Those three women, I mean.'

I said nothing.

'Beauty is too nebulous,' she said. 'It's too subjective. It's just an opinion.'

I said nothing.

She said, 'What?'

'It's not just an opinion,' I said. 'Not with those three.'

'Then we're looking for two factors. Two things that

interacted. They were beautiful and they were also something else.'

'Maybe they were pregnant,' I said.

We examined the proposition. They were girlfriend material. It was a base town. These things happen. Mostly by accident, but sometimes on purpose. Sometimes women think that moving from one base town to another with a baby is better than living alone in the base town where they were born. A mistake, probably, but not for all of them. My own mother had been OK with it, for instance.

I said, 'Shawna Lindsay was desperate to get out, according to her kid brother.'

Deveraux said, 'But I can't see why Janice May Chapman would have been. She wasn't born here. She chose this place. And she wouldn't have needed a guy to get her out anyway. She could have just sold up and driven away in her Honda.'

'Accident, then,' I said. 'With her, anyway. One other thing we didn't see in her house was birth control. Nothing in the medicine cabinet.'

No response.

I asked, 'Where do you keep yours?'

'Bathroom shelf,' she said. 'There are no medicine cabinets here.'

'Did Rosemary McClatchy want to get out of town?'

'I don't know. Probably. Why wouldn't she?'

'Did the doctor test for pregnancy?'

'No,' Deveraux said. 'I'm sure they would have in a big city. But not here. Merriam signed the certificate and gave us the cause of death, that's all. The fifty-cent opinion.'

I said, 'Chapman didn't look pregnant.'

'Some women don't, for months.'

'Would Rosemary McClatchy have told her mother?'

'I can't ask her,' Deveraux said. 'Absolutely not. No way. I can't put that possibility into Emmeline's mind. Because suppose Rosemary wasn't pregnant? It would taint her memory.'

'There was something Shawna Lindsay's brother wasn't telling me. I'm sure of it. Maybe something big. You should talk to him. His name is Bruce. He wants to join the army, by the way.'

'Not the Marines?'

'Apparently not.'

'Why? Did you trash the Marines to him?'

'I was very fair.'

'Would he talk to me? He seems very hostile.'

'He's OK,' I said. 'Ugly, but OK. He seems drawn towards the military. He seems to understand command structure. You're a Marine and a sheriff. Approach it right and he might stand up and salute.'

'OK,' she said. 'Maybe I'll try it. Maybe I'll go see him today.'

'All three of them could have been accidental,' I said. 'The big decisions might have come afterwards. About what to do, I mean. If they all three liked the status quo they might have chosen a different route. Or they might have been persuaded.'

'Abortion?'

'Why not?'

'Where would they get an abortion in Mississippi? You'd have to drive north for hours.'

'Which is maybe why Janice Chapman got dressed before four in the morning. An early start. Maybe she had a long trip ahead of her. Maybe her boyfriend was driving her somewhere. For an afternoon appointment, perhaps. Then an overnight stay. Maybe she was thinking ahead, to the reception counter. The waiting room. So she put on something appropriate. Stylish, but reasonably demure. And maybe she packed a bag. That's something else we didn't see in her house. Suitcases.'

'We'll never know for sure,' Deveraux said. 'Unless we find the boyfriends.'

'Or the boyfriend, singular,' I said. 'It might have been the same guy.'

'With all three of them?'

'It's possible.'

'But it makes no sense. Why would he set up an appointment at an abortion clinic for them and then murder them before they got a mile down the road? Why not just go through with the appointment?'

'Maybe he's the kind of guy who can't afford either a pregnant girlfriend or an association with an abortion clinic.'

'He's a soldier. Not a preacher. Or a politician.'

I said nothing.

Deveraux said, 'Maybe he wants to be a preacher or a politician later.'

I said nothing.

'Or maybe he's got preachers or politicians in the family. Maybe he has to avoid embarrassing them.'

There was a creak from a floorboard outside in the hall, and then a soft knock on my door. I recognized the sound immediately. The same as the morning before. The old guy. I pictured his slow shuffling tread, the slow tentative movement of his arm, the muted low-energy impact of his papery knuckles on the wood.

Deveraux whispered, 'Oh, shit.'

Now we *were* like teenagers. Now we were rushing and fumbling. Deveraux rolled off the bed and grabbed an armful of clothing, which happened to include my pants, so I had to wrestle them back from her, which spilled the other garments all over the place. She tried to collect them and I tried to get my pants on. I got tangled up and fell back on the bed and she made it to the bathroom but left a breadcrumb trail of socks and underwear behind her. I got my pants more or less straight and the old guy knocked again. I limped across the floor and kicked clothes towards the bathroom as I went. Deveraux darted out and collected them up. Then she ducked back in again and I opened the door.

The old guy said, 'Your fiancée is on the phone for you.'

Loud and clear.

FORTY-SIX

I padded downstairs barefoot, wearing only my pants. I took the call alone in the back office behind the reception counter, as before. It was Karla Dixon on the line. My old colleague. The financial wizard. She had been a founder member of the original 110th Special Unit. My second pick, after Frances Neagley. I guessed Stan Lowrey had passed on my question about money from Kosovo, and Dixon was calling back direct, to save time.

I asked, 'Why did you have to say you were my fiancée?'

She asked back, 'Why, did I interrupt something?'

'Not exactly. But she heard.'

'Elizabeth Deveraux? Neagley told us about her. You two are getting it on already?'

'And now I've got some explaining to do.'

'You need to take care there, Reacher.'

'Neagley always thinks that.'

'This time she's right. The sergeants' network is all lit up. Red hot. Deveraux is being checked out, big time.'

'I know that,' I said. 'Garber already told me. Waste of time.'

'I don't think so. It all suddenly went quiet.'

'Because there's nothing there.'

'No, because there is. You know how bureaucracy works. It's easy to say no. Silence means yes.'

'What would they find if they checked you out?'

'Plenty.'

'Or me?'

'I hate to think.'

'So there you go,' I said. 'Nothing to worry about.'

'Believe me, there's something wrong there, Reacher. I mean it. Maybe something real big. My advice would be to stay away from her.'

'Too late for that. I don't buy it, anyway. She was a good little jarhead.'

'Who told you that?'

'She did.'

Silence on the line.

I said, 'What else?'

Dixon said, 'There's no money coming out of Kosovo. None at all. Whoever's worrying about that is on a wild-goose chase. It's not a factor.'

'You sure?'

'Completely.'

'They're wondering if Joe is telling me anything.'

'Wild-goose chase,' she said again. 'Treasury wouldn't know, anyway. Unless it was billions and billions. Which it isn't. It isn't even dollars and cents. It's nothing. Someone's panicking, that's all. They're thrashing around. They're looking for something that isn't there.'

'OK, good to know,' I said. 'Thanks.'

'That was the good news,' she said.

'What's the bad news?'

'Related information,' she said. 'A friend of a friend got into the Kosovo files, and they're plenty thick right now.'

'With what?'

'Among other things, two local women disappeared without a trace.'

Dixon told me that over the last year two Kosovan women had simply vanished. There was no local explanation. No family troubles. Both were unmarried. Both had been within range of the U.S. Army's local footprint. Both had fraternized.

'Girlfriend material,' Dixon said.

'Good looking?' I asked.

'I didn't see photographs.'

I asked, 'Was there an investigation?'

'Under the radar,' Dixon said. 'We're not there at all, remember, as far as the rest of the world is concerned. So they flew a guy in from Germany. Supposedly on his way to Italy for some NATO crap, but Kosovo was the real destination. The travel arrangements are still on file.'

'And?'

'As a patriotic American you'll be glad to hear that every last member of the U.S. armed forces was as innocent as a newborn baby. No crimes were committed by anyone in uniform.'

'So the case was closed?'

'Tighter than a trout's asshole.'

'Who was the investigator?'

'Major Duncan Munro.'

*   *   *

I finished the call with Dixon and went back upstairs. Deveraux wasn't in my room. I padded back to hers and found the door locked. I heard the shower running. I knocked but got no response. So I showered and dressed and went back fifteen minutes later and found nothing but silence. I walked up to the diner, but she wasn't there either. Her car was not in the department lot. So I just stood there on the sidewalk, with nowhere to go, and no one to talk to, and nothing to do, completely unaware that the hour that would change everything had just ticked down from sixty minutes to fifty-nine.

FORTY-SEVEN

I loitered on the sidewalk for half of that hour. Mostly I leaned on a wall and didn't move. A professional skill. Necessary in my line of work. I'm good at it. But I know people who are better. I know people who have waited hours or days or weeks for something to happen.

I was waiting for the old guy with the tape measure to show up and open the shirt shop. Which he did, eventually. I pushed off my wall and crossed the street and followed him inside. He fussed with locks and lights and I made straight for his pile of button-downs. I found the same thing I was wearing and took it to the counter.

The old guy said, 'Stocking up?'

I said, 'No, the first one got dirty.'

He leaned in and peered at my pocket. I saw his eyes trace the curl of blood. Down and up. He said, 'I'm sure that would wash out. Cold water, maybe a little salt.'

'Salt?'

'Salt helps with bloodstains. With cold water. Hot water sets them.'

'I don't think the Toussaint's hotel offers a very sophisticated laundry service,' I said. 'Actually I don't think they offer any kind of laundry service at all. They don't even offer coffee in the lounge.'

'You could take the shirt home with you, sir.'

'How?'

'Well, in your suitcase.'

'Easier just to replace it.'

'But that would be very expensive.'

'Compared to what? How much do suitcases cost?'

'But you would keep a suitcase for ever. You would use it over and over again for many years.'

I said, 'I think I'll just take the new shirt. No need to wrap it.'

I paid the guy and then ducked into his changing cubicle and pulled the curtain. I took off the old shirt, put on the new, and came back out.

'Got a trash can?' I asked.

The guy paused a beat in surprise and then ducked down and came back up with a knee-high metal canister. He held it out uncertainly. I balled up the dirty shirt and hit a three-pointer from about ten feet. The guy looked horrified. Then I headed back across the street to the diner for breakfast. And for a little more purposeful loitering. I knew my best chance of running into Deveraux would be right there. A woman who ate like she did couldn't stay away for long. It was just a matter of time.

In the end it was a matter of less than twenty minutes. I ate eggs and was halfway through my third cup of coffee when she came in. She saw me from the doorway and paused. The whole world paused. The atmosphere went solid. She was in uniform again, and her hair was tied back. Her face was a little set in place. A little immobile. She looked wonderful.

I took a breath and kicked the facing chair out. She didn't react. I saw her eyes move as she considered her options. She looked at all the tables. Most of them were unoccupied. But evidently she decided that to sit on her own might cause a scene. She was worried about voters. Worried about her reputation. So she came over to me. She pulled the chair out another foot and sat down, quiet and reserved, knees tight together, hands in her lap.

I said, 'I don't have a fiancée. I don't have any kind of other girlfriend.'

She didn't answer.

I said, 'It was just an MP colleague on the phone. They're all playing a game with the undercover thing. Apparently it amuses them. My CO calls himself my uncle.'

No answer.

'I can't prove a negative,' I said.

'I'm hungry,' she said. 'This is the first time in two years I've missed breakfast.'

'I apologize for that,' I said.

'Why? There's no need, if what you're saying is true.'

'It is true. I'm apologizing on behalf of my colleague.'

'Was it your sergeant? Neagley?'

'No, it was a woman called Karla Dixon.'

'What did she want?'

'To tell me that no one is running a financial scam out of Fort Kelham.'

'How would she know?'

285

'She knows everything about anything with a dollar sign in front of it.'

'Who thought there was a financial scam out of Kelham?'

'The brass. I suppose it was a theoretical possibility. Like you said, they're desperate.'

'If you had a fiancée, would you cheat on her?'

'Probably not,' I said. 'But I'd want to, with you.'

'I've been burned before.'

'Hard to believe.'

'Yet true. Not a good feeling.'

'I understand,' I said. 'But you weren't being burned last night.'

She went quiet. I saw her thinking. *Last night.* She waved to the waitress and ordered French toast. The same as the day before.

'I called Bruce Lindsay,' she said. 'Shawna Lindsay's little brother. Did you know they have a phone?'

'Yes,' I said. 'I've used it. Karla Dixon was returning a call I made from it.'

'I'm heading over there this afternoon. I think you're right. He has something to tell me.'

Me. Not us.

I said, 'It was a fellow officer's lame joke. That's all.'

She said, 'I'm afraid there's a problem with the finger-prints. From Janice Chapman's house, I mean. My own fault, as a matter of fact.'

'What kind of problem?'

'Deputy Butler has a friend over there at the Jackson PD. From back when he took the course. I encourage him to get her to do our processing for us, on the quiet, to save ourselves the money. We don't have the budget here. But Butler's friend screwed up this time, and I can't ask him to ask her to do it over. That would be a step too far.'

'Screwed up how?'

'She got her file numbers mixed. Chapman's data went to a case about a woman called Audrey Shaw, and we got Audrey Shaw's data. The wrong person entirely. Some kind of federal government worker. Which Chapman definitely wasn't, because there's no federal government work here, and Chapman didn't work anyway. Unless Audrey Shaw was the previous owner of Chapman's house, in which case it was Butler's own screw-up, looking for prints in the wrong places, or yours, for letting him.'

'No, Butler did a good job,' I said. 'He looked in all the right places. Those prints weren't from a previous owner, not unless she sneaked back in and used Chapman's toothbrush in the middle of the night. So it's just one of those things, I guess. Shit happens.'

'Tell me again,' she said. 'About that phone call.'

'It was Major Karla Dixon of the 329th,' I said. 'With information for me. That's all.'

'And the fiancée thing was a joke?'

'Don't tell me the Marines are better comedians, too.'

'Is she good looking?'

'Pretty nice.'

'Was she ever your girlfriend?'

'No.'

Deveraux went quiet again. I could see a decision coming. It was almost there. And I was pretty sure it was going to turn out OK. But I didn't find out. Not right then. Because before she could speak again the stout woman from the department's switchboard room crashed in through the diner door and stopped dead with one hand on the knob and one on the jamb. She was out of breath. She was panting. Her chest was heaving. She had run all the way. She called out, 'There's another one.'

FORTY-EIGHT

Deputy Butler had been on his way to relieve Pellegrino for the middle watch at Fort Kelham's gate, and a mile out he had happened to glance to his left, and he had seen a forlorn shape low down in the scrub perhaps a hundred yards north of the road. Five minutes after that he had been on the horn to HQ with the bad news, and ninety seconds after taking the message the dispatcher had made it to the diner. Deveraux and I were in her car twenty seconds after that, and she put her foot down hard and drove fast all the way, so we were on the scene less than ten minutes after Butler had first chanced to turn his head.

Not that speed made any difference.

We parked nose to tail behind Butler's car and got out. We were on the main east–west road, two miles beyond the last of Carter Crossing itself, one mile short of Kelham, out in an open belt of scrubland, with the forest that bordered Kelham's fence well ahead of us and the forest that flanked the railroad track well behind us. It was the middle of the morning and the sky was clear and blue. The air was warm and the breeze was still.

I could see what Butler had seen. It could have been a rock, or it could have been trash, but it wasn't. It was small in the distance, dark, slightly humped, slightly elongated, pressed down, deflated. It was unmistakable. Judging its size was difficult, because judging the exact distance was difficult. If it was eighty yards away, it was a small woman. If it was a hundred and twenty yards away, it was a large man.

Deveraux said, 'I hate this job.'

Butler was standing out in the scrub, halfway between the dark shape and us. We set out walking towards him, and then we passed him without a word. I figured the overall distance was going to be close to dead on a hundred yards, which made the shape neither a small woman nor a large man. It was going to be something in between. A tall woman, or a short man.

Or a teenager, maybe.

Then I recognized the distorted proportions.

And I started to run.

At twenty yards out I was sure. At ten yards out I was certain. At ten feet out I had absolute visual confirmation. No possible doubt. It was Bruce Lindsay. The ugly boy. Sixteen years old. Shawna Lindsay's little brother. He was on his front. His feet were apart. His hands were down by his sides. His giant head was turned towards me. His mouth was open. His deep-set eyes were dark and dead.

We followed no kind of crime-scene protocol. Deveraux and I trampled the area and touched the corpse. We rolled it over and found an entry wound on the left side of the rib cage, up high, close to the armpit. No exit wound. The bullet had come in, shredded the heart, shattered the spine, had deflected and tumbled and was still in there somewhere.

I knelt up and scanned the horizon. If the kid had been walking east, he had been shot from the north, almost certainly by a rifleman who had exited Kelham's fence-line woods and had been patrolling the open belt of scrub. The quarantine zone.

Deveraux said, 'I talked to him this morning. Just an hour ago. We had an appointment at his house. So why was he here?'

Which was a question I didn't want to answer. Not even to myself. I said, 'He had a secret to keep, I guess. About Shawna. He knew you'd get it out of him. So he decided to be somewhere else this afternoon.'

'Where? Where was he going?'

'Kelham,' I said.

'This is open country. If he was heading for Kelham he would have been on the road.'

'He was shy about strangers seeing him. Because of the way he looked. I bet he never walked on the roads.'

'If he was shy with strangers, why would he risk going to Kelham? There must be a dozen strangers in the guardhouse alone.'

I said, 'He went because I told him it would be OK. I told him soldiers would be different. I told him he'd be welcome there.'

'Welcome there for what? They don't offer guided tours.'

The kid was wearing canvas pants, a little like mine,

and a plain sweatshirt in navy blue, with a dark warm-up jacket over it. The jacket had fallen open when we rolled him. I saw folded paper in the inside pocket.

I said, 'Take a look at that.'

Deveraux slid the paper out of the pocket. It looked like an official document, heavy stock, folded three times. It looked old, and I was sure it was. About sixteen years old, almost certainly. Deveraux unfolded it and scanned it and said, 'It's his birth certificate.'

I nodded and took it from her. The State of Mississippi, a male child, family name Lindsay, given name Bruce, born in Carter Crossing. Born eighteen years ago, apparently. It might have withstood a hasty glance, but not further scrutiny. The alteration was not skilful, but it had been patient. Two digits had been carefully rubbed away, and then two others had been drawn in to replace them. The ink matched well, and the style matched well. Only the breached surface of the paper gave it away, but that was enough. It stood out. It drew the eye.

'My fault,' I said. 'My fault entirely.'

'How?'

Go straight to Kelham, I had said. *There are recruiters on every post. As soon as you've got something in your hand that proves you're eighteen years old, they'll let you in and never let you out again.*

The kid had taken it literally. I had meant he would have to wait. But he had gone ahead and made himself eighteen years old, right there and then. He had manufactured something to have in his hand. Probably at the same kitchen table where I had sat and talked and drunk iced tea. I pictured him, head down, concentrating, tongue between his teeth, maybe wetting the paper with a drop of water, scraping the old numbers off with the tip of a dinner knife, blotting the damp patch, waiting for it to dry, finding the right pen, calculating, practising, and then drawing in the new numbers. The numbers that would get him through Kelham's gate. The numbers that would get him accepted.

All on my dime.

I started walking back towards the road.

Deveraux came after me.

I told her, 'I need a gun.'

She said, 'Why?'

I stopped again and turned and looked east and scoped it out. Fort Kelham was a giant rectangle north of the road and its fence ran through a broad belt of trees that extended a couple hundred yards each side of the wire. It looked like the whole place had been hacked out of the same kind of old forest that lay south of the road, but I guessed the opposite was true. I guessed Kelham had been laid out on open ground fifty years before, and then farmers had stopped ploughing short of the fence, so the trees had come afterwards. Like new weeds. Not like the old woods to the south. The new trees thinned here and there, but mostly they provided deep cover wherever it was needed. Easy enough for a small force to stay concealed among them, slipping outward into the open belt of scrub when necessary, then slipping back inward and on through the fence for rest or resupply.

I started walking again. I said, 'I'm going to find this quarantine squad that everyone claims doesn't exist.'

'Suppose you do?' Deveraux said. 'It will be your word against theirs. Your word against the Pentagon's, basically. You'll say the squad existed, they'll say it didn't. And the Pentagon has the bigger microphone.'

'They can't argue with physical evidence. I'll bring back enough body parts to convince anyone.'

'I can't let you do that.'

'They shouldn't have shot the kid, Elizabeth. That was way out of line, whoever they are. They opened the wrong door there. That's for damn sure. What lies on the other side is their problem, not ours.'

'You don't even know where they are.'

'They're in the woods.'

'In camouflage with binoculars. How would you even get near them?'

'They have a blind spot.'

'Where?'

'Close to Kelham's gate. They're looking for the kind of intruder who already knows he can't get through the gate. So they're not looking there. They're looking farther afield.'

'The guardhouse watches the gate.'

'No, the guardhouse watches what approaches the gate. I'm not going to approach the gate. I'm going to find the gap. Too far in the rear of the mobile force, too far in advance of the guardhouse.'

'They're shooting people, Reacher.'

'They're shooting the people they see. They won't see me.'

'I'll give you a ride back to town.'

'I'm not going back to town. I want a ride in the other direction. And a firearm.'

She didn't answer.

I said, 'I'm prepared to do it without either thing if necessary. Slower and harder, but I'll get it done.'

She said, 'Get in the car, Reacher.'

No indication where she planned to take me.

We got in the car and Deveraux backed it away from Butler's cruiser and then she took off forward, east, towards Kelham. The right direction, as far as I was concerned. We covered most of the last mile and I said, 'Now head off across the grass. To the edge of the woods. Like you just saw something.'

She said, 'Straight at them?'

'They're not here. They're north and west of here. And they wouldn't shoot at a police vehicle anyway.'

'You sure about that?'

'Only one way to find out.'

She slowed and turned the wheel and thumped down off the road on to hard-packed dirt. The road was in a gap shaped like an hourglass. Two hundred yards north of it Kelham's new trees ran away from us in a gentle curve, and two hundred yards south of it the old woods ran away from us in a symmetrical pattern. Deveraux headed north and east, at an angle of forty-five degrees relative to the pavement, bucking and bouncing, and then she steered through a wide turn across the dirt and came to a stop with the flank of the car right next to the woods. My door was six feet from the nearest tree.

I said, 'Gun?'

'Jesus,' she said. 'This whole thing is illegal on so many different levels.'

'But like you told me, it's their word against mine. If there's anyone to shoot, they'll say there wasn't. The more shooting, the more denying.'

She took a breath and let it out and pulled the shotgun from its scabbard between our seats. It was an old Winchester Model 12, forty inches long, seven pounds in weight. It was nicked and worn but dewy with oil and polish. It could have been fifty years old, but it seemed well looked after. Even so, I worry about guns I have never fired. Nothing worse than pulling a trigger and having nothing happen. Or missing.

I asked her, 'Does it work?'

She said, 'It works perfectly.'

'When did you last fire it?'

'Two weeks ago.'

'At what?'

'At a target. I make the whole department requalify every year. And I need to be able to kick their butts, so I practise.'

'Did you hit the target?'

'I destroyed the target.'

I asked, 'Did you reload?'

She smiled and said, 'There are six in the magazine and one in the breech. I have spares in the trunk. I'll give you as many as you can carry.'

'Thank you.'

'It was my father's gun. Take care of it.'

'I will.'

'Take care of yourself, too.'

'Always.'

We got out of the car and she stepped around to the trunk and opened the lid. It was a messy trunk. There was dirt in it. Some kind of earth. But I spent no time worrying about tidiness, because there was a metal box bolted to the floor behind the seat-back bulkhead. For a woman built like Deveraux, it was a long way forward. She went up on tiptoes and bent forward at the waist and leaned in. Which manoeuvre looked fabulous from behind. Absolutely, truly spectacular. She flipped up the lid of the box and scrabbled with her fingernails and came back out with a carton of twelve-gauge shells. She straightened up and handed it to me. Fifteen rounds remaining. I put five in each pants pocket and five in my shirt pocket. She watched me do it. Then her eyes went wide and she said, 'You washed your shirt.'

I said, 'No, I bought a new one.'

'Why?'

'It seemed polite.'

'No, why did you buy a new one instead of washing the old one?'

'I went through this already. With the guy in the store. It seemed logical to me.'

'OK,' she said.

'You have a great ass, by the way.'

'OK,' she said again.

'I just thought I'd mention it.'

'Thank you.'

'We good now? You and me?'

She smiled. 'We always were,' she said. 'I was just yanking your chain, that's all. If she'd said she was your girlfriend I might have taken it seriously. But fiancée? That's ridiculous.'

'Why?'

'No woman would agree to marry you.'

'Why not?'

'Because you're not marriage material.'

'Why not?'

'How long have you got? The laundry issue alone could take an hour.'

'How do you do yours?'

'There's a pay launderette in the next alley past the hardware store.'

'With detergent and stuff?'

'It's not rocket science.'

'I'll think about it,' I said. 'I'll see you later.'

'Make sure you do, OK? We have a train to catch to-night.'

I smiled and nodded once and took a last look around, and then I stepped into the trees.

FORTY-NINE

At forty inches the Winchester was too long for easy transport through a forest. I had to carry it two-handed, upright in front of me. But I was glad to have it. It was a fine old piece. And fairly definitive. Twelve-gauge lead shot settles most disputes at the first time of asking.

It was March in Mississippi and there were enough new leaves on the trees to deny me a clear view of the sky. So I navigated by guesswork. Or dead reckoning, as some people prefer to call it. Which is hard to do, in a forest. Most right-handed people end up walking wide counterclockwise circles, because most right-handed people have left legs fractionally shorter than their right legs. Basic biology and geometry. I avoided that particular peril by stepping to the right of every tenth tree I came to, whether I thought I needed to or not.

The vegetation was dense, but not impossible. There was some underbrush and a lot of leaf litter. The trees were deciduous. I have no idea what kind they were. I don't know much about trees. The trunks were of various thicknesses and mostly three or four feet apart. Most of their lower limbs had died back in the gloom.

There wasn't much light down there. There were no paths. No sign of recent disturbance.

I had one circumstance working in my favour and two against. The negatives were that I was making a lot of noise, and I was wearing a bright white shirt. I was far from inconspicuous. No camouflage. No silent approach. The positive was that I had to be approaching them from their rear. They had to be hunkered down just inside the edge of the woods. They had to be looking outward. They were looking for journalists and busybodies and other unexplained strangers. Anyone walking purposefully towards them was fair game. But I would be coming up on them from behind.

And I figured I wouldn't be dealing with too many guys all at once. They would be split into small units. Minimum of two, maximum of four men in each. They would be mobile. No hides or bivouacs. They would be sitting on fallen logs or leaning on trees or squatting on the floor, looking out past the last of the growth into the bright daylight, always ready to move left or right to change their angle, always ready to range outward to meet a threat.

And I figured the small mobile units would be widely scattered. Thirty miles of fence is a lot of ground to defend. You could put a full-strength company in those woods, and one four-man unit would end up a thousand yards from its nearest neighbour. And a thousand yards in a wood is the same thing as a thousand miles. No possibility of immediate support or reinforcement. No covering fire. Basic rule of thumb: rifles and artillery are useless in a wood. Too many trees in the way.

I slowed down after advancing two hundred paces roughly north and west. I figured I must be approaching the first obvious viewpoint, at about nine o'clock on a notional dial, well above the road funnel, just inside a bulge that commanded a sweeping view west and south. Almost certainly it was the viewpoint that Bruce Lindsay had been seen from. He would have been on their left, easily visible from more than a mile away. They had stepped out, and advanced, and stood off maybe a couple of hundred yards from him. Maybe they had shouted a warning or an instruction. Maybe his response had been slow or confused or contradictory. So they had shot him.

I looped away wide to my right and then crept in on what I hoped was a straight line behind where I thought the first viewpoint would be. I moved through the trees like I was slipping through a crowd, easing left, easing right, leading with one shoulder, and then the other. I kept my eyes moving, side to side, and up and down. I watched the floor pretty carefully. Nothing I could do to avoid most of the stuff down there, but I didn't want to trip, and I didn't want to step on anything thicker than a broom handle. Dry wood can crack very loud when it breaks.

I kept on going until I sensed daylight ahead. Almost the edge of the wood. I looked left, looked right, and moved a cautious pace onward and found myself to be partly right and partly wrong. Right, because where I was standing was indeed an excellent viewpoint, and wrong, because it was unoccupied.

I stood a yard back from the last of the trees and found

myself looking southwest. The field of view was wide and wedge-shaped. The road to Carter Crossing ran diagonally across it at a distance. Nothing was moving on it, but if something had been I would have seen it very clearly. Likewise I would have seen anything in the fields up to a quarter-mile either side of the road. It was a great viewpoint. No question about that. I couldn't understand why it was abandoned. It made no tactical sense. There were many hours of daylight left. And as far as I knew nothing had changed at Kelham. No new strategic imperative had presented itself. If anything the situation was worse than ever for Bravo Company.

The state of the ground betrayed deep unseriousness too. There were cigarette butts stamped into the earth. There was a candy-bar wrapper, balled up and tossed. There were clear footprints, similar to the ones I had seen alongside the bled-out journalist on old man Clancy's land. I wasn't impressed. Army Rangers are trained to leave no sign behind. They're supposed to move through landscapes like ghosts. Especially when tasked to a sensitive mission of dubious legality.

I backed away, deep into the trees again, and I got myself all lined up and moved on north. I stuck to a route maybe fifty yards inside the edge of the wood. I watched for lateral paths leading back in towards Kelham's fence. I didn't see any. No real surprise. Covert entry and exit was probably arranged way to the north, at a remote spot at the tip of the reservation, far from any location in regular use.

I detoured again two hundred yards later, back to

where the trees thinned, to a spot with a worse view of the road but a better view of the fields. Again, an excellent vantage point. Again, unoccupied. And never occupied, as far as I could tell. No cigarette butts. No candy wrappers. No footprints.

I backed away once more, to my original line, and tried again two hundred yards later. Still nothing. I began to wonder if I was dealing with less than a full company. But to put fewer men on a thirty-mile perimeter made no sense to me. I would want more. Two full companies. Or three. And I'm a cheapskate, compared to the Pentagon. If I wanted five hundred men, the brass would want five thousand. Any kind of normal planning, that wood should have been crowded. Like Times Square. I should have been shot in the back long ago.

Then I began to wonder about watch changes and meal times. Possibly the apparent undermanning left certain spots unoccupied at certain times. But I was sure those spots would be occupied most of the time. They were too good to waste. If the mission was to detect potential hostiles approaching Kelham's perimeter, then the full 360 would have to be broken down into useful vantage points, and any of the three I had seen would qualify. So I guessed sooner or later I would find someone coming or going.

I turned around and moved deeper into the woods again. I got halfway back to my original line, and stopped walking. I just stood still and waited. For ten whole minutes I heard nothing at all. Then twenty. Then thirty. The breeze rattled leaves, and tree branches

303

moved and groaned, and tiny animals scuttled. Nothing else.

Then I heard footsteps and voices, far ahead and on my left.

FIFTY

I moved west and got behind an inadequate tree about as wide as my leg. I leaned my left shoulder on it. I levelled the shotgun. I aimed down the barrel at the approaching sounds. I kept both eyes open. I went completely quiet and still.

There were three men coming, I thought. Slow, relaxed, undisciplined. They were strolling. They were shooting the shit. I heard ragged scuffling from their feet in the leaves. I heard their voices, low and conversational and bored. I couldn't make out their words, but their tone betrayed no stress and no caution. I heard brambles wrenching and tearing, and twigs crunching and snapping, and I heard hollow clunks that I took to be plastic M16 stocks hitting trunks as the guys squeezed themselves through narrow gaps between trees. This was no kind of an orderly advance. These were not first-rate infantry soldiers. My mind ran on, like it does at times, and I saw myself writing an after-action memo criticizing their demeanour. I saw myself in a meeting at Benning, enumerating their deficiencies to a panel of senior officers.

The three men seemed to be tracking south, staying parallel to the edge of the wood, maybe twenty yards from it. No question that they were heading back to one of the viewpoints I had already scoped out. I couldn't see the men. Too many trees. But I could hear them pretty well. They were reasonably close. They were coming level with me, about thirty yards away, to my left.

I rolled around the skinny tree I was leaning on and kept myself behind them. I didn't follow them. Not immediately. I wanted to be sure there were no more of them coming. I didn't want to insert myself into a moving column. I didn't want to be the fourth guy in a big procession, with three guys ahead of me and an unknown number behind. So I stayed where I was, standing still and listening hard. But I was hearing nothing except the three guys wandering south. Nothing in the north. Nothing at all. Just natural sounds. Wind, leaves, insects.

The three guys were on their own.

I let their sound get about thirty yards down the track and then I moved after them. I picked up their physical trail easily enough. They were on an informal route that had been beaten through the underbrush by the passage of feet, back and forth, over a couple of days. There were damp turned-over leaves, and broken twigs. There was a general wash of organic matter to the margins of a meandering path about twelve inches wide. Faint, but noticeable. Very noticeable, in fact, compared to the rest of the forest floor. Compared to what I had seen elsewhere, that path looked like I-95.

* * *

I followed them all the way. I matched their pace easily enough. I didn't worry about making noise, as a matter of logic. As long as I was quieter than any two of them, then none of the three would hear me. And it was easy to be quieter than any two of them. It would have been hard to be noisier, in fact, short of firing the Winchester a couple of times and singing the national anthem.

I let myself get a little closer. I put a spurt on and got within twenty yards of them. Still no visual contact, except for one fleeting glimpse of a narrow back in camouflage BDUs, and a black glint of what I took to be an M16 barrel. But I could hear them clearly. There were definitely three of them. One was older than the others, by the sound of it, and possibly in command. One wasn't saying much, and the third was nasal and hyped up. I still couldn't make out words, but I knew they weren't saying anything worth listening to. The tenor and rhythm of their conversation told me so. There were low sarcastic murmurs, and rejoinders, and occasional barks of cheap laughter. Just three guys, passing the time.

They did not detour over to the third of the three viewpoints I had seen. They kept on going right past it, ambling, almost certainly in single file. I heard the first guy's voice louder, as he tossed comments back over his shoulder to the next two in line behind him, whose replies I could hardly hear at all, as they were projected forward and away from me. But I still sensed that nothing of importance was being said. They were bored, possibly tired, and mired in a routine task they were already familiar with. They anticipated no danger and no hazard.

They passed the second viewpoint, too. They strolled on south, and I followed them, two hundred yards along the trail, and then I heard them turn right and crash onward towards the first viewpoint. Nine o'clock on the notional dial. The place where Bruce Lindsay's killers had been hiding out, almost certainly.

I made it to the turn they had taken, and I waited there, on the main track. I heard them stop twenty yards west of me, which was exactly where I had been before, just inside the edge of the wood, where the candy wrapper and the footprints and the cigarette butts were. I moved towards them, three yards, five, and then I stopped again. I heard one of them belch, which produced laughter and general hilarity, and I guessed they had indeed moved north for their scheduled meal, and were now back on station again. I heard one of them take a leak behind a tree. I heard splashing against the kind of leathery, hairy leaves that grew down on the forest floor. I heard rifle barrels parting thin eye-level branches, as they peered out west at the open land ahead of them. I heard the scratch and clunk of a Zippo lighter, and a moment later I smelled tobacco smoke.

I took a breath and moved on, closer and closer, left and right through the trees, five more yards, then six, then seven, leading with my left elbow, then my right, swimming through the crowded space, the Winchester shotgun held upright in front of me. The three guys had no idea I was there. I could sense them ahead of me, unaware, standing still, looking outward, going quiet, settling in, their lunch hour excitement over. I held my breath and moved up one tree closer to them, silently, then another tree, then another, and then finally I got my first clear sight of them.

And I had no clue what I was looking at.

FIFTY-ONE

There were three men, as I had thought. They were fifteen feet from me. The width of a room. They all had their backs to me. One was grey-haired and heavy. He was wearing Vietnam-era olive drab fatigues. They were too tight on him. He was carrying an M16 rifle and I could see the butt of a Beretta M9 semi-automatic pistol in a webbing holster on his belt. A nine-millimetre handgun. Standard U.S. Army issue, as was the M16. The guy had old paratrooper boots on his feet, and no hat on his head.

The second guy was younger and a little taller but not much thinner. He was sandy-haired, and he was wearing what I was sure were Italian army combat fatigues. Similar to ours, but different. Better cut. He was carrying an M16 by its top handle. Right-handed. No sidearm. He was wearing black athletic sneakers. No hat. He had a small backpack in non-matching camouflage.

The third guy was wearing 1980s-issue U.S. Army woodland pattern camouflage BDUs. He wasn't fat. Far from it. He was a runt. Maybe five feet six, maybe a hundred and forty pounds. Lean and wiry and hardscrabble and nervous. He was carrying an M16 too. Civilian shoes on his feet, no hat, no sidearm. He was the smoker. There was a lit cigarette between the first two fingers of his left hand.

At first the Italian battledress made me wonder if they were some kind of a weird NATO force. But the first guy's Vietnam fatigues didn't fit with any current 1997 scenario, however screwed up international politics might have been by then, and neither did the third guy's street shoes, nor did their collective lack of combat headgear, or their lack of portable lunch rations, or their completely unprofessional behaviour. I didn't know what they were. My mind ran through random possibilities, like a departures board runs through flights at an airport. I was surprised they didn't hear the clacking and ticking from inside my head.

I looked at them again, left to right, and then right to left.

I couldn't figure it out.

Then finally I understood: they were amateurs.

The Mississippi backwoods, next to Tennessee and Alabama. Civilian militias. Pretend soldiers. Men who like to run around in the woods with guns, but like to say they're defending some vital thing or other. Men who like to shoot the shit in the surplus store, right after their bulk purchase of old fatigues and Italian battle-dress.

And men who like to buy their guns at country gun stores. At certain country gun stores in particular. Because certain country gun stores are near military

311

bases, and therefore some of them have something special for sale under the counter. All it takes is someone on the inside, and believe me, there is always someone on the inside. A steady stream of M16s and Berettas and worse is written off every year as lost or damaged or otherwise unusable, whereupon it is destroyed, except it isn't. It's hustled out the back door in the dead of night and an hour later it's under the counter at the gun shop.

I have arrested many people, often in groups larger than the one in front of me, but I have never been very good at it. The best arrests run on pure bluster, and I get self-conscious if I have to rant and rave. Better for me to land an early sucker punch, to shut them down right at the very beginning. Except that shouting *freeze freeze freeze* makes me a little self-conscious too. The words come out a little tentative. Almost like a request.

But I had with me the greatest conversation-stopper ever made: a pump-action shotgun. At the cost of one unfired shell, I could make the kind of sound that would freeze any three men to any three spots in the world.

The most intimidating noise ever heard.

Crunch-crunch.

My ejected shell hit the leaves at my feet and the three guys froze solid.

I said, 'Now the rifles hit the deck.'

Normal voice, normal pitch, normal tone.

The sandy-haired guy dropped his rifle first. He was pretty damn quick about it. Then went the older guy, and last of the three came the wiry one.

'Stand still now,' I said. 'Don't give me a reason.'

Normal voice, normal pitch, normal tone.

They stood reasonably still. Their arms came up a little, out from their sides, slowly, and they ended up a small distance from their bodies, where they held them. They spread their fingers. No doubt they spread their toes inside their boots and sneakers and shoes. Anything to appear unarmed and undangerous.

I said, 'And now you take three big paces backward.'

They complied, all three guys, all three taking exaggerated stumbling steps, and all three ending up more than a body's length from their rifles.

I said, 'And now you turn around.'

FIFTY-TWO

I had never seen any of them before. After the slow spin the older guy had ended up facing me on my left. He was completely unknown to me. He was just a guy, not very significant, a little pouchy and worn. The guy in the middle was the sandy-haired one. He was like the older man would have been, had he grown up twenty years later and in better circumstances. Just a guy, a little soft and civilized. The third guy was different. He was what you get when you eat squirrels for four generations. Smarter than a rat and tougher than a goat, and jumpier than either one.

I tucked the Winchester's stock up in my right armpit and pulled my elbow back and held the gun one-handed. I aimed it less than perfectly at the guys on the right. But then, it was a twelve-gauge shotgun. My aim didn't need to be perfect.

I used my left arm as a communications aid and looked at the older guy and said, 'Now comes the part where you take out your sidearm and hand it to me.'

He didn't respond.

I said, 'And here's how you're going to do it. You're

314

going to pull it out of the holster with one finger and one thumb, and then you're going to juggle it around and reverse it in your hand, and you're going to point it at yourself, OK?'

No response.

I said, 'Second prize is I shoot you in the legs.'

Normal voice, normal pitch, normal tone.

No response. Not at first. I thought about wasting another shell and pumping the gun again, but in the end I didn't need to. The old guy wasn't a hero. He hopped right to it after a second's thought. He did the finger and thumb thing, and he got the gun reversed in his hand, and he pressed its muzzle to his belly.

I said, 'Now find the safety and set it to fire.'

It was hard to do backwards, but the guy succeeded.

I said, 'Hold the barrel with your thumb and first two fingers. Get your ring finger loose. Now get it back there in the trigger guard. Right back there. Pressing backward on the trigger.'

The guy did it.

I asked, 'Now what do you know?'

He didn't answer.

I said, 'Any kind of struggle, you get a bullet in the gut. That's what you know. Any kind of struggle at all. We clear on that? You understand?'

The guy nodded.

I said, 'Now move your arm and bring the gun out towards me. Slowly and carefully. Keep it on the same line all the way. Keep it pointing right at yourself. Keep your ring finger hard on the trigger.'

The guy did it. He got the gun a couple of feet out from

his centre mass, and I stepped in and took it from him. Just pulled it right out of his hand, as smooth as you like. I stepped back and he dropped his arm and I swapped hands. The Winchester went to my left, and I held the Beretta in my right.

And breathed out.

And smiled.

Three prisoners taken and disarmed, all without a shot being fired.

I looked at the old guy and asked, 'Who are you people?'

He swallowed twice and then he got some kind of backbone back, and he said, 'We're on a mission, and it's the kind of mission civilians should stay away from, if they know what's good for them.'

'Civilians as opposed to what?'

'As opposed to military personnel.'

'Are you military personnel?'

The old guy said, 'Yes, we are.'

I said, 'No, you're not. You're a shower of make-believe shit.'

He said, 'It's an authorized mission.'

'Authorized by who?'

'By our commander.'

'Who authorized him?'

The guy started to hem and haw and bluster. He started talking and stopped again a couple of times. I crossed the Winchester's barrel with the Beretta and pointed the handgun straight at the guy. I wasn't sure it worked. I never trust a gun I haven't fired myself. But it felt right and it weighed right. The safety catch was off.

I knew that for sure. And the guy was flinching pretty good. And he should know better than anyone whether the piece worked. Because it was his. I laid my finger hard on the trigger. The guy saw me do it. But still he didn't say anything.

Then the sandy-haired guy spoke up. The soft one. He said, 'He doesn't know who authorized the mission, and he's too embarrassed to admit it. That's why he isn't saying anything. Can't you see that?'

'He'd rather get shot than be embarrassed?'

'None of us knows who authorized anything. Why would we?'

I asked, 'Where are you from?'

'First tell me who you are.'

'I'm a commissioned officer in the United States Army,' I said. 'Which means that if your so-called mission was authorized by the military, then you must currently be under my command, as the senior officer present. Right? That would be logical, wouldn't it?'

'Yes, sir.'

'Where are you from?'

'Tennessee,' the guy said. 'We're the Tennessee Free Citizens.'

'You don't look very free to me,' I said. 'Right now you look kind of detained.'

No answer.

I asked, 'Why did you come down here?'

'We got word.'

'What word?'

'That we were needed here.'

'How many of you came?'

317

'There are sixty of us.'

'Twenty teams for thirty miles?'

'Yes, sir.'

I asked, 'What instructions did you get when you got here?'

'We were told to keep people away.'

'Why?'

'Because it was time to step up and help the nation's military. Which is every patriot's duty.'

'Why did the nation's military need your help?'

'We weren't told why.'

'Rules of engagement?'

'We were supposed to keep people away, however we had to do it.'

'Did you kill that kid this morning?'

Silence for a long, long moment.

Then the runt on my right spoke up.

He said, 'You mean the black boy?'

The old guy said, 'This mission is *fully* authorized.'

I said, 'I mean the African-American teenage male, yes.'

The guy with the sandy hair glanced urgently at his buddies. First one, then the other. Rapid movements of his head. He said, 'None of us should answer questions about that.'

I said, 'At least one of you should.'

The old guy said, 'This mission is fully authorized at the very highest level possible. There is no higher level than the level that authorized this mission. Whoever you are, mister, you are making a very big mistake.'

I said, 'Shut up.'

The guy with the sandy hair looked straight at the runt and said, 'Don't say anything.'

I looked at the runt and said, 'Say what you like. No one will believe you anyway. Everyone knows a pussy like you is just there for the ride.' I turned away. Back to the old guy.

The runt said, 'I shot the black boy.'

I turned back.

I asked him, 'Why?'

'He was acting aggressive.'

I shook my head. 'I saw the corpse,' I said. 'The bullet hit high under his arm. No damage to the arm itself. I think he had his hands up. I think he was surrendering.'

The runt sniffed and said, 'I suppose it could have looked that way.'

I uncrossed the Winchester and the Beretta. I raised the handgun. I pointed it at the little guy's face.

I said, 'Tell me about yesterday.'

He looked straight at me.

Calculation in his little rat eyes.

He decided I wasn't going to shoot.

He said, 'We were north of here yesterday.'

'And?'

'I guess you could say I'm two for two this season.'

'Who applied the field dressing?'

The sandy-haired guy said, 'I did. It was an accident. We were just following orders.'

I turned back to the runt and said, 'Tell me again. About sighting in on a sixteen-year-old boy with his hands up.'

319

I moved my aim half an inch upward. The exact centre of his forehead.

The guy grinned and said, 'I suppose he might have been waving.'

I pulled the trigger.

The gun worked fine. Just fine. Exactly as it should. The sound of the shot cracked and hissed and rolled. Birds flew up in the sky. The spent case ejected and bounced off a tree and hit me hard in the thigh. The runt's head blew apart and wet-slapped the leaves behind him, and he went down vertically, his skinny butt to his heels, and then he bounced slackly and spilled over in the kind of boneless tangle only the recently and violently dead can achieve.

I waited for the sound to die away and for my hearing to come back and I looked at the two survivors and I said, 'Your alleged mission has just been terminated. As of right now. And the Tennessee Free Citizens has just been disbanded. As of this moment. They're totally out of business now. You two run along and spread that news. You've got thirty minutes to haul your sorry asses out of my woods. You've got an hour to get out of this state altogether. All fifty-nine of you. Any slower than that, I'll send a Ranger company after you. Now beat it.'

The two survivors just stood there for a second, completely still, pale and shocked and afraid. Then they came to. And they ran. They really hustled. I listened to them go until their noise faded away to nothing. It took a long time, but then they were gone and I knew they wouldn't be back. They had taken a casualty, and they had no appetite for that kind of thing. I was sure they would make a martyr of the guy, but I was equally sure they would take great pains to avoid sharing his glorious fate. Blood and brains are realities, and realities are unwelcome visitors in the world of make-believe.

I clicked the safety on the Beretta and put it in my pants pocket. I untucked my shirt and let the tails hide it. Then I headed back the way I had come, leading with one shoulder and then the other, as I slipped between the trees with the Winchester upright in front of me.

FIFTY-THREE

Elizabeth Deveraux was waiting exactly where she had left me, right next to her car, six feet from the tree line. I stepped out of the woods right in front of her and she jumped a little, but then she gathered herself pretty quickly. I guessed she didn't want to insult me by being surprised I had made it. Or she didn't want to show she had been anxious. Or both. I kissed her on the lips and handed back the Winchester and she asked, 'What happened?'

I said, 'They're some kind of a citizens' council from Tennessee. Some kind of a half-assed amateur backwoods militia. They're leaving now.'

'I heard a handgun.'

'One of them was so overcome with regret he committed suicide.'

'Did he have things to regret?'

'More than most.'

'Who brought them here?'

I said, 'That's the big question, isn't it?'

*   *   *

I returned her spare shotgun ammunition from my pockets. She made me put it in the trunk myself. Then we drove back to town. My new Beretta dug into my thigh and my stomach all the way. We passed through the black half of Carter Crossing, and then we thumped over the railroad track, and then we pulled into the Sheriff's Department's lot. Home base for Deveraux. Safety. She said, 'Go get a cup of coffee. I'll be back soon.'

'Where are you going?'

'I have to give Mrs Lindsay the news about her son.'

'That won't be easy.'

'No, it won't.'

'Want me to come with you?'

'No,' she said. 'That wouldn't be appropriate.'

I watched her drive away, and then I headed to the diner for coffee. And for the phone. I kept my mug close at hand on the hostess station and dialled Stan Lowrey's office. He picked up himself. I said, 'You're still there. You've still got a job. I don't believe it.'

He said, 'That stuff is getting old, Reacher.'

'You'll look back on it like the dying embers of a happy time.'

'What do you want?'

'From life in general? That's a big question.'

'From me.'

'I want many things from you,' I said. 'Specifically I want you to check some names for me. In every database you can find. Mostly civilian, if you can, including government stuff. Call the D.C. police and try to get

323

them to help. The FBI too, if there's anyone over there still speaking to you.'

'On the up and up or on the quiet?'

'On the very quiet.'

'What names?'

'Janice May Chapman,' I said.

'That's the dead woman, right?'

'One of several.'

'And?'

'Audrey Shaw,' I said.

'Who is she?'

'I don't know. That's why I want you to check her out.'

'In connection with what?'

'She's a loose end connected to another loose end.'

'Audrey Shaw,' he said, slowly, as if he was writing it down.

Then he said, 'What else?'

I asked, 'How far away is Garber's office from yours?'

'It's on the other side of the stairwell.'

'I need him on the line. So go get him and drag him over by the scruff of his raggedy old neck.'

'Why not just call him direct?'

'Because I want him on your line, not his.'

No answer, except a plastic thump as he laid down the phone on his desk, and a grunt as he stood up, and a hiss as his chair cushion recovered its shape. Then silence, which was expensive, because I was on a pay phone. I fed it another quarter and waited. Whole minutes passed. I started to think Garber was sitting tight. Refusing to come. But then I heard the phone lift up off the desk and the familiar voice asked, 'What the hell do you want now?'

'I want to talk to you,' I said.

'So call me. We have switchboards now. And extensions.'

'They're listening to your line. I think that's pretty obvious, isn't it? You're a pawn here, the same as me. Therefore someone else's line is safer.'

Garber was quiet for a beat.

'Possible,' he said. 'What have you got for me?'

'The boots on the ground outside of Kelham were an unofficial force. A local citizens' militia. Evidently part of some weirdo network of true patriots. Apparently they were here to defend the army from unjustified harassment.'

'Well, Mississippi,' he said. 'What do you expect?'

'They were from Tennessee, actually,' I said. 'And you're missing the point. They didn't just happen to be here. They weren't just passing by on a whim. They weren't here for a vacation. They were deployed here. They have a contact somewhere who knew exactly when, and exactly where, and exactly how, and exactly why they would be needed. Who would have that kind of information?'

'Someone who had all the facts from the get-go.'

'And where would we find such a person?'

'Somewhere high up.'

'I agree,' I said. 'Any idea who?'

'None at all.'

'You sure? You need to put me in the loop here if you can.'

'I'm sure. You're already in the loop as much as I am.'

'OK, go back to your office. Five minutes from now I'm going to call you. You can ignore what I say, because it won't mean much. But stay on the line long enough to let the tape recorders roll.'

'Wait,' Garber said. 'There's something I have to tell you.'

'Like what?'

'News from the Marine Corps.'

'What kind of news?'

'There's some kind of issue with Elizabeth Deveraux.'

'What kind of issue?'

'I don't know yet. They're playing hard to get. They're making a real big deal about access. The file she's in is apparently some super-toxic thing. Highest category, biggest deal in the world, and similar bullshit. But word is there was some big scandal about five years ago. The story is Deveraux got some other Marine MP fired for no good reason. Rumours say it was personal jealousy.'

'Five years ago is three years before she quit. Was she honourably discharged?'

'Yes, she was.'

'Voluntary separation or involuntary?'

'Voluntary.'

'Then there's nothing there,' I said. 'Don't worry about it.'

'You're thinking with the wrong part of your body, Reacher.'

'Five minutes,' I said. 'Be back at your desk.'

*　　*　　*

The waitress freshened my cup and I drank most of the new brew while I counted three hundred seconds in my head. Then I stepped back to the phone and dialled Garber direct. He answered and I said, 'Sir, this is Major Reacher reporting from Mississippi. Can you hear me?'

Garber said, 'Loud and clear.'

I said, 'I have the name of the individual who ordered the Tennessee Free Citizens to Kelham. That order became part of a criminal conspiracy in that it resulted in two homicides and two felony assaults. I have an appointment I need to keep at the Pentagon the day after tomorrow, and then I'll return to base immediately afterwards and I'll get JAG Corps involved at that point in time.'

Garber was on the ball. He caught on fast and played his part well. He asked, 'Who was the individual?'

I said, 'I'll keep that strictly to myself for the next forty-eight hours, if you don't mind.'

Garber said, 'Understood.'

I dabbed the cradle to end the call, and then I dialled a new number. Colonel John James Frazer's billet, deep inside the Pentagon. The Senate Liaison guy. I got his scheduler and made a twelve o'clock appointment with him, in his office, for the day after next. I didn't say why, because I couldn't. I didn't have a real reason. I just needed to be somewhere in the giant building. As bait in a trap.

Then I sat at a table and waited for Deveraux. A woman who ate like she did wouldn't be long.

FIFTY-FOUR

Deveraux came in thirty minutes later, looking pale and drawn. Death messages are never pleasant. Especially when lightning strikes twice, against a mother who is already angry. But it's all part of the job. Bereaved relatives are always angry. Why wouldn't they be?

Deveraux sat down and blew a long sad breath at me.

'Bad?' I asked.

She nodded.

'Terrible,' she said. 'She's not going to vote for me ever again, that's for sure. I think if I had a house, she'd burn it down. If I had a dog, she'd poison it.'

'Can't blame her,' I said. 'Two for two.'

'It will be three for three soon. That woman is going to take a midnight stroll on the railroad tracks. I guarantee it. Within a week, probably.'

'Has that happened before?'

'Not often. But the train is always there, once a night. Like a reminder that there's a way out if you need one.'

I said nothing. I wanted to remember the midnight train in a happier context.

She said, 'I want to ask you a question, but I'm not going to.'

'What question?'

'Who put those idiots in the woods?'

'Why aren't you going to ask it?'

'Because I'm assuming there's a whole bunch of things here, all interconnected. Some big crisis on the base. A part answer wouldn't make sense. You'd have to tell me everything. And I don't want to ask you to do that.'

'I couldn't tell you everything even if I wanted to. I don't know everything. If I knew everything I wouldn't be here any more. The job would be done. I'd be back on post doing the next thing.'

'Are you looking forward to that?'

'Are you fishing?'

'No, I'm just asking. I've been there myself, don't forget. Sooner or later we all hit the moment when the light goes out. I'm wondering if it's happened to you yet. Or if it's still to come.'

I said, 'No, I don't really want to get back on post. But that's mostly because of the sex, not the work.'

She smiled. 'So who put those idiots in the woods?'

'I don't know,' I said. 'Could have been a number of people. Kelham is a pie the same as any other pie, and there are lots of folks with their fingers in it. Lots of interests, lots of angles. Some of them are professional, and some of them are personal. Maybe five or six of them pass the crazy test. Which means there are five or six different chains of command terminating in five or six very senior officers somewhere. Any one of them could feel threatened in some way bad enough to

329

pull a stunt like this. And any one of them would be quite capable of doing it. You don't get to be a very senior officer in this man's army by being a sweet guy.'

'Who are the five or six?'

'I wouldn't have the faintest idea. That's not my world. From where they are, I'm just a grunt. I'm indistinguishable from a private first class.'

'But you're going to nail him.'

'Of course I'm going to nail him.'

'When?'

'Day after tomorrow, I hope. I have to go to D.C. Just for a night, maybe.'

'Why?'

'I got on a line I knew to be tapped and said I knew a name. So now I have to go hang out up there and walk the walk and see what comes out of the woodwork.'

'You made yourself the bait in a trap?'

'It's like a theory of relativity. Same difference if I go to them or they come to me.'

'Especially when you don't even know who they are, let alone which one of them is guilty.'

I said nothing.

She said, 'I agree. It's time to shake something loose. If you want to know if the stove is hot, sometimes the only way to find out is to touch it.'

'You must have been a pretty good cop.'

'I still am a pretty good cop.'

'So when did your light go out? With the Marines, I mean. When did you stop enjoying it?'

'About where you are now,' she said. 'For years you've

laughed off the small things, but they come so thick and fast that eventually you realize an avalanche is made up of small things. Snowflakes, right? Things don't get much smaller than that. Suddenly you realize that small things *are* big things.'

'No single specific thing?'

'No, I got through fine. I never had any trouble.'

'What, all sixteen years?'

'I had some minor speed bumps here and there. I dated the wrong guy once or twice. But nothing worth talking about. I made it to CWO5, after all, which is as high as it goes for some of us.'

'You did well.'

'Not bad for a country girl from Carter Crossing.'

'Not bad at all.'

She asked, 'When are you leaving?'

'Tomorrow morning, I guess. It will take me all day to get there.'

'I'll have Pellegrino drive you to Memphis.'

'No need,' I said.

'Agree for my sake,' she said. 'I like to get Pellegrino out of the county as often as possible. Let him wreck his car and kill a pedestrian in some other jurisdiction.'

'Has he done that here?'

'We don't have pedestrians here. This is a very quiet town. Quieter than ever right now.'

'Because of Kelham?'

'This place is dying, Reacher. We need that base open, and fast.'

'Maybe I'll make some headway in D.C.'

'I hope you do,' she said.

331

'We should have lunch now.'

'That's why I came in.'

Deveraux's lunch staple was chicken pie. We ordered a matched pair and were halfway through eating them when the old couple from the hotel came in. The woman had a book, and the man had a newspaper. A routine pit stop, like dinner. Then the old guy saw me and detoured to our table. He told me my wife's brother had just called. Something very urgent. I looked blank for a second. The old guy must have thought my wife came from a very large family.

'Your brother-in-law Stanley,' he said.

'OK,' I said. 'Thanks.'

The old guy shuffled off and I said, 'Major Stan Lowrey. A friend of mine. He and I have been TDY at the same place for a couple of weeks.'

Deveraux smiled. 'I think the verdict is in. Marines were better comedians.'

I started eating again, but she said, 'You should call him back if it's very urgent, don't you think?'

I put my fork down.

'Probably,' I said. 'But don't eat my pie.'

I went back to the phone for the third time and dialled. Lowrey answered on the first ring and asked, 'Are you sitting down?'

I said, 'No, I'm standing up. I'm on a pay phone in a diner.'

'Well, hold on tight. I have a story for you. About a girl called Audrey.'

FIFTY-FIVE

I leaned on the wall next to the phone. Not because I was necessarily worried about falling down with shock or surprise. But because Lowrey's stories were usually very long. He fancied himself a raconteur. And he liked background. And context. Deep background, and deep context. Normally he liked to trace everything back to a seminal point just before random swirls of gas from the chartless wastes of the universe happened to get together and form the earth itself.

He said, 'Audrey is a very ancient name, apparently.'

The only way to knock Lowrey off his discursive stride was to get your retaliation in first. I said, 'Audrey was an Anglo-Saxon name. It's a diminutive of Aethelthryth or Etheldreda. It means noble strength. There was a Saint Audrey in the seventh century. She's the patron saint of throat complaints.'

'How do you know shit like this? I had to look it up.'

'I know a guy whose mother is called Audrey. He told me.'

'My point is, it's no longer a very common name.'

'It was number 173 on the hit parade at the last

333

census. It's slightly more popular in France, Belgium and Canada. Mostly because of Audrey Hepburn.'

'You know this because of a guy's mother?'

'His grandmother too, actually. They were both called Audrey.'

'So you got a double ration of knowledge?'

'It felt like a double ration of something.'

'Audrey Hepburn wasn't from Europe.'

'Canada isn't in Europe.'

'They speak French there. I've heard them.'

'Of course Audrey Hepburn was from Europe. English father, Dutch mother, born in Belgium. She had a UK passport.'

'Whatever, what I'm saying is, if you would ever let a guy get a word in edgewise, if you search for Audreys you don't get too many hits.'

'So you found Audrey Shaw for me?'

'I think so.'

'That was fast.'

'I know a guy who works at a bank. Corporations have the best information.'

'Still fast.'

'Thank you. I'm a diligent worker. I'm going to be the most diligent unemployed guy in history.'

'So what do we know about Audrey Shaw?'

'She's an American citizen,' Lowrey said.

'Is that all we know?'

'Caucasian female, born in Kansas City, Missouri, educated locally, went to college at Tulane in Louisiana. The Southern Ivy League. She was a liberal arts student and a party girl. Middling GPA. No health problems, which I imagine means slightly more than it says, for a party girl from Tulane. She graduated on schedule.'

'And?'

'After graduation she used family connections to get an intern's job in D.C.'

'What kind of intern's job?'

'Political. In a Senate office. Working for one of her home-state Missouri guys. Probably just carrying coffee, but she was called an assistant to an assistant executive director of something or other.'

'And?'

'She was beautiful, apparently. She made strong men weak at the knees. So guess what happened?'

'She got laid,' I said.

'She had an affair,' Lowrey said. 'With a married man. All those late nights, all that glamour. The thrill of working out the fine print in trade deals with Bolivia. You know how it is. I don't know how those people stand the excitement.'

'Who was the guy?'

'The senator himself,' Lowrey said. 'The big dog. The record gets a little hazy from that point onward, because obviously the whole thing was covered up like crazy. But between the lines it was a torrid business. Between the sheets too, probably. A real big thing. People say she was in love.'

'Where are you getting this from, if the record is hazy?'

'The FBI,' Lowrey said. 'Plenty of them still talk to me. And you better believe they keep track of things like this. For leverage. You notice how the FBI budget

335

never goes down? They know too many things about too many politicians for that to ever happen.'

'How long did the affair last?'

'Senators have to run for re-election every six years, so generally they spend the first four rolling around on the couch and the last two cleaning up their act. Young Ms Shaw got the last two of the good years and then she was patted on the butt and sent on her way.'

'And where is she now?'

'This is where it gets interesting,' Lowrey said.

I pushed off the wall and looked over at Deveraux. She seemed OK. She was eating what was left of my pie. She was craning across the table and picking at it. Demolishing it, actually. In my ear Lowrey said, 'I've got rumours and hard facts. The rumours come from the FBI and the hard facts come from the databases. Which do you want first?'

I settled back against the wall again.

'The rumours,' I said. 'Always much more interesting.'

'OK, the rumours say young Ms Shaw felt very unhappy about being discarded in the way she was. She felt used and cheap. Like a Kleenex. She felt like a hooker leaving a hotel suite. She began to look like the kind of intern that could cause serious trouble. That was the FBI's opinion, anyway. They keep track of that stuff too, for different reasons.'

'So what happened?'

'In the end nothing happened. The parties must have reached some kind of mutual accommodation. Everything went quiet. The senator was duly re-elected and Audrey Shaw was never heard from again.'

'Where is she now?'

'This is where you ask me what the hard facts say.'

'What do the hard facts say?'

'The hard facts say Audrey Shaw isn't anywhere any more. The databases are completely blank. No records of anything. No transactions, no taxes, no purchases, no cars or houses or boats or trailers, no snowmobiles, no loans or liens or warrants or judgements or arrests or convictions. It's like she ceased to exist three years ago.'

'Three years ago?'

'Even the bank agrees.'

'How old was she then?'

'She was twenty-four then. She'd be twenty-seven now.'

'Did you check the other name for me? Janice May Chapman?'

'You just spoiled my surprise. You just ruined my story.'

'Let me guess,' I said. 'Chapman is the exact reverse. There's nothing there more than three years old.'

'Correct.'

'They were the same person,' I said. 'Shaw changed her identity. Part of the deal, presumably. A big bag of cash and a stack of new paperwork. Like a witness protection programme. Maybe the real witness protection programme. Those guys would help a senator out. It would give them an IOU to put in their back pocket.'

'And now she's dead. End of story. Anything else?'

'Of course there's something else,' I said. There was

one last question. Big and obvious. But I hardly needed to ask it. I was sure I knew the answer. I felt it coming right at me, hissing through the air like an incoming mortar round. Like an artillery shell, aimed and ranged and fused for an air burst right next to my head.

I asked, 'Who was the senator?'

'Carlton Riley,' Lowrey said. 'Mr Riley of Missouri. The man himself. The chairman of the Armed Services Committee.'

FIFTY-SIX

I got back to the table just as the waitress was putting down two slices of peach pie and two cups of coffee. Deveraux started eating immediately. She was a whole chicken pie ahead of me, and she was still hungry. I gave her a lightly edited recap of Lowrey's information. Everything, really, except for the words Missouri, Carlton, and Riley.

She asked, 'What made you give him Audrey Shaw's name in the first place?'

'Flip of a coin,' I said. 'A fifty-fifty chance. Either Butler's buddy screwed up her case numbers or she didn't. I didn't want to assume one way or the other.'

'Does this stuff help us?'

Small words, but big concepts. *Help*, and *us*. It didn't help me. Not with Janice May Chapman, anyway. With Rosemary McClatchy and Shawna Lindsay, I wasn't so sure any more. Lowrey's news cast a strange new light on them. But Lowrey's news helped Deveraux, that was for damn sure. With Chapman, at least. It decreased the chances about a billionfold that her local population was involved with her in any way at all. Because it increased the chances about a billionfold that mine was.

I said, 'It might help us. It might narrow things down a little. I mean, if a senator has a problem, which of the five or six chains of command is going to react?'

'Senate Liaison,' she said.

'That's where I'm going. The day after tomorrow.'

'How did you know?'

'I didn't.'

'You must have.'

'It was just a random choice. I needed a reason to be there, that's all.'

'Wait,' she said. 'This makes no sense. Why would the army get involved if a senator had a problem with a girl? That's a civilian matter. I mean, Senate Liaison doesn't get involved every time a politician loses his car keys. There would have to be a military connection. And there's no military connection between a civilian senator and his civilian ex-girlfriend, no matter where she lives.'

I didn't answer.

She looked at me. 'Are you saying there *is* a connection?'

I said, 'I'm not saying anything. Literally. Watch my lips. They aren't moving.'

'There can't be a connection. Chapman wasn't in the army, and there certainly aren't any senators in the army.'

I said nothing.

'Did Chapman have a brother in the army? Is that it? A cousin? A relative of some kind? Jesus, is her *father* in the army? What would he be now, mid-fifties? The

340

only reason to stay in at that age is if you're having fun, and the only way to have fun at that age is to be a very senior officer. Is that what we're saying here? Chapman was a general's daughter? Or Shaw, or whatever her real name was?'

I said nothing.

She said, 'Lowrey told you she got the intern job because of family connections, right? So what else can that mean? We're talking about having an actual senator who owes you favours here. That's a big deal. Her father must be a two-star at least.'

I said nothing.

She looked straight at me.

'I can tell what you're thinking,' she said.

I said nothing.

'I didn't get it right,' she said. 'That's what you're thinking. I'm on the wrong track. Chapman had no relatives in uniform. It's something else.'

I said nothing.

She said, 'Maybe it's the other way around. Maybe the senator is the one with a relative in uniform.'

'You're missing the point,' I said. 'If Janice May Chapman was a sudden short-term problem who required a sudden short-term solution, why was she killed in exactly the same way as two other unconnected women six and nine months previously?'

'Are you saying it's a coincidence? Nothing to do with the senator connection?'

'It could be that way,' I said.

'Then why the big panic?'

'Because they're worried about blowback. In general.

They don't want any kind of taint coming near a particular unit.'

'The one with the senator's relative in it?'

'Let's not go there.'

'But they weren't worried about blowback before? Six and nine months ago?'

'They didn't know about six and nine months ago. Why would they? But Chapman jumped out at them. She had two kinds of extra visibility. Her name was in the files, and she was white.'

'Suppose it wasn't a coincidence?'

'Then someone was very smart,' I said. 'They took care of a sudden short-term problem by copycatting an MO that had been used before in two unconnected cases. Excellent camouflage.'

'So you're saying there could be two killers here?'

'Possible,' I said. 'Maybe McClatchy and Lindsay were regular everyday homicides, and Chapman was made to look like them. By someone else.'

We finished our desserts and drank our cups of coffee. Deveraux told me she had work to do. I asked her if she would mind if I went to see Emmeline McClatchy one more time.

'Why?' she asked.

'Boyfriends,' I said. 'Apparently both Lindsay and Chapman were stepping out with a soldier who owned a blue car. I'm wondering if McClatchy is going to make it a trifecta.'

'That's a long walk.'

'I'll find a shortcut,' I said. I was beginning to piece

342

together the local geography in my head. No need to walk three sides of a square, first north to the Kelham road, then east, then south again to the McClatchy shack. I was already roughly on the same latitude. I figured I could find a way across the railroad track well short of the official crossing. A straight shot east. One side of the square.

Deveraux said, 'Be gentle with her. She's still very upset.'

'I'm sure she always will be,' I said. 'I imagine these things don't fade too fast.'

'And don't say anything about pregnancy.'

'I won't,' I said.

I headed south on Main Street, in the general direction of Dr Merriam's office, but I planned to turn east well before I got there. And I found a place to do just that within about three hundred yards. I saw the mouth of a dirt road nested in the trees. It had a rusted fire hydrant ten yards in, which meant there had to be houses somewhere farther on. I found the first one a hundred feet later. It was a tumbledown, swaybacked affair, but it had people living in it. At first I thought they were the McKinney cousins, because it was that kind of a place, and because it had a black brush-painted pick-up truck standing on a patch of dirt that might once have been a lawn. But it was a different make of truck. Different age, different size, but the same approach to maintenance. Clearly northeastern Mississippi was not fertile ground for spray-painting franchises.

I passed two more places that were similar in every

343

way. The fourth house I came to was worse. It was abandoned. It had a mailbox entirely hidden by tall grass. Its driveway was overgrown. It had bushes and brambles up against the door and the windows. It had weeds in the gutters, and green slime on the walls, and a cracked foundation pierced by creeper tendrils thicker than my wrists. It was standing alone in a couple of acres of what once might have been meadow or pasture, but was now nothing more than a briar patch crowded with sapling trees about six feet tall. The place must have been empty for a long time. More than months. A couple of years, maybe.

But it had fresh tyre tracks across its turn-in.

Seasonal rains had washed dirt down various small slopes and left a mirror-smooth puddle of mud in the dip between the road and the driveway. Seasonal heat had baked the mud to powder, like cement straight from the bag. A four-wheeled vehicle had crossed it twice, in and out. Broad tyres, with treads designed for use on regular pavement. Not new, but well inflated. The tread pattern was exactly captured. The marks were recent. Certainly put there after the last time it had rained.

I detoured a couple of steps to avoid leaving footprints next to the tyre marks. I jumped over the dip and fought through a tangle of waist-high crap until I got next to the driveway. I could see where the tyres had crushed the weeds. There were broken stalks. They had bled dark-green juice. Some of the stronger plants had not broken. They had whipped back upright, and some of them were smeared with oil from the underside of an engine.

Whoever had rolled down the driveway had not

344

entered the house. That was clear. None of the rampant growth around the doors or the windows had been disturbed. So I walked on, past the house, past a small tractor barn, out to the space behind. There was a belt of trees ahead of me, and another to my left, and another to my right. It was a lonely spot. Not directly overlooked, except by birds, of which there were two in the air above me. They were turkey vultures. They were floating and looping endlessly.

I moved on. There was a long-abandoned vegetable garden, ringed by a rusted rabbit fence. An archaeologist might have been able to tell what had been grown there. I couldn't. Further on was a long high mound of something green and vigorous. An old hedge, maybe, untrimmed for a decade and run to seed. Behind it were two utilitarian structures, placed there so as not to be visible from the house, presumably. The first structure was an old wooden shed, rotting and listing and down at one corner.

The other structure was a deer trestle.

FIFTY-SEVEN

The deer trestle was a big thing, built in an old-fashioned A-frame style from solid timbers. It was at least seven feet tall. I could have walked under the top rail with no trouble at all. I guessed the idea was to back up a pick-up truck and dump a dead animal out of the bed on to the dirt between the A-frames, and then to tie ropes to the animal's hind legs, and then to flip the ropes up over the top rail, and then to use muscle power or the pick-up itself to haul the animal up in the air so that it hung vertically and upside down, ready for the butcher's knife. Age-old technology, but not one I had ever used. If I wanted a steak, I went to the Officers' Club. Much less work.

The trestle could have been fifty years old or more. Its timbers were mature, seasoned, and solid. Some kind of native hardwood. There was a little green moss growing on its northern exposures, which faced me. Its top rail had been worn to a smooth polish over the years, by the ropes that had run over it. There was no way of knowing how long ago it had last been used. Or how recently.

But the dirt between its spread legs had been

disturbed, and recently. That was clear. The top two or three inches had been dug up and removed. What should have been beaten and blackened earth as old as the frame itself was now a shallow pit about three feet square.

There was no other useful evidence in the yard. None at all, except for the missing dirt, and the tyre marks that had not come from a pick-up truck or any other kind of utilitarian vehicle. The shed next to the trestle was empty. And I checked the house again as I passed by on the trip back to the road, just to be sure, but it had not been entered. The windows were filmed with grey organic scum, which also lay less visibly on the siding and the doors and the door handles. Nothing had been touched. No marks, no smears. There were misty spider webs everywhere, unbroken. There was vegetation of every kind, some of it thorned and brawny, some of it limp and delicate, all of it growing exactly where it wanted to, up stoops, across doorways, none of it pushed aside or cut back or otherwise disturbed.

I stopped at the mouth of the driveway and parted the long grass around the mailbox with my hands. The mailbox was a standard Postal Service item, standard size, once painted grey, now no colour at all, flecked with rust in fine lines where the curve of the sheet metal had stressed the enamel finish. It was set on a post that had started its service as a six-by-six, but was now wizened away to a twisted baulk that retained only its core. There had been a name on the box, spelled out in stick-on letters printed on forward-leaning rectangles, in a style popular long ago. They had been peeled off, possibly as a last gesture when the home was abandoned, but they had left dry webs of adhesive residue behind, like fingerprints.

There had been eight letters on the box.

I jumped the ditch again and continued east. I passed two more houses, widely spaced, occupied, but in no kind of good condition. After the last one the road narrowed and its surface went pitted and lumpy. It burrowed into a wall of trees and ran on straight. The trees crowded in from the sides and left a thoroughfare barely a yard wide. I pressed on regardless, whipped and clawed by branches. Fifty paces later I came out the other side and found the railroad track right there in front of me, running left to right, blocking my path. At that location it was up on a raised earth berm about a yard high. The terrain in that part of Mississippi looked pretty flat to the human eye, but straining locomotives see things differently. They want every dip filled in, and every peak shaved level.

I scrambled up the yard of earth and crunched over the ballast stones and stood on a tie. To my right the track ran straight all the way south to the Gulf. To my left it ran straight north, all the way to wherever it went. I could see the road crossing far in the distance, and the old water tower. The rails either side of me were burnished bright by the passage of iron wheels. Ahead of me were more low trees and bushes, and beyond them was a field, and beyond the field were houses.

I heard a helicopter, somewhere east and a little

north. I scanned the horizon and saw a Blackhawk in the air, about three miles away. Heading for Kelham, I assumed. I listened to the *whap-whap-whap* of its rotor and the whine of its turbine, and I watched it maintain direction but lose height as it came in to land. Then I scrambled down the far side of the earth berm and headed onward through the next belt of trees.

I hiked across the field that came after that and stepped over a wire and found myself on a street I figured was parallel with Emmeline McClatchy's. In fact I could see the back of the house with the beer signs in the windows. The ad-hoc bar. But between it and me were other houses, all surrounded by yards. Private property. In the yard dead ahead of me two guys were sitting in white plastic chairs. Old men. They were watching me. By the look of them they were taking a break from some kind of hard physical labour. I stopped at their fence line and asked, 'Would you do me a favour?'

They didn't answer in words, but they cocked their chins up like they were listening. I said, 'Would you let me walk through your yard? I need to get to the next street.'

The guy on the left asked, 'Why?' He had a fringe of white beard, but no moustache.

I said, 'I'm visiting with a person who lives there.'

'Who?'

'Emmeline McClatchy.'

'You with the army?'

I said, 'Yes, I am.'

'Then Emmeline doesn't want a visit from you. Nor does anyone else around here.'

'Why not?'

'Because of Bruce Lindsay, most recently.'

'Was he a friend of yours?'

'He surely was.'

'Bullshit,' I said. 'He told me he had no friends. You all called him deformed and shunned him and made his life a misery. So don't get up on your high horse now.'

'You got some mouth on you, son.'

'More than just a mouth.'

'You going to shoot us too?'

'I'm sorely tempted.'

The old guy cracked a grin. 'Come on through. But be nice to Emmeline. This thing with Bruce Lindsay shook her up all over again.'

I walked the depth of their yard and heard the Blackhawk again, taking off from Kelham, far in the distance. A short visit for somebody, or a delivery, or a pick-up. I saw it rise above the treetops, a distant speck, nose down, accelerating north.

I stepped over a wire fence at the end of the yard. Now I was in the bar's lot. Still private, technically, but in principle bars welcome passers-by rather than run them off. And the place was deserted, anyway. I looped past the building and made it out to the street unmolested.

And saw an army Humvee easing to a stop outside the McClatchy house.

FIFTY-EIGHT

A Humvee is a very wide vehicle, and it was on a very narrow dirt road. It almost filled it, ditch to ditch. It was painted in standard green and black camouflage colours, and it was very clean. Maybe brand new.

I walked towards it and it came to a stop and the motor shut off. The driver's door opened and a guy climbed down. He was in woodland-pattern BDUs and clean boots. Since before the start of my career battledress uniform had been worn with subdued name tapes and badges of rank, and like everything else in the army the definition of *subdued* had been specified within an inch of its life, to the point where names and ranks were unreadable from more than three or four feet away. An officer-led initiative, for sure. Officers worried about snipers picking them off first. The result was I had no idea who had just gotten out of the Humvee. Could have been a private first class, could have been a two-star general. Three-stars and above don't drive themselves. Not usually. Not on business. Not off duty either. They don't do much of anything themselves.

But I had a clear premonition about who the guy was.

An easy conclusion, actually. Who else was authorized to be out and about? He even looked like me. Same kind of height, same kind of build, similar colouring. It was like looking in a mirror, except he was five years my junior, and it showed in the way he moved. He was bouncing around with plenty of energy. An impartial judge would have said he looked young and over-exuberant. The same judge would have said I looked old and over-tired. Such was the contrast between us.

He watched me approach, curious about who I was, curious about a white man in a black neighbourhood. I let him gawp until I was six feet away. My eyesight is as good as it ever was, and I can read subdued tapes from further than I should, especially on bright sunlit Mississippi afternoons.

His tapes said: *Munro. U.S. Army.*

He had little black oak leaves on his collar, to show he was a major. He had a field cap on his head, the same camouflage pattern as his blouse and his pants. He had fine lines around his eyes, which were about the only evidence he wasn't born yesterday.

I had the advantage, because my shirt was plain. Civilian issue. No name tape. So I stood there for a moment in silence. I could smell diesel from his ride, and rubber from its tyres. I could hear its engine tick as it cooled. I could hear the breeze in Emmeline McClatchy's shade tree.

Then I stuck out my hand and said, 'Jack Reacher.'

He took it and said, 'Duncan Munro.'

I asked, 'What brings you here?'

He said, 'Let's sit in the truck a spell.'

*   *   *

A Humvee is equally wide inside, but most of the space is taken up by a gigantic transmission tunnel. The front seats are small and far apart. It was like sitting in adjacent traffic lanes. I think the separation suited both our moods.

Munro said, 'The situation is changing.'

I said, 'The situation is always changing. Get used to it.'

'The officer in question has been relieved of his command.'

'Reed Riley?'

'We're not supposed to use that name.'

'Who's going to know? You think this truck is wired for sound?'

'I'm just trying to maintain protocol.'

'Was that him in the Blackhawk?'

Munro nodded. 'He's on his way back to Benning. Then they're going to move him on and hide him away somewhere.'

'Why?'

'There was some big panic two hours ago. The phone lines were burning up. I don't know why.'

'Kelham just lost its quarantine force, that's why.'

'That again? There never was a quarantine force. I told you that.'

'I just met them. Bunch of civilian yahoos.'

'Like Ruby Ridge?'

'But less professional.'

'Why do people do stupid shit like that?'

'They envy our glamorous lives.'

'What happened to them?'

'I chased them away.'

'So then someone felt he had to withdraw Riley. You're not going to be popular.'

'I don't want to be popular. I want to get the job done. This is the army, not high school.'

'He's a senator's son. He's making his name. Did you know the Marine Corps employs lobbyists?'

I said, 'I heard that.'

'This was our version.'

I looked out my window at the McClatchy place, at its low roof, its mud-stained siding, its mean windows, its spreading tree. I asked, 'Why did you come here?'

'Same reason you chased the yahoos away,' Munro said. 'I'm trying to get the job done.'

'In what way?'

'I checked out the other two women you mentioned. There were FYI memos in the XO's files. Then I cross-referenced bits and pieces of information I picked up along the way. It seems like Captain Riley is something of a ladies' man. Since he got here he's had a string of girlfriends longer than my dick. It's likely both Janice Chapman and Shawna Lindsay were on the list. I want to see if Rosemary McClatchy will make it three for three.'

'That's why I'm here, too.'

'Great minds think alike,' Munro said. 'Or fools never differ.'

'Did you bring his picture?'

He unbuttoned his right breast pocket, just below his name. He pulled out a slim black notebook and opened

354

it and slid a photograph from between its pages. He handed it to me, arm's length across the transmission tunnel.

Captain Reed Riley. The first time I had seen his face. The photograph was in colour, possibly taken for a passport or some other civilian document that prohibited headgear or other visual obstructions. He looked to be in his late twenties. He was broad but chiselled, somewhere halfway between bulky and slender. He was tanned and had very white teeth, some of which were on display behind an easy grin. He had brown hair buzzed short, and wise empty eyes creased at the corners with webs of fine lines. He looked steady, competent, hard, and full of shit. He looked exactly like every infantry captain I had ever seen.

I handed the picture back, arm's length across the transmission tunnel.

I said, 'We'll be lucky to get a definitive ID. I bet all Rangers look the same to old Mrs McClatchy.'

'Only one way to find out,' Munro said, and opened his door. I got out on my side and waited while he looped around the stubby hood. He said, 'I'll tell you something else that came up with the cross-referencing. Something you might like to know. Sheriff Deveraux is not a lesbian. She's a notch on Riley's bedpost too. Apparently they were dating less than a year ago.'

And then he walked on ahead of me, to Emmeline McClatchy's door.

Emmeline McClatchy opened up after Munro's second knock. She greeted us with polite reserve. She remembered me from before. She paid close attention as Munro introduced himself, and then she invited us inside, to a small room that had two wooden wheelback chairs either side of a fireplace, and a rag rug on the floor. The ceiling was low and the dimensions were cramped and the air smelled of cooked food. There were three framed photographs on the wall. One was Martin Luther King, and one was President Clinton, and the third was Rosemary McClatchy, from the same series as the picture I had seen in the Sheriff's Department's file, but possibly even more spectacular. A friend with a camera, one roll of film, a sunny afternoon, a frame, a hammer and a nail, and that was all that was left of a life.

Emmeline and I took the chairs by the fireplace and left Munro standing on the rug. In the tiny room he looked as big as I felt, and just as awkward, and just as clumsy, and just as alien. He took the photograph from his pocket again and held it face down against his chest. He said, 'Mrs McClatchy, we need to ask you about your daughter Rosemary's friends.'

Emmeline McClatchy said, 'My daughter Rosemary had lots of friends.'

Munro said, 'In particular one young man from the base she might have been seeing.'

'Seeing?'

'Stepping out with. Dating, in other words.'

'Let me see the picture.'

Munro bent down and handed it over. She held it this way and that in the light from the window. She studied it. She asked, 'Is this man suspected of killing the white girl?'

Munro said, 'We're not sure. We can't rule him out.'

'Nobody brought pictures to me when Rosemary was killed. Nobody brought pictures to Mrs Lindsay when Shawna was killed. Why is that?'

Munro said, 'Because the army made a bad mistake. There's no excuse for it. All I can say is it would have been different if I had been involved back then. Or Major Reacher here. Beyond that, all I can do is apologize.'

She looked at him, and so did I. Then she looked at the picture again and said, 'This man's name is Reed Riley. He's a captain in the 75th Ranger Regiment. Rosemary said he commanded Bravo Company, whatever that is.'

'So they were dating?'

'Almost four months. She was talking about a life together.'

'Was he?'

'Men will say anything to get what they want.'

'When did it end?'

'Two weeks before she was killed.'

'Why did it end?'

'She didn't tell me.'

'Did you have an opinion?'

Emmeline McClatchy said, 'I think she got pregnant.'

FIFTY-NINE

There was silence in the small room for a moment, and then Emmeline McClatchy said, 'A mother can always tell. She looked different. She acted different. She even smelled different. At first she was happy, and then later she was miserable. I didn't ask her anything. I thought she would come to me on her own. You know, in her own good time. But she didn't get the chance.'

Munro was quiet for a beat, like a mark of respect, and then he asked, 'Did you ever see Captain Riley again after that?'

Emmeline McClatchy nodded. 'He came by to offer his condolences, a week after her body was found.'

'Do you think he killed her?'

'You're the policeman, young man, not me.'

'I think a mother can always tell.'

'Rosemary said his father was an important man. She wasn't sure where or how. Politics, perhaps. Something where image matters. I think a black girlfriend was a good thing for Captain Riley, but a pregnant girlfriend wasn't.'

*   *   *

Emmeline McClatchy wouldn't be pushed any further. We said our goodbyes and walked back to the Humvee. Munro said, 'This is looking real bad.'

I asked him, 'Did you speak to Shawna Lindsay's mother too?'

'She wouldn't say a word to me. She chased me away with a stick.'

'How solid is the information about Sheriff Deveraux?'

'Rock solid. They dated, he ended it, she wasn't happy. Then Rosemary McClatchy was next up, as far as I can piece it together.'

'Was it his car that got wrecked on the track?'

'According to the Oregon DMV it was. Via the plate you found. A blue 57 Chevy. A piece of shit, not a show car.'

'Did he have an explanation?'

'No, he had a lawyer.'

'Can you prove he was Janice Chapman's boyfriend too?'

'Not beyond a reasonable doubt. She was a party girl. She was seen with a lot of guys. She can't have been dating all of them.'

'She was known as a party girl at Tulane, too.'

'Is that where she went?'

'Apparently.'

He smiled. 'If all the Tulane coeds were laid end to end, I wouldn't be in the least surprised.'

'Did you know she wasn't really Janice Chapman?'

'What do you mean?'

'She was born Audrey Shaw. She changed her name three years ago.'

'Why?'

'Politics,' I said. 'She was coming off a two-year affair with Carlton Riley.'

I left him with that piece of information, and walked away south. He drove away north. This time I didn't cut through anyone's yard. I walked around the block, like a responsible citizen, and stepped over the wire and hiked across the field and found the dirt track through the trees. I was back on Main Street less than twenty minutes later. Five minutes after that I was inside the Sheriff's Department. One minute after that I was in Deveraux's office. She was behind her desk. The desk was covered in a sea of paper.

I said, 'We need to talk.'

SIXTY

Deveraux looked up at me, a little alarmed. Something in my voice, maybe. She said, 'Talk about what?'

I asked her, 'Did you ever date a guy from the base?'

'What base? You mean Kelham?'

'Yes, Kelham.'

'That's kind of personal, isn't it?'

'Did you?'

'Of course not. Are you crazy? Those guys are my biggest problem. You know how it is between a military population and local law enforcement. It would have been the worst kind of conflict of interest.'

'Do you socialize with any of them?'

'No, for the same reason.'

'Do you know any of them?'

'Barely,' she said. 'I've toured the base and met some of the senior officers, in a formal way. Which is to be expected. They're trying to deal with the same kind of problems I am.'

'OK,' I said.

'Why are you asking?'

'Munro was at the McClatchy place. Rosemary McClatchy and Shawna Lindsay seem to have dated the same guy. Janice Chapman also, probably. Munro heard you had dated the guy too.'

'That's bullshit. I haven't dated a guy in two years. Couldn't you tell?'

I sat down.

'I had to ask,' I said. 'I'm sorry.'

'Who was the guy?'

'I can't tell you.'

'You have to tell me. Don't you think? McClatchy and Lindsay are my cases. Therefore it's relevant information. And I have a right to know if some guy is taking my name in vain.'

'Reed Riley,' I said.

'Never heard of him,' she said.

Then she said, 'Wait a minute. Did you say Riley?'

I didn't answer.

She said, 'Oh my God. Carlton Riley's son? He's at Kelham? I had no idea.'

I said nothing.

'Oh my God,' she said again. 'That explains a whole lot.'

I said, 'It was his car on the railroad track. And Emmeline McClatchy thinks he got Rosemary pregnant. I didn't ask her. She came right out with it.'

'I need to talk to him.'

'You can't. They just choppered him out of there.'

'To where?'

'What's the most remote army post in the world?'

'I don't know.'

'Neither do I. But a buck gets ten that's where he'll be tonight.'

'Why would he say he dated me?'

'Ego,' I said. 'Maybe he wanted his pals to believe he had collected the whole set. The four most beautiful women in Carter Crossing. The Brannan brothers at the bar told me he was a big dog and always had arm candy.'

'I'm not arm candy.'

'Maybe not on the inside.'

'His father probably knows the guy Janice Chapman had the affair with. They're right there in the Senate together.'

I said nothing.

She looked right at me.

She said, 'Oh, no.'

I said, 'Oh, yes.'

'The same woman? Father and son? That's seriously messed up.'

'Munro can't prove it. Neither can we.'

'We can infer it. This all is way too much hoopla for a theoretical worry about blowback in general.'

'Maybe,' I said. 'Maybe not. Who knows how these people think?'

'Whatever, you can't go to D.C. Not now. It's far too dangerous. You'll be walking around with the world's biggest target on your back. Senate Liaison has got a lot invested in Carlton Riley. They won't let you screw things up. Believe me, you're nothing to them compared to a good relationship with the Armed Services Committee.'

She said all that and then her phone rang and she picked up and listened for a minute. She covered the mouthpiece with her palm and said, 'This is the Oxford PD asking about the dead journalist. I want to tell them the proven perpetrator was shot to death by police after resisting arrest, case closed.'

I said, 'Fine with me.'

So she told them that, and then she had to call a whole long list of state departments and county authorities, so I wandered out of her office and she got so busy I didn't talk to her again until dinner at nine o'clock.

At dinner we talked about her father's house. She ordered her cheeseburger and I got a roast beef sandwich and I asked her, 'What was it like growing up here?'

'It was weird,' she said. 'Obviously I didn't have anything to compare it to, and we didn't get television until I was ten, and we never went to the movies, but even so I sensed there had to be more out there. We all did. We all had island fever.'

Then she asked where I grew up, so I went through as much of the long list as I could remember. Conceived in the Pacific, born in West Berlin when my father was assigned to the embassy there, a dozen different bases before elementary school, education all over the world, cuts and bruises picked up fighting in hot wet alleys in Manila healing days later in cold wet quarters in Belgium, near NATO headquarters, then running across the original assailants a month later in San Diego and resuming the conflict. Then eventually West Point, and a restless, always-moving career of my own, in some of the same places but in many new and different places too, in that the army's global footprint was not identical to the Marine Corps'.

She asked, 'What's the longest you were ever in one spot?'

I said, 'Less than six months, probably.'

'What was your dad like?'

'He was quiet,' I said. 'He was a birdwatcher. But his job was to kill people as fast and efficiently as possible, and he was always aware of it.'

'Was he good to you?'

'Yes, in an old-fashioned way. Was yours?'

She nodded. 'Old-fashioned would be a good way to describe it. He thought I'd get married and he'd have to come all the way to Tupelo or Oxford to visit me.'

'Where was your house?'

'South on Main Street until it curves, and then first on the left. A little dirt road. Fourth house on the right.'

'Is it still there?'

'Just about.'

'Didn't it rent again?'

'No, my dad was sick for a spell before he died, and he let the place go. The bank that owned it wasn't paying attention. It's more or less a ruin now.'

'All overgrown, with slime on the walls and a cracked foundation? A big old hedge in back? Eight letters on the mailbox?'

'How do you know all that?'

'I was there,' I said. 'I passed by on my way to the McClatchy place.'

She didn't answer.

I said, 'I saw the deer trestle.'

She didn't answer.

I said, 'And I saw the dirt in the trunk of your car. When you gave me the shotgun shells.'

SIXTY-ONE

The waitress came by and picked up our empty plates and took our orders for pie. Then she went away again and Deveraux was left looking at me, a little crestfallen. A little embarrassed, I thought. She said, 'I did a stupid thing.'

I said, 'What kind of stupid thing?'

'I hunt,' she said. 'Now and then. Just for fun. Deer, mostly. Just for something to do. I give the meat to the old folks, like Emmeline McClatchy. They don't eat well otherwise. Pork, sometimes, if a neighbour is butchering a pig. If the neighbour thinks to share. But that doesn't always happen. Sometimes the neighbours can't afford to share.'

'I remember,' I said. 'Emmeline had deer meat in the pot when we were there the first time. She offered us lunch. You declined.'

She nodded. 'No point in giving and then taking away. I got that deer a week ago. I couldn't take it back to the hotel, obviously. So I used my dad's place. I always have, since I came back here. That's a good trestle. But then you came up with your theory about Janice Chapman.

I didn't know you very well at that point. I thought you might get on the phone to HQ. I had visions of Blackhawks in the air, finding every trestle in the county. So I sent you off to ID the wrecked car so you would be out of the way for an hour, and I went over and dug up the blood.'

'Tests would have proved it came from an animal.'

'I know,' she said. 'But how long would that have taken? I don't even know where the nearest lab is. Atlanta, maybe. It could have taken two weeks or more. And I can't afford to be under a cloud for two weeks or more. I literally can't afford it. This is the only job I have. I don't know where I'd get another one. And voters are weird. They always remember the suspicion, and they never remember the outcome.'

I thought about my old pal Stan Lowrey, back on post, with his want ads. A brave new world, for all of us.

'OK,' I said. 'But it was a fairly dumb thing to do.'

'I know it was. I panicked a little bit.'

'Do you know other hunters? And other trestles?'

'Some.'

'Because I still think that's how those women were killed. I don't see how it could be done any other way.'

'I agree. Which is why I panicked.'

'So sooner or later we might need to get those Blackhawks in the air.'

'Unless we find Reed Riley first and ask him some questions.'

'Reed Riley is gone,' I said. 'He's probably army liaison at Thule Air Force Base by now.'

'Which is where?'

'Northern Greenland,' I said. 'The top of the world. It's certainly the air force's most remote place. I was there once. I was on a C5 that had a problem. We had to land there. It's part of the distant early-warning system. No sunlight for four months of the year. They've got radar that can see a tennis serve three thousand miles away.'

'Did you get their phone number?'

I smiled. 'We're going to have to do it another way. I'll see what comes out of the woodwork the day after tomorrow.'

She said nothing in reply to that. We ate our pie slowly. We had time to kill. At that point the midnight train was probably just easing its way out of the yards in Biloxi.

Deveraux was still worried about the old man in the hotel, and she didn't want to repeat her charade at the top of the stairs, so I gave her my key and we left the diner separately, ten minutes apart, which left me with the check and time for a third cup of coffee. Then I strolled down the street and nodded to the guy behind the desk and headed up the stairs and tapped on my own door. Deveraux opened up instantly and I stepped inside. She had taken her shoes and her gun belt off, but everything else was still in place. Uniform shirt, uniform pants, ponytail. All good.

We went at it like a junkie heats a spoon, half-fast, half-slow, full of intense anticipation, willing to make the investment, barely able to wait for the payoff. She started by taking the elastic out of her hair, shaking it loose, smiling at me from behind its thick dark curtain.

She undid the first three buttons on her shirt, and the weight of her name plate and badges and stars dragged the loose material askew and showed me a deep triangle of bare skin. I took off my shoes and my socks and pulled my shirt tails out of my pants. She put one hand on the fourth button on her shirt, and the other on the button on the waistband of her pants, and she said, 'Your choice.'

Which was a tough choice to make, but I thought long and hard about it and came to a firm conclusion. I said, 'Pants,' and she popped the button and a long minute later she was barefoot and bare-legged in just her tan uniform shirt. I said, 'Now you get the same choice,' and she went the other way and I took off my shirt. This time she asked about my shrapnel scar, and I gave her the short version, which was all about unfortunate timing at the start of my career, and a routine liaison visit to a Marine encampment in Beirut, Lebanon, and being passed by a truck which then blew itself up near the barracks entrance, a hundred yards from where I was standing.

She said, 'I heard about an army MP there. That was you?'

I said, 'I'm not sure who else was there.'

'You went into the ruin and helped people.'

'Only by accident,' I said. 'I was looking for a medic. For myself. I could see what I had eaten for dinner the night before.'

'You got the Silver Star.'

'And blood poisoning,' I said. 'I could have done without either thing.'

370

I undid my waistband button and she undid the last of her shirt buttons and then we were in nothing but our underwear. That state of affairs did not endure long. We set my shower running and climbed into the tub together and pulled the curtain. We grabbed soap and shampoo and lathered up and washed each other up and down, side to side, inside and out. No one on earth could have faulted our standards of hygiene, or our approach to insuring them. We stayed in the shower until Toussaint's tank ran cool, and then we grabbed enough towels to make sure we wouldn't put puddles in my bed, and then the serious business began. She tasted warm and slick and soapy, and I'm sure I did too. She was lithe and strong and full of energy. We were very patient. I figured the midnight train was by then north of Columbus, south of Aberdeen, maybe forty miles and forty minutes away.

And forty minutes is a good long time. Halfway through it there was precious little we didn't know about each other. I knew the way she moved, and what she liked, and what she loved. She knew the same about me. I got to know the way her heart hammered against her ribs, and the way her ribs moved as she panted, and the difference between one kind of panting and another. She got to know equivalent facts about me, the early-warning catch in my throat, the things to do to make my skin flush red, where I liked to be touched, and what drove me absolutely crazy.

Then we began, a long slow build-up, with a time certain in mind, like an invading army approaching a D-Day H-Hour, like infantrymen watching the beach come closer, like pilots seeing the target grow large in the bomb sights. Long and slow, closer and closer, long and slow, for five whole minutes. Then eventually faster and harder, faster and harder, faster and harder. The glass on my bathroom shelf began to tinkle right on cue. It shook and rattled. The pipes in the walls made muffled metallic sounds. The French doors shook, one sound from the wood, another from the glass, a third from the latch. The floorboards vibrated like drum skins, a discarded shoe rolled right side up, her sheriff's star beat a tiny tattoo against the wood, the Beretta in my pocket thumped and bounced, the bedhead beat on the wall in a rhythm not our own.

The midnight train.

Right on time.

All aboard.

But this time it was different.

And wrong.

Not us, but the train. Its sound was not the same. Its pitch was low. It was suddenly slowing hard. Its distant rumble was overlaid with the binding, grinding, screeching howl of brakes. I saw in my mind iron blocks jammed against the rims, locked wheels, long showers of superheated sparks in the night-time air, one car after the other slamming and buffeting the next in front, as the mile-long length telescoped together behind the slowing locomotive. Deveraux slipped out from under me and sat up straight, her eyes nowhere, listening hard. The grinding howl kept on going, loud, mournful, primitive, impossibly long, and then eventually it started to fade, partly because the train's momentum had carried it far beyond the crossing, and partly because it was finally almost at a stop.

By my side Deveraux whispered, 'Oh, no.'

SIXTY-TWO

We dressed fast and were out on the street two minutes later. Deveraux stopped and took two flashlights from her trunk. She lit one up and gave one to me. We used the alley between the hardware store and the pharmacy, past Janice Chapman's sad pile of sand, between the loan office and Brannan's bar, and out to the beaten earth beyond. She walked on ahead of me. Almost limping. Which didn't surprise me. I was on my knees. But she kept on going, dogged, committed, reluctant but determined to serve.

She was going to the railroad track, of course. She scrambled up the packed stones and stepped over the bright steel on to the ties. She turned south. I followed her. I figured the engineer would be about twenty minutes behind us. I figured his train would weigh about eight thousand tons. And I knew a little about trains that weigh eight thousand tons. Sometimes MPs are traffic cops like any other cops, but our traffic is specialized, in that it includes tank trains, which usually weigh about eight thousand tons, and part of directing traffic at that level is understanding it takes a tank train about a mile to stop even in a panic. And it takes an average man twenty minutes to walk a mile, so we would get there twenty minutes before the engineer did.

Which was not a privilege.

Although I doubted there would be much left to find.

We pressed on, almost jogging, trying to match awkward strides to the intervals between the ties. Our flashlight beams bounced and swung, through a fading cloud of smoke left behind by the train's tortured brakes. I figured we were headed right where I had already walked twice that day, where the path through the field to the east crossed the track before heading into the woods to the west. Deveraux's own childhood street, in effect, more or less. She must have been thinking about the same place, because as we approached the spot she slowed right down and started playing her flashlight beam carefully left and right.

I did the same thing, and it fell to me to find it. All that was left. Except, I supposed, a red pulverized mist that must have filled the air and touched everything within a hundred yards, a molecule here, a molecule there.

It was a human foot, amputated just above the ankle. The cut was clean and straight. Not ripped or torn or ragged. It was a neat straight line. That line had been hit by some unbelievable instantaneous shockwave, some kind of savage subsonic pulse, like an acoustic weapon. I had seen such a thing before. And so had Deveraux. Most traffic cops have.

The shoe was still in place. A polished black item, plain and modest, with a low heel and a strap and a button. The stocking was still in place under it. Its top edge looked like it had been trimmed with scissors. Under its beige opacity was dark ebony skin, ending neatly in what looked like a plaster-cast cross-section displayed in a medical school lecture hall. Bone, veins, flesh.

'Those were her church shoes,' Deveraux said. 'She was a nice woman at heart. I am so, so sorry this happened.'

'I never met her,' I said. 'She was out. That was the first thing the kid ever said to me. My mom's out, he said.'

We sat on a tie about five yards north of the foot and waited for the engineer. He joined us fifteen minutes later. There wasn't much he could tell us. Just the lonely glare of the headlight, and the briefest subliminal flash of a white lining inside a black coat falling open, and then it was all over long ago.

'Her church suit,' Deveraux said. 'Black gabardine, white lining.'

Then the engineer had slammed on the brakes, as he was required to by railroad policy and federal regulations and state laws, all of which were a totally pointless waste of time, in his opinion. Stress on the train, stress on the track, and for what? A mile's walk, and nothing when he got there. It had happened to him before.

He and Deveraux exchanged various reference numbers and names and addresses, again as per regulations, and Deveraux asked him if he was OK or wanted help in any way, but he brushed the concerns aside and set off walking north again, a mile back to his cab, not at all shaken up, just weary with routine.

*　　　*　　　*

We walked back to Main Street, past the hotel, to the Sheriff's Department. No one was on duty at night, so Deveraux let us in with a key and turned on the lights. She called Pellegrino and told him to come back in on overtime, and she called the doctor and told him he had more duties to perform. Neither one was happy, but both were quick. They arrived almost together within a matter of minutes. Maybe they had heard the train too.

Deveraux sent them off together to collect the remains. We waited, not saying much, and they were back within half an hour. The doctor left again for his office, and Deveraux told Pellegrino to drive me to Memphis. Much earlier than I had planned, but I would have wanted it no other way.

SIXTY-THREE

I didn't go back to the hotel. I left directly from the Sheriff's Department, with nothing except cash in one pocket and the Beretta in the other. We saw no passing traffic. No big surprise. It was the dead of night, and we were far from anywhere. Pellegrino didn't talk. He was mute with fatigue, or resentment, or something. He just drove. He used the same route I had come in on, first the straight-shot east–west road through the forest, and then the minor road I had ridden in the old Chevy truck, and then the dusty two-lane I had ridden in the sagging Buick sedan. We crossed the state line into Tennessee, and passed by Germantown, where I had gotten out of the lumber guy's pick-up, and then we headed through the sleeping southeast suburb and arrived in downtown Memphis, still well before dawn. I got out at the bus depot and Pellegrino drove away without a word. He went around a block and I heard his motor beating between buildings, and then it faded to nothing and he was gone.

The early start gave me a big choice of buses, but the first of them didn't leave for an hour. So I quartered the surrounding low-rent blocks, looking for an all-night diner, and I found a choice of two. I picked the same place I had used for lunch three days previously. It was cheap, and it hadn't killed me. I got coffee from a crusted pot, and bacon and eggs from pans that had been hot since the Nixon administration. Fifty minutes later I was in the back of a bus, heading north and east.

I watched the sun come up through the window on my right, and then I slept for the rest of the six-hour ride. I got out at the same place I had gotten in three days before, at the depot on the edge of the town close to the post where I was based. The town bore no obvious similarity to Carter Crossing, but all the same elements were there. Bars, loan offices, auto parts, gun shops, used-stereo stores, each one of them thriving on the supportive stream of Uncle Sam's military dollars. I walked past them all and headed into open country, stopping at the diner half a mile out for lunch, then continuing onward. I was back on post and in my quarters before two o'clock in the afternoon, which was much earlier than I had expected, and which gave me the chance to improve my plan a little.

The first thing I did was take a long hot shower. Deveraux's scent came up at me in the steam. I dried off and dressed in full-on Class A uniform, soup to nuts. Then I called Stan Lowrey and asked him for a ride back to the bus depot. I figured if I hurried I could get to D.C. by dinner time, which was about twelve hours ahead of schedule. And I told Lowrey to make no secret of where I was going. I figured the more people who knew, and the longer I was there, the better chance things would have to come crawling out of the woodwork.

Washington D.C. at seven o'clock on a Monday evening was going quiet. A company town, where the company was America, and where work never really stopped, but where it moved into quiet confidential locations after five in the afternoon. Salons, bars, fancy restaurants, townhouse parlours, those locations were unknown to me, but I knew the neighbourhoods most likely to contain them. So I skipped the kind of distant chain hotels a lowly O4 like me would normally use, and I headed for the brighter lights and the cleaner streets and the higher prices south of Dupont Circle. Not that I was intending to pay for anything. Legend had it there was a fancy place on Connecticut Avenue with a glitch in its back office, whereby uniformed guests were automatically billed to the Department of the Army. Some one-time conference arrangement that had never been cancelled, or some embittered veteran in charge of the ledgers, no one knew. But the legend said you could be in Arlington Cemetery before the charges caught up with you.

I walked there slowly, in the centre of every sidewalk I used. I was vigilant without appearing to be so. I used store windows as mirrors and gazed around innocently at every crosswalk light. No one was paying me any attention. I was crowded and jostled at times, but only by normal busy people rushing ahead to the next thing on their long agendas. I got to the hotel without any trouble and checked in under my real name and rank, and the legend held up, in that I was asked for no charge card or deposit. All I had to do was sign a piece of paper, which I did, as clearly and legibly as possible. No point in being the bait in a trap, and then hiding your light under a bushel. Not that I had ever been sure what a bushel was. Some kind of a small barrel, I assumed. In which case the light would go out anyway, for want of oxygen.

I rode the elevator to my room and hung my Class A coat on a hanger and called down and asked for dinner to be delivered. Thirty minutes later I was eating a sirloin steak, which would also be billed to the Pentagon. Thirty minutes after that I left the tray in the corridor and went out for a walk, just trawling, just seeing if my passage would pull anyone out of the shadows behind me. But no one reacted, and no one followed. I walked around the Circle and then quartered the blocks beyond it, passing the Iraqi Embassy at one extreme and the Colombian at the other. I saw men and women I took to be federal agents of various kinds, and men and women out of uniform but clearly military, and men and women in uniform, from all four branches of the service, and numerous private citizens in serious suits, but none of them made a move against me. None of them was even slightly interested. I was part of the furniture.

So I went back to the hotel, and I went to bed in my luxurious room, and I waited to see what would happen the next day, which would be Tuesday, the eleventh of March, 1997.

SIXTY-FOUR

I woke up at seven and let the Department of the Army buy me a room service breakfast. By eight I was showered and dressed and out on the street. I figured this was when the serious business would begin. A noon appointment at the Pentagon for a guy based as far away as I was made it likely I would have stayed in town the night before, and Washington hotels were easily monitored. It was that kind of a city. And I wasn't hiding my light under any kind of a small barrel. So I half expected opposition in the lobby, or right outside the street door. I found it in neither place. It was a fresh spring morning, the sun was out, the air was warm, and everything I saw was benign and innocent.

I made a show of strolling out to a newspaper kiosk, even though the hotel supplied publications of every type. I bought a *Post*, and a *Times*, and I lingered and loitered over making change, all slow and unconcerned, but there was no approach and no attack. I carried the papers to a coffee shop and sat at an outside table, in full view of the whole world.

No one looked at me.

By ten o'clock I was full of coffee and had read the ink off both broadsheets and no passer-by had shown any interest in me. I began to think I had outsmarted myself with my choice of hotel. A transient O4 would normally stay in a different kind of place, of which there were simply too many to call. So I began to think it likely the opposition would be focusing on the end of my journey, not a stop along the way. Which would be more efficient for them, anyway. They knew exactly where I was going, and exactly when.

Which meant they would be waiting for me in or around the Pentagon, at or before twelve o'clock. The belly of the beast. Much more dangerous. Less than three miles away, but a different planet in terms of how they would do things.

It was still a beautiful morning, so I walked. Any day could be the last of life or liberty, so small pleasures were always worth pursuing. I went south on 17th Street, past the Executive Office building next to the White House, down the side of the Ellipse, and on to the Mall. I turned away from George Washington's monument and headed for Abraham Lincoln's. I looped left of the old guy and found my way on to the Arlington Memorial Bridge and stepped out over the broad waters of the Potomac. Plenty of people were making the same trip by car. No one else was doing it on foot. The morning joggers were long gone, and the afternoon joggers were still at work.

I stopped halfway across and leaned on the rail. Always a wise precaution on a bridge. Nowhere for a follower to hide. They had to keep on coming. But there was no one behind me. No one ahead of me, either. I gave it five minutes, resting on my elbows like a contemplative soul, but no one came. So I moved on again, another three hundred yards, and I arrived in Virginia. Straight ahead of me in the distance was Arlington National Cemetery. The main gate. I was there five minutes later. I walked into the sea of white stones. Immediately there were graves all around me. Always the best way to approach the Department of Defense. Through the graveyard. For purposes of perspective.

I detoured once to pay my respects to JFK, and again to pay my respects to the Unknown Soldier. I walked behind Henderson Hall, which was a high-level Marine place, and I came out the cemetery's south gate, and there it was: the Pentagon. The world's largest office building. Six and a half million square feet, thirty thousand people, more than seventeen miles of corridors, but just three street doors. Naturally I wanted the southeast entrance. For obvious reasons. So I looped around, staying alert, keeping my distance, until I was able to join the thin stream of people coming in from the Metro station. The stream got thicker as it funnelled towards the doors. It turned out to be a decent crowd. The right kind of people, for my particular purposes. I wanted witnesses. Arrests go bad all the time, sometimes accidentally, sometimes on purpose.

But I got in OK, despite a little uncertainty in the lobby. What I thought was an arrest team turned out to be a new watch coming on duty. A temporary manpower surplus. That was all. So I made it to 3C315 unmolested. Third floor, C ring, nearest to radial corridor number three, bay number fifteen. John James Frazer's office. Senate Liaison. There was no one in there with him. He was all alone. He told me to close the door. I did. He told me to sit down. I did.

He said, 'So what have you got for me?'

I said nothing. I had nothing to say. I hadn't expected to get that far.

He said, 'Good news, I hope.'

'No news,' I said.

'You told me you had the name. That's what your message said.'

'I don't have the name.'

'Then why say so? Why ask to see me?'

I paused a beat.

'It was a shortcut,' I said.

And right there the meeting died on its feet. There was really nothing more to say. Frazer put on a big show of being tolerant. And patient. He called me paranoid. Then he laughed a little. About how I couldn't even get arrested. Then he tried to look concerned. About my state of health, maybe. And certainly about my appearance. The hair and the stubble. He put on the kind of brusque and manly voice an uncle uses with a favourite nephew.

He said, 'You look terrible. There are barbershops here, you know. You should go use one.'

'I can't,' I said. 'I'm supposed to look like this.'

'Because of the undercover role?'

'Yes.'

'But you're not really undercover, are you? I heard the local sheriff rumbled you immediately.'

385

'I think it's worth continuing for the general population. The army is not real popular with them at the moment.'

'Anyway, I expect you'll be withdrawn now. In fact I'm surprised you haven't been withdrawn already. When did you last get orders?'

'Why would I be withdrawn?'

'Because matters appear to be resolved in Mississippi.'

'Do they?'

'I think so. The shootings outside of Kelham were clearly a case of an excess of zeal from an unofficial and unauthorized paramilitary force from another state. The authorities in Tennessee will take care of all that. We can't really stand in their way. Our powers are limited.'

'They were ordered there.'

'No, I don't really think so. Those groups have extensive underground communications. We think it will prove to be a civilian initiative.'

'I don't agree.'

'This is not debate class. Facts are facts. This country is overrun with groups like that. Their agendas are decided internally. There's really no doubt about that.'

'What about the three dead women?'

'The perpetrator has been identified, I believe.'

'When?'

'The news became public three hours ago, I think.'

'Who is it?'

'I don't have all the details.'

'One of ours?'

'No, I believe it was a local person. Down there in Mississippi.'

I said nothing.

Frazer said, 'Anyway, thank you for coming in.'

I said nothing.

Frazer said, 'This meeting is over, major.'

I said, 'No, colonel, it isn't.'

SIXTY-FIVE

The Pentagon was built because World War Two was coming, and because World War Two was coming it was built without much steel. Steel was needed elsewhere, as always in wartime. Thus the giant building was a monument to the strength and mass of concrete. So much sand was needed for the mix it was dredged right out of the Potomac River, not far from the rising walls themselves. Nearly a million tons of it. The result was extreme solidity.

And silence.

There were thirty thousand people the other side of Frazer's closed door, but I couldn't hear any of them. I couldn't hear anything at all. Just the kind of hissing quiet typical of a C ring office.

Frazer said, 'Don't forget you're talking to an officer senior to you in rank.'

I said, 'Don't forget you're talking to an MP authorized to arrest anyone from a newborn private to a five-star general.'

'What's your point?'

'The Tennessee Free Citizens were ordered to

Kelham. That's clear, I think. And I agree, they acted with an excess of zeal when they got there. But that's on the guy who gave the order, as much as it's on them. More so, in fact. Responsibility starts at the top.'

'No one gave any orders.'

'They were dispatched at the same moment I was. And Munro. We all converged. It was one single integrated decision. Because Reed Riley was there. Who knew that?'

'Perhaps it was a local decision.'

'What was your personal position?'

'Purely passive. And reactive. I was ready to handle the fallout, if any. Nothing more.'

'You sure?'

'Senate Liaison is always passive. It's about putting out fires.'

'Is it never proactive? Never about cutting firebreaks ahead of time?'

'How could I have done that?'

'You could have seen the danger coming. You could have made a plan. You could have decided to defend Kelham's fence from pesky civilians asking awkward questions. But you couldn't ask the Rangers to do that themselves. No commander on earth would recognize that as a legal order. So you could have called some unofficial buddies. From Tennessee, say, which is your home state. Where you know people. That's possible, isn't it?'

'No, that's ridiculous.'

'And then to integrate your whole approach you could have decided to tap MP phones, to monitor things, and to give yourself an early warning in case anything seemed to be heading in the wrong direction.'

'That's ridiculous too.'

'Do you deny it?'

'Of course I deny it.'

'So humour me,' I said. 'Let's talk theoretically. If a person did those two things, what would you think?'

'What two things?'

'Called Tennessee, and tapped phones. What would you think?'

'That laws were broken.'

'Would a person do one thing and not the other? Speaking as a professional soldier?'

'He couldn't afford to. He couldn't afford to have an unauthorized force in the field without a way of knowing if it was close to being discovered.'

'I agree,' I said. 'So whoever deployed the yahoos also tapped the phones, and whoever tapped the phones also deployed the yahoos. Am I making sense? Theoretically?'

'I suppose so.'

'Yes or no, colonel?'

'Yes.'

I asked, 'How good is your short-term memory?'

'Good enough.'

'What was the first thing you said to me when I came in here today?'

'I told you to close the door.'

'No, you said hello. Then you told me to close the door.'

'And then I told you to sit down.'

'And then?'

He said, 'I don't recall.'

'We had a minor discussion about how busy this place is at noon.'

'Yes, I remember.'

'And then you asked me what news I had.'

'And you didn't have any.'

'Which surprised you. Because I had left a message in which I told you I had the name.'

'I was surprised, yes.'

'What name?'

'I wasn't sure. It might have concerned anything.'

'In which case you would have said *a* name. Not *the* name.'

'Perhaps I was humouring your delusion that someone did in fact send those amateurs to Mississippi. Because it seemed important to you.'

'It was important to me. Because it was true.'

'OK, I respect your convictions. I suggest you find out who.'

'I have found out who.'

He didn't reply.

'You slipped up,' I said.

He didn't answer.

'I didn't leave you a message,' I said. 'I made an appointment. With your scheduler. That was all. I didn't give a reason for it. I just said I needed to see you at noon today. The only time I mentioned anything about names and the Tennessee Free Citizens was on a completely separate call with General Garber. Which evidently you were listening to.'

The hissing quiet in the little office seemed to change in pitch. It went low and ominous, like a real thrumming silence.

Frazer said, 'Some things are too big for you to understand, son.'

'Probably,' I said. 'I'm not too clear about what happened in the first trillionth of a second after the Big Bang. I can't make the quantum physics work. But I can get by with a lot of other things. For instance, I understand the Constitution of the United States pretty well. You ever heard of the First Amendment? It guarantees the freedom of the press. Which means any old journalist is entitled to approach any old fence he likes.'

'That guy was from some radical pinko rag in a college town.'

'And I understand you're lazy. You've spent years kissing Carlton Riley's ass, and you don't want to start over with a new guy. Not now. Because that would involve actually doing your damn job.'

No reply.

I said, 'The second human being your boys killed was an underage recruit. He was on his way to try to join the army. His mother killed herself the same night. I understand both of those things. Because I saw what was left. First one, and then the other.'

No reply.

I said, 'And I understand you're doubly arrogant. First you thought I wouldn't figure out your genius scheme, and then when I did, you thought you could deal with me all by yourself. No help, no back-up, no arrest teams.

Just you and me, here and now. I have to ask, how dumb are you?'

'And I have to ask, are you armed?'

'I'm in Class A uniform,' I said. 'No sidearm is carried with Class A uniform. You'll find that in the regulations.'

'So how dumb are you?'

'I didn't expect to be in this situation. I didn't expect to get this far.'

'Take my advice, son. Hope for the best, plan for the worst.'

'You got a gun in your desk?'

'I have two guns in my desk.'

'You going to shoot me?'

'If I have to.'

'This is the Pentagon. There are thirty thousand military personnel outside your door. They're all trained to run towards the sound of gunfire. You better have a story ready.'

'You attacked me.'

'Why would I?'

'Because you're obsessed about who shot some ugly black kid in the back of beyond.'

'I never told anyone he was ugly. Or black. Not on the phone. You must have gotten that from your Tennessee buddies.'

'Whatever, you're obsessed. I ordered you to leave but you attacked me.'

I leaned back in his visitor chair. I stretched my legs out in front of me. I let my arms hang down. I got good and relaxed. I could have fallen asleep. I said, 'This doesn't look like a very threatening posture, does it? And I weigh about two-fifty. You'll have a problem moving me before 3C314 and 3C316 get in here. Which will take them about a second and a half. And then you'll have to deal with the MPs. You kill one of their own in dubious circumstances, they'll tear you apart.'

'My neighbours won't hear. No one will hear a thing.'

'Why? You got suppressors on those guns?'

'I don't need suppressors. Or guns.'

Then he did a very strange thing. He stepped over and took a picture off his wall. A black and white photograph. Himself and Senator Carlton Riley. It was signed. By the senator, I assumed. Not by him. He stepped away from the wall and laid the picture on his desk. Then he stepped back again and pincered his fingertips and worried the nail out of the plaster.

'Is that it?' I said. 'You're going to prick me to death with a pin?'

He put the nail next to the photograph.

He opened a drawer and took out a hammer.

He said, 'I was in the middle of rehanging the picture when you attacked me. Fortunately I was able to grab the hammer, which was still close at hand.'

I said nothing.

'It will be very quiet,' he said. 'One solid blow should do it. I'll have plenty of time to arrange your body whatever way I need to.'

'You're insane,' I said.

'No, I'm committed,' he said. 'To the future of the army.'

394

SIXTY-SIX

Hammers are very evolved items. They haven't changed for years. Why would they? Nails haven't changed. Nails have been the same for ever. Therefore a hammer's necessary features were worked out long ago. A heavy metal head, and a handle. All you need, and nothing you don't. Frazer's was a claw design, a framing hammer, maybe twenty-eight ounces. A big ugly thing. Total overkill for picture hanging, but such mismatches of tool and purpose are common in the real world.

It made for a decent weapon, though.

He came at me with it cocked in his right hand like a nightstick. I scrambled up out of my chair pretty fast, any idea of embarrassing him with an inappropriate postmortem position abandoned long ago. Sheer instinct. I don't scare easy, but humans are very evolved too. A lot of what we do is hard-wired right back to the mists of time. Right back to where my pal Stan Lowrey liked to start a story.

Frazer's office was small. Its free floor space was smaller still. Like fighting in a phone booth. How it was going to go would depend on how smart Frazer was.

And I figured he was plenty smart. He had survived Vietnam, and the Gulf, and years of Pentagon bullshit. You don't do any of that without brains. I figured he was an easy seven out of ten. Maybe an eight. In no imminent danger of winning the Nobel Prize, but definitely smarter than the average bear.

Which helped me. Fighting morons is harder. You can't guess what they're going to do. But smart people are predictable.

He swung the hammer right to left, waist height, a standard opening gambit. I arched back and it missed me. I figured next he would slash back the other way, left to right, same height, and he did, and I arched back again, and he missed again. An exploratory exchange. Like moving pawns on a chessboard. He was breathing strangely. Ferocity, not a throat problem. Nothing for Saint Audrey to worry about. It was ferocity, and excitement. He was a warrior at heart, and warriors love nothing more than the fight itself. It consumes them. They live for it. He was smiling, too, in a feral way, and his eyes were seeing nothing except the hammer head and my midsection beyond it. There was a sharp tang of sweat in the air, something primitive, like a night-time rodent's lair.

I dodged forward half a step, and he matched it with a backward move of his own that left us in the middle of the floor, which was important. To me. He wanted me back against the wall, and I didn't want to be there.

Not yet, anyway.

He swung the hammer a third time, scything it hard, making it look like he meant it, which he didn't. Not yet.

I could read the pattern. It was in his eyes. I arched back and the hammer head buzzed by an inch from my coat. Twenty-eight ounces, on a long handle. The momentum of the miss carried it way around. His shoulders turned ninety degrees and he twisted at the waist. He used the torque to come right back at me. With some arm extension this time. He forced me back. I ended up close to the wall.

I watched his eyes.

Not yet.

He was a warrior. I wasn't. I was a brawler. He lived for the tactical victory. I lived to piss on the other guy's grave. Not the same thing. Not the same thing at all. A different focus. He swung for the fourth time, same angle, same height. He was like a fastball pitcher, getting me used to one thing before unleashing another thing entirely. Inside, inside, inside, and then the splitter away. But Frazer wouldn't go low. He would go high. Low would be better, but he was only a seven out of ten. Maybe an eight. But not a nine.

He swung a fifth time, same height, same angle, so hard that the tines of the claw made a raw thrumming sound as they moved through the air, stopping as the hammer stopped. He swung a sixth time, same height, same sound, more extension. I was very close to the wall. No real place to go. Then came the seventh swing, same height, same angle, same sound.

Then came his eyes.

They flicked upward, and the eighth swing aimed high, right at the side of my head. Right at my temple. I saw a glint off the hammer's inch-wide striking face.

Twenty-eight ounces. Nearly two pounds in weight. It would have punched a very neat hole through the bone.

But it didn't, because my head wasn't there when it arrived.

I dropped vertically, eight inches on to bent and pre-set knees, four inches so the swing would miss me, and another four as a margin of safety, and I heard the rush of air above me, and I felt the miss drag him around in a wild part-circle, and I started back up, and then we were into a whole new set of calculations. We had done the three dimensions. We had done in and out, back and forth, and up and down. Now we were ready for the fourth dimension. Time. The only remaining questions were how fast could I hit him, and how fast was he spinning?

And they were crucial questions. For him especially. I was twisting as I rose and my elbow was already moving fast and it was a certainty I was going to hit him with it in the neck. A mathematical certainty. But which part of the neck? The answer was, whichever part was there when the blow landed. Front, side, back, it was all the same to me. But not to him. For him, some parts would be worse than others.

The twenty-eight ounces had first pulled his arms away from his shoulders, in a kind of Olympic hammer-throwing way, and then they had pulled his trailing shoulder hard, in a kind of whip-cracking way, so he was well into a serious but uncontrolled spin by then. And my elbow was doing pretty well by that point. A muscle memory thing. It happens automatically. If in doubt, throw the elbow. Maybe a childhood thing. My weight was behind it, my foot was braced, and it was going to land, and it was going to land hard. In fact it was going to land very hard. It was already scything and clubbing downward. And it was accelerating. It was going to be a vicious blow. It was going to be the kind of vicious blow he might survive if he took it on the side of the neck, but not on the back. A blow like that on the back of the neck would be fatal. No question. Something to do with how the skull joins the vertebrae.

So it was all about time, and speed, and rotation, and eccentric orbits. It was impossible to predict. Too many moving parts. At first I thought he was going to take it mostly on the side. On the angle, really, but with the ratio tilted towards maybe surviving it. Then I saw it was going to be closer to fifty-fifty, but the twenty-eight ounces suddenly pulled him off in some new direction, and from that point onward there was no doubt he was going to take it on the back of the neck and nowhere else. No doubt at all. The guy was going to die.

Which I didn't regret.

Except in a practical sense.

SIXTY-SEVEN

Frazer went down by his desk, not hitting it, making a sound no louder than a fat guy sitting down on a sofa. Which was safe enough. No one calls the cops when a fat guy sits down on a sofa. There was carpet on the floor, some kind of a Persian thing most likely left behind by a previous occupant long dead of a heart attack. Under the carpet would be pad, and under that was solid Pentagon concrete. So sound transmission was strictly contained. *No one will hear a thing*, Frazer had said. *You got that right*, I thought. *Asshole.*

I pulled the illicit Beretta from my Class A coat pocket and held it on him for a long moment. Just in case. Hope for the best, plan for the worst. But he didn't move. No way could he. Maybe his eyelids. His neck was loose right at the top. He had taken no vertebrae with him. His skull was attached to the rest of him by nothing but skin.

I left him where he was for the time being and was about to step into the centre of the room to start scoping things out when the door opened.

And in walked Frances Neagley.

*   *   *

She was in woodland-pattern BDUs and she was wearing latex gloves. She glanced around the room once, twice, and she said, 'We need to move him near where the picture was.'

I just stood there.

'Quickly,' she said.

So I got myself going and I hauled him over to where he might plausibly have fallen while he was hanging the picture. He could have gone over backward and hit his head on the edge of the desk. The distances were about right.

'But why would he?' I said.

'He was banging in the nail,' Neagley said. 'He flinched when he saw the claw coming at him on the backswing. Some knee-jerk reaction. A reflex. He couldn't help it. He got his feet tangled up in the rug and over he went.'

'So where's the nail now?'

She took it off the desk and dropped it at the base of the wall. It tinkled faintly against the gutter of tile beyond the edge of the rug.

'And where's the hammer?'

'It's near enough,' she said. 'Time to go.'

'I have to erase my appointment.'

She showed me diary pages from her pocket.

'Already in the bag,' she said. 'Let's go.'

Neagley led me down two flights of stairs and through the corridors at a pace somewhere between moderate and brisk. We used the southeast entrance to get outside and then we headed straight for the parking lot, where we stopped among the reserved spaces, and Neagley unlocked a large Buick sedan. It was a Park Avenue. Dark blue. Very clean. Maybe new.

Neagley said, 'Get in.'

So I got in, on to soft beige leather. Neagley backed up and swung the wheel and headed for the exit, and then we were through the barrier, and pretty soon after that we were on a bunch of highway ramps, and then we were through the last of them and on a six-lane road heading south, just one car among a rolling thousand.

I said, 'The inquiry desk has a record of me coming in.'

'Wrong tense,' Neagley said. 'It had a record. It doesn't any more.'

'When did you do all that?'

'I figured you were OK as soon as you were one on one with the guy. Although I wish you hadn't talked so much. You should have moved to the physical much sooner. You have talents, honey, but talking ain't top of the list.'

'Why are you even here?'

'I got word.'

'What word?'

'The story of this crazy trap. Walking into the Pentagon like that.'

'Word from where?'

'From way down in Mississippi. From Sheriff Deveraux herself. She asked for my help.'

'She called you?'

'No, we had a séance.'

'Why would she call you?'

'Because she was worried, you idiot. As was I, as soon as I heard.'

'There was nothing to worry about.'

'There could have been.'

I asked, 'What did she want you to do?'

'She wanted me to watch your back. To make sure you were OK.'

'I don't think I told her what time the appointment was.'

'She knew what bus you were on. Her deputy told her what time he'd gotten you to Memphis, and so it was easy enough to figure out what line you would take.'

'How did that help you this morning?'

'It didn't help me this morning. It helped me yesterday evening. I've been on you since you left the bus depot. Every minute. Nice hotel, by the way. If they ever catch up with me for the room service, you owe me big money.'

I said, 'Whose car is this?'

'It belongs to the motor pool. As per procedure.'

'What procedure?'

'When a senior staff officer passes away, his department-owned car is returned to the motor pool. Where it is immediately road tested to determine what remedial work needs to be done before it can be reissued. This is the road test.'

'How long will it last?'

'About two years, probably.'

'Who was the officer?'

'It's a fairly new car, isn't it? Must have been a fairly recent death.'

'Frazer?'

'It's easier for the motor pool to do the paperwork first thing in the morning. We were all counting on you. If anything had gone wrong we'd all have had red faces.'

'I might have arrested him instead.'

'Same thing. Dead or busted, it makes no difference to the motor pool.'

'Where are we going?'

'You're due on post. Garber wants to see you.'

'Why?'

'I don't know.'

'That's three hours away.'

'So sit back and relax. This might be the last rest you get for a spell.'

'I thought you didn't like Deveraux.'

'Doesn't mean I wouldn't help her if she was worried. I think there's something wrong with her, that's all. How long have you known her?'

'Four days,' I said.

'And I bet you could already tell me four weird things about her.'

I said, 'I should try to call her, if she's worried.'

'I already tried,' Neagley said. 'From the scheduler's phone. While you were giving Frazer all that theoretical shit. I was going to tell her you were nearly home and dry. But she didn't answer. A whole Sheriff's Department, and no one picked up.'

'Perhaps they're busy.'

'Perhaps they are. Because there's something else you need to know. I checked a rumour from the sergeants' network. The ground crew at Benning says the

404

Blackhawk that came in from Kelham on Sunday was empty. Apart from the pilots, of course. No passenger, is what they meant. Reed Riley didn't go anywhere. He's still on the post.'

SIXTY-EIGHT

I took Neagley's advice and relaxed through the rest of the ride. It took a lot less than three hours. The Buick was much faster than a bus. And Neagley pushed it much harder than a bus driver would. I was back on post by three-thirty. I had been gone exactly twenty-four hours.

I went straight to my quarters and took off the fancy Class As and cleaned my teeth and took a shower. Then I put on BDUs with a T-shirt and went to see what Garber wanted.

Garber wanted to show me a confidential file from the Marine Corps. That was the purpose of his summons. But first came a short question-and-answer session. It didn't go well. It was very unsatisfactory. I asked the questions, and he refused to answer them.

And he refused to make eye contact.

I asked, 'Who did they arrest in Mississippi?'

He said, 'Read the file.'

'I would like to know.'

'Read the file first.'

'Do they have a good case or is it bullshit?'

'Read the file.'

'Was it the same guy for all three women?'

'Read the file first.'

'Civilian, right?'

'Read the damn file, Reacher.'

He wouldn't let me take the file away. It had to remain under his personal control at all times. Under his eye throughout, technically, but he didn't follow the letter of the law on that point. He stepped out of his office and closed the door quietly and left me alone with it.

It was about a quarter of an inch thick, cased in a jacket that was a different shade of khaki than the army uses. Better quality, too. It was smooth and crisp, only a little scraped and scuffed by the passage of time. It had red chevrons on all four edges, presumably denoting some elevated level of secrecy. It had a white stick-on label with a USMC file number printed on it, and a date five years in the past.

It had a second label with a name printed on it.

DEVERAUX, E.

Her name was followed by her rank, which was CWO5, and her service number, and her date of birth, which was fairly close to mine. Near the bottom edge of the jacket was a third stick-on, slightly misaligned, taken from a long roll of pre-printed tape. I guessed it was supposed to say *Do Not Open Unless Authorized* but it had been cut at the wrong interval so that in reality it said *Open Unless Authorized Do Not*. Bureaucracy can be full of accidental humour.

But the contents of the file were not funny.

The contents started with her photograph. It was in colour, and maybe a little more than five years old. Her hair was buzzed very short, like she had told me. Probably a number two clipper, grown out a week or so, like a soft dark halo. Like moss. She looked very beautiful. Very small and delicate. The short hair made her eyes enormous. She looked full of life, full of vigour, in control, in command. Some kind of a mental and physical plateau. Late twenties, early thirties. I remembered them well.

I laid the photograph face down on my left and looked at the first sheet of printed words. They were typewritten. An IBM machine, I guessed, with the golf ball. Common in 1992. And there were still plenty around in 1997. Computer word processing was happening, but like everything else in the military it was happening slowly and cautiously, with a great deal of doubt and suspicion.

I started reading. Immediately it was clear that the file was a summary of an investigation conducted by a USMC Brigadier General from their Provost Marshal's office, which oversaw their MP business. The one-star's name was James Dyer. A very senior man, for what appeared to be nothing more than a personnel issue. A personal dispute, in fact, between two Marine MPs of equal rank. Or, technically, a dispute between one Marine MP and two others, for a total of three. On one side of the issue were a woman named Alice Bouton and a man named Paul Evers, and on the other side of the issue was Elizabeth Deveraux.

Like every summary I had ever read this one began

with a bald narrative of events, written neutrally and patiently, without implication or interpretation, in language anxious to be clear. The story was fairly simple. Like a sub-plot from daytime TV. Elizabeth Deveraux and Paul Evers were dating, and then they weren't, and then Paul Evers and Alice Bouton were dating, and then Paul's car got trashed, and then Alice got dishonourably discharged after a financial irregularity came to light.

That was the narrative of events.

Next came a digression into Alice Bouton's situation. Like a sidebar. Alice was indisputably guilty, in General Dyer's opinion. The facts were clear. The evidence was there. The case was solid. The prosecution had been fair. The defence had been conscientious. The verdict had been unanimous. The amount in question had been less than four hundred dollars. In cash, taken from an evidence locker. Proceeds from an illegal weapons sale, confiscated, bagged up, logged in, and awaiting exhibition in an upcoming court martial. Alice Bouton had taken it and spent it on a dress, a purse, and a pair of shoes, in a store close to where she was based. The store remembered her. Four hundred bucks was a lot of money for a jarhead to spend on an outfit, back in 1992. Some of the larger denomination bills were still in the store's register when the MPs came calling, and the serial numbers matched the evidence log.

Case closed.

Sidebar over.

Next up was General Dyer's interpretation of the three-way turmoil. It was painstaking. It was prefaced with a cast-iron guarantee that all conclusions were amply supported by data. Conversations had been had, interviews had been conducted, information had been gathered, witnesses had been consulted, and then everything had been cross-referenced and cross-checked, and anything supported by fewer than two independent sources had been omitted. A full court press, in other words. You could take it to the bank. The guarantee ended with a long emphasized paragraph. I could picture the IBM machine bucking and rocking on the desk as the golf ball slammed back and forth, supplying the furious underline. The paragraph confirmed Dyer's belief that everything about to be described was courtroom-ready, should further action be deemed necessary or desirable.

I turned the page and started in on the analysis. Dyer wrote in a plain style, and did not inject himself into the narrative. Given the preceding page, any reader would understand that the content might not be 100 per cent forensically proven fact, but that equally it was very far from scuttlebutt or rumour. It was solid information. It was known as much as anything was knowable. Hence Dyer never wrote *I believe* or *I think* or *It seems likely*. He just told the story.

Which went like this: Elizabeth Deveraux had been seriously pissed when Paul Evers dumped her for Alice Bouton. She had felt slighted, disregarded, disrespected, and insulted. She was a woman scorned, and her subsequent behaviour seemed determined to prove the cliché true in every respect. She victimized the new couple by bad-mouthing them everywhere she could, and by manipulating workloads whenever she could, to stop them getting downtime together.

Then she drove Paul Evers's car off a bridge.

Evers's car was nothing special, but it represented a significant investment on his part, and it was essential to his social life, given that no one wants to stay on post all the time. Deveraux had retained a key for it, and late one night had driven it away and steered it carefully beyond a bridge abutment and let it roll over a thirty-foot drop into a concrete flood sluice. The impact had almost totalled the car, and heavy rain later that night had finished the job.

Then Deveraux had turned her attention to Alice Bouton.

She had started by breaking her arm.

General Dyer's two-independent-sources rule meant that the circumstances were not precisely described, because the attack had not been witnessed, but Bouton claimed Deveraux had been the assailant, and Deveraux had never denied it. The medical facts were beyond dispute. Bouton's left elbow had been dislocated and both bones in her left forearm had been snapped. She had been in a hard cast for six long weeks.

And Deveraux had spent those six long weeks pursuing the theft allegation with demonic intensity. Except that *pursuing* was the wrong word, initially, because at the outset there was nothing to pursue. No one knew anything had been stolen. Deveraux had first inventoried the evidence lockers and audited the paperwork. Only then had she discovered the discrepancy. And then she had made the allegation. And then she had pursued it, like an obsession, with the ultimate result being as described in General Dyer's sidebar. The court martial, and the guilty verdict.

There was a huge uproar in the Marine MP community, of course, but Bouton's guilty verdict had insulated Deveraux from any kind of formal criticism. What would have looked like a vendetta had the verdict been different was left looking like a good piece of police work entirely in keeping with the Marine Corps' sense of ethics and honour. But it was a fine line. General Dyer had been in no doubt that the case involved major elements of personal retribution.

And, unusually for such reports, he had attempted to explain why.

Again, he confirmed that conversations had been had, and interviews had been conducted, and information had been gathered, and witnesses had been consulted. The participants in these new discussions had included friends and enemies, acquaintances and associates, and doctors and psychiatrists.

The salient factor was held by all to be Alice Bouton's unusual physical beauty.

All were agreed that Bouton had been an exceptionally good looking woman. Words quoted included gorgeous, stunning, spectacular, heart-breaking, knock-out, and incredible.

All the same words applied equally to Deveraux too, of course. All were agreed on that point also. No question. The psychiatrists had concluded that therein lay the explanation. General Dyer had translated their clinical language for the casual reader. He said Deveraux couldn't take the competition. She couldn't stand not to be clearly and definitively the most beautiful woman on the post. So she had taken steps to make sure she was.

I read the whole thing one more time, front to back, and then I butted all the pages neatly together and closed the jacket on them, and Garber came back into the room.

SIXTY-NINE

The first thing Garber said was, 'We just heard from the Pentagon. John James Frazer was found dead in his office.'

I said, 'Dead how?'

'Looks like a freak accident. Apparently he fell and hit his head on the desk. His staff got back from lunch and found him on the floor. He was doing something with a picture of Carlton Riley.'

'That's bad.'

'Why?'

'This is not a great time to lose our Senate Liaison.'

'Did you read the file?'

I said, 'Yes, I did.'

'Then you know we don't need to worry about the Senate any more. Whoever replaces Frazer will have plenty of time to learn the job before the next thing comes along.'

'Is that going to be the official line?'

'It's the truth. She was a Marine, Reacher. Sixteen years in. She knew all about cutting throats. She knew how to do it, and she knew how to pretend she didn't.

414

And the car alone proves it. Right there, what more is there to say? She wrecks Paul Evers's car, and she wrecks Reed Riley's. Same MO. Same exact reason. Except this time she's only one of four beautiful women. And Munro says Riley dates her and then dumps her for the other three in succession. So this time she's three times as mad. This time she goes beyond breaking arms. This time she has her own private deer trestle behind an empty house.'

'Is that going to be the official line?'

'It's what happened.'

'So what next?'

'It's purely a Mississippi matter now. We have no dog in the fight, and we have no way of knowing what will happen. Most likely nothing will happen. My guess is she won't arrest herself, and she won't give the State Police any reason to either.'

'So we're going to walk away?'

'All three of them were civilians. They're nothing to do with us.'

'So the mission is terminated?'

'As of this morning.'

'Is Kelham open again?'

'As of this morning.'

'She denies dating Riley, you know.'

'She would, wouldn't she?'

'Do we know anything about General Dyer?'

'He died two years ago after a long and exemplary career. He never put a foot wrong. The man was stainless.'

'OK,' I said. 'I'll take steps.'

'Towards what?'

'Towards wrapping up my involvement.'

'Your involvement is already wrapped up. As of this morning.'

'I have private property to recover.'

'You left something there?'

'I thought I was heading right back.'

'What did you leave?'

'My toothbrush.'

'That's not important.'

'Will the DoD reimburse me?'

'For a toothbrush? Of course not.'

'Then I have a right to recover it. They can't have it both ways.'

He said, 'Reacher, if you draw one iota more attention to this thing there won't be anything I can do to help you. Right now some very senior people are holding their breath. We're one inch away from news stories about a senator's son dating a three-time killer. Except neither one of them can afford to say anything about it. Not him, for one reason, and not her, for another. So we'll probably get away with it. But we don't know yet. Not for sure. Right now it's still in the balance.'

I said nothing.

He said, 'You know she's good for it, Reacher. A man with your instincts? She was only pretending to investigate. I mean, did she get anywhere with it? And she was playing you like a violin. First she was trying to get rid of you, and when you wouldn't go, she switched to keeping you close. So she could monitor your progress. Or the lack of it. Why else would she even talk to you?'

I said nothing.

He said, 'The bus is long gone, anyway. To Memphis. You'd have to wait until tomorrow now. And you'll see things differently tomorrow.'

I asked, 'Is Neagley still on the post?'

He said, 'Yes, she is. I just made a date to have a drink with her.'

'Tell her she's taking the bus home. Tell her I'm taking the company car.'

He asked, 'Do you have a bank account?'

I said, 'How else would I get paid?'

'Where is it?'

'New York. From when I was at West Point.'

'Move it to somewhere nearer the Pentagon.'

'Why?'

'Involuntary separation money comes through quicker if you bank in Virginia.'

'You think it will come to that?'

'The Joint Chiefs think war is over. They're singing along with Yoko Ono. There are big cuts coming. Most of them will fall on the army. Because the Marines have better PR, and because the navy and the air force are a whole different thing altogether. So the people right above us are making lists, and they're making them right now.'

'Am I on those lists?'

'You will be. And there will be nothing I can do to stop it.'

'You could order me not to go back to Mississippi.'

'I could, but I won't. Not you. I trust you to do the right thing.'

SEVENTY

I met Stan Lowrey on my way off the post. My old friend. He was locking his car just as I was unlocking the Buick with the key I'd collected from the motor pool. I said, 'Goodbye, old pal.'

He said, 'That sounds final.'

'You may never see me again.'

'Why? Are you in trouble?'

'Me?' I said. 'No, I'm fine. But I heard your job is vulnerable. You might be gone when I get back.'

He just shook his head and smiled and walked on.

The Buick was an old lady's car. If my grandfather had had a sister, she would have been my great-aunt, and she would have driven a Buick Park Avenue. But she would have driven it slower than me. The thing was as soft as a marshmallow and twice as buttery inside, but it had a big motor. And government plates. So it was useful on the highway. And I got on the highway as soon as I could. On I-65, to be precise. Heading south, down the eastern edge of a notional corridor, not down the western edge through Memphis. I would be approaching from a side I

418

had never seen before, but it was a straighter shot. And therefore faster. Five hours, I figured. Maybe five and a half. I would be in Carter Crossing by ten thirty at the latest.

I went south all the way through Kentucky in the last of the daylight, and then it got dark pretty quickly as I drove through Tennessee. I hunted around for a mile and found the switch and turned on my headlights. The broad road took me through the bright neon of Nashville, fast and above the fray, and then it took me onward through open country, where it was dark and lonely again. I drove like I was hypnotized, automatically, not thinking anything, not noticing anything, surprised every time I came to by the hundred-mile bites I had been taking out of the journey.

I crossed the line into Alabama and stopped at the second place I saw for gas and a map. I knew I would need to head west off an early Alabama exit and I needed a map with local details to show me where. Not the kind of large-scale plan you can buy ahead of time. The sheet I bought unfolded neatly and showed me every farm track in the state. But it showed me nothing more than that. Mississippi was just a blank white space on the edge of the paper. I narrowed down my target area and found a choice of four east–west routes. Any one of them might have been the road that led onward past Kelham's gate to Carter Crossing. Or none of them might. There could have been all kinds of dog-leg turns waiting for me on the other side of the line. A regular maze. No way of knowing.

Except that Kelham had been built in the 1950s, which was still a time of big wars and mass mobilizations. And DoD planners have always been a cautious bunch. They didn't want some reservist convoy from New Jersey or Nebraska getting lost in unfamiliar parts. So they put discreet and coded signs here and there, marking the way to and from every major installation in the nation. Their efforts intensified after the Interstate system was begun. The Interstate system was formally named for President Eisenhower, for a very good reason. Eisenhower had been Allied Supreme Commander in Europe during World War Two, and his biggest problem had not been Germans. It had been getting men and material from point A to point B across lousy and unmarked roads. He was determined his successors should not face similar problems should land war ever come to America. Hence the Interstate system. Not for vacations. Not for commerce. For war. And hence the signs. And if those signs had not been shot up or trashed or stolen by the locals, I could use them like homing beacons.

I found the first of the signs at the next exit I came to. I came off the ramp and struck out west on a concrete ribbon lined here and there with low-rent malls and auto dealers. After a time the commercial enterprises died back and the road reverted to what I guessed it had been before, which was a meandering rural route through what looked like pretty country. There were trees and fields and the occasional lake. There were summer camps and vacation villages and the occasional inn.

There was a bright moon high in the sky, and it was all very picturesque.

I drove on but saw no more DoD signs until I was in Mississippi, and only one more after that. But it was a bold and confident arrow pointing straight ahead, with the number 17 embedded in the code below it, indicating just seventeen more miles to go. The clock in my head said five past ten. If I hustled, I would arrive ahead of schedule.

SEVENTY-ONE

Evidently the DoD engineers had been just as concerned about the westward approach to Kelham as the eastward. The road was the same in both directions. Same width, same material, same camber, same construction. I recognized it ten miles out. Then I sensed the trees and the fence in the darkness to my right. Kelham's southeastern corner. Bottom right on a map.

The southern perimeter slid by my window, and I waited for the gate to arrive. I saw no reason why it wouldn't be at the exact midpoint of the fence. The DoD liked neatness. If there had been a hill in the way, army engineers would have removed it. If there had been a swamp in the way, army engineers would have drained it.

In the end I guessed that actually there had been a small valley in the way, because after a couple of miles the road stayed level only by mounting a causeway about six feet high. The land all around was lower. Then the causeway widened dramatically on my right and became a huge fan-shaped concrete elevation floating above the grade. Like a gigantic turn-in, like the mouth of a wide new road. It started out about the size of an end-on football field. Maybe wider, but then it got a little narrower. It met the old road at a right angle, but there were no sharp edges. No sharp turns. The turns were shallow, easing gently through graceful, generous curves. To accommodate tracked vehicles, not Buicks, however lumbering.

But if the fan shape was the mouth of a new road, then that new road dead-ended fifty yards later, at Fort Kelham's gate. And Fort Kelham's gate was a heavy-duty affair. That was for damn sure. Physically it was stronger than anything I had seen outside a combat zone. It was flanked by fortifications and the guardhouse, which was also a serious affair. It had nine personnel in it. The county's interests were represented by the lone figure of Deputy Geezer Butler. He was sitting in his car, which was parked at an angle on the cusp of the farther curve, in a kind of no-man's-land, where the county's road became the army's.

But the army's heavy steel barriers were wide open, and the army's road was in use. The base was all lit up and alive, and the whole scene looked exactly like business as usual. People were coming and going, not a big crowd, but no one was lonely. Most were driving, but some were on motorbikes. More were coming than going, because it was close to ten-thirty, and there were early starts tomorrow. But some hardy souls were still venturing out. Instructors, probably. And officers. Those who had it easy. I braked behind two slower cars and someone came out the gate and pulled in behind me and I found myself stuck in a little four-car convoy. We were swimming against the tide, going west, heading for the other side of the tracks. Possibly the last of many such convoys that evening.

I sensed the bottom-left corner coming up, Kelham's southwestern limit, and I tried to identify the blind spot I had used two days before, but it was too dark to see. Then we were out in the open scrub. I saw Pellegrino in his cruiser, coming the other way, driving slow, trying to calm the returning traffic with his presence alone. Then we were rolling through the black half of town, and then we were bouncing over the railroad track, and then we were pulling a tight left in behind Main Street, and then we were parking on the beaten earth in front of the bars, and the auto parts places, and the loan offices, and the gun shops, and the secondhand stereo stores.

I got out of the Buick and stood on the open ground halfway between Brannan's bar and the lines of parked cars. The open ground was being used as a kind of common thoroughfare. There were guys in transit from one bar to another, and there were guys standing around talking and laughing, and both groups were merging and separating according to some complex dynamic. No one was walking directly from place to place. Everyone was looping back towards the cars, pausing, shooting the shit, slapping backs, comparing notes, shedding one buddy and picking up another.

And there were plenty of women, too. More than I would have believed possible. I had no idea where they had all come from. Miles around, probably. Some were paired off with soldiers, others were in larger mixed groups, and some were in groups of their own. I could see about a hundred guys in total, and maybe eighty women, and I guessed there might be similar numbers inside. The men were from Bravo Company, I assumed, still on leave and anxious to make up for lost time. They were exactly what I would have expected to see. Good guys, well trained, by day performing at 100 per cent of their considerable capacities, by night full of energy, full of goodwill, and full of high spirits. They were all in their unofficial off-duty uniform of jeans, jackets and T-shirts. Here or there a guy would look a little pinched and wary compared to the others, which most likely meant he was on the promotion track, and clearly some guys needed the spotlight more than others, but overall they were precisely what a good infantry unit looks like when it comes out to play. There was plenty of buzz going on, and plenty of noise, but I sensed no frustration or hostility. There was nothing negative in the air. They didn't blame the town for their recent incarceration. They were just glad to get back to it.

But even so I was sure local law enforcement would be holding its breath. In particular I was sure Elizabeth Deveraux would still be on duty. And I was definitely sure where I would find her. She needed a central location, and a chair and a table and a window, and something to do as time ticked away. Where else would she be?

I eased my way through the thin crowd and stepped left of Brannan's bar and into the alley. I skirted Janice Chapman's pile of sand and followed the dog-leg and came out on to Main Street between the hardware store and the pharmacy. Then I turned right and walked up to the diner.

The diner was almost completely full that night. It was practically heaving, compared to how I had seen it before. Like Times Square. There were twenty-six customers. Nineteen of them were Rangers, sixteen of them in four groups of four at four separate tables, big guys sitting tight together, shoulder to shoulder. They were talking loud, and calling back and forth to each other. They were keeping the waitress busy. She was running in and out of the kitchen, and she probably had been all day long, dealing with the pent-up demand for something other than army chow. But she looked happy. The gates were finally open. The river of dollars was flowing again. She was getting her tips.

The other three Rangers were dining with their girl-friends, face to face at tables for two, leaning in, heads together. All three men looked happy, and so did all three women. And why not? What could be finer than a romantic dinner at the best restaurant in town?

The old couple from the hotel were in there too, at their usual table for four, almost hidden by the groups of Rangers all around them. The old lady had her book, and the old guy had his paper. They were staying later than normal, and I guessed they were the only service workers in town not at that very moment camped out behind their cash registers. But none of the guys from Kelham needed a bed for the night, and Toussaint's offered no other facilities. Not even coffee. So it made sense for the owners to wait out the noise and the disruption somewhere safe and familiar, rather than listen to it all out their back windows.

Then deeper into the room and right of the aisle and alone at the rearmost table for two was Major Duncan Munro. He was in BDUs and his head was bent over a meal. On the spot, just in case, even though his involvement in Kelham's affairs had been terminated hours before, presumably. He was a good MP. Professional to the end. I guessed he was on his way back to Germany, and was waiting for transport.

And Elizabeth Deveraux was there, of course. She was on her own at a table closer to the window than I had seen her choose before. On the spot, vigilant, just in case, paying attention, not willing to let the mayhem filter out from behind Main Street on to Main Street itself. Because of the voters. She was in uniform, and her hair was up in its ponytail. She looked tired, but still spectacular. I watched her for a beat, and then she looked up and saw me and smiled happily and kicked a chair out for me.

I paused another beat, thinking hard, and then I stepped over and sat down opposite her.

SEVENTY-TWO

Deveraux didn't speak at first. She just looked me over, top to bottom, head to toe, maybe checking me for damage, maybe adjusting to the sight of me in uniform. I was still in the BDUs I had put on that afternoon, after getting back from D.C. A whole new look.

I said, 'Busy day?'

She said, 'Real busy since ten o'clock this morning. They opened the gates and out they came. Like a flood.'

'Any trouble?'

'None of them would pass a field sobriety test on their way home, but apart from that everything's cool. I've got Butler and Pellegrino out and about, just to show the flag. Just in case.'

'I saw them,' I said.

'So how did it go up there?'

'Inconclusive,' I said. 'Very bad timing on my part, I'm afraid. Just one of those freak things. The guy I went to see died in an accident. So I got nothing done.'

'I figured,' she said. 'I was getting regular updates from Frances Neagley, until things got busy here. From eight until ten this morning you were drinking coffee

428

and reading the newspaper. But something must have happened during those hours. My guess would be around nine o'clock. Mail call, maybe. But whatever, somebody must have reached a conclusion about something, because an hour later it all let loose. It was back to business as usual here.'

I nodded.

'I agree,' I said. 'I think new information was released this morning. Something definitive, I guess.'

'Do you know what it was?'

I said, 'By the way, thank you for worrying. I was very touched.'

'Neagley was just as worried as I was,' she said. 'Once I told her what you were doing, that is. She didn't need much persuading.'

'In the end it was safe enough,' I said. 'It got a little tense around the Pentagon. That was the worst of it. I hung around there for quite a time. I came in through the cemetery. Behind Henderson Hall. You know that place?'

'Of course I do. I was there a hundred times. They have a great PX. It feels like Saks Fifth Avenue.'

'I got talking with a guy there. About you and a one-star called James Dyer. This guy said Dyer knew you.'

'Dyer?' she said. 'Really? I knew him, but I doubt if he knew me. If he did, then I'm flattered. He was a real big deal. Who was the guy you were talking to?'

'His name was Paul Evers.'

'Paul?' she said. 'You're kidding. We worked together for years. In fact we even dated once. One of my

429

mistakes, I'm afraid. But how amazing that you bumped into him. It's a small world, right?'

'Why was he a mistake? He seemed OK to me.'

'He was fine. He was a really nice guy. But we didn't really click.'

'So you dumped him?'

'More or less. But it felt close to mutual. We both knew it wasn't going to work. It was just a question of who was going to speak first. He wasn't upset, anyway.'

'When was this?'

She paused to calculate.

'Five years ago,' she said. 'Feels like yesterday. Doesn't time fly?'

'Then he said something about a woman called Alice Bouton. His next girlfriend after you, apparently.'

'I don't think I knew her. I don't recall the name. Did Paul seem happy?'

'He mentioned something about car trouble.'

Deveraux smiled. 'Girls and cars,' she said. 'Is that all guys ever talk about?'

I said, 'Reopening Kelham means they're sure the problem is on your side of the fence, you know. They wouldn't have done it otherwise. It's a Mississippi matter now. That will be the official line, from this point forward. It's not one of us. It's one of you. You got any thoughts on that?'

'I think the army should share its information,' she said. 'If it's good enough for them, it would be good enough for me too.'

'The army is moving on,' I said. 'The army won't be sharing anything.'

She paused a beat.

'Munro told me he got new orders,' she said. 'I suppose you have, too.'

I nodded. 'I came back to tie up a loose end. That's all, really.'

'And then you'll be moving on. To the next thing. That's what I'm thinking about right now. I'll think about Janice Chapman tomorrow.'

'And Rosemary McClatchy, and Shawna Lindsay.'

'And Bruce Lindsay, and his mother. I'll do my best for all of them.'

I said nothing.

She asked, 'Are you tired?'

I said, 'Not very.'

'I have to go help Butler and Pellegrino. They've been working since dawn. And anyway, I want to be on the road when the last of the stragglers start to head home. They're always the toughest guys, and the drunkest.'

'Will you be back by midnight?'

She shook her head.

'Probably not,' she said. 'We'll have to manage without the train tonight.'

I said nothing in reply to that, and she smiled once more, a little sadly, and then she got up and left.

The waitress finally got to me five minutes later and I ordered coffee. And pie, as an afterthought. She treated me a little differently from before. A little more formally. She worked near a base, and she knew what the black oak leaves on my collar meant. I asked her how her day had gone. She said it had gone very well, thank you.

'No trouble at all?' I asked.

'None,' she said.

'Even from that guy in back? The other major? I heard he could be a handful.'

She turned and looked at Munro. She said, 'I'm sure he's a perfect gentleman.'

'Would you ask him to join me? Get him some pie, too.'

She detoured via his table, and she delivered my invitation, which involved a lot of elaborate pointing, as if I was inconspicuous and hard to find in the crowd. Munro looked over quizzically, and then he shrugged and got up. Each of the four Ranger tables fell silent as he passed, one after the other. Munro was not popular with those guys. He had had them sitting on their thumbs for four solid days.

He sat down in Deveraux's chair and I asked him, 'How much have they told you?'

'Bare minimum,' he said. 'Classified, need to know, eyes only, the whole nine yards.'

'No names?'

'No,' he said. 'But I'm assuming that Sheriff Deveraux must have given them solid information that clears our guys. I mean, what else could have happened? But she hasn't arrested anybody. I've been watching her all day.'

'What has she been doing?'

'Crowd control,' he said. 'Watching for signs of friction. But it's all good. No one is mad at her or the town. It's me they're gunning for.'

'When are you leaving?'

'First light,' he said. 'I get a ride to Birmingham,

Alabama, and then a bus to Atlanta, Georgia, and then I fly Delta back to Germany.'

'Did you know Reed Riley never left the base?'

'Yes,' he said.

'What do you make of that?'

'It puzzles me a little.'

'In what way?'

'Timing,' he said. 'At first I thought it was a decoy move, like politics as usual, but then I got real. They wouldn't burn a hundred gallons of Jet-A on a decoy move, senator's son or not. So he was still scheduled to leave when the Blackhawk departed Benning, but by the time it arrived at Kelham the orders had changed. Which means some big piece of decisive information came in literally while the chopper was in the air. Which was two days ago, on Sunday, right after lunch. But they didn't act on it in any other way until this morning, which is Tuesday.'

'Why wouldn't they?'

'I don't know. I see no reason for a delay. It feels to me like they were evaluating the new data for a couple of days. Which is usually wise. Except in this instance it makes no sense at all. If the new data was strong enough to make a snap decision to keep Riley on the post Sunday afternoon, why wasn't it strong enough to open the gates Sunday afternoon? It doesn't add up. It's as if they were ready to act privately on Sunday, but they weren't ready to act publicly until this morning. In which case, what changed? What was the difference between Sunday and today?'

'Beats me,' I said. Which was disingenuous. Because

433

there was really only one answer to that question. The only material difference between Sunday afternoon and Tuesday morning was that I had been in Carter Crossing on Sunday afternoon, and I had been eight hundred miles away on Tuesday morning.

And no one had expected me to come back again.

What that meant, I had no idea.

SEVENTY-THREE

The waitress was overworked and slow, so I left Munro to receive the pies alone and I headed back to the dog-leg alley. I came out between Brannan's bar and the loan office and saw that a few cars had left and the crowd on the open ground had thinned considerably, much more so than the few absent cars could explain, so I figured people were inside at that point, drinking away their last precious minutes of freedom before heading home for the night.

I found most of them inside Brannan's bar itself. The place was packed. It was seriously overcrowded. I wasn't sure if Carter County had a fire marshal, but if it did, the guy would have been having a panic attack. There must have been a hundred Rangers and fifty women in there, back to back, chest to chest, holding their drinks up neck-high to avoid the crush. There was a roar of sound, a loud generalized amalgam of talk and laughter, and behind it all I could hear the cash drawer slamming in and out of the register. The river of dollars was back in full flow.

I spent five minutes fighting my way to the bar, on a random route left and right through the crowd, checking faces as I went, some up close, some from afar, but I didn't see Reed Riley. The Brannan brothers were hard at work, dealing beer in bottles, taking money, making change, dumping wet dollar bills into their tip jar, passing and repassing each other in their cramped space with moves like dancers. One of them saw me and did the busy-barman thing with his chin and his eyes and the angle of his head, and then he recognized me from our earlier conversation, and then he remembered I was an MP, and then he leaned in fast like he was prepared to give me a couple of seconds. I couldn't remember if he was Jonathan or Hunter.

I asked him, 'Have you seen that guy Reed? The guy we were talking about before?'

He said, 'He was in here two hours ago. By now he'll be wherever the shots are cheapest.'

'Which is where?'

'Can't say for sure. Not here, anyway.'

Then he ducked away to continue his marathon and I fought my way back to the door.

I got back to the diner sixteen minutes after I left it and found that the pies had been delivered in my absence and that Munro was halfway through eating his. I picked up my fork and he apologized for not waiting. He said, 'I thought you were gone.'

I said, 'I often take a walk between courses. It's a Mississippi thing, apparently. Always good to blend in with the local population.'

He said nothing in reply to that. He just looked a little bemused.

I asked, 'What are you doing in Germany?'

'Generally?'

'No, specifically. As in, when you get there first thing in the morning the day after tomorrow, what's on your desk?'

'Not very much.'

'Nothing urgent?'

'Why?'

'Three women were killed here,' I said. 'And the perp is running around free as a bird.'

'We have no jurisdiction.'

'Remember that picture in Emmeline McClatchy's parlour? Martin Luther King? He said all that needs to happen for evil to prevail is that good men do nothing.'

'I'm a military cop, not a good man.'

'He also said the day we see the truth and cease to speak is the day we begin to die.'

'That stuff is way above my pay grade.'

'He also said that injustice anywhere is a threat to justice everywhere.'

'What do you want me to do?'

'I want you to stay here,' I said. 'One more day.'

Then I finished my pie and went looking for Elizabeth Deveraux again.

It was eleven thirty-one when I left the diner for the second time. I turned right and walked up to the Sheriff's Department. It was locked up and dark. No vehicles in the lot. I kept on going and turned the corner on to the

Kelham road. There was a stream of traffic coming out from behind Main Street. One car after another. Some were full of women and turning left. Most were full of Rangers and turning right, at least three and sometimes four guys in each car. Bravo Company, going home. Maybe they had a midnight curfew. I glanced down to the acre of beaten dirt and saw every single car except my Buick in motion. Some were just starting up and backing out. Others were manoeuvring for position, getting in line, getting ready to join the convoy.

I kept on walking, on the left-hand shoulder, keeping my distance from the traffic heading for Kelham. A lot of beer had been consumed, and the designated driver concept was not big in 1997. Not in the army, anyway. Dust was coming up off the road, and bright headlight beams were cutting through it, and motors were roaring. Two hundred yards ahead of me cars were thumping over the railroad track and then accelerating away into the darkness.

Deveraux was right there, sitting in her car on the far side of the crossing. She was facing me. She was parked with her wheels on the shoulder of the road. I walked towards her, with Bravo Company overtaking me all the way, maybe ninety of them in thirty cars in the minute it took me to reach the railroad. By the time I got there the stream was already thinning behind me. The last of the stragglers were passing me by, five and ten and twenty seconds between each one. They were driving fast, chasing after their more punctual friends.

I waited for a break in the traffic long enough to get me safely over the track, and Deveraux opened her door

438

and got out to meet me. We stood there together, lit up bright by the oncoming headlights. She said, 'Five more minutes and they'll all be gone. But I have to wait until Butler and Pellegrino get back. I can't go off duty before they do. That wouldn't be fair.'

I asked, 'When will they get back?'

'The train takes a whole minute to pass a given point. Which doesn't sound like much, but it feels like an hour when you've been working all evening. So they'll try to make it before midnight.'

'How long before midnight?'

She smiled. 'Not long enough, I'm afraid. Five to, maybe. We wouldn't get home in time.'

I said, 'Pity.'

She smiled wider.

She said, 'Get in the car, Reacher.'

She started the motor and waited a moment as the last of the Bravo Company stragglers sped by. Then she eased off the shoulder, and manoeuvred out to the humped crown of the pavement, and then she turned a tight right that put us up on the crossing, sideways to the road, facing north up the railroad track, directly in line with it. She put a light foot on the gas and steered carefully and got her right-hand wheels up on the right-hand rail. Her left-hand wheels were down on the ties. The whole car was tilted at a decent angle. She drove on, not fast, not slow, but decisive and confident. She went straight, one hand on the wheel, one hand in her lap, past the water tower, then onward. Her left-hand wheels pattered over the ties. Her right-hand wheels ran smooth. A fine piece of car control. Then she braked gently, one side up, one side down, and she came to a neat stop.

On the track.

Twenty yards north of the water tower.

Right where Reed Riley's car had waited for the train.

Where the broken glass began.

I said, 'You've done this before.'

She said, 'Yes, I have.'

SEVENTY-FOUR

She said, 'This is the tricky part. It's all about momentum now.' She turned the wheel hard to the left and just as the front right-hand tyre came down off the right-hand rail she hit the gas and the pulse of acceleration popped the front left-hand tyre up over the left-hand rail. The whole car squirmed for a second, and she kept her foot light on the pedal, and the other wheels followed suit, two, three, four, with separate squelching sounds, side-wall rubber against steel, and then she stopped again and parked in the dirt very close to and exactly parallel with the track. The first of the ballast stones were about five feet from my window.

She said, 'I love this spot. No other way to get to it, because of the ditch. But it's worth the trouble. I come here quite often.'

'At midnight?' I asked.

'Always,' she said.

I turned and looked out the back window. I could see the road. More than forty yards away, less than fifty. At first there was nothing happening. No traffic. Then a car flashed past east to west, left to right, away from

Kelham, towards town, moving fast. A big car, with lights on its roof and a shield on its door.

'Pellegrino,' she said. She was watching too, now. Right at my side. She said, 'He was probably holed up a hundred yards away, and as soon as that last straggler passed him he counted to ten and hightailed it for home.'

I said, 'Butler was parked right at Kelham's gate.'

'Yes, Butler is the one with a race on his hands. And our fate *in* his hands. As soon as he passes us, I guarantee we're alone in the world. This is a small town, Reacher, and I know where everyone is.'

The clock in my head said eleven forty-nine. Butler's plight involved a complex calculation. He was three miles away and wouldn't hesitate to drive at sixty, which meant he could be home in three minutes. But he couldn't start that three-minute dash until the last straggler got at least within headlight range of Kelham. And that last straggler might be driving pretty slow at that point, having had a skinful of beer and having seen Pellegrino parked menacingly on the side of the road. My guess was Butler would be through in eleven minutes, which would be midnight exactly, and I said so.

'No, he'll have jumped the gun,' Deveraux said. 'The last ten minutes have been fairly quiet. He'll have moved off the gate five minutes ago. That's my guess. He might not be far behind Pellegrino.'

We watched the road.

All quiet.

I opened my door and got out of the car. I stepped right on the edge of the rail bed. The left-hand rail was no more than a yard away. It was gleaming in the moonlight. I figured the train was ten miles south of us. Passing through Marietta, maybe, right at that moment.

Deveraux got out on her side and we met behind the Caprice's trunk. Eleven fifty-one. Nine minutes to go. We watched the road.

All quiet.

Deveraux stepped back around and opened a rear door. She checked the back seat. She said, 'Just in case. We might as well be ready.'

'Too cramped,' I said.

'You don't like doing it in cars?'

'They don't make them wide enough.'

She checked her watch.

She said, 'We won't make it back to Toussaint's in time.'

I said, 'Let's do it right here. On the ground.'

She smiled.

Then wider.

'Sounds good to me,' she said. 'Like Janice Chapman.'

'If she did,' I said. I took off my BDU jacket and spread it out on the weeds, as long and wide as it would go.

We watched the road.

All quiet.

She took off her gun belt and stowed it on the rear seat of the car. Eleven fifty-four. Six minutes. I knelt down and put my ear on the rail. I heard a faint metallic whisper. Almost not there at all. The train, six miles south.

We watched the road.

We saw a hint of a glow in the east.

Headlights.

Deveraux said, 'Good old Butler.'

The glow grew brighter, and we heard rushing tyres and a straining engine in the silence of the night. Then the glow changed to delineated beams and the noise grew louder and a second later Butler's car flashed left to right in front of us and thwacked over the crossing without slowing down at all. He went airborne on the lee side and crashed back to earth with a yelp of rubber and a cloud of dust. Then he was gone.

Four minutes to go.

We were neither refined nor elegant. We wrenched our shoes off and pulled our pants down and abandoned all adult sophistication in favour of pure animal instinct. Deveraux hit the deck and got comfortable on my jacket and I went down right on top of her and propped myself up on my palms and watched for the glimmer of the train's headlight in the distance. Not there yet. Three minutes to go.

She wrapped her legs around my hips and we got going, fast and hard from the first moment, anxious, desperate, insanely energetic. She was gasping and panting and rolling her head from side to side and grabbing fistfuls of my T-shirt and hauling on it. Then we were kissing and breathing both at the same time, and then she was arching her back and grinding her head on the ground, straining her neck, opening her eyes, looking at the world behind her upside down.

Then the ground began to shake.

As before, just faintly at first, the same mild constant

444

tremor, like the beginning of a distant earthquake. The stones in the rail bed next to us started to scratch and click. The ties started to tremble. The rails themselves started to sing, humming and keening and whispering. The ties jumped and shuddered. The ballast stones crunched and hopped. The ground under my hands and knees danced with big bass shudders. I looked up and gasped and blinked and squinted and saw the distant headlight. Twenty yards south of us the old water tower started to shake and its elephant's trunk started to sway. The ground beat on us from below. The rails screamed and howled. The train whistle blew, long and loud and forlorn. The warning bells at the crossing forty yards away started to ring. The train kept on coming, unstoppable, still distant, still distant, then right next to us, then right on top of us, just as insanely massive as before, and just as impossibly loud.

Like the end of the world.

The ground shook hard under us and we bounced and bucketed whole inches in the air. A bow wave of air battered us. Then the locomotive flashed past, its giant wheels five feet from our faces, followed by the endless sequence of cars, all of them hammering, juddering, strobing in the moonlight. We clung together, the whole long minute, sixty long seconds, deafened by the squealing metal, beaten numb by the throbbing ground, scoured by dust from the slipstream. Deveraux threw her head back under me and screamed soundlessly and jammed her head from side to side and beat on my back with her fists.

Then the train was gone.

I turned my head and saw the cars rolling away from me into the distance at a steady sixty miles an hour. The wind dropped, and the earthquake quieted down, first to gentle tremors again, and then to nothing at all, and the bells stopped dead, and the rails stopped hissing, and the night-time silence came back. We rolled apart and lay on our backs in the weeds, panting, sweating, spent, deaf, completely overwhelmed by sensations internal and external. My jacket had gotten balled up and crumpled under us. My knees and hands were torn and scraped. I imagined Deveraux was in an even worse state. I turned my head to check and saw she had my Beretta in her hand.

SEVENTY-FIVE

The Marine Corps never liked the Beretta as much as the army did, so Deveraux was handling mine with proficiency but less than total enthusiasm. She dumped the magazine, ejected an unfired round, checked the chamber, racked the slide, and then put the whole thing back together again. She said, 'I'm sorry. It was in your jacket pocket. I wondered what it was. It was digging into my ass. I'm going to have a bruise.'

'In which case it's me that's sorry,' I said. 'Your ass deserves nothing but the best. It's a national treasure. Or a regional attraction, at the very least.'

She smiled at me and stood up, unsteady, and went in search of her pants. Her shirt tail hung down, but not far enough. No bruise yet. She asked, 'Why did you bring a gun?'

'Habit,' I said.

'Were you expecting trouble?'

'Anything's possible.'

'I left mine in the car.'

'So did lots of dead people.'

'It's just the two of us here.'

'As far as we know.'

'You're paranoid.'

'But alive,' I said. 'And you haven't arrested anyone yet.'

'The army can't prove a negative,' she said. 'Therefore they must know who it was. They should tell me.'

I said nothing in reply to that. I followed her lead and staggered to my feet and picked up my pants. We got dressed, hopping from foot to foot together, and then we perched side by side on the Caprice's rear bumper and laced our shoes. Getting back to the road was no real problem. Deveraux did it in reverse, backing up on to the track like parallel parking, then backing all the way to the crossing, and then turning the wheel and taking off forward. We were in my hotel room five minutes later. In bed. She went straight to sleep. I didn't. I lay in the dark and stared at the ceiling and thought.

Mostly I thought about my last conversation with Leon Garber. My commanding officer. An honest man, and my friend, as far as I knew. But cryptic. *It's the truth*, he had said. *She was a Marine, Reacher. Sixteen years in. She knew all about cutting throats. She knew how to do it, and she knew how to pretend she didn't.* Then he had gotten a little impatient. *A man with your instincts*, he had said, about me. Later I had pushed the issue. *You could order me not to go back to Mississippi*, I had said. *I could*, he had said. *But I won't. Not you. I trust you to do the right thing.*

The conversation replayed endlessly in my head.

The truth.

Instincts.

The right thing.

In the end I fell asleep very late and completely un-sure whether Garber had been telling me something, or asking me something.

My long-held belief that there is no better time than the second time was put to a severe test when we woke up, because the fifth time was also pretty terrific. We were both a little stiff and sore after our outdoor extravaganza, so we took it gently, long and slow, and the warmth and the comfort of the bed helped a lot. Plus neither one of us knew whether there would ever be a sixth time, which added a little poignancy to the occasion. Afterwards we lay quiet for a while, and then she asked me when I was leaving, and I said I didn't know.

We ate breakfast together in the diner, and then she went to work, and I went to use the phone. I tried to call Frances Neagley at her desk in D.C., but she wasn't back yet. Probably still on an all-night bus somewhere. So I dialled Stan Lowrey instead, and got him right away. I said, 'I need you to do something else for me.'

He said, 'No jokes this morning? About how you're surprised I'm still here?'

'I didn't have time to think of any. I wanted Neagley, not you. You should try to get hold of her as soon as you can. She's better than you at this kind of shit.'

'Better than you, too. What do you need?'

'Fast answers,' I said.

'To what questions?'

'Statistically speaking, where would we be most likely to find U.S. Marines and concrete flood sluices in close proximity?'

'Southern California,' Lowrey said. 'Statistically speaking, almost certainly Camp Pendleton, north of San Diego.'

'Correct,' I said. 'I need to trace a jarhead MP who was there five years ago. His name is Paul Evers.'

'Why?'

'Because his parents were Mr and Mrs Evers and they liked the name Paul, I guess.'

'No, why do you want to trace him?'

'I want to ask him a question.'

Lowrey said, 'You're forgetting something.'

'Like what?'

'I'm in the army, not the Marine Corps. I can't get into their files.'

'That's why you need to call Neagley. She'll know how to do it.'

'Paul Evers,' he said, slowly, like he was writing it down.

'Call Neagley,' I said again. 'This is urgent. I'll get back to you.'

I hung up with Lowrey and shovelled more coins into the slot and called the Kelham number Munro had given Deveraux, right back at the beginning. The call went through to some guy who wasn't Munro. He told me Munro had left at first light, in a car to Birmingham, Alabama. I said I knew that had been the plan. I asked the guy to check if it had actually happened. So the guy called the visiting officers' quarters and came back to me and said no, it hadn't actually happened. Munro was still on the post. The guy gave me a number for his room and I hung up and redialled.

Munro answered and I said, 'Thank you for sticking around.'

He said, 'But what am I sticking around for? Right now I'm just hiding out in my room. I'm not very popular here, you know.'

'You didn't join the army to be popular.'

'What do you need?'

'I need to know Reed Riley's movements today.'

'Why?'

'I want to ask him a question.'

'That could be difficult. As far as I know he's going to be pretty much tied up all day. You might be able to grab him over lunch. If he gets time for lunch, that is. And if he does, it will be very early.'

'No, I need him to come to me. In town.'

'You don't understand. The mood has changed here. Bravo Company is out from under the cloud. Riley's father is flying in for a visit.'

'The senator? Today?'

'ETA close to one o'clock this afternoon. Billed as an off-the-record celebration of what the guys are doing in Kosovo.'

'How long will it last?'

'You know what politicians are like. The old guy is supposed to watch some training crap in the afternoon, but dollars to doughnuts he'll get a real hard-on and want to hang around all night drinking with the boys.'

'OK,' I said. 'I'll figure something out.'

'Anything else?'

'Well, since you've got nothing to do except sit around all day, you could tell me a couple of things.'

'What things?'

The phone started beeping at me and I said, 'Why don't you call me back on the government's dime?' I read out the number from the dial and hung up. I walked to my table to pay the breakfast check and by the time I got back to the phone it was ringing.

'What things?' Munro said again.

'Impressions, mainly. About Kelham. As in, is there a good reason for Alpha Company and Bravo Company to be based there?'

'As opposed to where else?'

'Anywhere else east of the Mississippi River.'

'Kelham is pretty isolated,' Munro said. 'Helps with the secrecy thing.'

'That's what they told me, too. But I don't buy it. There are secrets on every base. They could keep the lid on this thing anywhere. Kosovo is not even interesting. Who would even listen? But they chose Kelham a year ago. Why did they do that? Have you seen anything about Kelham that would make it the only choice?'

'No,' Munro said. 'Not really. It's adequate, no question. But not essential. I assume it was about sending four hundred extra wallets to a dying town.'

'Exactly,' I said. 'It was political.'

'What isn't?'

452

'One more thing,' I said. 'You're clear about how Janice Chapman ended up in that alley, right?'

'I hope so,' he said. 'Based on what I saw last night, Chief Deveraux operates an exclusion zone in terms of Main Street itself. She makes sure all the action happens between the bars and the railroad track. Therefore both Main Street and the alley would have been deserted. Therefore the perp must have stopped on Main Street and carried the corpse in from that direction.'

'How long would it have taken?'

'Doesn't matter. No one was there to see. Could have been a minute, could have been twenty.'

'But why there? Why not somewhere else, ten miles away?'

'The body was supposed to be found, I guess.'

'Plenty of lonelier places it would still have been found. So why there?'

'I don't know,' Munro said. 'Maybe the perp was constrained in some way. Maybe he had company, somewhere close by. Like the diner, or one of the bars. Maybe he had to duck out and take care of it real fast. Maybe he couldn't be gone for long without somebody noticing. So maybe he had to trade safety for speed. Which would dictate a nearby location.'

'Can you give me another day?' I said. 'Can you be here tomorrow?'

'No,' he said. 'I'm going to get my butt kicked bad for being one day late. I can't risk two.'

'Pussy,' I said.

He laughed. 'Sorry, man, but if you don't get it done today you're on your own.'

453

SEVENTY-SIX

Senator Carlton Riley's impending visit kept the town very quiet. It was as if Kelham's gates were locked again. I doubted that the leave order had been formally rescinded, but Rangers are good soldiers, and I was sure the base commander had dropped heavy hints about 100 per cent participation in the hoopla. I left the diner and found Main Street back to its previous torpor. My borrowed Buick was the only car parked on the block behind. It looked lonely and abandoned. I unlocked it and drove it around to the hotel and retrieved my toothbrush and settled my account at the desk. Then I got back behind the wheel and went exploring.

I started opposite the vacant lot between the diner and the Sheriff's Department. I headed south from there for two hundred yards, to where Main Street started to bend, driving fast but not stupid fast. I made the left into Deveraux's childhood street, and hustled along to her old house, fourth on the right. Total elapsed time, forty-five seconds.

I turned in over the dried mud puddle and drove down the overgrown driveway, past the tumbledown

454

house, through the back yard, past the wild hedge, to the deer trestle. I swung left and backed up and popped the trunk and got out.

Total elapsed time, a minute and fifteen seconds.

There were trees to my left and trees to my right and trees ahead of me. A lonely spot, even in the bright daylight. I mimed supporting a body's weight, cutting the wrist straps, cutting the ankle ties, carrying the body to the car, lowering it into the trunk. I fiddled around four more times, taking off imaginary pads and straps and belts and scarves from two wrists and two ankles. I stepped back to the trestle and picked up an imaginary bucket of blood and heaved it over to the car and wedged it in the trunk alongside the body.

I closed the trunk lid and got back in the driver's seat.

Total elapsed time, three minutes and ten seconds.

I backed up and turned and drove the length of the driveway again and headed back to Main Street. I drove the same two hundred yards I had driven before and stopped on the kerb between the hardware store and the pharmacy. Right at the mouth of the alley.

Total elapsed time, four minutes and twenty-five seconds.

Plus one minute to put the blood in the alley.

Plus another minute to put Janice May Chapman in the alley.

Plus fifteen seconds to get back where I started.

Total elapsed time, six minutes and forty seconds.

Touch and go.

Maybe long enough to stick in someone's mind, in a social situation, or maybe not.

I rewound the clock in my head to four minutes and twenty-five seconds and drove on north and then east, to the railroad crossing. I came to a stop right on top of it. New total, four minutes and fifty-five seconds. Plus a minute to carry Rosemary McClatchy to the ditch, and thirty seconds to get back to the car, and twenty seconds to get back where I started.

Total elapsed time, six minutes and forty-five seconds.

Fractionally longer, but in the same ballpark.

I didn't drive up to where Shawna Lindsay had been dumped, on the pile of gravel. No point. That destination was in a whole different category. That was a twenty-minute excursion, right there. It was the sole exception to the hurry-up rule. Therefore it had been undertaken under different circumstances. No company. No social situation. Plenty of time to thread cautiously along dark dirt roads between ditches, turning right, turning left, doing the deed, and then coming back again, just as slow, just as cautious.

But what was interesting about Shawna Lindsay's resting place was the car that carried her there. What kind of car could get through that neighbourhood twice, without attracting notice or comment? What kind of car was entitled to be there at that time of night?

I sat in the Buick for a spell and then I parked it outside the diner and went in and bought a new roll of quarters for the phone. I tried Neagley first and found her at her desk.

I said, 'You're late to work today.'

She said, 'But not by much. I've been here half an hour.'

'I'm sorry about the bus.'

'It was OK,' she said. Public transportation was tough for Neagley. Too much chance of inadvertent human contact.

I asked, 'Did you get a message from Stan Lowrey?'

'Yes, and I already traced the name for you.'

'In half an hour?'

'It was easy, I'm afraid. Paul Evers died a year ago.'

'How?'

'Nothing dramatic. It was an accident. A helicopter crashed at Lejeune. It was in the newspaper, actually. A Sea Hawk lost a rotor blade. Two pilots and three passengers died, one of which was Evers.'

I said, 'OK, plan B. The other name I want is Alice Bouton.' I spelled it out. I said, 'She's been a civilian for the last five years. She was discharged from the Corps without honour. So you better call Stan back. He's better than you at this kind of shit.'

'The only thing Lowrey has that I don't is a friend at a bank.'

'Exactly,' I said. 'That's why you need to call him. Corporations know about civilians better than we do.'

'Why are we doing this?'

'I'm checking a story.'

'No, you're clutching at straws. That's what you're doing.'

'You think?'

'Elizabeth Deveraux is as guilty as sin, Reacher.'

'You've seen the file?'

'Only the carbons.'

I said, 'But with a thing like this, you have to flip a coin.'

'As in?'

'As in, maybe she did it, maybe she didn't. We don't know yet.'

'We know, Reacher.'

'Not for sure.'

Neagley said, 'It's a good thing you don't own a car.'

I hung up with her and before I was a step away the phone rang on the wall, with the first good news of the day.

SEVENTY-SEVEN

It was Munro on the phone, and he wanted to tell me he had had a cup of coffee. Or more specifically he wanted to tell me he had talked to the steward who had brought him the cup of coffee. The conversation had been on the subject of the day's upcoming festivities, and Munro said the stewards expected to be very busy until after dinner, but no later than that, because the mess bar would be deserted all evening, because the last time the senator visited he had hosted everybody in town, at Brannan's bar, because politically it seemed more authentic, and no doubt the old guy would do the same thing again.

'OK,' I said. 'That's good. Riley will come to me after all. And his father. What time will dinner finish?'

'Scheduled to be over by eight o'clock, according to the steward.'

'OK,' I said again. 'I'm sure father and son will leave the base together. I want you on them from the moment they drive through the gate. But unobtrusively. Can you do that?'

'Could you?'

459

'Probably.'

'Then what makes you doubt I could?'

'Innate scepticism, I suppose,' I said. 'But whatever, keep your ear to the ground until eight tonight, and use this phone number as a contact if you need me. I'll be in and out of this diner all day long.'

'OK,' Munro said. 'I'll see you later. But whether or not you'll see me is a different question altogether.'

I hung up with Munro, and I asked the waitress to answer the phone for me if it rang again. I asked her to write down the callers' names on her order pad. Then it was all about waiting. For information, and for face to face encounters, and for decisive conclusions. I stepped out to the Main Street sidewalk and stood in the sun. Across the street the guy from the shirt store was doing the same thing. Taking a break, and tasting the air. On my left two old guys were on a bench outside the pharmacy, four hands piled on two canes between two sets of knees. Apart from the four of us the town was deserted. No hustle, no bustle, no traffic.

All quiet.

Until the goon squad from Kelham showed up.

There were four of them in total. They were Kelham's own local version of Senate Liaison, I guessed, preparing the ground the same way a Secret Service advance team prepares the ground ahead of a presidential visit. They came out of the mouth of the alley beyond the two old guys on the bench. I guessed they had just called on the Brannan brothers and alerted them to what was going to happen that night. Maybe they had made invoicing arrangements. In which case I wished the Brannan brothers the very best of luck. I imagined billing a Senate office was a long and frustrating experience.

The four guys were all officers. Two lieutenants, a captain, and a light colonel in the lead. He was fiftyish and fat. He was the kind of soft staff officer who looks ludicrous in battledress uniform. Like a civilian at a fancy-dress party. He stopped on the sidewalk and put his knuckles on his hips. He looked all around. He saw me. I was in battledress uniform too. On the face of it, I was one of his. He spoke over his shoulder to a lieutenant behind him. Too far to hear his voice, but I could read his lips. He said, *Tell that man to get his ass over here double-quick.* I guessed he would want to know why I wasn't back on the base, getting myself ready for 100 per cent participation in the hoopla.

The lieutenant's eyesight was not as good as mine. He approached most of the way full of one kind of body language, which changed fast when he got close enough to read my rank insignia. He stopped a respectful four feet away and saluted and said, 'Sir, the colonel would like a word with you.'

Normally I treat lieutenants well. I was one myself, not so very long ago. But right then I wasn't in the mood for nonsense. So I just nodded and said, 'OK, kid, tell him to step right up.'

The kid said, 'Sir, I think he would prefer it if you went to him.'

'You must be confusing me with someone who gives a shit what he prefers.'

461

The kid went a little pale and blinked twice and about-turned and headed back. He must have spent the walk time translating my response into acceptable terms, because there was no instant explosion. Instead the colonel paused a beat and then set off waddling in my direction. He stopped three feet away, and I saluted him very smartly, just to keep him confused.

He returned the salute and asked, 'Do I know you, major?'

I said, 'That depends on how much trouble you've been in, colonel. Have you ever been arrested?'

He said, 'You're the other MP. You're Major Munro's opposite number.'

'Or he's mine,' I said. 'Either way, I'm sure we both hope you have a great day.'

'Why are you still here?'

'Why wouldn't I be?'

'I was told all issues had been resolved.'

'The issues will be resolved when I say they are. That's the nature of police work.'

'When did you last get orders?'

'Some days ago,' I said. 'They came from Colonel John James Frazer at the Pentagon, I believe.'

'He died.'

'I'm sure his successor will have new orders for me in due course.'

'It could take weeks to install a successor.'

'Then I guess I'm stuck here.'

Silence.

Then the fat guy said, 'Well, stay out of sight tonight. Understand? The senator must not see a CID presence here. There are to be no reminders of recent suspicions. None at all. Is that clear?'

I said, 'Request noted.'

'It's more than a request.'

'Next up from a request is an order. But you're not in my chain of command.'

The guy rehearsed a reply, but in the end he didn't come out with anything. He just turned on his heel and waddled back to his pals. And at that point I heard the phone ring inside the diner, very faintly through the door, and I beat the waitress to it by a step.

SEVENTY-EIGHT

It was Frances Neagley on the line, from her desk in D.C. She said, 'Bouton is a very uncommon name, apparently.'

I said, 'Did Stan Lowrey tell you to say that?'

'No, Stan wants to know if she's related to Jim Bouton, the baseball pitcher. Which she probably is, at least distantly, given how rare the name is. I, however, am basing my conclusion on an hour's solid work, which turned up no Boutons at all, much less any Alice Boutons. Having said that, right now I can't get any further than three years back with the Marines, which would miss her anyway, and if she was dishonourably discharged she probably didn't get the kind of job or income that would show up in too many other places.'

'She probably lives in a trailer park,' I said. 'Nowhere near Pendleton, either. Southern California is too expensive. She must have moved.'

'I have a call in to the FBI. And to a pal in USMC personnel command, for the ancient history. And Stan is hassling his banker friend, for the civilian stuff. Although she might not have had a bank account. Not if she lived in a trailer park. But whatever, I just wanted to let you know we're on it, that's all. We'll have more later.'

'How much later?'

'Tonight, I hope.'

'Before eight o'clock would be good.'

'I'll do my best.'

I hung up the phone and decided to stay in the diner, for lunch.

And inevitably Deveraux came in less than ten minutes later, in search of her own lunch, and, possibly, in search of me. She stepped inside and paused in front of the window, with the light behind her. Her hair lit up like a halo. Her shirt was very slightly translucent. I could see the curve of her waist. Or sense it, at least. Because I was familiar with it. I could see the swell of her breast.

She saw me staring, and she started towards me, and I kicked the opposite chair out an inch. She sat down and brought the backlight with her. She smiled and said, 'How was your morning?'

I said, 'No, how was yours?'

'Busy,' she said.

'Making any progress?'

'With what?'

'Your three unsolved homicides.'

'Apparently the army solved those homicides,' she said. 'And I'll be happy to do something about them as soon as the army shares its information.'

I said nothing.

She said, 'What?'

'You don't seem very interested in finding out who did it, that's all.'

'How can I be interested?'

'The army says it was a civilian.'

'I understand that.'

'Do you know who it was?'

'What?'

'Do you know who it was?'

'Are you saying I do?'

I said, 'I'm saying I know how these things work. There are some people you just can't arrest. Mrs Lindsay would have been one of them, for instance. Suppose she'd gone the other way and gotten tooled up and gone and shot somebody. You wouldn't have arrested her for it.'

'What are you saying?'

'I'm saying in any town there are people the sheriff won't arrest.'

She was quiet a long moment.

'Maybe,' she said. 'Old man Clancy might be one of them. But he didn't cut any throats. And I'd arrest anyone else, whoever they were.'

'OK,' I said.

'Maybe you think I'm bad at my job.'

I said nothing.

'Or maybe you think I've lost my edge because we have no crime here.'

'I know you have crime here,' I said. 'I know you always did. I'm sure your father saw crimes I can't even imagine.'

'But?'

'You don't have investigation here. And you never did. I bet ninety-nine times out of a hundred your father knew exactly who did what, right down to the details. Whether he could do anything about it was a different issue. And I bet the one case in a hundred where he didn't know who did it went unsolved.'

'You're saying I'm a bad investigator.'

'I'm saying County Sheriff is not an investigator's job. It needs other skills. All kinds of community stuff. And you're good at it. You have a detective for the other things. Except right now you don't.'

'Any other issues, before we order?'

'Just one,' I said.

'Which is?'

'Tell me again. You never dated Reed Riley, right?'

'Reacher, what is this?'

'It's a question.'

'No, I never dated Reed Riley.'

'Are you sure?'

'Reacher, please.'

'Are you?'

'I didn't even know he was here. I told you that.'

'OK,' I said. 'Let's order.'

She was mad at me, obviously, but she was hungry, too. More hungry than mad, clearly, because she stayed at the table. Changing tables wouldn't have been enough. She would have had to storm out emphatically, and she wasn't prepared to do that on an empty stomach.

She ordered the chicken pie, of course.

I ordered grilled cheese.

She said, 'There are things you aren't telling me.'

I said, 'You think?'

'You know who it is.'

I said nothing.

'You do, don't you? You know who it is. So this whole thing wasn't about me knowing who it is. It was about you knowing who it is.'

I said nothing.

'Who is it?'

I didn't answer.

'Are you saying it's someone I won't arrest? Who won't I arrest? It makes no sense. I mean, obviously it's a great idea for the army to dump the blame on someone they know will never be arrested. I get that. Because if there's no arrest, there can be no charge, no interview, no trial, and no verdict. Hence no facts. So everyone can just walk away and live happily ever after. But how could the army know who I wouldn't arrest? Which is nobody, by the way. So this whole thing is crazy.'

'I don't know who it is,' I said. 'Not for sure. Not yet.'

SEVENTY-NINE

We finished our lunch without saying much more. Then we had pie. Peach, naturally. And coffee. I asked her, 'Did the Kelham PR squad come see you?'

She nodded. 'Just before I came out for lunch.'

'So you know what's happening tonight.'

'Eight o'clock,' she said. 'Everyone on best behaviour.'

'You OK with that?'

'They know the rules. If they stick to them, I won't give them any trouble.'

Then the phone rang. Deveraux whipped around and stared at it, as if she had never heard it ring before. Which was possible. I said, 'It's for me.'

I walked over and picked up. It was Munro. He said, 'I have the transportation details, if you're interested. Reed Riley doesn't own a car any more, as you know, so he's borrowing a plain olive drab staff car. He'll be driving with his father as his only passenger. The motor pool has been told to have the car ready at eight o'clock exactly.'

'Thanks,' I said. 'Good to know. Is there a return ETA?'

'There's an eleven o'clock curfew tonight. Unofficial, all done in whispers, but it'll happen. A few beers is authentic. Too many is embarrassing. That's the thinking. So people will be leaving town from ten-thirty onwards. The senator's plane is scheduled to be wheels-up at midnight.'

'Good to know,' I said again. 'Thanks. Has he arrived yet?'

'Twenty minutes ago, in an army Lear.'

'Has the hoopla started yet?'

'First pitch in about an hour.'

'Will you bring me your interview notes?'

'Why?'

'There are a couple of things I want to check. As soon as the senator looks like he's going to stay put for ten minutes, would you bring them down to me in the diner?'

Munro agreed to do that, so I hung up the phone and walked back to the table, but by then Deveraux was already getting up to leave. She said, 'I'm sorry, I have to get back to work. I've got a lot to do. I have three homicides to solve.'

Then she pushed past me and walked out the door.

Waiting. I passed some of the time by taking a walk. I looped around the Sheriff's Department building and entered the acre of beaten earth behind Main Street from the top. The railroad track on my left was silent. The stores and bars on my right were all open, but they had no customers. The bars all had cleaners working in them, all of them black women over forty, all of them

470

bent low over mops and pails, all of them supervised by anxious owners well aware that a U.S. senator would be passing by, and maybe even dropping in. Brannan's was getting more attention than most. Furniture was being moved, refrigerators were being topped off, trash was being hauled out. Even the windows were being wiped.

Across the alley from Brannan's the loan office was doing no business at all. Shawna Lindsay had worked there before she died, and evidently she had been replaced by another young woman, less beautiful, but possibly just as good with her numbers. She was sitting on a high stool behind a counter, with a lit-up Western Union sign behind her head. I had time to kill, so on a whim I went inside. The woman looked up as the door opened, and she smiled like she was happy to see me. Maybe I was the only customer of the day so far.

I asked her how the system worked, and after a little back and forth I understood I could call my bank on the phone and order money to be sent to any such office in America. I would need a password for the bank, and either ID or the same password for the office. This was 1997, remember. Things were still pretty casual back then. I knew there were all kinds of banks close to the Pentagon, because thirty thousand people all in one place was a big market to exploit. I decided next time I was in D.C. I would move my account to one of them, and find out its phone number, and register a password. Just in case.

I thanked the young woman and moved on, to the next place in line, which was a gun shop. I bought spare ammunition for the Beretta, nine-millimetre

Parabellums in a box of twenty, and a spare magazine to put fifteen of them in. I checked that it fit and worked, which it did. Most guys who don't check new equipment are still alive, but by no means all of them. I replaced the round I had put through the skinny runt's head, and then I put the gun back in one pocket and the new magazine and the four loose rounds in the other.

And that was it for shopping. I didn't need a used stereo, and I didn't need auto parts. So I dog-legged through Janice Chapman's alley and walked back to the diner. The waitress met me at the door and told me she had taken no calls for me. I stood there for a second, unsure, and then I picked up the phone, fed it a quarter and dialled the Treasury Department switchboard. The same number I had called from the old yellow phone in the Lindsay kitchen. The same woman answered. Middle-aged, and elegant.

She asked, 'How may I direct your inquiry?'

I said, 'Joe Reacher's office, please.'

I heard the same scratching and clicking, and the same minute of dead air. Then the young woman I was sure wore a plaid skirt and a white sweater picked up and said, 'Mr Reacher's office.'

I asked, 'Is Mr Reacher there?'

She recognized my voice immediately, probably because it was just like Joe's. She said, 'No, I'm sorry, he's not back yet. He's still in Georgia. I think. At least, I hope.'

'You sound worried,' I said.

'I am, a little.'

'Don't be,' I said. 'Joe's a big boy. He can handle

472

whatever Georgia throws at him. I don't even think he's allergic to peanuts.'

Then I hung up and walked deep into the room and holed up at the rearmost table for two. I just sat there, waiting for Munro, counting off the time in my head.

Munro showed up more or less exactly as promised, an hour after our earlier phone call, plus five minutes for the drive. He parked a plain car on the kerb and came in and found me in the gloom at the back of the room. He unbuttoned his top pocket and slid out the slim black notebook I had seen before. He put it on the table and said, 'Keep it. No one else is going to want it. No one is saving a permanent place for it in the National Archives.'

I nodded. 'Some colonel just told me there are to be no reminders of recent suspicions.'

Munro nodded in turn. 'I just got the same speech. And that guy is real mad at you, by the way. Did you offend him somehow?'

'I certainly hope so.'

'He's writing a report for Garber.'

'We always need toilet paper.'

'Plus copies all over. You're going to be famous.' He looked straight at me for a second, perhaps regretfully, and then he headed back to his car. I opened the little black book and started to read.

EIGHTY

Munro's handwriting was cramped and neat and meticulous. It filled about fifty of the small pages. His method was to record two or three conversations at a time, and then to summarize them before moving on to the next two or three. That way both his raw materials and his conclusions were preserved side by side, the latter for ease of reference, the former for reconfirming the latter. A circular system, safe, diligent, and conscientious. He was a good cop. Reed Riley's photograph was still in the book, wedged tight into the spine after the last note and before the first blank page. I realized he had been using it as a bookmark.

The focus of all fifty pages was Janice May Chapman. It had emerged early on that she and Riley had been dating. Not that Riley had said anything about her. Or about anything else, either. He had lawyered up at the start and confined his answers to name, rank, and number. No big deal for an investigator of Munro's quality. He had spoken to every man in Bravo Company and teased out the facts from the blind sides and the unguarded rear. He had taken fragments of passing mentions and put them all together and woven them into a solid and reliable narrative.

Riley's men had talked about him in a way I had heard many times before. He was too young to be a legend, too unproven to be a star, but he had some kind of celebrity charisma, partly because of who his father was, and partly because of his own personality. But he wasn't liked. The conversations as recorded were loyal to a fault, but it was institutional loyalty, not personal loyalty, all of it filtered through any soldier's traditional hatred for the military police. No one had a bad thing to say about the guy, but no one had a good thing to say either. By reading between the lines of what was and wasn't said I saw that Riley was a grandstander and a show pony, and that he was impatient, reckless, careless, and full of entitlement. No big deal in a low-temperature environment like Kosovo, but he would have been accidentally shot in the back or blown up with a faulty grenade on his first day if he had been a generation older in Vietnam. That was for damn sure. Better men than Riley had suffered that fate.

Before Chapman it was clear he had dated Shawna Lindsay. They had been seen together many times. And before Lindsay he had dated Rosemary McClatchy. They too had been seen together many times, in the bars, in the diner, riding around in the blue 57 Chevy. There was a faint twice-removed reek of testosterone in Munro's notes, as one young man after another had chortled about the big dog mowing them down in sequence, all the best looking women in town, just like that, wham bam, thank you ma'am.

And according to Bravo Company, that prestigious sequence had begun with Elizabeth Deveraux. She was well known at Kelham, because of an early courtesy visit at the start of the mission. Back then training had been intense, and there had been no leave or downtime, but the big dog had snuck out at night and nailed the prize. That triumph had been revealed one evening during Bravo Company's first tour to Kosovo, over drinks around a fire. Again, I could almost hear the voices first-hand, full of chuckling delight at the way the rest of the regular 75th training grunts thought Deveraux was a lesbian, and at the way the boys of Bravo Company secretly knew better, because of their big dog, their alpha male, and his irresistible ways. They didn't like the guy, but they admired him. Personality, and charisma. And hormones too, I guessed.

There was nothing else of interest in the notebook. I spent some time looking at Riley's picture again, and then I squared the whole thing away in my own top pocket, and I went back to waiting.

The rest of the afternoon was long and fruitless. The hours passed, and no one called, and no one came, and the town stayed quiet. At one point I heard some faint live-firing noise from the east, and I guessed the hoopla at Kelham was going swimmingly. From time to time I drank a cup of coffee and ate a slice of pie, but mostly I just rested in a semi-vegetative state, eyes open but half asleep, breathing low, saving energy, like hibernation. Local people came and went in ones and twos, and at six o'clock Jonathan and Hunter Brannan came in for an early dinner, to fuel up ahead of their busy evening, which I thought was wise, and two or three others I took to be bar owners did the same thing, and some of what I took to be their cleaners stopped by before heading home, and at seven o'clock Main Street went dark outside the window, and at seven-thirty the old couple from the hotel came in for their meal, she with her book, he with his paper.

Then a minute later Stan Lowrey called on the phone, and the evening began to unravel.

EIGHTY-ONE

Lowrey started out by apologizing for the extreme lateness of his warning, and then he said he had just heard from an MP friend at Fort Benning in Georgia, where the 75th Ranger Regiment was based. Apparently a lieutenant colonel from their remote detachment at Kelham had phoned home and told his bosses there were still two CID majors on the scene locally, one on the post itself and one in town, the latter a prize pain in the ass, and because his bosses were determined that Senator Riley be shown nothing but a good time, they had dispatched a babysitting squad to muzzle the said CID majors for the remaining duration of the senator's visit. Just in case. Lowrey said the squad had left Benning in a Blackhawk helicopter some time ago, and therefore might well have already arrived at Kelham.

'MPs?' I said. 'They won't mess with me.'

'Not MPs,' Lowrey said. 'Regular Rangers. Real tough guys.'

'How many?'

'Six,' Lowrey said. 'Three for you and three for Munro, I guess.'

'Rules of engagement?'

'I don't know. What does it take to muzzle you?'

'More than three Rangers,' I said. I scanned the street out the window and saw nothing moving. No vehicles, no pedestrians. I said, 'Don't worry about me, Stan. It's Munro I'm concerned about. I need two pairs of hands tonight. It's going to make it harder if he gets hung up.'

'Which he will,' Lowrey said. 'You will too, probably. Word is these guys aren't kidding around.'

'Would you call him for me and give him the same warning?' I asked. 'If they haven't already gotten to him, that is.' I recited Munro's VOQ number, and I heard the scratch of a pencil as Lowrey wrote it down. Then I asked, 'Has your pet banker come through on Alice Bouton yet?'

'Negative,' Lowrey said. 'He's been busy all day. But Neagley is still on it.'

'Call her and tell her to take her thumb out her ass and get me some results. Tell her if I'm busy with the GI Joes when she calls she's authorized to leave a message with the waitress.'

'OK, and good luck,' Lowrey said, and hung up. I stepped out to the sidewalk and looked up and down the street. Nothing doing. I guessed the Rangers would look for me first in one of the bars. Probably Brannan's. If I was planning to make trouble, that was where I would be. So I looped around through the dog-leg alley and scanned the acre of ground from deep in the shadows.

And sure enough, there was a Humvee parked right there, big and green and obvious. I guessed the plan was to frogmarch me over to it and throw me in the back and drive me out to Kelham, and then to stash me in whatever room Munro was already locked up in. Then the plan would be to wait until the senator's Lear left at midnight, and let us out again, and apologize most sincerely for the misunderstanding.

Everyone has a plan until they get punched in the mouth.

I eased out around the corner of Brannan's bar and looked in through the window. The place was sparkling clean. Tables and chairs were neatly arrayed, all around a focal point I assumed would be occupied by the senator and his son. Acolytes would sit close by, and there was plenty of open space where the less well connected could stand. Jonathan and Hunter Brannan were behind the bar, looking well rested and well nourished after their early dinner.

Three guys in BDUs were talking to them.

They were Rangers, each one of them a decent size, and none of them a rookie. One of them was a sergeant, and two of them were specialists. Their uniforms had seen plenty of wear, and their boots were clean but creased. Their faces were tanned and lined and blank. They were professional soldiers, pure and simple. Which was a dumb expression, because professional soldiers were all kinds of things, none of which was pure, and none of which was simple. But ultimately it didn't matter exactly what two of them were, because the sergeant was in charge. And I had never met a sergeant who was less than well aware that there were eighteen ranks above him in the hierarchy, all the way up to the commander-in-chief, and that they all made more money than he did, in exchange for making policy decisions.

In other words, whatever a sergeant did, there were eighteen groups of people ready, willing, and waiting to criticize him.

I eased back into the shadows and headed back to the diner.

There were three customers still in the place, the old couple from Toussaint's and the guy in the pale suit I had seen once before. Three was a good number, but not a great number. On the other hand the demographics were close to perfect. Local business people, solid citizens, mature, easily outraged. And the old couple at least were guaranteed to stay for hours, which was good, because I might need hours, depending on Neagley's progress, or the lack of it.

I came in the door and stopped by the phone and the waitress shook her head at me, to tell me there had been no incoming calls. I used the phone book and found the number for Brannan's bar, and then I put a quarter in the slot and dialled. One of the Brannan brothers answered and I said, 'Let me speak to the sergeant.'

I heard a second of surprise and uncertainty, and then I heard the phone being reversed on the bar, and I heard the click of nails and the thump of palms as the receiver was passed from hand to hand, and then a voice said, 'Who is this?'

I said, 'This is the guy you're looking for. I'm in the diner.'

No answer.

I said, 'This is the part where you want to put your

481

hand over the mouthpiece long enough to ask the bar-men where the diner is, so you can send your guys to check while you keep me talking on the phone. But I'll save you the trouble. The diner is about twenty yards west of you and about fifty yards north. Send one guy through the alley on your left and the other counterclockwise out of the lot and around the Sheriff's Department building. You personally can come in through the kitchen door, which should be pretty close to where you parked your truck. That way you've got me covered in every direction. But don't worry. I'm not going anywhere. I'll wait for you right here. You'll find me at a table in back.'

Then I hung up and walked to the rearmost table for four.

EIGHTY-TWO

The sergeant was the first in. Shortest distance, biggest investment. He came through the kitchen door slowly and cautiously and let it swing shut behind him. I half-turned in my seat and raised my hand in greeting. I was about seven feet away from him. Then one of the specialists came in the front. From the alley, I assumed. Second shortest distance. A minute later the third guy was there, a little out of breath. Longest distance, biggest hurry.

They stood there, filling the aisle, two to my right and one to my left.

'Sit down,' I said. 'Please.'

The sergeant said, 'Our orders are to take you to Kelham.'

I said, 'That isn't going to happen, sergeant.'

No answer.

The clock in my head showed a quarter to eight.

I said, 'Here's the thing, guys. To take me out of here against my will would involve a considerable amount of physical commotion. At a rough guess we would bust up at least three or four tables and chairs. There might be personal injuries too. And the waitress will assume we're Bravo Company personnel. Because no one else from Kelham has leave right now. Believe me, she keeps track of stuff like that, because her income depends on it. And she knows Bravo's company commander is expected right there in Brannan's bar at any minute. So it would be entirely natural for her to head around there to complain. And to get that done she'd almost certainly have to interrupt a moment of intimacy between father and son. Which would be a big embarrassment for all concerned, especially you.'

No answer.

'Sit down, guys,' I said.

They sat down. But not where I wanted them to. They weren't dumb. That was the problem with a volunteer army. There were selection criteria. I was in an aisle seat at my table for four, facing the door. If they had all joined me at the same table, I would have had freedom of movement. But they didn't all join me at the same table. The sergeant sat down face to face with me, but the specialists sat across the aisle, one each side of a table for two. They pulled their chairs out at an angle, one of them ready to intervene if I made a break one way, and the other ready if I broke the other way.

'You should try the pie,' I said. 'It's really good.'

'No pie,' the sergeant said.

'You better order something. Or the waitress might throw you out for loitering. And if you refuse to go, she knows who to call.'

No answer.

I said, 'There are members of the public here, too. You really can't afford to attract attention.'

Stalemate.

Ten minutes to eight.

The phone by the door stayed silent.

The waitress came by and the sergeant shrugged and ordered three pies and three cups of coffee. Two more people came in the door, both of them civilians, one of them a young woman in a nice dress, the other a young man in jeans and a sport coat. They took a table for two, three along from the specialists and directly opposite the old couple from the hotel. They didn't look much like the kind of folks who would get straight on the phone with their Congressman because of a little public mayhem, but the more warm bodies in the room the better.

The sergeant said, 'We're happy to sit here all night, if that's what it takes.'

'Good to know,' I said. 'I'm going to sit here until the phone rings, and then I'm going to leave.'

'I'm sorry, but I can't let you communicate with anyone. Those are my orders.'

I said nothing.

'And I can't let you leave. Unless you agree to go to Kelham.'

I said, 'Didn't we just have this discussion?'

No response.

The phone didn't ring.

Five minutes to eight.

At eight o'clock the guy in the pale suit paid his check and left, and the old lady from the hotel turned a page in her book. Nothing else happened. The phone stayed quiet. At five past eight I began to hear noise outside, behind

485

me, the sound of cars and crunching tyres, and I sensed a change in the night-time air, like pressure building, as Bravo Company started to arrive in town, first in ones and twos, then by the dozens. I assumed Reed Riley had led the parade in his borrowed staff car, with his father in the seat beside him. I assumed the old guy was at that moment stationed at Brannan's door, greeting his son's men, ushering them in, grinning like an idiot.

The three Rangers boxing me in had eaten their pies one at a time, with the other two always alert and watchful. They were pretty good. By no means the worst I had ever seen. The waitress collected their plates. She seemed to sense what was going on. Every time she passed by she gave me a concerned look. There was no doubt whose side she was on. She knew me, and she didn't know them. I had tipped her many times, and they hadn't, not even once.

The noise from outside continued to build.

The phone didn't ring.

I spent the next few minutes thinking about their Humvee. I knew that like every other Humvee in the world it would have a big General Motors diesel in it, and I knew that like every other Humvee in the world it would have a three-speed automatic transmission in it, and I knew that like every other Humvee in the world it would weigh north of four tons, all of which I knew would make it good for about sixty miles an hour, tops. Which I knew wasn't race-car fast, but which I knew was fifteen times faster than walking, which I knew was a good thing.

I waited.

Then, just after eight-thirty, three things happened. The first was unfortunate, and the second was unprecedented, and the third was therefore awkward.

First, the young couple left. The girl in the nice dress, and the boy in the sport coat. He laid money on the table, and they got up together and walked out holding hands, fast enough to suggest that an evening prayer meeting was not the next item on their agenda.

And second, the old couple left. She closed her book, he folded his paper, and they got up and shuffled out the door. Back to the hotel, presumably. Far earlier than ever before. No obvious reason, except possibly a sudden hopeless intuition that old man Riley would cancel the Lear and decide on an early night in town.

At that point the waitress was in the kitchen, which left just four people in the room, one of which was me, and three of which were my babysitters.

The sergeant smiled and said, 'Just us now.'

I didn't answer.

He said, 'No members of the public.'

I didn't answer.

He said, 'And I don't think the waitress is the complaining type. Not really. She knows this place could end up on the shit list easy as anything. For a month. Or two. Or for however long it takes to put her on welfare.'

He was leaning forward across the table. Closer to me than before. Looking straight at me. His two men were leaning forward across the aisle, elbows on knees, hands loose, feet planted, watching me.

Then the third thing happened.

The phone rang.

EIGHTY-THREE

The three Rangers were good. Very good. The phone was a traditional old item with a big metal bell inside, which rang for a whole lazy second before adding a reverberation tail that took another whole lazy second to die away, whereupon the sequence would repeat itself endlessly until either the call was answered or the caller gave up. An old-fashioned, comforting sound, familiar for a hundred years. But on this occasion before the first ring was halfway over all three Rangers were in motion. The guy directly to my left was instantly on his feet, lunging behind me, putting big hands on my shoulders, pressing me down into my seat, hauling me back past the vertical, keeping me in a weak and inefficient position. The sergeant opposite me was instantly leaning forward, grabbing my wrists, pressing them into the tabletop with the flat of his hands. The third guy came up out of his chair and balled his fists and blocked the aisle, ready to hit me anywhere he could if I moved.

A fine performance.

I offered no resistance.

I just sat there.

Everyone has a plan, me included.

The phone rang on.

Three rings later the waitress came out of the kitchen. She paused a beat and took one look and then pushed past the Ranger in the aisle and headed for the phone. She picked up and listened and glanced my way and started talking, looking at me the whole time, as if she was describing my current predicament to someone.

To Frances Neagley, I assumed.

Or I hoped.

The waitress listened again for a moment and then trapped the phone between her ear and her shoulder and took out her order pad and her pen. She started writing. And kept on writing. Practically an essay. She started a second page. The guy behind me kept the pressure on. The sergeant kept hold of my wrists. The third guy moved closer. The waitress made shapes with her mouth as she concentrated on spelling unfamiliar words. Then she stopped writing and checked back through what she had, and she swallowed once and blinked twice as if the next part of her task was going to be difficult.

She hung up the phone. She tore out her two written pages and held them as if they were hot. She took a step towards us. The guy behind me took his weight off my shoulders. The sergeant let go of my wrists. The third guy sat down again.

The waitress walked the length of the aisle, right into our little group, a fifth member, and she shuffled one written page on top of the other, and she checked the three guys' collars, and she focused on the sergeant. The man in charge.

She said, 'I have a two-part message for you, sir.'

The guy nodded at her and she started reading.

She said, 'First, whoever you are, you should let this man go immediately, for both your own sake and the army's, because, second, whoever you are and whatever your orders and whatever you think on this occasion, he's likely to be right and you're likely to be wrong. This message comes from an NCO of equal rank, with nothing but the army's and your best interests at heart.'

Silence.

The sergeant said, 'Noted.'

Nothing more.

Neagley, I thought. *Good try.*

Then the waitress leaned forward and put her second handwritten page face down on the table and slid it towards me, fast and easy, the same way she had slid a million diner checks before. I trapped it under my left palm and kept my right hand ready.

No one moved.

The waitress stood still for a second, and then she walked back to the kitchen.

I used the ball of my left thumb and curled the top of the paper upward, like a guy playing poker, and I read the first two lines of my message. Seven words. The first of them was a Latin preposition. Typical Neagley. *Per*. Meaning in this context *According to*. The next six words were *United States Marine Corps Personnel Command*. Which meant that whatever information was contained in the rest of the note had come straight from the horse's mouth. It would be reliable. It would be definitive. It would be solid gold.

It would be good enough for me.

I let the top of the paper slap back down against the tabletop. I spread my thumb and my first two fingers and pincered them together and folded the note one-handed, blank side out, message side in. I crisped the fold with my right thumbnail and jammed the note in my right top pocket, behind Munro's little black book, below my name tape.

Ten minutes to nine in the evening.

I looked at the Ranger sergeant and said, 'OK, you win. Let's go to Kelham.'

EIGHTY-FOUR

We went out through the kitchen, single file, and we used the diner's rear door, because that was the fastest route back to their Humvee. The sergeant led the way. I was sandwiched between the two specialists. One of them kept his hand flat on my back, pushing, and the other had hold of the front of my jacket, pulling. The night air felt sharp, neither warm nor cold. The acre of bare ground was jammed with parked cars. There were people fifty yards to my right, all of them men, all of them in uniform, all of them quiet and on best behaviour, all of them clustered in a rough semicircle around the front of Brannan's bar, like a living halo behind the head of a saint, or an overspill crowd watching a prize fight. Most had bottles of beer in their hands, probably purchased elsewhere and carried back within sight of the main attraction. I guessed the senator was loving the attention, and I guessed his son was pretending not to.

The Humvee looked wide and massive in among the regular rides. Which it was. Parked next to it at a respectful interval was a plain sedan painted flat green. Reed Riley's borrowed staff car, I assumed, second into the lot and put next to the truck for the sake of the tough-guy image. Instinctive, for a politician.

The sergeant slowed a step and the rest of us bunched up behind him, and then we struck off again on a new vector, straight towards the truck, not fast, not slow. No one paid us any attention. We were just four dark figures, and everyone else was facing in the other direction.

The Humvee was not locked. The sergeant opened the left rear door and the specialists crowded behind me and left me no option but to get in. The interior smelled of canvas and sweat. The sergeant waited until the specialists were on board, one of them in the front passenger seat, the other across the wide transmission tunnel next to me in the back, both of them turned watchfully towards me, and then he climbed into the driver's seat and hit the button and started the engine. It idled for a second with a hammer-heavy diesel rattle, and he settled himself in his seat, and got ready to move off. He turned the headlights on. He put the transmission in gear. He rolled forward, the ride lumpy, the steering vague, the speed low. He headed north across the rough ground, towards the Kelham road, past the ranks of parked cars, past the back of the Sheriff's Department building. He checked his mirror out of sheer habit, and he glanced left, and he prepared to turn right thirty yards ahead.

I asked, 'What are you guys trained for?'

He said, 'Man-portable shoulder-launch surface-to-air defence.'

'Not police work?'

'No.'

493

'I could tell,' I said. 'You didn't search me. You should have.'

I came out with my Beretta in my right hand. I reached forward and bunched his collar in my left hand tight enough to choke him. I hauled him back hard against his seat. I jammed the muzzle of the gun hard into the back of his right shoulder, directly above his armpit. Humvees are built pretty solid, including the seat frames. I had the guy pulled and pushed rigid against an immovable object. He wasn't going anywhere. He wasn't even going to breathe, unless I let him.

I said, 'Let's all sit still and stay calm.'

They all did both things, because of where I had the gun. His ear or his neck would not have worked. They would not have believed I was prepared to shoot the guy dead. Not one soldier against another, however desperate I was supposed to be. But a non-fatal wound through the soft flesh just to the right of his shoulder blade was plausible. And terrible. It would have ended his career. It would have ended his life as he knew it, with nothing ahead of him but crippling pain and disability checks and left-handed household utensils.

I let out half an inch of his collar but kept him tight against the seat back.

I said, 'Turn left.'

He turned left, on to the east–west road.

I said, 'Drive on.'

He drove on, into the die-straight tunnel through the trees, away from Kelham, towards Memphis.

I said, 'Faster.'

He sped up, and pretty soon the big truck was rattling

494

and straining close to sixty miles an hour. And at that point we entered the realm of simple arithmetic. It was nine o'clock in the evening, and that road was about forty miles long, and the chances of meeting traffic on it were low. I figured a thirty-minute, thirty-mile drive would meet all our needs.

'Keep on going,' I said.

The guy kept on going.

Thirty minutes later we were at some featureless point thirty miles west of Carter Crossing and maybe ten miles short of the minor road that led up towards Memphis. I said, 'OK, this is far enough. Let's stop here.'

I kept on hauling his collar one way and I kept on pushing the other way with the gun and the guy stepped off the gas and coasted and braked to a stop. He put the transmission in Park and took his hands off the wheel and sat there like he knew what was coming next, which maybe he did, and maybe he didn't. I turned my head and looked at the guy next to me and said, 'Take your boots off.'

And at that point they all knew what was coming next, and there was a pause, like a mutiny brewing, but I waited it out until the guy next to me shrugged and bent to his task.

I said, 'Now your socks.'

The guy peeled them off and balled them up and stowed them in his boots, like a good soldier should.

I said, 'Now your jacket.'

He took his jacket off.

I said, 'Now your pants.'

There was another long, long pause, but then the guy hitched his butt up off the seat and slid his pants down over his hips. I looked at the guy in the front passenger seat and said, 'Same four things for you.'

He got right to it, and then I made him help his sergeant out. I wasn't about to let the guy fold forward and away from me. Not at that point. When they were done I turned back to the guy next to me and I said, 'Now get out of the truck and walk forward twenty paces.'

His sergeant said, 'You better hope we never meet again, Reacher.'

'No, I hope we do,' I said. 'Because after suitable reflection I'm sure you'll want to thank me for not hurting you in any way at all. Which I could have, you hopeless amateur.'

No reply.

'Get out of the truck,' I said again.

And a minute later all three of them were standing on the road in the headlight beams, barefoot, pantless, in nothing but T-shirts and boxers. They were thirty miles from where they wanted to be, which under the best of conditions was a seven- or eight-hour walk, and going barefoot on a rural road was no one's definition of the best of conditions. And even if by some miracle there was passing traffic, they stood no chance of hitching a ride. No chance at all. No one in his right mind would stop in the dark for three wildly gesticulating bare-legged men.

I climbed through to the driver's seat and reversed a hundred yards and then turned around and headed back the way we had come, with nothing but engine noise and the sour smell of boots and socks for company. The clock in my head showed nine thirty-five, and I figured if the reduced payload let the Humvee hit sixty-five miles an hour I would be in Carter Crossing again at three minutes past ten.

EIGHTY-FIVE

In the event the big GM diesel gave me a little better than sixty-five miles an hour, and two minutes short of ten o'clock I pulled up and hid the truck in the last of the trees and walked the rest of the way. A man on foot can be a lot stealthier than a four-ton military vehicle, and safety is always the best policy.

But there was nothing to hide from. Main Street was quiet. There was nothing to see except light in the diner's window and my borrowed Buick and Deveraux's Caprice parked nose to tail in front of it. I guessed Deveraux was keeping half an eye on the situation but not worrying too much about it. The senator's presence all but guaranteed a quiet and untypical night.

I stayed on the Kelham road and skipped Main Street itself and looped around behind it on a wide and cautious radius. I kept myself concealed behind the last row of parked cars and walked down level with Brannan's bar. The crowd at the door was still there. I could see maybe fifty guys clustered in the same semicircle I had seen before. Past them I could see a big crowd inside the bar itself, some guys standing and some, I assumed, sitting at the tables further into the room, although I had no direct view of the latter group. I moved closer, squeezing between parked cars and pick-up trucks, with the hubbub ahead of me getting a little louder with each step. But not much louder. The noise was a lot lower in level and a lot more polite and restrained than it would have been on any other night. Best behaviour.

I crossed an open lane between the first row of cars and the second and eased onward between a twenty-year-old Cadillac and a beat-up GMC Jimmy and a soft voice right next to me said, 'Hello, Reacher.'

I turned and saw Munro leaning against the far side of the Jimmy, neatly in the shadow, nearly invisible, relaxed and patient and vigilant.

'Hello, Munro,' I said. 'It's good to see you. Although I have to say I didn't expect to.'

He said, 'Likewise.'

'Did Stan Lowrey call you?'

He nodded. 'But a little too late.'

'Three guys?'

He nodded again. 'Mortarmen from the 75th.'

'Where are they now?'

'Tied up with telephone wire, gagged with their own T-shirts, locked in my room.'

'Good work,' I said. Which it was. One against three, no warning, taken by surprise, but a satisfactory result none the less. I was impressed. Munro was nobody's fool. That was clear.

He asked, 'Who did you get?'

'An anti-aircraft crew.'

'Where are they?'

'Walking back from halfway to Memphis with no shoes and no pants.'

He smiled, white teeth in the dark. He said, 'I hope I never get posted to Benning.'

I asked, 'Is Riley in the bar?'

'First to arrive, with his dad. They're holding court big time. Tab must be three hundred bucks by now.'

'Curfew still in place?'

He nodded. 'But it's going to be a last-minute rush. You know how it is. The mood turned out to be pretty good, and no one will want to be the first to leave.'

'OK,' I said. 'Your job is to make sure Riley is the last to leave. I need him to be the very last car out of here. And not by a second or two, either. By a minute at least. Do whatever it takes to make that happen, will you? I'm depending on it.'

With anyone else I might then have gone ahead and sketched out a few alternative ways to accomplish that goal, like suggestions, anything from puncturing a tyre to asking for the old guy's autograph, but by then I was beginning to realize Munro didn't need help. He would think of all the same things I could, and maybe a few more besides.

He said, 'Understood.'

'And then your job is to go sit on Elizabeth Deveraux. I need her to be under your eye throughout. In the diner, or wherever. Again, whatever it takes.'

'Understood,' he said again. 'She's in the diner right now, as it happens.'

'Keep her there,' I said. 'Don't let her go out on traffic

patrol tonight. Tell her with the senator behind them the guys will behave.'

'She knows that. She gave her deputies the night off.'

'Good to know,' I said. 'And good luck. And thanks.'

I squeezed back between the Cadillac and the Jimmy and crossed the open lane and threaded through the rearmost rank of cars and walked out of the lot the same way I had come in. Five minutes later I was just past the railroad crossing, hidden in the trees on the side of the road that led to Kelham, waiting again.

Munro's assessment of the collective mood turned out to be correct. No one left as early as ten thirty, because of the weird dynamic surrounding the senator. I had seen similar things before. I was pretty sure no one from Bravo Company would have pissed on the guy if he was on fire, but everyone seemed fascinated by his alien presence, and no doubt everyone still had the base commander's instructions ringing in his ears. *Be nice to the VIP. Show him some respect.* So no one peeled away early. No one wanted to go first. No one wanted to stand out. So ten thirty came and went with no movement on the road. None at all.

As did ten thirty-five.

Ten forty, likewise.

Then at ten forty-five the dam broke and they came in droves.

I heard noise like a muted version of an armoured division firing up and I saw exhaust smoke and crisscross headlight beams far in the distance as they all started jockeying for position and funnelling out of

501

the lot. Lights swung towards me in an endless chain and thirty seconds later the lead car thumped over the crossing and sped on by. It was followed by all the others in sequence, too many to count, each just yards from the one in front, like stock cars on a racetrack straightaway. Engines roared and wheezed and worn tyres pattered over the rails and I smelled the sweet sharp tang of unleaded gasoline. I saw the old Cadillac and the GMC sport utility I had squeezed between, and I saw Chevys and Dodges and Fords and Plymouths and Jeeps and Chryslers, sedans and pick-up trucks and four-wheel-drives and coupés and two-seaters. They kept on coming, an unbroken stream, heading home, relieved, exuberant, their duty done.

Ten minutes later the stream was thinning and the gaps between cars were lengthening and in the distance I could see late stragglers moving out. The last dozen vehicles took a whole minute to pass me by. None of them was a flat green staff car. The final tail-end charlie was an old Pontiac sedan, scarred and sagging. I watched it approach. *As soon as he passes us, I guarantee we're alone in the world*, Deveraux had said. The old Pontiac thumped quietly over the track on soft tyres, and then it was gone.

I stepped out of the trees and faced east and saw tiny red tail lights disappearing into the darkness. The noise faded behind them and the exhaust smoke drifted and cleared. I turned the other way and far in the distance and right on cue I saw a lone pair of headlights click on. I saw their beams bounce and swing, side to side, up and down, and I saw them lead the way north, out through the lot, and then I saw them swing towards me and bounce twice more as the wheels behind them climbed up off the dirt and on to the blacktop.

The clock in my head showed one minute to eleven.

I walked west, back over the railroad crossing, ten yards towards the town, and then I stopped and stepped out to the crown of the road and raised my hand high, palm out, like a traffic cop.

EIGHTY-SIX

The headlight beams picked me up maybe a hundred yards out. I felt the hot light on my face and on my palm and I knew Reed Riley could see me. I heard him lift off the gas and slow down. Pure habit. Infantrymen spend a lot of time riding in vehicles, and many of their journeys are enabled or directed or otherwise interrupted by guys in BDUs waving them through or pointing them left or pointing them right or bringing them to a temporary standstill.

I stayed right where I was, my hand still raised, and the flat green staff car came to a stop with its front bumper a yard from my knees. By then my eye line was high above the headlights, and I could see Riley and his father side by side behind the windshield glass. Neither one looked surprised or impatient. Both looked prepared to waste a minute on a matter of routine. Riley looked exactly like his photograph, and his father was an older version, a little thinner, a little larger in the ears and the nose, a little more powdered and presentable. He was dressed like a jerk, like every other visiting politician I had ever seen. He was wearing a khaki canvas Ike jacket over a formal shirt with no tie. The jacket had a United States Senate roundel on it, as if that safe and insulated branch of the legislature was a combat unit.

I stepped around to Reed Riley's door, and he wound his window down. His face started out one way, and then it changed when he saw the oak leaves on my collar. He said, 'Sir?'

I didn't answer. I took one more step and opened the rear door and got in the back seat behind him. I closed the door after me and shuffled over to the centre of the bench and both men craned around to look at me.

'Sir?' Riley said again.

'What's going on here?' his father asked.

'Change of plan,' I said.

I could smell beer on their breath and smoke and sweat in their clothing.

'I have a plane to catch,' the senator said.

'At midnight,' I said. 'No one will look for you before then.'

'What the hell does that mean? Do you know who I am?'

'Yes,' I said. 'I do.'

'What do you want?'

'Instant obedience,' I said. I took out the Beretta for the second time that evening, fast, smooth, like a magician. One minute my hand was empty, and the next it was full of dull steel. I clicked the safety to fire, a small sound, but ominous in the silence.

The senator said, 'You're making a very serious mistake, young man. As of right now your military career is over. Whether it gets any worse than that is entirely up to you.'

'Be quiet,' I said. I leaned forward and bunched Reed Riley's collar in my hand, the same way I had with the sergeant from Benning. But this time I put the muzzle of the gun in the hollow behind his right ear. Soft flesh, no bone. Just the right size.

'Drive on,' I said. 'Very slowly. Turn left on the crossing. Head up the railroad line.'

Riley said, 'What?'

'You heard me.'

'But the train is coming.'

'At midnight,' I said. 'Now hop to it, soldier.'

It was a difficult task. Instinctively he wanted to lean forward over the wheel for a better view out the front. But I wouldn't let him. I had him hauled back hard against the seat, pulled and pushed. But even so, he did OK. He rolled forward and spun the wheel hard and crabbed diagonally up on to the rise. He lined it up and felt his right front tyre hit the groove in the pavement. He eased forward, dead straight, and the edge of the blacktop fell away under us. His right-hand tyres stayed up on the rail. His left-hand wheels were down on the ties. A fine job. As good as Deveraux.

'You've done this before,' I said.

He didn't answer.

We rolled on, less than walking pace, radically tilted, the right side of the car up and running smooth, the left side down and rising and falling over the ties like a boat on a swell. We rolled past the old water tower, then ten more yards, and then I said, 'Stop.'

'Here?'

'It's a good spot,' I said.

He braked gently and the car stopped, right on the line, still tilted over. I kept hold of his collar and kept the gun in place. Ahead of me through the windshield the rails ran straight north to a vanishing point far in the distance, like slim silver streaks in the moonlight.

I said, 'Captain, use your left hand and open all the windows.'

'Why?'

'Because you guys already stink. And it's only going to get worse, believe me.'

Riley scrabbled blindly with his fingers and first his father's window came down, then mine, then the one opposite me.

Fresh night air came in on the breeze.

I said, 'Senator, lean over and turn the lights off.'

It took him a second to find the switch, but he did it.

I said, 'Now turn the engine off and give me the key.'

He said, 'But we're parked on the railroad track.'

'I'm aware of that.'

'Do you know who I am?'

'You asked me that before. And I answered. Now do what you're told. Or do I have to make a campaign contribution first? In which case please consider my contribution to be not shooting your son through the knee.'

The old guy made a small sound in his throat, the kind of thing I had heard once or twice before, when jokes turned out not to be jokes, when dire situations turned from bad to worse, when nightmares were revealed to be waking realities. He leaned sideways and twisted the key and pulled it and held it out to me.

'Toss it on the back seat,' I said.

He did so, and it landed next to me and skittered down the slope of the cushion made by the tilt of the car.

I said, 'Now both of you put your hands on your head.'

The senator went first, and I pulled the Beretta back to let his son follow suit. I let go of his collar and sat back in my seat and said, 'What's the muzzle velocity on a Beretta M9?'

The senator said, 'I have no idea.'

'But your boy should. We spent a lot of time and money training him.'

'I don't remember,' Riley said.

'Close to thirteen hundred feet per second,' I said. 'And your spinal cords are about three feet from me. Therefore about two-thousandths of a second after either one of you moves a single muscle, you're either dead or crippled. Get it?'

No response.

I said, 'I need an answer.'

'We get it,' Riley said.

His father said, 'What do you want?'

'Confirmation,' I said. 'I want to be sure I have this thing straight.'

EIGHTY-SEVEN

I picked up the car key and put it in my pocket. I spread my left leg wide and braced my foot and got comfortable on the tilted bench. I said, 'Captain, you lied to your men about dating Sheriff Deveraux, am I right?'

Riley's father said, 'What possible basis do you have for interrogating us?'

'Forty-nine minutes,' I said. 'Then the train gets here.'

'Are you mad?'

'A little grumpy, that's all.'

He said, 'Son, don't say a word to this man.'

I said, 'Captain, answer my question.'

Riley said, 'Yes, I lied about Deveraux.'

'Why?'

'Command strategy,' he said. 'My men like to look up to me.'

I said, 'Senator, why were Alpha Company and Bravo Company moved from Benning to Kelham?'

The old guy huffed and puffed for a minute, trying to convince himself to hold fast, but in the end he said, 'It was politically convenient. Mississippi always has its hand out. Or in someone else's pocket.'

'Not because of Audrey Shaw? Not because you thought your boy deserved a little gift to celebrate his new command?'

'That's ridiculous.'

'But it happened.'

'Purely a coincidence.'

'Bullshit.'

'OK, it was a side benefit. I thought it might be fun. But nothing more. Decisions of that magnitude are not based on trivialities.'

I said, 'Captain, tell me about Rosemary McClatchy.'

Riley said, 'We dated, we broke up.'

'Was she pregnant?'

'If she was, she never said anything to me about it.'

'Did she want to get married?'

'Come on, major, you know any one of them would marry any one of us.'

'What was she like?'

'Insecure,' he said. 'She drove me nuts.'

'How did you feel when she was killed?'

'Bad,' he said. 'It was a bad thing to happen.'

'Now tell me about Shawna Lindsay.'

But at that point the senator decided they had taken all the shit they were going to take from me. He twisted around to dress me down, and then he remembered he was not supposed to move, and so he bounced back again like a stupid old mare against a new electric fence. He stared forward and breathed hard. His son didn't move. So they were taking a little shit from me, at least. Mainly the part nine millimetres wide. Thirty-five hundredths of an inch, in real money. A little smaller than a .38, a lot bigger than a .25. That's how much shit they were taking.

The old man took another breath.

He said, 'That matter has been resolved, I believe. The Lindsay girl. And the other one.'

I said, 'Captain, tell me about the dead women in Kosovo.'

His father said, 'There are no dead women in Kosovo.'

I said, 'Seriously? What, they live for ever?'

'Obviously they don't live for ever.'

'Do they all die in their sleep?'

'They were Kosovan women and it happened in Kosovo. It's a local matter. Just like this is a local matter, right here, right now. A local person has been identified. The army is not under a cloud. That's what we were celebrating tonight. You should have been there. Success is something to be happy about. I wish more people understood that.'

I said, 'Captain, how old are you?'

Riley said, 'I'm twenty-eight.'

I said, 'Senator, how would you feel if your son was still a captain at thirty-three?'

The old guy said, 'I would be very unhappy.'

'Why?'

'It would represent failure. No one stays five years at the same rank. You'd have to be an idiot.'

I said, 'That was their first mistake.'

'What?'

'You heard me.'

'What do you mean, their? Who are they?'

'Do you have a grandfather?'

511

'Way back.'

'So did I. He was my granddad. But of course he was also lots of other kids' granddad too. There were about ten of us, I think. Four separate families. It always came as a surprise to me, even though I knew.'

'What the hell are you talking about?'

'It's the same thing with Senate Liaison. There's us, and there's the brass in Washington, and there's you. Like a grandfather. Except you're the Marine Corps' grandfather too. And they have their own Senate Liaison. They're probably a lot better than ours. They're probably willing to do whatever it takes. So you turned to them for help. But they made a number of mistakes.'

'I read the report. There were no mistakes.'

'Five years in the same rank? Deveraux is not the kind of person who spends five years in the same rank. Like you said, you'd have to be an idiot. And Deveraux is not an idiot. My guess is she was a CWO3 five years ago. My guess is she got two promotions since then. But your Marine Corps boys went ahead and wrote CWO5 on a file that was supposed to be five years old. They used an old picture but they didn't back off her terminal rank. Which was a mistake. They were in too much of a rush.'

'What rush?'

'Janice Chapman was white. Finally you had one people were going to take seriously. And she was linked to you. There was no time to waste.'

'What are you talking about?'

'This whole thing was about too much rush. You worked like crazy, and teased us about access to give yourself more time. But finally you got it done just after lunch on Sunday. The file was complete. The word came through while the chopper was in the air. So it went back empty. But then you waited until Tuesday before you released it for public scrutiny. I had a rather big-headed explanation for that. I thought it was because I was here on Sunday but not on Tuesday. But that wasn't the reason. You needed two days to make it look old. That was the reason. You had to scrape it up and scuff it around.'

'Are you saying that file was a forgery?'

'I know, you're shocked. Maybe you've known for nine months, or six, or maybe just a week or so, but we all know now.'

'Know what?' Reed Riley said.

I turned towards him. He was staring forward too, but he knew I was talking to him. I said, 'Maybe Rosemary McClatchy was insecure because her beauty was all she had, so maybe she got jealous, and maybe that's where you got the idea for the vengeful woman. And she was pregnant too, and you'd already checked out the local sheriff, because that's what an ambitious company commander does, and it was easier for you than most, because of your connections, so you knew about the empty house, and you're a sick bastard, so you took poor pregnant Rosemary McClatchy there and you butchered her.'

No response.

'And you liked it,' I said.

No response.

'So you did it again. And you got better at it. No more dumping them in the ditch by the railroad track. You

513

were ready for something more adventurous. Maybe something more appropriate. Maybe Shawna Lindsay also had delusions of marriage, and maybe she was talking about living in a little house together, so you dumped her on a construction site. You could drive through that neighbourhood any time you liked. You always had. The big dog, out on the prowl, in his old blue car. Part of the scenery.'

He said, 'I broke up with Shawna weeks before she died. How do you explain that?'

'You ask them back, they come running, right?'

No answer.

I said, 'And you dumped Janice Chapman behind a bar for the same reason. She was a party girl. And maybe you set yourself a little extra challenge that night. Third time lucky. Variety is the spice of life. Maybe you told the guys you were hitting the head, and you snuck out and did it in the same time you need to take a leak. Six minutes and forty seconds would be my guess. Which is not plausible. Not for Deveraux. That's where the alternative theory starts to falter. Did nobody think about how she's built? She couldn't lift a full-grown woman off a deer trestle. She couldn't carry a corpse to a car.'

Senator Riley said, 'The file is genuine.'

I said, 'It started out with its feet on the ground. Someone thought up a neat little story. The jealous woman, the broken arm. The missing four hundred dollars. It was quite subtle. Conclusions would be drawn by the reader. But then someone chickened out. They didn't want subtle any more. They wanted a flashing red light. So you retyped the whole thing to include a car. Then

514

you got on the phone and told your son to go put his own car on the train track.'

'That's crazy.'

'There was no other reason behind the stuff with the car. The car was senseless. It served no other purpose. Other than to nail the lid shut on Deveraux as soon as anyone opened that file.'

'That file is genuine.'

'They went too far with the dead people. James Dyer, maybe. We could buy that. He was a senior officer. Health maybe not the best. But Paul Evers? Too convenient. As if you were scared of people asking questions. Dead people can't answer. Which brings us to Alice Bouton. Is she going to be dead too? Or is she going to be still alive? In which case, what would she tell us if we asked her about her broken arm?'

'The file is completely genuine, Reacher.'

'Can you read, Senator? If so, read this for me.' I slid the folded diner check from my pocket and tossed it in his lap.

He said, 'I'm not allowed to move.'

I said, 'You can pick it up.'

He picked it up. It shook in his hand. He looked at the back. He looked at the front. He turned it right way up. He took a breath. He asked, 'Have you read it? Do you know what it says?'

I said, 'No, I haven't looked at it. I don't need to know. Either way I've got enough to nail you.'

He hesitated.

I said, 'But don't fake anything. I'll read it right after you, just to check.'

He took a breath.

He read out, 'Per United States Marine Corps Personnel Command.'

He stopped.

He said, 'I need to know this is not classified material.'

'Does it matter?'

'You're not cleared for classified material. Neither is my son.'

'It's not classified material,' I said. 'Keep reading.'

He said, 'Per United States Marine Corps Personnel Command there was no Marine named Alice Bouton.'

I smiled.

'They invented her,' I said. 'She didn't exist. Very sloppy work. It makes me wonder if I was wrong. Maybe you watered down the subtlety in two separate stages. And maybe the car came first. Maybe it was Alice Bouton you wrote in at the last minute. Without enough time to steal a real identity.'

The old guy said, 'The army had to be protected. You must understand that.'

'The army's loss is the Marine Corps' gain. And you're their granddaddy too. So professionally you didn't give a damn. It was your son you were protecting.'

'It could have been anyone in his unit. We'd do this for anyone at all.'

'Bullshit,' I said. 'This was a fantastic amount of corruption. This was exceptional. This was unprecedented. This was about the two of you, and no one else.'

No answer.

I said, 'By the way, it's me who's protecting the army.'

I didn't want to shoot them, obviously. Not that there

would be much left for the pathologist to examine, but a cautious man takes no unnecessary risks. So I dropped the gun on the seat beside me and came forward with my right hand open, and I got it flat on the back of the senator's head, and I heaved it forward and bounced it off the dashboard rail. Pretty hard. The human arm can pitch a baseball at a hundred miles an hour, so it might get close to thirty with a human head. And the seat belt people tell us that an untethered impact at thirty miles an hour can kill you. Not that I needed the senator dead. I just needed him out of action for a minute and a half.

I moved my right hand over and got it under Reed Riley's chin. His hands came down off his head to tear at my wrist and I replaced them with my own left hand, open, jamming down hard on the top of his head. Push and pull, up and down, left hand and right hand, like a vice. I was crushing his head. Then I slid my right hand up over his chiselled chin until the heel of my hand lodged there and I clamped my palm over his mouth. His skin was like fine sandpaper. He had shaved early that morning, and now it was close to midnight. I slid my left hand over his brow until its heel caught on the ridge below his hairline. I stretched down and clamped his nose between my finger and thumb.

And then it was all about human nature.

He thought he was suffocating. First he tried to bite my palm, but he couldn't get his mouth open. I was clamping too hard. Jaw muscles are strong, but only when they're closing. Opening was never an evolutionary priority. I waited him out. He clawed at my hands. I waited him out. He scrabbled in his seat and drummed his heels. I waited him out. He arched his back. I waited him out. He stretched his head up towards me.

I changed my grip and twisted hard and broke his neck.

It was a move I had learned from Leon Garber. Maybe he had seen it somewhere. Maybe he had done it somewhere. He was capable of it. The suffocation part makes it easy. They always stretch their heads up. Some kind of a bad instinct. They put their necks on the line all by themselves. Garber said it never fails, and it never has for me.

And it succeeded again a minute later, with the senator. He was weaker, but his face was slick with blood from where I had broken his nose on the dashboard rail, so the effort expended was very much the same.

EIGHTY-EIGHT

I got out of the car at eleven twenty-eight exactly. The train was thirty-two miles south of us. Maybe just crossing under Route 78 east of Tupelo. I closed my door but left all the windows open. I tossed the key into Reed Riley's lap. I turned away.

And sensed a figure wide on my left.

And another, wide on my right.

Good moves by someone. I had the Beretta, and I could hit one or the other of them, but not both of them. Too much lateral travel between rounds.

I waited.

Then the figure on my right spoke.

She said, 'Reacher?'

I said, 'Deveraux?'

The figure on my left said, 'And Munro.'

I said, 'What the hell are you two doing here?'

They converged on me, and I tried to push them away from the car. I said, 'Why are you here?'

Deveraux said, 'Did you really think I was going to let him keep me in the diner?'

'I wish he had,' I said. 'I didn't want either of you to hear anything about this.'

'You made Riley open the windows. You wanted us to hear.'

'No, I wanted fresh air. I didn't know you were there.'

'Why shouldn't we hear?'

'I didn't want you to know what they were saying about you. And I wanted Munro to go back to Germany with a clear conscience.'

Munro said, 'My conscience is always clear.'

'But it's easier to play dumb if you really don't know the answer.'

'I never had a problem playing dumb. Some folks think I am.'

Deveraux said, 'I'm glad I heard what they were saying about me.'

Eleven thirty-one. The train was twenty-nine miles south of us. We walked away, on the ties, between the rails, leaving the flat green staff car and its passengers behind us. We walked past the old water tower and made it to the crossing. We turned west. Forty yards away Deveraux's cruiser was parked on the shoulder. Munro wouldn't get in. He said he would walk on down to Brannan's bar, where he had left a car he had borrowed. He said he needed to get back to Kelham as soon as possible, to square things away with the captured mortarmen, and then to hit the sack ahead of his early start the next morning. We shook hands quite formally, and I thanked him most sincerely for his help, and then he moved away and within ten paces he was lost to sight in the dark.

Deveraux drove me back to Main Street and parked outside the hotel. Eleven thirty-six in the evening. The train was twenty-four miles away. I said, 'I checked out of my room.'

She said, 'I still have mine.'

'I need to make a phone call first.'

We used the office behind the reception counter. I put a dollar bill on the desk and dialled Garber's office. Maybe the tap was still in place, and maybe it wasn't. It made no difference to me. I got a lieutenant on the line. He said he was the senior person on duty. He said in fact he was the only person on duty. Night crew. I asked him if he had paper and pencil handy. He said yes to both. I told him to stand by to take dictation. I told him to mark the finished product urgent and to leave it front and centre on Garber's desk, for immediate attention first thing in the morning.

'Ready?' I asked him.

He said he was.

I said, 'A tragedy occurred late last night in sleepy Carter Crossing, Mississippi, when a car carrying United States Senator Carlton Riley was struck by a passing train. The car was being driven by the senator's son, U.S. Army Captain Reed Riley, who was based at nearby Fort Kelham, Mississippi. Senator Riley, of Missouri, was chairman of the Senate's Armed Services Committee, and Captain Riley, described by the army as a rising star, was in command of an infantry unit regularly deployed on missions of great sensitivity. Both men died instantly in the accident. Carter County

Sheriff Elizabeth Deveraux confirmed that local drivers regularly attempt to beat the train across the road junction, in order to avoid a long and inconvenient delay, and it is believed that Captain Riley, recently posted to the area and adventurous in spirit, simply mistimed his approach to the crossing.'

I paused.

'Got that,' the lieutenant said, in my ear.

'Second paragraph,' I said. 'The senator and his son were returning to Fort Kelham after helping the nearby town celebrate Sheriff Deveraux's successful resolution of a local homicide investigation. The killing spree had lasted nine months and the five victims included three local women in their twenties, a local teenage boy, and a journalist from nearby Oxford, Mississippi. The male perpetrator, responsible for all five deaths, is described as a militia member and a white supremacist from neighbouring Tennessee, and was shot to death earlier in the week, in a wooded area close to Fort Kelham, by local police, while resisting arrest.'

'Got that,' the lieutenant said again.

'Start typing,' I said, and hung up.

Eleven forty-two in the evening. The train was eighteen miles away.

Room seventeen was as plain as room twenty-one had been. Deveraux had made no attempt to personalize it. She had two battered suitcases propped open for clothes storage, and a spare uniform was hanging off the curtain rail, and there was a book on the night table. And that was it.

We sat side by side on her bed, a little shell-shocked, and she said, 'You did everything you could. Justice is done all around, and the army doesn't suffer. You're a good soldier.'

I said, 'I'm sure they'll find something to complain about.'

'But I'm disappointed with the Marine Corps. They shouldn't have cooperated. They stabbed me in the back.'

'Not really,' I said. 'They tried their best. They were under tremendous pressure. They pretended to play ball, but they put in a bunch of coded messages. Two dead people and an invented one? That thing with your rank? Those mistakes had to be deliberate. They made it so the file wouldn't stand up. Not for long. Same with Garber. He was ranting and raving about you, but really he was acting a part. He was acting out what the reaction was supposed to be. He was challenging me to think.'

'Did you believe the file, when you first saw it?'

'Honest answer?'

'That's what I expect from you.'

'I didn't instantly reject it. It took me a few hours.'

'That's slow for you.'

'Very,' I said.

'You asked me all kinds of weird questions.'

'I know,' I said. 'I'm sorry.'

Silence.

The train was fifteen miles away.

She said, 'Don't be sorry. I might have believed it myself.'

Which was kind of her. She leaned over and kissed me.

I went and washed the last dry traces of Carlton Riley's blood off my hands, and then we made love for the sixth time, and it worked out perfectly. The room began to shake right on cue, and the glass on her bathroom shelf began to tinkle, and her French door trembled, and her floor quivered, and her room door creaked, and our abandoned shoes hopped and moved, and her bed shook and bounced and walked tiny fractions. And at the very end of it I was sure I heard a sound like a cymbal crash, vanishingly brief and faint and distant, like an instant metallic explosion, like molecules reduced to atoms, and then the midnight train was gone.

Afterwards we showered together, and then I dressed and got ready to head home, to face the music. Deveraux smiled bravely and asked me to drop by any time I was in the area, and I smiled bravely and said I would. I left the hotel and walked up to the silent diner and climbed into the borrowed Buick and drove east, past Fort Kelham's impressive gate, and then onward into Alabama, and then north, no traffic, night-time hours all the way, and I was back on post before dawn.

I hid out and slept four hours and emerged to find that my hasty dictation to Garber's night crew had been adopted by the army more or less word for word as the official version of events. Tones everywhere were hushed and reverent. There was talk of a posthumous Distinguished Service Medal for Reed Riley, to recognize his time in an unspecified foreign country, and his father was to have a memorial service in a grand D.C. church the following week, to recognize who knew what.

I got neither medal nor memorial. I got thirty minutes with Leon Garber. He told me right away the news was not good. The fat staff officer from Kelham's PR squad had done the damage. His call to Benning had bounced around, mostly upward, at a very bad time, and it had been followed by a written report, and as a result of both I was on the involuntary separation list. Garber said under the circumstances it would be the work of a moment to get me taken off again. No doubt about that. I could extract a price for my silence. He would broker the deal, gladly.

Then he went quiet.

I said, 'What?'

He said, 'But your life wouldn't be worth living. You'd never get promoted again. You'd be terminal at major if you lived to be a hundred. You'd be deployed to a storage depot in New Jersey. You can get off the separation list, but you'll never get off the shit list. That's how the army works. You know that.'

'I covered the army's ass.'

'And the army will be reminded of that every time it sees you.'

'I have a Purple Heart and a Silver Star.'

'But what have you done for me lately?'

Garber's clerk gave me a sheet of paper explaining the procedure. I could do it in person at the Pentagon, or I could do it by mail. So I got back in the Buick and headed for D.C. I had to return the car to Neagley anyway. I got there a half-hour before the banks closed, and I picked one at random and moved my account. They offered me my choice of a toaster oven or a CD player.

I took neither one, but I asked for their phone number and I registered a password.

Then I headed over to the Pentagon. I chose the main concourse entrance, and I got halfway to the door, and then I stopped. The crowd carried on around me, oblivious. I didn't want to go in. I borrowed a pen from an impatient passer-by and I signed my form and I dropped it in a mailbox. Then I walked through the graveyard and out the main gate to the tangle of roads between it and the river.

I was thirty-six years old, a citizen of a country I had barely seen, and there were places to go, and there were things to do. There were cities, and there was countryside. There were mountains, and there were valleys. There were rivers. There were museums, and music, and motels, and clubs, and diners, and bars, and buses. There were battlefields and birthplaces, and legends, and roads. There was company if I wanted it, and there was solitude if I didn't.

I picked a road at random, and I put one foot on the kerb and one in the traffic lane, and I stuck out my thumb.

61 HOURS

By Lee Child

A Jack Reacher Thriller

'Explodes into one of the best thrillers I've read for ages'
Independent on Sunday

GET READY FOR THE MOST EXCITING COUNT-DOWN OF YOUR LIFE

HOUR SIXTY-ONE
Icy winter in South Dakota. A bus skids and crashes in a gathering storm. On the back seat: Jack Reacher, hitching a ride to nowhere.

HOUR THIRTY-ONE
A small town is threatened by sinister forces. One brave woman is standing up for justice. If she's going to live to testify, she'll need help from a man like Reacher. Because there's a killer coming for her.

HOUR ZERO
Has Reacher finally met his match? He doesn't want to put the world to rights. He just doesn't like people who put it to wrongs.

'A new and believable hero . . . when we thought all the heroes had been written'
Observer

WORTH DYING FOR

By Lee Child

A Jack Reacher Thriller

'His is an ironclad storytelling ethos, a gift for narrative that grips like the proverbial vice . . . If anyone can put down *Worth Dying For* after the first few pages, then they shouldn't really be reading thrillers at all'
Independent

Has Jack Reacher finally met his match?

61 Hours ended with Reacher trapped in a desperate situation from which escape seemd impossible. Even for him.

Was that really the end of the road for the maverick loner?

'. . . one of the great storytellers of the thriller genre'
The Times